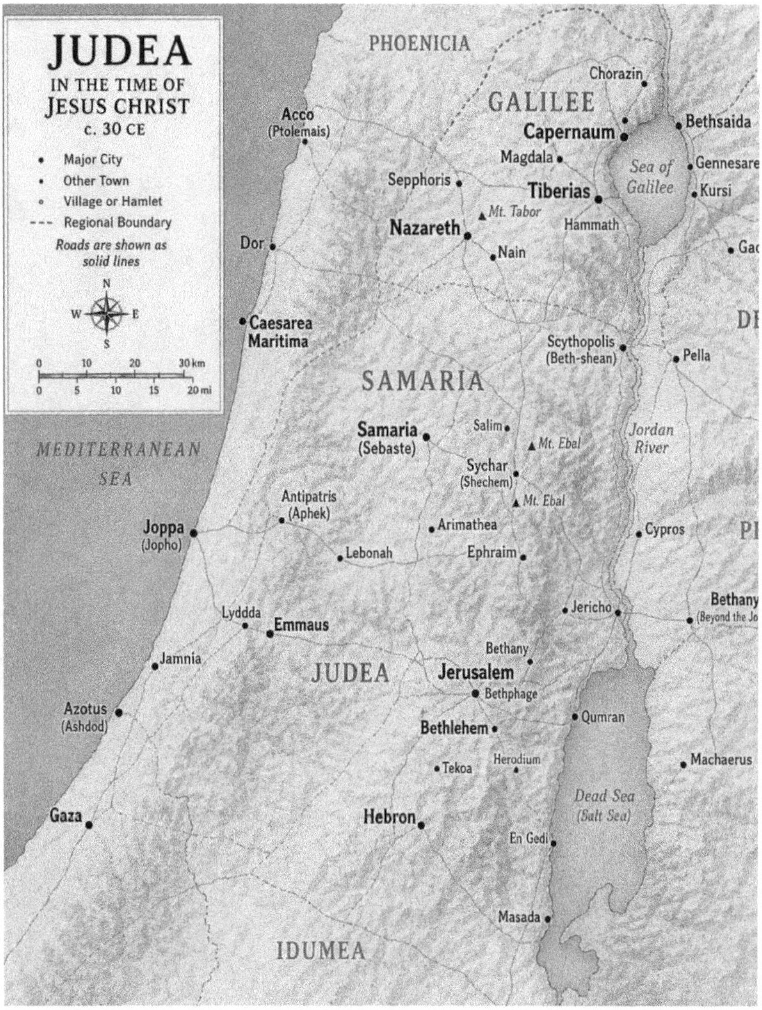

JUDEA

IN THE TIME OF

JESUS CHRIST

c. 30 CE

- Major City
- Other Town
- Village or Hamlet
- --- Regional Boundary

Roads are shown as solid lines

N W E S

0 10 20 30 km

0 5 10 15 20 mi

PHOENICIA
GALILEE
Chorazin
Acco
(Ptolemais)
Capernaum
Bethsaida
Magdala
Sea of Galilee
Gennesare
Sepphoris
Tiberias
Kursi
Mt. Tabor
Hammath
Nazareth
Dor
Nain
Caesarea Maritima
Scythopolis
(Beth-shean)
Pella
SAMARIA
MEDITERRANEAN SEA
Samaria
(Sebaste)
Salim
Mt. Ebal
Jordan River
Sychar
(Shechem)
Mt. Ebal
Antipatris
(Aphek)
Joppa
(Jopho)
Arimathea
Cypros
Lebonah
Ephraim
Jericho
Bethany
(Beyond the Jo
Lyddda
Emmaus
Bethany
Jamnia
JUDEA
Jerusalem
Bethphage
Azotus
(Ashdod)
Qumran
Bethlehem
Tekoa
Herodium
Machaerus
Dead Sea
(Salt Sea)
Gaza
Hebron
En Gedi
Masada
IDUMEA

The Book of Lazarus: A Biblical Horror

By Walter Shank

TABLE OF CONTENTS

Dedicated to my beautiful wife and family.

"**Jesus Christ** why don't you come save my life now. Open my eyes, blind me with your light now." Tool, Opiate

Part I: Resurrection

i

It was the same nightmare that had haunted her for the last few nights, but it was no less terrifying. Her young body lay uncomfortably askew across the bed. In response to the returning nightmare, she writhed and squirmed. She was half wrapped in her own twisted, knotted, soiled clothing and left disheveled from her last tedious, unnecessary sexual union. A warm breeze blew in from a solitary open window, chilling the copious sweat that beaded on her bare legs, arms and brow.

Behind her rapid eye movement, she was running. Hand in hand with her brother, Lazarus. More than running. They were sprinting from nebulous boulder to nebulous boulder in a wide, dark field. Hiding. Sprinting, then hiding. They were sprinting and hiding from an indomitable, foreboding spirit. Boulder after boulder that they were using as cover from the powerful being was instantly reduced to a shower of pebbles and ash from the charged bolts of lightning that shot from its eyes.

While gripping onto Lazarus' hand tightly, Mary dropped behind a great, massive hunk of stone and stopped to catch her breath for a brief moment. Her heart pounded like a frantic, distant war drum in her ears. She could feel and hear an audible deep, warm hum coming closer and closer. The phenomenon vibrated her eyeballs in their sockets and rumbled deep in her chest. Her voice warbled in her throat and ears when she turned Lazarus' face to hers and screamed, "We have to move!"

Mary and Lazarus located their next hiding spot, sitting nondescript in the gloomy distance. The sickening vibration and hum gained in intensity as the spirit came upon them. Right as they pushed off from the hard-packed ground with their bare feet, the stone that they had been hiding behind, (which had seemed enormous enough to hide a few houses), exploded into a confetti of showering pebbles and rubble. The shriek from the lightning strike that struck the stone made her eardrums throb and her vision went pure black.

This caused Mary and Lazarus to both falter in their stride to the next stone. To instinctually brace for the possible fall, they extended their hands out.Mary did stumble and fall to the ground. Lazarus, who was a few cubits (1 cubit = 18 inches) ahead of her when she fell, scrambled back to her. He grabbed his sister by the arm and pulled her away from the approaching, brilliant specter. Neither the brother nor the sister was aware that the angel following them had only one single-minded interest; that was in Lazarus and Lazarus alone.

The siblings ran as fast as their limited human legs could propel them. When they came closer to the next stone, they saw that it was, in fact, a small, wooden shack. Both Lazarus and Mary ducked in the only opening and huddled in the dark corner of the structure. They were hyperventilating and holding onto one another. Listening with fear over their own labored breathing and hammering hearts for their relentless pursuer. Their own shaking hands had been placed over their own terrified mouths.

Precious, elongated seconds played out, like measured, ringing hammer strikes on a blacksmith's anvil. Their breathing and hearts had begun to slow back down to a near normal pace.

Then, the hair on them that wasn't soaked in a coating of anxious sweat, lifted from their heads and arms, as though elevated by static electricity. The nauseating hum grew in strength from outside of the shack in a remarkable crescendo that shook the entire structure. A glow that was quickly becoming blinding, seeped in through every fracture of their temporary domicile.

Outside, in one swift motion, the floating, droning, glowing spirit took its appendage, that could've been an arm or a wing, and barely swept it to one side through the air. The application of the slightest effort of a gesture, caused every stick of the shack to blow away the same direction its hand (or wing) went. This left just the terrified set of siblings crouching in the dirt, holding onto each other for dear life.

Lazarus quivered and screamed while clutching onto Mary, "You can't have my sister!"

The winged, perplexing thing cocked what could've been its head to one side quizzically for a moment, as though confused by the little human's assumption. It idled. Crackling and emanating a frightening power while hovering close to the pair. Bobbing up and down marginally. Studying them. An uncomfortable amount of time underneath the thing's scrutiny passed, before it began to draw even nearer to them. Floating onward. Determined to have its prize. Coming to a stop only about five cubits from them.

Brother and sister started to paw at each other, trying to hold on tighter. Trying to disappear. However, it wasn't possible for the laws of physics-even within the parameters of a nightmare-to change and accommodate their desire to vanish. They both began to whimper and scream frail, feckless threats at what was coming. The constant, eclipsing hum blotted out every other sound, though. At this proximity, the vibrating behind the power made their teeth chatter and their vision blur. All over their bodies, little stings and pinches nipped at their skin.

As always in this nightmare, there wasn't any form to behold. It was more like an imposing backlight, framing a vague suggestion of a human-like silhouette with multiple sets of wings poking out and folding all around it. The figure moved in a simple gesture of reaching out to the siblings, with what could've been construed as an open hand. Then, without any further hesitation, it snatched its fingers closed in a forceful fist. Mary, all of a sudden, looked about and realized she was holding nothing! No one! No physical body!! Her brother was gone!!!

The spirit turned away slowly, as though bored, now that it had completed its mission of retrieval. It had acquired its bounty of one brother. Uninterested in anything more. As though it intended to leave Mary alone in this limbo.

Still utterly flummoxed as to what just happened, Mary screamed at its back, "What have you done with Lazarus!?"

It remained ignorant of her question and continued to drift away. On to its next scheduled bounty.

Mary chased after it and screamed again, “Where is my brother!?”

Still, this evoked nothing resembling an answer from the brother-snatching, humming, electrified, glowing ghost.

Now, as usual in this reoccuring nightmare, she picked up a fragment of rock from one of the stones that had hid them, before it was blown to smithereens. She hurled it at the angel, while screaming demands again for the return of Lazarus. The stone passed right through it, as though through mist. However, this time, the spirit did spin around in slow response to gaze upon her.

Mary looked back up at the thing in pure, rageful defiance. It regarded her, like she was a boring, yet bothersome bug. She then screamed into the vibrating void of the angel’s presence, “What have you done with Lazarus!?”

That's when, as was typical in this strange, terrifying dream, the spirit took both of what could've been its hands, palms touching and proceeded to spread them outwards to both the left and the right.

Underneath her feet the Earth suddenly opened up. She reached for a rough, crumbling ledge in a laughable, futile gesture. Her stomach jumped up into her throat as she fell, and fell, and fell in an endless drop. She seemed to fall forever with her screams echoing in her own ears. Following her all the way down until...

ii

Her body jolted awake in reaction to the return of the nightmare. From head to toe, her body was covered in slimy sweat. Small dribbles of semen rested, half dried, but still very tacky on her stomach. She rolled her terrible tasting tongue around the inside of her cesspool of a mouth, tasting stale wine and male sweat. Her disorientation was replete and close to blinding.

Even so, as a means of habit, her bloodshot eyes flicked over to the large, wooden carved storage chest in the corner of her room. Seeing that it had been pulled back in place gave her a tiny, but welcome relief.

In a tentative manner, she got up from the tousled mattress, wiped off her abdomen with the lower corner of her robe and went to the wash basin. The water from the pitcher was tepid, but still felt blessedly refreshing as she splashed her face and swabbed the back of her neck. She felt grime in all of her creases, so she was compelled to eagerly continue with an aggressive washing of her **complete** self. The lover she chose for the previous evening, who usually tended to other, literal fields, could've used a wash himself before his visit to her earlier.

They can't all be perfumed princes, she thought in a cynical voice to herself as she scrubbed the dried spunk off of her belly.

Even the perfumed princes aren't princes, another thought invaded. This one came in the maternal, reprimanding voice of her older sister.

No, she agreed with herself. None were chivalrous, like in the fables her sister and herself had told one another as children. She chuckled without a smidge of mirth at this observation. Princes, soldiers, manservants. All men, regardless of stasis, are looking to conquer. Pining for comfort, but lacking the ability to reciprocate such comfort. She had only just buried her brother after all, but she still craved the temporary escape from the dismal reality of the last four days. No matter how frivolous, rough or odorous that escape may be.

Who she really wanted to escape with and, would comfort gladly, without any reciprocal benefits, was away from Bethany right now. Preaching abroad somewhere with his apostles. A perfect man that was so unattainable for her, it made her tenacious for him all the more. There was also an undeniable touch of anger that tinted these irrational feelings of hers, in a significant way towards the Lord. After all, her sister, Martha, and herself had sent word to the Messiah of their brother's illness well over a week ago. Begging for him to come to their brother's aid. Provide a miracle, or something. In an unfortunate turn of events, Lazarus succumbed to his sickness within a few days of his sister's messenger pigeon being sent out to find and alert Jesus.

It had been the sister's one and only shared hope.

Mary began to weep at the thought of her brother's helpless corpse at this very moment. Laying in that dank tomb. Hot hour after hour. Day after day.

Rotting away in an ultra slow succession. Being eaten away by vermin on the exterior and bugs on the interior. The thought made her want to wretch and weep in concurrent actions.

Outside, the day was currently receding into late afternoon, judging from the reddish orange hue of daylight. Puffy clouds were gathering in the West, lit up peach, with grim, pocketed shadows of gray by the imposing sunset. She must've only dozed for a few hours. Fruit that had been set out this morning was withering in a carved wooden bowl on a small, circular table. Flies were hopping about, busy suckling at the juicy, forming decay.

Still feeling dirty from her pungent encounter, she tore off her soiled robe and undergarments over her head. She then proceeded to take the entire wash basin and pour it over the top of her naked body. Her eyes were squeezed closed against the outside world for a few moments. She stood in an apathetic, dripping puddle. Goose pimples popped out in stark bumps on her tanned flesh. Inside of her, there was an unfulfillable desire to wake up from what she had woken up to.

Birds screeched and chirped incessant, annoying songs outside, which wasn't unusual. Neither was the constant bubbling gaggle of people flowing up and down the streets of Bethany. Nor a random, ephemeral passing buzz of a curious fly cruising by her ear. There was something altered about her surroundings, though.

Mary's eyes snapped open and when they did she was startled to see her older sister, Martha, standing as still as a stone in the threshold to her room. She was holding a tiny unfurled, rectangular note in her hands. Regarding Mary with her bare forearms held up tight beneath her heavy breasts. A resting pained look of judgement, pity and exhaustion was all the more prevalent as she surveyed the rest of Mary's room. The puddle Mary stood dripping in. The rumpled condition of the mattress. An unmistakable stink of body odor and experimental sex that hung in the room, like a gaudy, blaring, offensive tapestry. On the table sat two fine wine cups, one half full, one knocked over, its contents dripping slowly off of the edge of the table and staining the floor. Then, Martha's focus came back to her sister.

Mary stared back at Martha. Hungover and soaking wet, but still maintaining a strong-willed, default defiance.

Martha sighed out a loud exasperated sigh, rolled the little strip of note back up and tucked it in her pocket. Upon entering the room, she started the conversation by being passive, "Sorry to interrupt your....washing up afterwards, but-"

"Is th-this t-truly imp-p-portant?" Mary interjected in a tired, chattering voice. Cold and wet exposed skin had gotten her starting to shiver.

"Yes, it is sister," Martha volleyed back to Mary, as she began to tour the room. She lowered her voice down to a conspiratorial whisper, patting where she had stuffed the note and leaning in, "I have just received word, sister. Our Lord Jesus comes to Bethany."

Mary gasped and flushed in newfound delight at the thought of being close to the Lord, Jesus. Thinking upon his touch and his distinct smell caused her head to swoon and she faltered in her stance. Before she went tumbling to the floor naked, she steadied herself by placing her hand upon the nearby small table.

Martha picked up the toppled wine cup and continued, speaking in the same low, quiet tone, "He is currently on his way to Bethany. To the house of 'a friend', according to the note." Mary, glanced over and out of the open window. *Who was the friend?* she pondered. Martha continued, "Would you care to join me in meeting him there, or do you have another fragrant-" She sniffed for dramatic effect and brought her hand up to her nose in a polite, theatrical gesture indicating a bad smell had been detected "-escapade planned?"

Without a verbal reply, Mary broke from her leaning stance against the table, in the lukewarm puddle and stumbled over to her wardrobe to retrieve a fresh set of clothes. Something special. It would have to be the robe dyed in fine Phoenician purple *Argaman*. The best one she owned. The one that Jesus himself had said she'd looked like an angel in.

Upon seeing her sister's sense of urgency, Martha nodded curtly and responded, "Good. I will be waiting for you." She marched out of the room without another word.

Mary remained silent. Instead, she just rang out her saturated, dark hair over the decent, spread out puddle and began fashioning it into a quick braid. She pulled a silk patterned shawl over her damp hair and sat down to slip on a pair of worn leather sandals.

Upon standing to leave, another wave of dizziness and nausea washed over her all of a sudden. Most likely, this was a typical side effect brought on from her escalated drinking, coupled with debaucherous sex that lasted well through the night and into the late morning. Irregular, drunken sleep, and extreme sadness. That was the prognosis. She steadied herself against the table again and waited for the swell of vertigo to pass. New droplets of sweat sprouted up all over her exposed skin and chilled her. Breathing in deep through her nose and slowly out through her mouth proved to be a little helpful.

After a few moments, the intensity of Mary's bout of dizziness began to dissipate. She wiped at her eyes with aggressive, irritated swipes and rotated her head from side to side (as though that would clear the fog in there), then she left the sordid mess of her room behind. In a fugue state, she zigzagged through the hallways. Nodding mechanically at various maids and servants as she went to meet her impatient, but stern sister, who was waiting by the front door.

Martha was giving some common orders to a tiny, old woman named Hannah, a servant of the house since time immemorial. Hannah's frail hands wrung together as she nodded to Martha's instructions. In all honesty, the old woman knew the protocol and the inner workings of this house better than anyone, making the fact that Martha was telling her anything as nothing more than a silly formality.

Mary approached and surprised Martha by wrapping her arms around her and hugging her tight. Martha embraced her back, with just as much heartfelt enthusiasm. When they pulled away, there were tears rising up in Martha's coffee colored eyes. Tears pooled in Mary's hazel, bloodshot eyes as well. Mary was breathing hard, like she had just run a marathon. Before Martha could question what was happening, Mary's eyes rolled up in her head and she fell backwards, hitting her cranium upon the hard, mosaic floor. *SMACK!*

"Good Heavens!" Martha exclaimed and leapt on top of her sister. She was making attempts to rouse her by calling her name, shaking her by the shoulders and slapping her cheeks with enough force so as not to hurt her. When there wasn't any response, Martha slapped harder, once and waited. Mary remained unconscious.

Some surrounding servants, as well as friends and family, who were populating the house for the purpose of consoling the sister's in their time of grief, gathered around Martha. Voicing genuine concern. Asking what had happened to Mary.

Martha stood up and they all took a step or two back. She wiped the salty moisture from her cheeks and composed herself as once again as the Lady of the House. Mary remained stinking hungover and unconscious on the floor.

"I have to go," Martha announced to the room. Some of those who heard her nodded their heads up and down. Martha added to no one in particular, "Please, watch over her."

In direct response to Martha's request, a few members of family and staff knelt down by Mary. A servant girl immediately began fanning the unconscious Mary with the apron she had tied around herself. Another of the concerned staff members held Mary's hand, stroking her clammy skin and whispering to her checked out ears. Martha nodded in succinct approval that this was as good as it was going to get and made for the door.

Phillip and Caleb approached her. Caleb was a familiar face from her childhood, yet he wasn't well known to her. He seemed nice enough, even if there was a weasel-like, sinister quality about him that she could never quite put her finger on. On the other hand, she had known big, burly Phillip for most of her life and held a special fondness for him in her heart. Maybe at some other time in her life, what she felt for him could blossom into love, but now was not the time for such flights of fancy. Now was mainly set aside for grief and keeping the house from descending into turmoil.

Both Phillip and Caleb offered to accompany Martha through the streets of Bethany, wherever she was going.

"That truly isn't necessary," Martha replied in a polite decline of the offer. She felt comfortable bringing Phillip to where Jesus and his apostles were hiding. Caleb on the other hand, she wasn't so sure of.

Martha's cousin, a fellow sympathizer for the Lord, pulled Martha aside while the main focus of the room was being spent on Mary and urged her in a discreet, rushed whisper in her ear, "Martha, take them. Our Lord is in danger here. You may be in danger too if found in his company."

With reluctance, Martha acquiesced to this logic. After all, Jesus had been, in fact, threatened with stones the last time he had visited Bethany. She also had to admit to herself that some masculine protection, especially from the handsome Phillip, and traveling company would be very welcome.

With that, the party of three stepped out into the late afternoon to traverse the dusty grid leading outside of Bethany. All the while, being heightened in awareness to the threat of Roman soldiers and Temple Priests patrolling the same streets in search of those who would dare to align their allegiance with The Son of God, Jesus.

iii

They arrived some time later at the modest house of Simon the Leper. Dried out and thirsty from their small journey. The dolomitic limestone pathway leading up towards the solid Aleppo pine door, felt a bit warmer through the soles of their sandals as opposed to the miles of hard packed earth that they had been walking now for furlongs (1 furlong = 220 yards). Random placement of fig and olive trees provided sporadic shade until the groves thickened towards the back of the property, giving way to a graceful, sloping hillside. Beyond that was a horizon that was getting painted with darker pastels upon each passing minute.

A weary Martha, Phillip and Caleb approached the large, unfinished door. Martha rapped her little knuckles upon the thick, splintered pine. After a polite knock and waiting for a few long moments, the door cracked open, revealing just a thin sliver of dark interior.

"Hello?" Martha called into the slim void with an obvious apprehensiveness included in her inquiry.

The door swung open on squealing hinges and she found herself being scooped up into a huge bear hug by the apostle, Peter. Her dirty feet dangled above the ground two full handbreadths (1 handbreadth = 4 inches). His robe was an unpleasant, scratchy pad of roughspun, unwashed wool. He smelled of fish, sleeping in the wild and not bathing. In a deep, rumbling voice he was blubbering and laughing, at the same time. Saying into Martha's ear that he was sorry over and over again.

Martha felt another set of meaty arms envelope Peter and herself, "I'm so sorry about Lazarus, Martha." The soft voice of John warmed her left ear with his breath. He smelled worse than Peter, but she didn't care. It was good to see them and feel the genuine empathy expressed through their words and their embrace.

Once removed from their arms, one by one, the remainder of the twelve greeted Martha and her male traveling companions. Each apostle offered their personal condolences for the loss of Lazarus. Judas Iscariot being the last. His condolence was imparted with an awkward hug and a sneer, but that was probably to be expected. All of the apostles looked very hungry and filthy. They were, after all, in hiding.

Peter relayed that the homeowner, Simon the Leper, had self-sequestered for the evening, but had left his kind regards to be passed on.

Once everyone had exchanged their formalities, the three newcomers washed their feet and calves. Then onto their hands and forearms. The water, even though dirty and populated by a few flies, was cool and rejuvenating. Martha even splashed her face and the back of her neck, prompting Caleb and Phillip to follow suit.

After being refreshed, Martha was met again by a grinning Peter. He was jovial, but that was normal for Peter. "I'll take you to Him," he said. Phillip and Caleb abandoned their washing. Peter told them both where they could find food and drink while they afforded Martha the courtesy of a private meeting with the Lord.

Peter then took her by the hand and led her with a tiny lit candle pinched between a set of dirty, fishhook scarred fingers. Doing most of the talking, he managed to squeeze in a couple of quick, funny anecdotes as he guided her down a slim hallway to a room at the rear of the house. As they got closer to where Jesus was waiting, Peter's demeanor changed and he became more grim and stoic. He took his unclipped, filthy fingernail and tapped the door.

Martha didn't hear anything, but Peter answered with a demure reply of, "Yes, my Lord."

In a smooth arc, Peter swung the door open. There, kneeling on the floor was Jesus with his back to the door. Praying. Mouthing an earnest prayer to his Heavenly Father. Big drops of sweat dotted his forehead. His hands were white knuckled and clasped beneath his disheveled beard.

"My Lord," Martha broached timidly, as she entered the small guest room.

"Amen," the Messiah whispered, finishing up. He stood from kneeling, turned to her and held his arms open to her. The pull was magnetic and she felt as if she were floating towards him. He was smiling. Tears welling up and shaking in his deep brown eyes. She crashed into his embrace, like a tidal wave spawned from a turbulent maelstrom and dashing upon an unwavering, eternal rocky shore. Within the confines of his arms she was crying, taking in great big, snotty gulpfuls of air. He smelled like a nomad. Earthy and rank. Human and unpleasant.

Emotion came over her and Martha began to beat on Jesus' chest with the sides of her fists. "Why?! Why Lord?! If you had been here my brother would not have died!" She was jumbling her words through a mask of slime and tears. The beating she was trying to inflict had dissolved into weak, flimsy pattering. She had practically melted.

Jesus held Martha close, while shushing her and cooing soft reassurances to her. He was running his rough hand upon the back of her shawl and snagging his calluses upon the fine weave of the fabric.

Martha snapped her head up from his chest and looked up into his face through bleary, brown eyes. She gripped his robe in both of her tiny hands, as though he were going to fly away, or disappear. "But, even now I know that whatever You ask of God, God will give You," Martha bargained.

Jesus took his dirty thumbs and wiped away the tears on her cheeks. He then took the sleeve of his roughspun robe and wiped away at her messy nose and mouth, now that her momentary hysteria had subsided.

"Your brother will rise again," the Lord promised.

"I know that he will rise again in the Resurrection on the last day," she recited. Saying it as though it were elementary common knowledge.

She sniffed hard and wiped at her nose with her own sleeve. As she started composing herself, she noticed that the light of the entire room was dimming at considerable rapidity. As though the night was premature about imposing itself upon the world. Although, in fact, it wasn't the onset of twilight. Everything in existence was turning pitch black, except for Jesus and herself. He captured her brown eyes with his. Siphoning all of her focus. Shutting everything else out. She saw only his flawless face and he was holding her in his hypnotic, intense gaze. This left her completely unaware that their hands were entwined. She held her breath. The tips of her toes levitated over the woven prayer rug on the floor. An undeniable weightless feeling washed over her, like she was floating in a vast, currentless ocean.

There was a delayed effect that accompanied Jesus' powerful voice when he spoke, causing it to echo in Martha's mind after the words were mouthed in physical reality. As though her eyes and ears were operating on two different timelines. It was discombobulating, but captivating. Here is what Jesus said, "I am the Resurrection and the life. He who believes in Me, though he may die, he shall live." His electrifying deep brown eyes now blazed. "And whoever lives and believes in Me shall never die."

A meager light from a few flickering candles became visible just outside her periphery, as the solid darkness lifted. It had become night outside. She looked around the room as if seeing it for the first time. Time was lost to her. It felt like she had arrived five minutes prior, but outside showed that anywhere from one to two hours had been transpired.

"Do you believe this?" Jesus asked Martha.

Martha was caught in a state of confusion. "Huh?" She asked.

"Do you believe that whoever lives and believes in me shall never die?" The Lord repeated.

Immediately, the fog lifted from her mind. With crystal clear clarity she replied, believing with all of her mind, heart and spirit, "Yes, Lord, I believe that you are the Christ, the Son of God, who has come into this world."

With a genuine warmth to his eyes, Jesus smiled down at Martha. His eyes were deep, inviting pools, not ignited or blazing anymore. *How could one man be so perfect?* she wondered, taking in his hair, facial structure and what she could feel of his body through his dirty robes.

Jesus broke their contact and took a step back. "Where is Mary? Why did she not come with you?" He inquired.

Flustered, Martha answered, "Oh, she had fainted as we were leaving to come here." Her mind went to thoughts of wine glasses and the recent late nights for her sister. She took the liberty of inventing an excuse for Mary by saying, "I think my brother's death has been weighing heavily upon her."

Jesus raised an eyebrow at this proclamation. "Is that so?" He had heard rumors about Mary's proclivities long before she had washed his feet with her hair and tears at this very house. She was no less beautiful and enchanting to his imperfect human taste. The eternal spirit that he always knew himself to be, held disdain for the fact that Mary dealt with pain and strife by escaping deep into sex and alcohol. The human portion of Jesus that, up to this point, he had only known for thirty-three years, was intrigued and excited by her wantonness. Evil temptation. It must be true, Satan never rested.

"We must have Mary come at once," Jesus announced.

Martha's eyebrows knit together, "But, my Lord, she is not well," she used for her vague rebuttal.

"We shall see," He replied. He looked past her and called out, "Peter?" Martha looked back to the entry she had come through, (now what seemed like so long ago), then back to The Christ. Confusion was plastered all across her face.

In two breaths, Peter appeared on the threshold, crossing his arms across his chest. In a deep voice he said, "Yes my Lord." He smiled and gave Martha a confidential wink. She covered a smile, justifying his silliness.

Jesus ignored his comical theatrics. "I want you to take one of the men that escorted Martha here-"

"Phillip or Caleb?" Peter interjected.

"You pick," Jesus responded, sounding so tired. Peter's interrupting and constant jesting could be insufferable sometimes. Even to the long-suffering Lord. "Take whomever you choose, and go to the house of Martha and Mary. Bring Mary back here, discreetly."

Martha remained quiet and listening. Holding her breath as Peter nodded to his acceptance of the task without any further humor and turned to leave.

Jesus thought for a moment. "Peter?" Jesus called once more.

Peter poked his head around the corner to receive further instruction. "Take Martha with you," Jesus commanded his most fervent apostle.

Then, Jesus turned to Martha and looked down into her eyes, "Who else is there at your house?"

"Um, our servants, some family, friends," she offered in an innocent way. "Why?"

Peter now stepped all of the way into the small, cramped room. The Messiah went on to explain, "I think we can all agree that the less people that know of my presence here near Bethany, the better. It would be best if everyone thought I was still preaching abroad somewhere."

Jesus didn't need to mention the threats of stoning and execution that existed for him here. The Pharisees, Sadducees and Members of the Sanhedrin hated his logic. His parables. His miracles. Everything about him. With Roman occupation in Judea, in the form of Roman soldiers on patrol in the streets and Pontius Pilate taking up residence in Herod's Palace, the Temple and its government of the people were under constant scrutiny and threat of regime change. Jesus had formed a defiant movement amongst the constituents of the Temple, by means of his exclusive brand of preaching and providing a special brand of hope. For this reason, the Pharisees, Sadducees and Members of the Sanhedrin were engaged in a constant search for any reason to arrest and put Jesus on trial. Maybe even put him to death.

Martha nodded, “I’ll bring her back, my Lord. In secret.”

Jesus approved of her confidence. Once more, he stressed the need for stealth and discretion, embraced her again, then sent her back into the main entry room with Peter.

To Martha’s pleasure, Phillip ended up being the one selected to accompany Peter and Martha go back to Bethany for Mary. Caleb had found himself a scrap of unleavened bread and some soup. Also, at the moment, Caleb was engaged in a spirited, albeit suspicious conversation with Judas Iscariot.

As they walked out of the front door into a cloud dappled night, Peter was already regaling Martha with stories of fishes, great crowds and unbelievable miracles. It was good to laugh at his jokes and to hear his laugh in return.

Once they entered Bethany proper though, Peter became much less animated. Shark-like Holy Men and Roman soldiers patrolled the streets, hunting for that meddling Messiah or maybe even one of his followers. But, lucky for the trio, they had the cover of night and Martha's extensive knowledge of the shortcuts and alleys of Bethany to help conceal their mission.

At long last, they came to the street that Martha and Mary resided on. Peering outside of the opening to an alley and around the corner they could see a sizable procession approaching, consisting of Jewish High Priest Joseph ben Caiaphas, a sympathizer of the Sadducee’s, son-in-law of High Priest, Annas. He was a shrewd, damn-near-anorexic spectacle of pious righteousness, adorned in dyed purple and blue robes, with beads, precious gold and jewels adorned all over, and, of course, a leather bound phylactery box dangling upon his forehead. (Deut.11:18.) Annas, his father-in-law, a hideous, hunched over troll of a man holding onto a skinny, ginormous walking stick, was amongst the group as well. As well as a young Priest with a patchy copper beard and a boatload of ambition, named James ben Jonah. A cadre of soldiers on camels and horses, Annas, James and a few other Members of the Sanhedrin encircled The High Priest, Caiaphas. Some of the soldiers held torches aloft, the flickering flames glinting in spasmodical flashes off their armor and the sparkling luxury adorned on the

Priests. Caiaphas was speaking loudly to the makeshift militia about being on the lookout for that charlatan, Jesus.

Martha spun around and looked right into Peter's widened eyes. Then, in a harsh whisper, she told him, "You can't be here!"

Peter agreed. Nodding up and down in a vigorous way and looking back down the alley that they had come. He thought for a second, then turned back to Martha and grabbed her high up on each arm. Staring with intensity back at her, he relayed these instructions, "I will meet you just outside the city, back towards the House of Simon the Leper. One hour." She didn't have time to respond before he added, "Be careful."

Peter sprinted back down the alley.

Martha called out in a subdued voice after him, "You too." Just as Peter turned the corner out of the alleyway and disappeared. Leaving Phillip and herself to the figurative wolves, so to speak.

Martha could now hear the loud, shrill voice of Caiaphas proclaiming just around the corner to his cronies, "-Lazarus now dead four days, make no mistake, it's only a matter of time before Jesus and his *apostles*," he rolled this word in his mouth with extreme distaste, "show their blasphemous faces."

The surrounding party shifted and grumbled. Camels manipulated and rolled their mouths in rhythmic rotations around some decimated cud. Horses snorted, blowing clouds of clear mist out of their nostrils and floppy lips. Numerous torches crackled.

"Behold!" Caiaphas continued, holding up his bejeweled hand, "the home of the recently departed Lazarus and his sister's, who are in fact still living. Martha and Mary."

Martha felt her blood go cold. She also felt hot rage boiling up within her breast against this terrible man. It was obvious to anyone that he was being ambiguous about his motives. That he was there to search her house underneath the guise of concern for their mutual grief at the loss of her brother. Caiaphas was a treacherous snake and Martha knew she had to be very careful of how she tread in this metaphorical tall grass.

She covered her head with her plain shawl, looped her soft arm through Phillip's brawny arm and pulled him around the corner. Back onto her street. Just barely skirting the flickering edge of the firelight cast by the torches. Walking a hurried, but not too hurried as to be suspicious, curved path to the dark passage that ran down the length of her house. Martha's intention was to slip around the side of the house, and...in all honesty, she hadn't figured out the next part yet. Maybe, with Phillip here, in a perfect scenario, they would be able to get in, get Mary and get back out of town undetected.

Martha and Phillip were almost to the path of darkness that separated her from her nearest neighbor, when Phillip stepped in a sizable pile of camel scat and stumbled, causing some commotion. Soldier-laden camels and horses grunted. Turning their attention in the direction of Phillip and Martha.

Caiaphas snatched a torch from a soldier standing close by and raised it high aloft. The flickering edge lifted to reveal Martha and Phillip. Caught. Their pair of faces turned in shock to the group of conspirators, with their sinewy ring leader, Joseph ben Caiaphas, in the center of them all. A smug, satisfied smile cut deep creases to his sallow, sunken in face.

"Ah, how wonderful! Speak of the Devil! It is Martha, sister of Lazarus!!" he purred. Oil, or maybe venom, seemed to drip off of each and every syllable he spoke. "What a serendipitous delight to find you here, outside of your house, before I had to go and commission one of these fine gentlemen to knock on your door."

"Good evening, High Priest Caiaphas," she replied in a meek tone, giving a little bow of her head. She wiped at her eyes and regarded all of the men gathered there in support of Caiaphas' campaign with contempt. Phillip was shaking globs of camel crap off and wiping his sandals on the dusty boulevard, while some of Sadducees and soldiers chuckled at his unfortunate embarrassment. "To what do we owe this...visit?"

"Well, my dear," he began, "first, to offer my deepest sympathies for the loss of your brother." Mary nodded once to play along in accepting this lie. "Second, knowing that you have kept company with Jesus and some of his followers in the past, we," he looked around at his present company, then back to her, "are here to inspect your house for any of these," he rotated a spider like hand on a lanky wrist, searching for the correct phrase, "blasphemers of the law. Surely, I'm not the only one who has come to visit you or your sister in the four days since your brother has passed. By the way, where is your sister, Mary? Is she home?"

Some of the surrounding men muttered and snickered at some internal, private joke. The punchline seems to be spent at Mary's expense just from the mention of her name. It was obvious, their motivation behind the jest was only for the purposes of insulting and hurting.

Phillip, now abandoned rubbing the side of his soiled foot against the dirt packed road and squared his shoulders against the uninvited party. His fists, like knobby boulders, were clenched at his sides. He was digging his fingernails into the flesh of his palm and breathing in forceful exhalations through his nostrils.

"Do you have something to say big man?!" Caiaphas shrieked in the street. Each word raised a whole octave from the one spoken before. This outburst spooked the camels and horses, causing them to stamp and twirl in a skittish manner.

Martha quelled Phillip's reckless fury with a delicate, soft touch to his flexed arm. He looked down into her brown eyes and saw the worry they conveyed. Phillip slumped his shoulders and released a heavy sigh. Then, after shooting another truculent look at Caiaphas and his cronies, he returned to the futile effort of trying to un-soil his sandal and foot of the stubborn, sticky camel scat.

Martha turned back towards the group of unsavory men. "Mary is home. I fear she's not feeling well," she admitted. "As for Jesus or any of his apostles, I have not seen either in a very long time," she lied.

Caiaphas right eyelid twitched. "Mmmmmhmmm," he replied with a cadence of suspicion. Arching one eyebrow high to where it was almost even with his box of tidbits of sacred scripture. "Well let's just have a little look, shall we?"

The cadre closed in now and nudged both Phillip and Martha towards the front door. Martha groaned inside. She just had to play along and get rid of them. Fast. The sands in the hourglass were falling steadily.

iv

Mary was fanning herself and sipping some water from a clay cup. She had been nursing a pulsing migraine, when she heard someone scream out in front of the house, on the boulevard. She went to the door and cracked it ajar with only a fingerbreadth (1 fingerbreadth = 1 inch) to peer out onto the street.

She saw both Phillip and Martha with their backs to the door. They stood in front of a miniature imposing mob of ugly Roman soldiers and pious Sadducees. Some were holding torches high. All were creeping in closer, backing up Martha and Phillip in the direction of Mary peeking through the front door. At the present moment, Martha was explaining Mary's not feeling well and lying about not having seen Jesus or any of the apostles.

Mary closed the door without a sound and resumed her place atop a mound of pillows. Her mind raced. She was fanning herself in furious, fast little movements. Pretending at being aloof to what she knew was inevitable in arriving. A servant girl drifted into view and refilled her cup with boring, cool lemon water from a clay pitcher. Mary would've preferred wine in her cup, instead. The waifish little maid asked Mary if she was hungry and offered her some figs. The thought of any food made Mary queasy on top of the butterflies flapping in her guts. In a polite raising of her hand, she declined just as she heard the familiar creak of their front door opening.

Upon seeing torches and spears, some of the attending servants and guests froze in place. Some of those gathered along on the outer edge of the great receiving room fled out. Mary remained propped upon her little hill of silk pillows.

Martha and Phillip stood with about a dozen men with ill intent behind them. One of them Mary recognized as Joseph ben Caiaphas. Tall, smart as a whip, cruel, skinny and dangerous. She saw him in all actuality as a wretched wolf, disguised in a High Priest's costume. A nefarious false representation of what should've been righteousness. Another face among the rabble she knew to be Annas' ugly mug. An old, short degenerate man, sporting a bulging set of eyes that leered instead of looked. Covered in jewels and refinement. Using a tall, altitudinous walking stick with a tip that came close to scraping the ceiling.

With a subtle flick of his pointy chin, Caiaphas gestured to a few of the men accompanying him, to search the house.

The younger Priest, James, with a patchy, copper beard whispered a rebuttal to Caiaphas order in his ear, "The house is considered unclean in the eyes of the Law, my Lord. Lazarus just-"

Suddenly, the young Priest broke off from what he was saying in a high pitched, choked squeal. Extreme pain exploded from his groin, where Caiaphas had seized him. Squashing James' male bits and pieces in an unrelenting claw.

In a calm voice, Caiaphas spoke to the young, whimpering Priest, "James, shut up and search the house, you moron." Then, Caiaphas then released the set of mangled testicles.

The young Priest sucked in a sharp intake of air through his gritted teeth. With gentleness, he held a hand to his nether region while he limped away in the company of an armored Roman soldier, in order to pursue those that retreated deeper into the house.

Phillip made to step away and one of the stationed soldiers grabbed ahold of his arm in firm restraint. He looked at Phillip from an unimpressed, flat foreign set of eyes.

"May I wash off my foot?" Phillip rumbled through gritted teeth.

Staying mute, the soldier shook his head from side to side, restraining Phillip and his dirt-dusted, dung covered foot to the spot. Phillip resigned himself to praying and seeking for patience. With a loud exhale through his nose, Phillip crossed his arms over his barrel of a chest and ruminated.

Martha's eyes were wide, boring into her sister. She was trying to convey a secret message to her via telepathy, *Don't tell them anything!* Mary returned her gaze with the slightest of knowing nods. *I know!*

Caiaphas wrapped the creepy, long, ringed fingers of one hand around Martha's shoulders and, with a contradicting tenderness, ushered her to take a seat right next to her sister on the pillow mound. He took a step back, clasped those spider-like hands together and regarded them in contemplative silence, as one would gaze upon an alien insect before stepping on it. The two women and The High Priest stared at each other. Their two sets of vulnerable, quivering brown and hazel eyes tilted slightly upwards to look into Caiaphas' near black eyes. They remained this way, locked in a staring contest, while the rest of the house was being ransacked. The room, despite its colossal size, was taking on a bit of a claustrophobic atmosphere as it was being filled.

Martha realized she had been holding her breath since Caiaphas had laid his repulsive hand upon her shoulders. She exhaled through her mouth with audible disdain and reached over for her sister's hand. They clasped tight onto one another. Mary's hands were shaky and clammy to the touch.

As soon as all of the soldiers and Holy Men finished their sweep, satisfied that everyone in the house was in this room, Caiaphas' shrill voice rose above for all to hear, "Good evening. I am Joseph ben Caiaphas, High Priest of Judaea." He allowed the words carrying the weight of his position to bounce off the walls and sink into the attending ears. His black eyes scanned the nervous, annoyed and scared faces gathered. No one responded.

The High Priest had their attention and now began a tour of the room, sauntering amongst those assembled. "In light of the recent death of Lazarus, I suspect it's only a matter of time before Jesus, or his followers, or both come to pay their respects."

"We haven't seen Jesus!" Mary spoke up in imprudent defiance.

"Silence wench!" Caiaphas, all of a sudden, was hovering over the younger sister. His pitch black eyes blazed underneath bushy greying eyebrows.

Some of the surrounding men, including Phillip, stirred and made to advance upon the High Priest. Phillip was restrained even tighter and the remaining soldiers now leveled their spears. Martha and Mary grabbed and held onto each other. Women, children and men all alike clumped together in an instinctual display of self preservation. Very young children were now crying out loud from the unwarranted altercation, causing some of the parents to try to coo and shush the upset youngsters in a soft manner.

Caiaphas reached down with his creepy fingers. Mary flinched away from his bony hand, but he persisted in his effort as she shied from his touch. Then, he proceeded to take a strand of Mary's hair and began rolling it in methodical, tiny circles between his thumb, index and middle fingers. The same hair that had, according to rumors, washed the feet of Jesus with tears shed from the same head. "Should anyone here willingly conceal knowledge pertaining to the whereabouts of these blasphemers," he tossed the strand of Mary's hair, sniffed his fingers, grimaced and wiped those same fingers on the robe of a middle aged Sadducee standing nearby, "they will be treated as enemies of the law...and of God."

"Pfffft!" Someone amongst those gathered scoffed.

Caiaphas' black eyes snapped up towards the source of the noise. He pointed a long splinter of a finger in the direction of the heckler. "Who dares?" Caiaphas seethed.

No one moved a muscle. It seemed they were **all** holding their breath. Some of the younger children in the room were still fussing, contrary to their parent's efforts at consoling them. Long moments passed as Caiaphas searched the attending faces for inherent mischief, his sharp finger hovering from face to face until coming to land on the shifty, sweating countenance of a not well known, distant cousin to Martha and Mary.

"This one," Caiaphas said without taking his eyes off him.

With a flourish of steel and hard acacia wood, the nearest Roman soldier spun his spear around and smacked the cousin across the face with a loud *Crack!!* Women, men and children alike gasped and screamed. The assaulted cousin dropped to the ground in a lifeless heap. Blood began to pool around his head. His body lay there inert, but Mary noted a soft rise and fall to his rib cage. At least he was still breathing.

Those gathered and horrified by this harassment, now shifted as if to advance on the perpetrators. Two soldiers, including the one that had assaulted the cousin, now held the pointy end of their spears against the small crowd. Holding them at bay, while a Sadducee and another big soldier each grabbed an arm of the cousin, hoisted his torso off of the floor, then dragged the lower half of his unconscious body out of the house.

Where are they taking him? Mary wondered in an internal hopeless voice. "You monster!" She screamed out loud.

Martha gripped onto her sister and pulled her back, not wanting her to get bashed next. They were both being surrounded and held by other men and women when Martha wailed, "My Lord, no one has seen Jesus or any of his twelve in Bethany since they were threatened by you with stones!" She wiped at her nose and sniffed back an oncoming stream of snot. "We are not hiding anyone or anything. Please, leave us to grieve in peace."

Tears stood quivering in Martha's eyes before spilling over and trickling down her cheeks. Mary had effortlessly produced her own set of tears now, as well as a fair amount of the surrounding women and a couple of men, for that matter.

Annas leaned in now and gave quiet advice in Caiaphas' ear, "Neither Jesus nor his followers are here. We cannot pursue this further."

Caiaphas closed his great black eyes and drew in a long, calming breath. He pinched at the bridge of his nose between his eyes, feeling substantial pressure blooming there then radiating outwards to his temples. With people openly weeping now, he could feel it was giving him the beginning tremors of a migraine. His little box of selected bits of scripture were beginning to feel very heavy resting against his forehead.

After a moment spent in private frustration, Caiaphas opened his eyes and nodded in a curt dip of his chin to his father-in-law, who was waiting down by his shoulder. Once again, a joyless smile masked his face as he addressed the assembled fearful, "Don't make the mistake of confusing my enthusiasm to uphold the law with cruelty."

Sensing that this interrogation was running its course, the soldier restraining Phillip loosened his grip on him.

Caiaphas continued, "Jesus will show up and we will find him. It's only a matter of time." He had to clear his throat, then went on, "So, if anyone wants to confess to anything now, I strongly suggest you do so."

With that, he now paused and cupped a hand to his ear. Tears were starting to dry up now, but no one responded, other than a few sniffles.

"I see," the High Priest relented. "Well, if there is nothing else that anyone wants to confess to, we will leave you to your mourning." He now swept in close to Mary and Martha. With a soft whisper that could've been intended for them alone, he conveyed, "But, I will be watching very closely. Make no mistake."

No one else spoke. The soldier that had been restraining Phillip, now shoved him towards the rest of the victims. Phillip stumbled and fell into their folding, open arms. One by one, Roman soldiers and Holy Men disappeared out of the front entrance, into the soft, flickering torchlight being held outside. Camels grunted out loud at their return.

Caiaphas was at the threshold now, walking backwards in slow measured steps, staring fiery black coals at the sister's, but addressing everyone, "I bid you all, good evening." With these words uttered out to the ether, Caiaphas slammed the door, rattling the wood on its hinges and leaving an air of trauma and peril behind.

V

There wasn't any time to waste. Martha kept recalling Peter's hasty instructions, *One hour, just outside of town.* A huge chunk of that time was wasted now, thanks to Caiaphas and his goons. There was no time to waste in enacting the plan to get Mary, and, maybe Phillip, out of here without arousing any suspicions. She did love everyone here, but that didn't mean she trusted each and every one of them to not want to snitch in order to gain some minor favor with the High Priest.

"We must leave at once," she muttered to Mary's face. There was the barest movement to her mouth as though she was trying to ventriloquate the words. "Are you ready?"

Not aware of the plan concocted between her sister and the Lord, Mary asked at a non conspiratorial volume, "Where are we going?"

Martha reflexively wanted to shush Mary by forcing her hand over her mouth, but caught herself. At the same, regular volume to match, she spoke back, "Why, to grieve and pray, my sister, at the tomb of our brother."

Mary looked sick at the suggestion. She began to shake her head a little from side to side, "No, Martha. There's been too much distress today." She patted her hand with a light touch, attempting to coax her, "Tomorrow."

Martha now took her thumb and index finger and pinched her forgetful sister on top of the hand. Mary pulled back and made to protest, but Martha was staring pointed daggers into her. Through telekinesis, she was trying to force Mary to remember their conversation from this afternoon, before she had passed out. After an impatient moment for Martha, realization came and dawned upon Mary's face.

Martha's voice now dropped to a near whisper, "We can't just go out the front door. They'll be waiting for us to lead them."

Mary nodded in thoughtful contemplation. Then it came to her. "I'll get up first, then you will follow after waiting for a minute. I have a way out of here."

Martha added, "We have to bring Phillip with us."

With a stern frown upon her face and emphatic shaking of her head, Mary signaled a hard, *NO*. Then, she arose from their island of tufted pillows, smoothed out her robes and walked off nonchalantly in the direction of her room.

Martha wondered what, in fact, her sister had in mind for facilitating their escape. There was only a window looking out onto the street in her room. There's no way she could be planning on going out there. That would be too obvious. In her head, Martha was trying to keep count at a steady pace to sixty, before arising herself. She realized she had been holding her breath and exhaled out now in a slow dribble of air, through a little "O" formed by her mouth.

When she was positive enough time had passed, she stood up without ceremony and began to head in the same direction Mary had. Phillip spotted her en route and raised his eyebrows in question. That look asked *Where are you going?* And, also, *Do you need me to come with you*? She declined with a soft, subtle hand gesture. Phillip came over to her and cupped a large, calloused hand to her cheek. He gave off an amorous, protective intensity, while looking down into her chestnut colored eyes. A look that said, *Be careful.*

She leaned her soft face into his rough hand a little, nuzzling it in a loving manner and nodded, *I will.*

With difficulty they parted ways and Martha found herself walking down her own dim, gloomy hallway. She was running her fingertips along the textured wall of the corridor, which was something that old Hannah, the Main House Maid, had hated with a boiling passion since as far back as Martha could recall. Despite the regular, vehement hatred espoused by Hannah, it had never broken Martha of the habit. Now, while tracing her fingers along the wall and holding her breath, Martha came down to the third door on the left, which had been left cracked open a fingerbreadth or two.

A creak, that no doubt sounded louder than it was, announced her entry. Darkness covered her entire field of vision from floor to ceiling. Dim light from the hallway didn't penetrate at all into the room. After a long moment, her eyes adjusted to the gloom. Upon scanning around, she saw her younger sister, Mary in the corner, crouching down by a large, plain but sturdy storage chest. Martha closed the door behind her, and by way of dainty tiptoe, ambulated over by her sister.

Mary looked up at her older, more conservative sister and whispered, “Please don't tell anyone about this.”

Martha’s eyebrows knit together, confused. “Don’t tell anyone about what?” She whispered back.

Without a verbal answer, Mary dug her fingers behind the storage chest and, with a straining grunt, began to budge the chest away from the wall. Seeing that it wasn’t getting any easier for her younger sister after a few of these small efforts, Martha came over and helped her slide the heavy chest almost all of the way from the wall. This revealed a small, excavated hole in the wall, big enough for a man, or, put in better terms, a random paramour, to crawl through. It was dark on the other side of the miniature passageway. This was due to a piece of wood covering the opening from detection on the outside.

All of a sudden, it made perfect sense to Martha why Mary was so adamant against Phillip being involved at all in seeing this. “Oh Mary,” was all Martha could manage. Without a doubt, becoming privy to the lengths that were went to to achieve and conceal this level of promiscuity were jarring to the, by comparison, more prudish, older sister.

Mary rolled her eyes and slid the wood covering the exterior of the hole aside. Martha expected to see moonlight pouring through, but the darkness on the other side of the short tunnel remained. The younger, more promiscuous-by-a-landslide sister then put her shoulder against a solid rock that had been placed in front of the wood and shoved it far enough for them to slip by.

“Oh Mary,” Martha groaned in a maternal, reprimanding tone.

“Come on,” was all Mary said and she crawled through.

As Martha crouched, she thought of something and began to ask while looking back behind her, “Who's going to close-” then she saw a large iron handle had been fastened to the back of the chest. Installed there so that whatever random suitor, after he had spilled his seed and had his fun, could close the door behind himself, so to speak.

“Oh Mary,” Martha reiterated, full of sorrow.

“Sshhh,” was Mary’s reply from behind their house.

Both sisters pulled on the iron bar and slid the chest back into place. Then, Mary replaced the flat, wood cover, followed by the good sized rock, with Martha’s help, of course.

Mary meandered over to the perimeter fence, running her fingers lightly along the jasmine-covered fencing, feeling for a seam. A couple of mangy goats bleated in angry protest as they were chased away from their nocturnal perch. Martha watched, marveling at the audacious lengths that her sister had gone to in order to satiate the sin that plagued her. Mary found the panel and pushed her knee into the lower half. This caused the bottom of the panel to push outward towards the alley and the top to swivel inward towards their garden. Mary put her face to the top of the opening, fighting the flowers for a view, making sure the coast was clear of any of Caiaphas' henchmen, or Caiaphas himself for that matter.

After a few rounds of checking in each direction, numerous times, determining that no one was about, the sisters emerged out into an alley behind their house. To be safe, they would have to stick to the alleys nearly the entire way out of town. Now that they were free of everyone's eyes and ears, Martha took the lead. Zigzagging them both left, then right. Then right again.

They came to a point where they had to cross a wide, common street. Before attempting to cross, Martha cupped her hand and put it about her ear. After a long moment, she became aware of crackling torches and voices approaching from off to their left. The sisters pressed themselves against the shadowed wall, keeping silent and listening. In a common reflex that was natural to herself, Martha held her breath.

A couple of soldiers passed by engaged in conversation about someone who had crossed High Priest, Caiaphas earlier that evening. Mary and Martha thought that the voices were referring to their cousin, who had been bashed across the face earlier that evening. A gruff voice spoke, "That punk will think twice before scoffing at the High Priest again, eh?" Both voices chuckled. The other, even gruffer voice added, "Nope. Someone's going to have to chew the little nipper's lamb and spit it down his throat for him now." To this jest they both laughed and laughed and laughed. It faded as they continued on patrol down the street.

When all was clear, Martha and Mary bounded across the wide boulevard, into another alley straight across. Now it was not much farther. Martha's distress eased a fraction, as she felt the hard part of this plan was nearly over. It was just a few more prudent jogs to the left and right until they were successful in their escape from Bethany undetected.

vi

They continued on a cautious route that would bring them to the house of Simon the Leper. A waxing gibbous moon gave them some illumination, but not much. They both searched the dimmed landscape with widened pupils and the occasional whisper-scream of Peter's name. Martha had lost track of the time, but felt, for sure, it had been well over an hour since they had agreed to meet back in this general area. She began to believe that he had left or, worse yet, something unfortunate had happened. Thoughts and scenarios played out all at once as her mind ramped up.

Mary called out again to the empty topography, "Peter!"

In answer, surprising both sisters, a soft two note whistle called back to her. The sound of which, for sure, did not originate from the throat of a bird.

"Peter?" Martha now inquired, quickening her pace in the direction they had heard the sound. This was reckless. Neither her nor Mary stopped to wonder if this could be some crafty soldier or vagabond robber or a rogue Sadducee.

The whistle came again, louder. Fortunately, this was followed by Peter's shaggy head peeking around the edge of a large boulder.

Mary and Martha broke into a run. Peter, now fully emerged from behind the rock, holding his great arms wide open in a gesture that was emulative of Jesus. "Martha." He called out, relieved. "Mary."

They all came together in a fierce hug that involved each of the sisters being smothered by Peter's barrel chest. All they could smell was his dank, fishy robe and old body odor. It was unpleasant and comfortable at the same time. "I thought something had happened," Peter was saying. "It's been over an hour, but I couldn't leave." He rubbed their backs with a soothing touch and kissed the tops of their heads. "I couldn't leave," he repeated.

Martha murmured something against his chest. "What was that?" he asked, letting up a little.

Mary looked up into his bearded face, gripping onto his filthy robes, her face distressed and swollen, but still, her beauty was undeniable. "Caiaphas," she said. Peter stiffened. "He's looking for you. He's looking for all of you."

"He hunts for Jesus," Martha interjected, "or any who know where he is."

Peter absorbed this, put them both down and began to move. They both followed, doubling their steps to each one of his long strides. "Does anyone know that you left? Or where you are?" He demanded in a serious tone, which sounded so foreign coming from him.

Martha recalled seeing Phillip and declining his company, now knowing it was for the purpose of saving her sister the embarrassment of being viewed as a trollop by one of their childhood friends. She didn't think that Phillip would have thought much about it. He wasn't like that. Phillip, instead, was quiet and protective, but in no way was he judgemental. (She did think it was a good thing that Mary felt shame though, and went to such exorbitant lengths to conceal her carnal desires. That at least told Martha that Mary knew her behavior was wrong.) Martha knew, as well, without question that Phillip would not sabotage her or her sister.

"Phillip," Martha confessed. "I saw him," she looked at her sister, "before we met in your room."

Before Peter could question Phillip's discretion, Martha defended him implicitly. Stressing her trust in his loyalty. Mary, also, now took up lobbying for Phillip. This turned into a back and forth sort of rally of the duo on behalf of good old, stoic, incorruptible Phillip. Peter took in their declarations of adulation and accounts of Phillip's trustworthiness, nodding in approval, while quickening their pace. Scanning ahead and behind them. Listening beyond their voices. He felt hunted, like a rabbit being sniffed out by an innumerable pack of voracious foxes. Paranoia hovered as a sinister storm cloud does over his shoulder the whole way back to Simon's.

A twig snapped from somewhere behind them, cutting through their jabber and every other sound of the night. Peter grabbed them both and ducked behind a tree, holding a thick finger up to his lips.

Quiet.

They waited for long, stretched out seconds, listening with their ears perked up in the air. Martha was holding her breath. Peter and Mary's shaky breathing coming through their noses, was nigh on deafening among the rest of the quiet night.

Multiple advancing footsteps became audible and could be heard crunching on the hard ground. Coming closer. Soft, low voices were rising now over the steady, rhythmic patter of foot falls. These voices began to take on some not unfamiliar notes, prompting Martha, then Mary to perk their heads up to listen in earnest.

A deep rumble of voice, that could only belong to Phillip, was now heard saying, “I’m sure of it. Jesus instructed us to bring Mary back.”

Clearer and closer now, the sound of another familiar voice could be heard asking, “But, you’re sure they came back this way, instead of going to the tomb?”

Martha leaped out from their hiding spot into plain view. “Phillip!” was all she said, causing the big man and a few others in their small group to jump and gasp from being startled. Then, Martha ran to Phillip and crashed into his arms, as though it had been weeks since she’d seen him, as opposed to a little under an hour.

Realization quickly took over, though. Mary and Peter had now materialized. Everyone from both parties greeted one another with savage, relieved gusto, having escaped Bethany proper, despite its teeming to the brim with Caiaphas’ subordinates. The two groups now became one of eight individuals, friends and family alike. All sharing a deep love and profound dedication for the Messiah.

After a quick recap of the last sequence of events, from Phillip gathering a few he trusted, to devising and carrying out their own escape plan, to the present moment, they resumed their pilgrimage.

Meanwhile Mary and Martha filled them in on the finer details of their slick escape, remaining vague, though, about their exact point of exit. Just treating it as another little secret shared between sisters.

Through little lies and omissions of facts like this, Martha knew she was only enabling her little sister by helping her hide what she occasionally turned into. Which, crudely put, was nothing but a pro bono concubine. Just something to be used, even though she claimed to be using "them" as well. Martha couldn’t recall being reckless like that at any point in her youth, so it wasn’t always easy for her to relate with her younger sister on why she found the solace that she did through being hedonistic, slovenly and debaucherous. But now, despite her sinful nature, Martha needed her baby sister more than ever. This was even more true after losing their only brother, Lazarus.

Out of the gloom, pushed up against a mature grove of olive and sycamore fig trees, appeared the quaint, inviting house of Simon the Leper. Warm candlelight flickered behind thick wooden shutters. The winding limestone path, once again, led Martha and Phillip to the sturdy wooden door that opened before they got within knocking range.

Andrew, Peter's brother, also known as the first disciple, Thomas, Bartholomew and John now greeted them with great enthusiasm. Hugging Mary voraciously and spinning her around. One by one they greeted all of the others, beckoning each one to hurry and come inside.

vii

Once inside, after all of the greetings had been exchanged to completion by visitors and apostles alike, everyone gathered and beheld Jesus. The Lord was sitting in an unassuming posture at a table in the dining room, tearing little bits of bread off of a stale, half eaten loaf. He was dipping these pieces, letting them soak in a small dish of olive oil and balsamic vinegar, in a calm, methodical manner. Then he would place each piece with perfectly executed etiquette into his mouth and chew in a way that exhibited minimal joy.

When he caught sight of the small gathered group, in particular, Mary, he brightened and rose up from the table, abandoning his meager meal. While walking towards them and still chewing, he gently brushed his hands upon his dingy, spotted garments.

When the Lord approached, Mary fell to the floor, directing her face downward in humble prostration to Jesus. She said, "Lord, if you had been here, my brother would not have died." Her words then became thicker, and her body trembled. When she looked up to the Lord, he saw she was openly weeping without a hint of restraint. Others, now started sniffing and wiping at their moist eyes. Murmuring in low, subdued tones their respects for Lazarus.

Jesus' brown eyes glided up to the ceiling. He mouthed something quick and indecipherable. In a soft way, Jesus then reached down, grasped Mary by the wrists and helped her to her feet. Taking her up in his arms, he rocked her in a soothing back and forth, while allowing her emotional tidal wave of loss to subside. Her helpless feet dangled a full handbreadth above the tile.

As once tearful eyes in the room were starting to dry, a feeling of discomfort infiltrated the morose moment. Jesus and Mary were still locked in a borderline romantic embrace that would've been considered publicly inappropriate for a married couple. His lips hovered down by her ear, not speaking, but she nodded on occasion as if he was. The weeping participants now became an unsettled audience. Martha couldn't deny a weird, unexplainable twinge of jealousy pinching in her chest.

Peter cleared his throat in a theatrical sort of way. After another moment spent in embrace, Jesus set Mary back down. Upon doing so, the Lord had to spin around and adjust the front of his robes down by his waist. An embarrassing, unexpected and thoroughly unwelcome erection had begun to pulse in response to Mary's undeniable womanliness. The human part of Jesus persona was so annoying in that regard; how its sinful nature would always involuntarily try to betray his pure, righteous determinations. Despite his elevated spirituality and power, he still possessed all of the ordinary human functions that every other human did. There was always urine, everyday defecation, boogers, ear wax, belly lint, toe jam, bad breath and, yes, the occasional, obnoxious hard on.

After a quick, fervent prayer, and thinking of a whole slewful of unattractive things, Jesus regained his previous, flaccid composure. When he turned back around, he panned across all of their faces. Familiar faces. New faces. Both categories of faces were creased with worry and puffed up from four long days spent in despair. Deep emotion moved the Lord and troubled his spirit. Tears appeared as jiggling pools at the bottom of his eyes. "Where have you laid him?" He asked.

"In the family tomb, my Lord," Mary replied. "Come, we will show you."

viii

The family tomb, where Lazarus had been laid to rest, was located on the eastern outskirts of Bethany, facing out towards the Dead Sea. A nice little crypt consisting of a lower chamber and a ground level antechamber, tucked nicely into a picturesque courtyard. It was about an hour or so of walking for a caravan of almost twenty people from the house of Simon the Leper, to the tomb. Their chosen path also, not entirely by chance, curved wide around Bethany. Giving them ample cushion from those who sought to capture, interrogate and persecute.

Small conversations were being murmured in close proximity amongst the apostles and the rest of the company. They were all clustered together, sharing in each other's body heat. The night was gorgeous and clear, but held a chill to it as well. Martha snuggled in close to Phillip and Mary pressed her body up against Jesus. The warmth seemed to radiate off of The Messiah, as though he housed an interior magma core. Both sisters and Phillip told Jesus of encountering Caiaphas earlier in the evening, as well as the invasion upon their house, and the assault upon their family member. They told Him how the streets were crawling with Priests of the Temple and Roman soldiers, seeking to apprehend any one of them in a heartbeat.

Judas Iscariot, who had been all but non-existent up until this point, piped up from close behind them, "What?! Why do they seek all of us?"

Martha looked over her shoulder, out of the corner of her eye at him, and said, "Caiaphas is openly accusing all of you of sedition and blasphemy."

"What?!" Judas asked again, not believing he had heard her right. "This is absurd. We did nothing wrong!" He was beginning to become emotional and his voice was rising. Some of his spiritual brothers tried to shush him.

Peter gruffly commanded Judas to, "Lower your voice."

"No!" Judas shot back with a defiant gleam in his eye. Getting louder, he went on, "We're being hunted now because of Him!" He pointed his index finger right at Jesus.

Judas' actions and words had now drawn the concentrated ire of most of the group. Many of them attempted to argue at once, creating a cacophony of unintelligible gibberish. But, past the squabbling, there was the undeniably crystal clear voice of Jesus ringing in Judas' head. "You doubt, yet, you still follow? What is it that you believe, Judas?"

Jesus never turned around or broke the set pace of his footsteps as these words were uttered within Judas' mind alone. Undeterred, the Lord kept walking, being led along the path through the grove by the sisters.

Meanwhile, Judas' breath had caught in his throat. He stuttered out a weak attempt at an exonerating argument, which drew a few of his fellow apostles closer in, putting their hands upon on his shoulder or grabbing him sternly, high up on his arm.

Mary turned to peek over Jesus' shoulder at Judas and told him, "Be quiet, please."

A look of complete shock came over Judas' face, as he was blissfully silenced. Peter, along with some of the others, chuckled at the warranted rebuke behind their hands. Judas now faded to the back of the crowd, where Caleb was walking and watching. A sour grimace contorted Judas' features. To be talked to in such a way, by a woman (particularly, the type of woman that Mary was rumored to be) was egregious on so many levels to his natural trait of being an audacious chauvinist. But, to be honest, he wasn't a favorite of Mary's either.

Or Martha's.

Or really of anyone's, lately.

Jesus, however, came to the defense of Judas Iscariot. "Don't be too harsh on Judas. He is merely frightened and passionate about what he feels." As they emerged from the canopy, underneath the boughs of the grove, he raised his hand and directed their attention to the myriad of stars above. Referring to the well known hunter constellation overhead, Jesus made the comparison to Judas by saying, "Much like the brazen foolishness of Kesil (Orion), who vowed to hunt and kill all of the animals inhabiting the Earth, so too is the blind enthusiasm of our dear Judas."

When no one spoke, Jesus added to sum it up for all listening, "Forgive him. Lest you excuse yourself of all forgiveness, by wearing the heavy mantle of judgement. Truly, I say to you, by judgment cast shall judgement be put upon."

They all walked the rest of the way, for the most part, in silence. Pondering on this lesson from Jesus. Peter could relate to the paranoia that Judas was feeling. He felt it too. They all did. But, Judas' faltering allegiance was due to something else altogether. Whatever it was, it seemed like his loyalties were teetering towards being compromised.

They all passed underneath a stone archway, connected to a low perimeter wall, into the quaint courtyard. Slowly, they walked past three sets of flanking, mature trees and funneled together at the end of the pathway. There they clustered just outside the tomb's entrance. A massive round stone, four cubits in diameter and one cubit thick, covered the mouth of Lazarus' final resting place.

Upon arrival, Jesus wandered over by the giant stone sealing up the cave entrance and lightly brushed his fingertips over the rough, porous surface. Without warning he became overcome with extreme grief and wept aloud for his friend, Lazarus.

Phillip and Mary were heard remarking about how obvious it was how much Lazarus meant to the Lord. This, in turn, caused almost all in attendance to weep as well. But, besides some weeping, others could be heard saying, "Could not he who opened the eyes of the blind man have kept this man from dying?"

Jesus was moved to tears once again at the sight of nearly everyone gathered mourning the death of Lazarus. Once the spell had passed, Jesus straightened his back and cleared his throat. He now commanded in a reverberating, powerful voice, "Take away the stone."

Confusion took over and owned the next few moments for all attending. No one moved or spoke.

Jesus wiped his eyes, sniffed and repeated, "Take away the stone, I said."

Some of his apostles, even Caleb and Phillip, made to move in closer now to the gigantic stone in order to roll it aside. Mary and the rest appeared paralyzed by what was playing out before them. Almost, as if they were watching it all play out in a dream before them. Like they were merely waiting to wake up.

Martha approached Jesus trying to reason, "But, Lord, by this time there is a bad odor, for he has been there four days."

Jesus looked her square in the eye and asked, "Did I not tell you that if you believe, you will see the glory of God?" This left Martha stunned and speechless.

With her answer being that of confused silence, Jesus then turned and nodded in affirmation of his previous command to the men. With a few labored grunts, followed by some shoving and skidding, the stone began to move. Making a grinding sound, of stone on stone, that was a roar in the stillness of the night. The dark corners of the threshold became visible and a couple of the men leaped away from the opening in response to the scent of four days of gradual human decomposition.

Thank God he didn't die in the summertime, Peter thought.

It was a slow, but steady process. Fingerbreadth by grinding fingerbreadth, the hulking stone moved. Jesus' mouth moved in a constant, rapid, silent prayer. The women, and some of the men, huddled amongst one another whispering low rebukes about respect for the dead. Once the stone had been rolled fully to the side, it revealed a pitch black, small doorway.

At this point, Christ raised his gaze to the heavens and beseeched His Father, saying, "Father, I thank you that you have heard me. I know that you always hear me, but I said this for the benefit of the people standing here, that they may believe that you sent me."

A low rumble was initiated then. It could be heard and felt beneath their feet. The air took on a warm, electric, tingling quality. Hairs lifted off of their heads and arms, defying gravity. Everyone's eyes vibrated in their sockets, turning the outline of everything into a holographic. Wind whipped across the landscape, bringing some stinging sand and grit with it. It all reminded Mary of something reminiscent of her reoccurring nightmare.

In a loud voice that rose above everything and seemed to echo across the vast, mystic sands of eternity, Jesus commanded, "LAZARUS, HEAR MY VOICE AND COME OUT!!"

In that instant, everything ceased. From the active rumbling underground to the tickling, static fizz that danced a neurotic waltz on the air. Martha was currently holding her breath, getting some spotty neon orbs at the edges of her peripheral vision. Silence hung as tangible and as heavy as the stone that had once covered the tomb. Then, from deep in the black depths of the crypt, came a great, loud groan that sounded something like a detuned guitar strummed once by a young child.

It was nothing short of a pure miracle.

Lazarus had been, by all accounts, resurrected back to life, after four long days spent within the unknown realm of death.

"I'll heal your wounds, I'll set you free, I'm **Jesus Christ** on ecstasy."
NIN, Suck

Part II: Reintegration

i

After the initial inhuman groan came from the crypt, more, just as awful sounding calls of lamentation followed. These painful outcries were accompanied by a harsh sliding and grinding that could be heard echoing out from the darkness. A low, vague outline of a mummified corpse dragging its lower half out of the ground level antechamber became visible. The corpse's arm faltered at one point and it fell, causing its torso to smack, like a slab of dead weight, onto the ground. On a pair of shaky, half-gnawed arms it managed to push itself back up and continue its sluggish crawl.

Everyone at the scene stood paralyzed in shock and horror as the corpse advanced further out into the courtyard. The waxing gibbous moon gave medium illumination upon the animated abomination. One milky, colorless eye peeked out, rolling all about and unfocused, from between some putrid burial rags. Dirty bits of death shroud hung off of it in ragged tatters. Some parts of its blanched skin were visible and sprinkled with rodent bites. Nasty looking reddish brown wounds with an infected dark purple outline. Each one bloodless. Each one infested and abounding with pink maggots. As the body fully emerged from the tomb, it was visible to all that there were even a couple of stowaway rats still clinging onto its legs. Slinky, brown vermin getting in a few last minute greedy nibbles of juicy decomposition before retreating away from the group of humans, back to the safety of the tomb and the rest of their scavenging brethren.

All in attendance, except for Jesus, recoiled at the sight that was slogging out of the tomb towards them. Woman and man alike, gasped, not only in collective horror, but also, in unanimous antipathy. They all took a big, cautious step backwards.

Caleb, Martha's childhood acquaintance, who was normally more reserved in his character, proclaimed aloud from beside Judas Iscariot, "What matter of abomination is that?!!"

Jesus smiled. Sweat dotted his brow from the exertion of performing this incredible miracle, despite the coolness of the late night hour. With humility he looked up to heaven and said in a soundless phrase, "Thank you, Father."

Jesus then strode over to his struggling, crawling friend and reached down with a gentle touch. Lifting, the Lord tried to assist his friend,Lazarus to its unsteady feet.

Caleb continued to shout, his voice climbing to a near hysterical level, "What is dead should stay that way! It's unnatural!!"

Likewise, Judas cast his two lots in, by saying, "It goes against the natural order! It's an empty vessel to be inhabited!!"

This drew the attention of a few of the apostles, who then came over to *assist* in calming both Caleb and Judas down. Being told, *You can leave!* or *How dare you say such a thing about this incredible miracle!*

Stepping forward with trepidation, John, Andrew and Peter came to assist the Messiah with the struggling corpse, the resurrected Lazarus. The smell coming off of Lazarus repelled all three of them for the briefest of moments, but they persevered beyond their impulse to gag.

Mary was encompassed by the other women, while crying and saying, "Lazarus, I can't believe it! My poor brother."

Martha exhaled after what seemed like minutes. She wasn't aware that she had even been holding her breath. Her feet carried her towards her newly resurrected brother on, what could've been, an innocent, floating cloud.

Could it really be, Lazarus? Martha thought to herself.

Jesus was hugging the cadaver, happy and crying, while Lazarus' arms hung at its sides lifelessly. Peter moved in closer to what was once his friend and he wrapped his arms around them both. His unwavering love for Lazarus outweighed his disgust from Lazarus' decomposed mortal stench.

The thick, meaty smell of rot was not enough to keep Martha away either. She now found herself wretching and embracing her revived brother.

Lazarus was moaning in unintelligible syllables through the special cloth and strips of fine linen wrapped around his head. Martha reached up and began, in a frenetic haste, to unravel the burial dressings. Round and round. Little by little his lightly gnawed away face was revealed.

Mary walked up now, staring at her resurrected brother in bleary-eyed disbelief. Once its mouth was unwrapped, Lazarus exercised its maw, while making pained, garbled moans in numerous, strange voices. Every so often, its neck muscles would weaken and fail, allowing its head to roll and drop.

"Praise be to God," Peter lauded. It wasn't altogether unanimous, but most shared the same, although reluctant, sentiment.

ii

The rest of the night passed by in a slow, fever dream-like haze. At one point, they found themselves to the west of the Mount of Olives at the Kidron Stream. Lazarus was stripped down naked and being bathed by some of the attending women. Its flesh at the cuticle appeared to have receded back from its fingernails, giving the effect that they were long and tapering to a dull point. The attending ladies were paying special attention washing off all of the plump maggots first. From there they moved on to all of the nasty rat bites and patches of decomposed skin, scrubbing in energetic circles at its red splotched achromasia. A couple small chunks of the necrotic, pale flesh sloughed away from the outer edges of the wounds during this process and floated merrily down the stream.

Mary and some of the women busy bathing Lazarus, as well as a few of the men on the shore, vomited at the sight of this. Ribbons of the women's spew also flowed down the stream, chasing after the tidbits of Lazarus' body, which had most likely already been gobbled up by passing fish.

It didn't seem to hurt Lazarus, as chunks and pieces sloughed off of it. It still moaned in an incoherent gobbledygook, but it was seeming to become just a little bit more cognizant. The drifting, swimming focus of its eyes never appeared to land upon any fleeting moments of cognition. Those eyes, that were once some of the deepest auburn, now rested as white and as pale as the few parts of its unbitten flesh.

Once the ladies were satisfied that they had removed most of the reek of death from Lazarus, they dried its body with trepid efficiency and fashioned some garments to at least cover over its privates. The chill of the late hour and the early spring season didn't seem to phase Lazarus though. No gooseflesh dimpled its skin. No shivering chattered its brownish, splitting teeth. The body just stood with a strange stooped over posture that was never there in its pre-resurrected existence.

At this point, the time had come for Jesus and his twelve to part ways with the smaller party from Bethany. Late night, quick goodbyes amidst a few stifled yawns were traded for the most part between the companies. Jesus, however, pulled the sisters aside, and asked, "Tell me, do you both believe that you have witnessed the glory of God?"

Martha responded without hesitation, "Yes, without question, you are the Son of the Most High God." Then she fell to her knees and prostrated herself before the Lord.

Mary looked over at what used to be her brother. Its pasty, shrunken eyes rolled unfocused in their sockets. Its near naked body was swaying and its mouth was mumbling in multiple inarticulate voices. Not really sounding like a voice at all, but, more like its vocal cords were being manually manipulated by thick, dumb fingers, like a harp being strummed by Goliath. At the moment, John and Didymus (Thomas) flanked the body of Lazarus on either side, steadying it back upright when its footing became unsure.

"Mary?" Jesus pressed.

"Yes, Lord," she responded with a little hesitation, "It truly is a miracle."

Jesus could sense a slight falter of inflection in her tone and followed her eyes when they would flick over, conveying worry for her brother. He smiled as a doting father would to a scared, misguided daughter and told her, "He will get better. Be patient and have faith."

The Lord hugged Mary very tight. She spoke against his chest, muffling her words, "I know my Lord. You are the Messiah, and the Son of the Most High God."

Martha could now be felt wiggling her way in against Mary and Jesus. Jesus enveloped them both in a massive, emotional embrace, then expressed His unconditional love for the two sisters and Lazarus once more.

Unexplainable heat emanated out of the Messiah and while Martha rested her head against Him, she felt as if she could fall into a sound sleep right there. A mighty yawn cracked her jaw. Then, in involuntary imitation, Mary yawned wide, as well.

Jesus released them out of His arms and back to the cold night, "You must go. You still have a long walk back to Bethany."

They both nodded in sleepy agreement, then Martha's eyes shot open, "But my Lord, what if Lazarus is seen? What shall we say?"

Jesus took Martha by the shoulders and looked her square in the eye, attempting to embolden her, "You tell them what has transpired here tonight. Tell them of the miracle you have witnessed and the glory of the Almighty God."

Again, she nodded in affirmation, although she knew that an answer like that would only work for some, but not for the likes of Caiaphas or any of his wicked henchmen. Despite this fact, she was kind and agreed, just the same.

Jesus stepped away from both sisters now and engaged Lazarus. Telling it He loved it and that it had been lucky this night. Speaking into Lazarus' ear, Jesus told the resurrected ghoul that it had been touched by the glory of God.

Lazarus' milky eyes stayed out of focus, looking through the Christ, and it fell into him saying in a garbled set of voices, something like, "My Lord." Or maybe it said something else. In all honesty, it sounded like it said something closer to a name, *Michael?* Regardless, it wasn't the same voice that had once teased Martha and Mary, or came to their defense. This was a different product of decomposed vocal cords, vibrating and tearing by means of user error.

In response to thinking Lazarus spoke the words "my Lord", Jesus replied enthusiastically, "Yes! Yes, Lazarus! That's good." The Lord held Lazarus in an embrace and, over its shoulder, caught Mary's eye. Seeming as if to say to her with his expression, *See, he's going to be just fine.*

Mary could only perform an exhausted nod up and down. She felt as though she lay on the ground and slept right where she stood.

Lazarus then turned its head into The Messiah's neck. Grazing its deflated, purple lips upon the gamey skin there. In a genial way, Jesus stepped away, while pushing with his gentle hand against Lazarus' depleted chest. Through his hand Jesus noticed that his friend remained void of the normal, everyday tried and true beat of a heart. Which was alarming. Jesus felt a passing moment of concern, which didn't linger, but, instead became replaced by a sense of optimism and confidence in another miracle well done.

Everyone out of the two groups then finished up the last of their farewells. An insider nod was exchanged without a word between Caleb and Judas Iscariot, while the rest engaged in a few more tears. A quick laugh or two and many, many hugs. Then the sisters turned their sore feet, their putrid brother and the rest of their baffled entourage back home.

To Bethany.

And, unknowingly to them, Danger.

iii

The streets were mostly dead (pardon the pun). Wisely, they decided to split up their group into a couple smaller groups. Phillip went with Martha, Mary, and the half naked spectacle that was Lazarus.

Walking the hunched over corpse through the grid of Bethany wasn't much more different than pulling and tugging around on a strung marionette. Its eyes weren't getting any better at the skills of concentration and focus. Receding gums made its teeth look large in its sunken face. On a weakened neck, its head bobbed and dipped often. Rigored joints cracked and popped in a macabre concert with each movement. However, there were still definite traces of the stench of death and decay that clung to the body of Lazarus, leaving a trail of suspicion for arousal.

An announcing glow of an early morning, torch-wielding patrol would give them enough time to duck into an alley and avoid whoever was around the next corner. They would then get stuck trying to silence Lazarus' persistent moaning and groaning. Once, during one of these shushings, Phillip made to put a hand over the moaning mouth of Lazarus. In response, Lazarus opened its mouth as one would when about to take a bite. Phillip snatched his hand away. Recoiling in an instinctual act of self preservation and discomfiture.

Martha's head was a sleep deprived, tumultuous maelstrom, spinning in all directions. Still, her mind was aware enough to take note that the way out of the city had seemed much more treacherous and lengthy. Now, in the meager light before daybreak, the city felt like a ghost town.

By the time they had reached their front door, the early morning sky was beginning to lighten to a deeply bruised, purplish pink over the Eastern horizon. As suspected, their house was as quiet as a cave when they pushed the door open and that all too familiar creaking of the hinges ripped a stretching stentorian note through the quiet of the hour. In a hurry, they rushed Lazarus through the great entry room, past the tranquil atrium, into the hallway, and ending up at the back of the house. There, they barricaded themselves into Mary's room, by way of a key that Mary had produced, from what seemed like thin air.

Oh Mary, Martha thought, as she watched Mary lock the door, and on top of that, retrieve a small wooden wedge with her toe and firmly kick it into place beneath the door. The older, more chaste sister looked over to the storage chest and could only imagine some swarthy man crawling in while Mary was battening down the hatches. Making sure that there weren't any unexpected intrusions.

Phillip was trying to corral Lazarus, who was wandering the circumference of the room and working at its vocal cords through a series of raspy, guttural moans. That was all it could generate for speech at the moment. Strange, incoherent moaning and snapping its frightening teeth at nothing. Phillip caught Martha's gaze after one of these ineffective chomps at the air while she was making up a couple of makeshift beds for the two men out of the plethora of pillows in the room. They both shared the same sentiment from across the room, *Something wasn't right.*

This miracle was not feeling very miraculous at the moment.

But, what they needed more than answers to the millions of questions swirling in their minds right now, was sleep. Solid sleep. Morning light peeking in around the imperfect edges of the wooden window shutters brightened, causing Lazarus some physical and emotional distress when it came in close proximity to the beams. Phillip, being the tallest, unwrapped the headdress he'd been wearing and draped it over the single, westward-facing window, blocking out almost all of the strengthening daylight.

By the light of a single oil lamp they finished up in preparation for slumber. Martha sat with Lazarus' unconscious head upon her lap while she stroked the side of its head in a hypnotic, gentle tracing. A couple strands of hair came out due to her caressing and, with a tired lack of emotion, she flicked them away. Watching the long, individual, brittle brown hairs fall, like feathers from a tumbled nest.

The rest of the house was beginning to hustle and bustle out beyond the wedged, locked door. At one point, someone tried to knock politely, then enter. This startled Lazarus and it moaned out with its whitish gray tongue pressed up against the roof of its mouth. Its eyes were rolled all of the way up into its head. The door, however, didn't budge. As for the knocker, whoever it was, based on previous history, assumed that the moan most likely came from one of Mary's regular male visitors and left.

Extinguishing the solitary flame of the oil lamp left them bathed in the stench of rot and a lukewarm morning grey. Mary knocked out first and was lightly snoring in minutes. Phillip's breathing deepened next, indicating he was slipping into sleep. Martha, however, laid there for the longest time before drifting off. Fighting against the impending sleep that hammered at her eyes. Watching her brother's lifeless body lay there. The thought kept spinning around and around in her mind, *Something's not right! Something's not right! Something's not right!!*

iv

Mary was replaying a memory in her dream. One from her early childhood of watching her father and her brother sawing at the base of a big Aleppo pine. She remembered her father had called the type of saw they were using a "misery whip". Her father at one end of the saw and her brother, Lazarus at the other. Back and forth they labored at the trunk of this massive tree, sweating, but they weren't making the slightest dent in the bark.

At least, none that she could remember upon being awoken by the sound of rushed, raspy whispering. Her eyes fluttered in strong resistance to coming open. In her struggling mind, she could now recognize the whispering as belonging to her sister and Phillip. And the sawing that she had been dreaming of had been spawned by the sound of her own snoring. She also realized an acute awareness of the strong urge to urinate.

Sitting up, Mary rubbed her stinging eyes and stretched her arms over her head, feeling as though she hadn't slept nearly enough, or even at all. Upon opening her eyes, she saw only a little beyond the soft illumination of a single oil lamp beneath the worried, pallid faces of Phillip and Martha. Phillip's headdress was still draped over the only window, permitting thin, angling slivers of daylight to peek in around the edges. Other than that, the room was stifling and smelled like a corpse-riddled tomb.

Speaking of which, that was what drew Mary's attention next. The subject of Martha and Phillip's hurried, anxious sounding conversation. It laid in the corner of the room, by the heavy storage chest, on a small hill of pillows, back arched like a contortionist, pushing its sunken belly up towards the ceiling. Twitching involuntarily every few moments. Its lips were pulled away, revealing a wide mouthful of dingy, yellow teeth resting in purple, decayed, receding gums. Skeletal hands with long, pointy fingernails flexed in the air. Rigid fingers were splayed wide apart in a horrifying, statuesque pose.

Mary doubted that what she was looking at was real. Her mind winced and didn't want to accept what the eyes were seeing. She felt that she must still be trapped in a dream that was swiftly becoming a nightmare.

But, now Martha and Phillip, seeing that she was awake, scooted over closer beside her.

"How did you sleep?" Martha asked wearily.

"Not enough," was Mary's reply, picking flakes from the corner of her eye. "What time is it?"

"Three, maybe four in the afternoon. Could be later," came Phillip's hoarse whisper. He also offered the fact, "I'm starving."

Martha patted his hand, eliciting temporary patience from him. Turning back to Mary, Martha rubbed with aggressiveness at her swollen eyes. "Something isn't right," she blurted. "Lazarus-" the older sister couldn't say anymore as she shook her head and pressed her lips together to keep them from quivering.

"I mean look at him! He's not breathing for God's sake!" Phillip said in a frantic whisper.

Mary looked over to her brother's body and realized, to her surprise, Phillip was right! There was **ZERO** rise and fall to Lazarus' chest. Her brother's body remained locked and contorted. Its awful fingers spread apart. Its back arched into a cruel curve. Dark open pockets dotting its skin where the flesh had either been gnawed at or sloughed away. It honestly broke Mary's heart to see her brother transformed like this.

Without warning, a thought invaded Mary's sleep deprived mind, *We should have left him in the tomb.*

Mary admitted, of course, that she was eternally grateful that her brother had been, beyond all reasoning, resurrected. But, this...this was something else on a different level. She one hundred percent agreed with Martha. Just look at Lazarus! You didn't have to be a soothsaying wiseman to see that something was not right. "We must get word to Jesus," said Mary. "He'll know what to do."

"He is in hiding," Martha retorted, her eyes bulging out of her head. "Did he tell you where he was going?"

For certain, the answer was, *No.* Mary's hazel eyes cast themselves downward and she bit at her bottom lip in defeated consternation.

Phillip put a heavy sentimental hand on her shoulder and smiled at her with a hearty stoicness beneath his huge, bushy beard. “He can’t be far,” he rumbled.

The younger sister nodded up and down in a silent response. Her tired mind spun.

Martha, however, scoffed in frustration. “We need to think,” she emphasized, sounding on the verge of anger. “Where would he go?”

“Well, they’re looking for Him aren’t they?” Phillip asked.

“Yes,” Martha responded with a hint of uncontrollable irritation to her tone. “And?”

Phillip said in a calm manner, “I would think that would narrow down which direction he would go. At least a little.”

Mary lifted her head. Martha’s eyes widened with a smidgen of hope and she patted his hairy mitt with approval, saying, “Yes. They definitely wouldn’t be heading West towards Jerusalem.”

Phillip and Mary nodded along in unison in agreement to this statement.

Martha continued, “That leaves South to Hebron, or East towards Cyprus.” Getting lost in thought, she tapped at her furry, unscrubbed teeth.

“Or North, which would take him to Jericho,” Mary finished for her. “Maybe further. Possibly as far as Ephraim.”

“Yes,” Martha said in an absentminded way. After a moment of contemplation, she focused back in on them, and said with a nervous shrug, “We’ll just have to send word to the North, East and South. Hope for the best.”

It wasn’t much, but what other choice did they have besides sending urgent letters in all three directions? Just in hopes that word reached Jesus sooner rather than later? All while keeping Lazarus hidden from public view in the meantime?

They wouldn’t be able to keep up a juggling act like that for very long. Talk about spinning plates!

All three stared at the twisted, rigid body of Lazarus. In her personal silence, Martha prayed to God for help, while holding her breath, as a force of habit. Phillip was rummaging about the room for some passable substitution for the headdress that he had hung up over the window, in order to block out the daylight. (He was being considerate of not waking Lazarus by removing the shade.) Meanwhile, Mary was fussing with the pillows surrounding Lazarus, trying to ensure he was comfortable, even though he looked anything but.

Phillip continued to scavenge around Mary's room for something that would pass for a suitable headdress. But, Mary, being who she was, possessed fabrics that were either flamboyant in pattern or color. Or both. Nothing plain and masculine. No drab article of cloth left behind by some random scamp.

Martha had finished her prayer and was watching Phillip's dilemma unfold, until he was standing, helpless, with a shiny purple *Argaman* sash in one hand and a robe of *Tekhelet* blue stripes intersected by scarlet stripes in the other.

"Just take yours off of the window," Martha said. "I'm sure a little bit of daylight won't be enough to wake him." Referring to Lazarus.

In response, Phillip set Mary's ostentatious garments on the small table next to him. Relieved and ready to eat, he snatched his bit of colorless plain, sturdy wool from atop the window. This immediately cast a bright beam of late afternoon sunlight through a splintered gap in the wooden shutters. This bright beam of light landed in a searing, diagonal streak right across Lazarus' face!

The reaction from Lazarus was instantaneous. Sunken pale eyes snapped open. Its multiple voices joined up in a chorus of high banshee-like howls, erupting from his singular maw, causing their hands to fly up and cover their ears. Lazarus' body curled and spun away from the sliver of direct sunlight into a fetal position. Frail tendrils of smoke lifted and sashayed in lazy calligraphy on the air above him. Mary covered his body with her own as she reached out, snatching pillows and blankets to cover her smoldering brother with.

"Cover it!" Mary screamed at Phillip as Lazarus writhed in pain and squirmed underneath her. Phillip fumbled with the fabric. Dropping it to the floor, flustered. Martha rushed over to help him affix the thick, woolen fabric over the shutters again.

Once they had done it, with the room back to a near pitch black darkness, Lazarus lay for a few moments, restless and moaning from the pain.

Pain? From being burnt by sunlight? Martha was thinking. Her mind careened as to what other side effects they could expect from this "miracle". She inched over to the lump that was her brother. It was buried underneath a mass of girly shaded pillows. She reached down and made to move a large, tufted purple pillow aside. This resulted in a violent, reactionary flinch from Lazarus, causing the three of them to flinch as well and jump back a full cubit.

Coming close again, Martha knelt down and moved aside the pillow, revealing a perfect two inch wide, precise slash of third degree puckered, smoldering flesh running across the width of its face, from jaw to temple. Its ashen eyes had closed again, and Martha felt a sharp pang of undeniable shame for being relieved by that fact. In order of her own personal retribution, she leaned further down and brushed her lips upon her brother's bony, rancid cheek.

Behind dark purple-veined gray, sunken closed eyelids, it sensed and became enticed by Martha's unwashed flesh. It turned with its mouth open, ready to bite.

Martha pulled away in horror and pushed her brother's dead, smoking face back beneath the pillows with both hands. Following this with placing another large, tasseled pillow over the top of it. For a moment, it writhed, like a pit of snakes, beneath the softness. Its rigored joints cracking loud and offensively.

Upon standing and spinning around, Martha saw her sister making a break for the door. Phillip was close behind her, with an ambiguous bit of fabric that belonged to her sister, clutched in his hand. Martha's feet scooted as fast as they could carry her. The swish-swish of their garments in motion sounded as loud as a sandstorm howling across the Judaen landscape.

Mary was reaching to open her door, when they all heard a muffled growl of what sounded like an unholy animal come from behind them. Underneath the mass of feather stuffed pillows, a tremor began to shake. All of the rancid air felt as if it was being sucked from the interior of the room at a rapid rate.

After a tangled blur of sequenced motions, they suddenly found themselves positioned with their backs against Mary's bedroom door, out in the corridor. All three were breathing in great big gusts. All three sets of their tired eyes were full circle with fear. A comical, flamboyant bit of patterned fabric rested cattywampus atop Phillip's head, as a headdress.

There was a soft shuffling sound and a dim, flickering light coming from around the corner. It was the House Maid, Hannah, who had been a part of the house as far back as Mary or Martha could remember. At a slow and steady pace, she was making her way towards them with a small, skinny torch in her hand. This was used for lighting the corridor lamps. A duty of hers that came every day as afternoon bled into evening.

She slowed her approach as she came closer to them. Casting flickering firelight upon them and recognizing the disheveled state they were all in.

"Is everything alright ladies?" Hannah asked, arching an eyebrow high. Her shrewd perception was taking in the odd, shameless fact that Phillip was wearing something girly of Mary's.

Martha answered by exhaling in an overly enthusiastic tone, "Yes, Hannah! Never better!"

Hannah's age old, translucent eyes panned over them from one to the other. Her geriatric mind was piecing together a possible scenario of what could've transpired based on Mary's proclivities and the history of what goes on behind the closed door of her room. A judgmental expression pursed her lips into a downturned grimace. "Oh," Hannah said simply. Emotionless.

Mary played into this and leaned into Phillip, twirling a playful finger in his thick beard. Phillip's eyes, somehow, became larger. "Don't worry about tidying up my room, Hannah," Mary said, even throwing in a sinful giggle, "it's a real mess in there." Then, she slapped Phillip's face sadistically.

Martha let out a shocked yelp. Phillip was just stunned, mouth agape. Hannah's judgemental grimace deepened, as her assumptions were confirmed.

Hannah served them up a quick harrumph, turned up her nose and continued to go about her swing shift duties.

When Hannah was out of earshot, Martha barked out a quick relieved laugh, "Quick thinking Mary. But, strange. Why?" There was a slight, jealous edge to her voice.

Mary smiled and shrugged her shoulders, saying, "It got rid of her, didn't it?" She then produced a skinny, iron key from an inner pocket and locked the door to her room. A mild, low growl alerted both sister's fear once again, thinking it came from the corpse of their brother on the other side of the door.

Instead, Phillip grasped at his empty stomach as it clutched in hunger pangs. They all nodded in unspoken unison and made their way for a quick wash up. Compose themselves. Then, it was across the atrium to the kitchen. Once there was some food in their bellies, they could concentrate on getting a plan into motion.

Although, as they left, no one was around to hear another, not so mild, horrific, inhuman growl coming from beyond the bolted threshold of Mary's room.

V

In the meantime, Caleb was approaching the Temple with a couple of familiar faces that were in attendance for the previous night's "miracle". There was a palpable determination to the rhythm of their step. Worried expressions were cemented onto their sleep deprived faces. But, their eyes blazed red-rimmed with the fever of a fundamentalist conviction.

It was Joseph ben Caiaphas they searched for. He must know of this "sin against the natural order of the Law" as Caleb and his two stool pigeons had been parroting amongst themselves at length. All night. They had been circling the night's events over and over. Demonizing every minute spent. Deliriousness had partnered up with them long ago. Being sleep indigent, hungry and traumatized had left them well beyond the category of fanaticism.

A loud, bustling Temple buzzed beneath a monolithic ceiling. It was full of hopeful worshippers from all over Judaea offering pigeons, doves, goats and bulls as burnt offerings for sacrificial atonement. Roman soldiers decked out in their lorica segmentata/squamata with *Machaira* swords in thick leather scabbards affixed to their hips and carrying long, imposing *Pilum* javelins, hugged the perimeter. Pharisees, along with Sadducees peppered the crowd, some selling cakes and incense, some on their knees, tearing open their robes at the chest, screaming a ridiculous performative prayer up to a God. It did not make for the most ideal atmosphere to divulge a terrifying account of a freakish resurrection.

The trio weaved through the crowd for a long while without any luck in their search for the High Priest. Up, past the Nicanor Gate and the Brazen Altar, or Kebesh, they turned left, past The Twelve Steps coming up to The Firstborn Gate. Still no luck at finding Caiaphas here. They continued on in the same direction. Past the Lightning Gate. Turning right at Upper Gate. Another right to confirm that Caiaphas was not amongst those at Jeconiah Gate. It came as no surprise to them, by this time, that he was not present at Flame Gate either.

Finally, they came upon a sizable crowd, packed tight and congregated around a group of Priests performing a ritual known as a Sin Offering at Sacrifice Gate.

Seven Priests cloaked in black robes assembled together with fine, sharp blades clasped in their bejeweled hands as they approached a beast to be sacrificed upon a large stone altar. The animal, tethered in place with burly, rough rope, stamped its hooves in a skittish, futile effort to get away. A well off, rich looking man kneeled close by. His sweaty hands were clasped together in fervent, mumbled supplication. He was crying. Tears and snot ran in gross rivulets down his distressed face into his oiled beard.

Joseph ben Caiaphas was spotted finally. He was standing off to the side with his arms crossed, looking tall, whip-thin and fearful. His dark eyes were supervising over the beginning of ritual that must adhere to the parameters of the Mosaic Law in every aspect. That, after all, was what these sinners were paying for. The Priests were, in a finite way, the gatekeepers to God and with the right amount of coin, almost any sin could be forgiven. Plus, more than anything, Caiaphas was hyper focused on portraying an image of a peaceful, controlled Judaea to the Roman foreigner elites.

The large, horned animal blared in protest. Its insane eyes darted about and its legs bucked behind it in wild, fitful bursts. The sin committed must have been something truly heinous, considering the size and quality of the offering. Priests encircled the beast and faced out at the surrounding onlookers. Their sacrificial, glinting blades were held upright in front of them, catching a dull shine from the ambient firelight.

The stage was set. The crowd was baited, transfixed and thirsty for bloodshed.

Encrusted in an exorbitant amount of jewelry and practically swimming in his temple garb, Caiaphas glided away from the column he had been leaning against in a nonchalant manner, looking very much like an eel emerging from a small cave. The High Priest's arms came uncrossed and he held them open, palms up in a prideful gesture of meek prostration. He floated, dreamlike, into the formed circle. Coming closer to the rich sinner and attempting to distort his face in a mask of calm, entreating delight.

The clamoring of the surrounding crowd had died down significantly to an unbroken soft, rippling of a murmur. They watched in suspense as the impressive animal was being prepared for sacrifice. The man, or more aptly, the sinner who had paid a good amount of coin for the offering and an even greater amount for the High Priest of the Year to plead his case of repentance, wept bitter tears.

When Caiaphas felt that he held everyone's attention, his dark eyes lifted to the heavens. In a high, piercing voice that shook the rafters, "Most High God of the Heavens and Earth," Caiaphas let each syllable hang for a moment and echo, "we come before you today to, first, to say thank you God," a few of those with their heads bowed nodded in solemn unity, "Thank you for allowing us entry to your House, so that we may speak with you directly, God."

The beast screamed out loud on the altar. It was wrestling against the rough ropes it had been bound with, causing its hide to rip and bleed around the woven hemp restraints.

Caiaphas continued, "We come into your House today to beseech you on behalf of this mortal sinner." The rich man Caiaphas was referencing began to blubber in tongues and shake. "For the sin of conspiring to murder his fellow man, a friend, in order to pursue unfettered adultery with the victim's wife," this drew a few reprimanding hisses and a few gasps of satisfied shock, "We offer you this wonderful beast of the Earth in hope of making Atonement for this man's terrible crime." The accused man cried aloud and, in a wild theatrical gesture, tore at his hair and ripped his garments asunder.

At this point, the crowd surged in closer to the altar, in anticipation of what they really came for. The actual sacrifice. Carnage. They pressed in, smushing Caleb and his two associates up against one another. The potpourri of everyone's body odor and breath created a soup in the air that didn't want to be swallowed.

Now, the seven Priests turned towards the wailing animal. In rehearsed synchronization they all raised their short swords high above their heads, and waited for the cue.

This was Caiaphas' favorite part. Letting the last few moments of the Sin Offering's life stretch out over an uncomfortable amount of time, until those in attendance would begin to whisper. Shifting their feet from left to right. Looking from the High Priest, to the sacrificial animal, then, back to the High Priest. Becoming unsure if the kill was going to come.

"Most High God, you and you alone are the life," Caiaphas voice rang confident and shrill. On the utterance of the word "life", the seven Priests proceeded to slash and thrust at the beast in a display of choreographed panache and dizzying flourishes of steel, until the animal dropped to the ground. One of the participants slit deep into the screaming throat of the animal, releasing a solid fan of dark red blood all over the floor. The crowd cheered at the sight of the fresh gore.

The most prominent of the seven, the young Priest with a patchy copper beard, James ben Jonah, rose up from the midst of the other priests, as a viper props itself up amongst the tall grass about to strike. He pulled the sleeves up on both arms, revealing sinewy tanned forearms intersected with light blue veins. He held up his hands in the air, drawing even more abundant cheers of adulation from those gathered. With a disturbing amount of relish and gusto he then plunged his hands deep into the neck wound of the dying beast, while spewing phrases like *"Only God forgives!"* and *"Blood is life!"*. Tendrils of spit flung from his mouth. His eyes bulged out of his skull, while he swirled his fingers at length through the viscera.

Joseph ben Caiaphas' voice rang high above the raging din, "The blood is the life! Only you are capable of true forgiveness, God!!"

James then ripped his hand from the wound, splattering some of the onlookers, eliciting a few gasps. Following this, he, along with the other six, coated the entire altar with the poor animal's blood. A few of the surrounding Pharisees ripped at their own garments in unison with the big finish, making a real dramatic show of all of it.

"Amen!" Caiaphas concluded.

When the dust had settled and the feverish crowd had dissipated, in search of the next gruesome sacrifice to behold, the scene before Caleb was reduced to its most based, crudest form. The magic of the ritual had evaporated. All that was left was the seven disheveled, spent Priests with torn robes, half covered in blood and the lifeless carcass in front of the altar. Flies danced all about in the air by the hundreds.

The Holy Men were cleaning the blood from themselves, discussing whether to eat the animal or take it outside and burn it, when Caleb, with his cohorts in tow, entered their hemisphere. Caiaphas' back was turned to them as he gave some final words of business to the rich sinner, for whom the ritual had just been performed.

"My Lord, Caiaphas," Caleb interrupted with urgency clinging to his tone like tree sap. "There is a matter we must discuss with you at once."

Caiaphas finished what he was saying to the wealthy man, spun around and looked over at the three of them, unamused. He studied them for a moment, squinting his dark eyes. A lone, solid streak of animal blood glistened across the bridge of his nose.

Then, he said with the bored intent of brushing off these vagabonds, "Rituals for Sin Offerings are concluded for the day." His eyes crossed for a split second as he noticed the red sacrificial blood streaked across his nose. Peeved, he rubbed at the spot with the sleeve of his adorned robe while adding, "You can purchase offerings from one of the Priests and try to come back tomorrow. God be with you."

"No, High Priest Caiaphas," Caleb replied, amping up the urgency to eleven, drawing the concerned attention of James and a few others within the vicinity. Caleb leaned in closer, lowering his voice. "It's about Jesus."

Caiaphas' right eyebrow crept up high. Intrigued. "Well, let's see if what you have to say is as interesting as you make it seem."

vi

Caleb and company divulged everything they had seen a mere sunrise ago. Grisly details came forth in a spilling torrent from all three, sometimes from one at time, but, for the most part, their stories converged on top of one another's all at once. Their combined extreme hysteria came off as very convincing.

They had all migrated through the attending crowds. Winding away from the Sacrifice Gate and now, they sat outside the Hall of Priests, at the Nansia Tables. This choice was made on purpose in order to utilize the brutal cacophony of the busy, nearby Abottoir to conceal the details of their conversation.

Caiaphas, along with his father-in-law, Annas and the young Priest, James, acting as supporting witnesses, could not believe the account that was laid out before them. Their eyes increased in circumference until the story tellers had disclosed everything up to this present moment. The trio of Holy Men, all members or sympathizers of the Sanhedrin, were left speechless after the fantastical story had been regurgitated. Now they were chewing it all over before a full digestion of what they had just heard.

Annas moved in and probed again, "You are positive that you have no idea as to Jesus, or his apostles, whereabouts?"

"Yes, Rabbi," Caleb replied honestly. "He left after the...the resurrection."

Caiaphas asked with razor sharpness, "What direction?"

"East?" Caleb offered, unsure. At the same time, both of his partners contradicted one another, by saying, "North?" And "South?"

We're done here, Caiaphas thought. *This tree has been plucked of all of its fruit. For now.*

Annas leaned and whispered into his son-in-law's ear, "I suggest you call an urgent meeting of the Sanhedrin. At once."

Caiaphas nodded in silent, curt agreement to this suggestion. Then, Annas and the younger, ambitious James, thanked the three for confiding in them. Afterward, they took their leave from the group, heading straight in the direction of the Hall of Priests.

Through a filter of numbness, moving without thinking, Caiaphas reached to an inner pocket and pulled out a small tied satchel of fifty shekels (1 shekel = 11.4-20 grams) worth of silver. A good amount for ten commoners. "Such information should be rewarded handsomely," Caiaphas offered, but his mind was already turning the gears. The blurry, outer edges of a plan were beginning to form.

Caleb stood paralyzed with his two companions. All three were dumbfounded by the weight of silver that Caleb now held in his hands.

Caiaphas voice dripped with slimy oil upon their ears once more, "You will be sure to find us if you come across any further information, won't you?"

Caleb was peeking into the satchel, stunned into stupor. Both of his partners' faces crowded in around his own to also stare with disbelief at the wonderful sheen and glint of all of the beautiful silver staring back at them.

Caiaphas cleared his throat voluntarily and Caleb's eyes drifted up to him, regaining focus. Caiaphas squared up to him and commanded now, "Keep your eyes and ears open." The High Priest long fingers grasped him by the biceps. "Report back to me directly, with whatever you find."

Caleb nodded and whispered, "Yes, Rabbi."

"Good," Caiaphas said, releasing his grip on him. Oily once again, "There is sure to be more silver in it for you."

All three smiled and nodded their vigorous affirmations. Thanking Joseph ben Caiaphas over and over again, confirming their allegiance to the point of getting on the High Priest's nerves. But, he kept it oily and slick enough to lubricate them right out of the Temple. Monetarily induced smiles had been placed upon their faces and a furthering dark purpose had been planted within the corrupted soil of their hearts.

vii

Within the hour, in the Chamber of Hewn Stones, Caiaphas had assembled every available member of the Sanhedrin, in order to discuss what he just learned regarding Jesus and the unbelievable resurrecting of Lazarus. A select number of the seventy-one members were in attendance for this impromptu meeting. Gamaliel the Elder, the representing president in this chamber, or Nasi, sat ancient, tired and bored upon a towering throne in the center of a semi-circle dais.

The hard triple *CLACK! CLACK! CLACK!* of shellacked femur bone on femur bone, fresh from the Abottoir, echoed hollow in the Chamber. With precision, this cut off all presumptive murmuring and suspicious conversation. The source of the call to order came from Annas, but, in these walls he was the presiding Av Beit Din, or chief of the court. The old ogre stood hunched over, gripping the two long, fat bones. This piercing triple strike called the impromptu meeting to order.

Gamaliel started by clearing his throat of loose phlegm and saying, "I want to start by thanking all of you that could attend this meeting of the Greater Sanhedrin on such short notice."

This drew a ripple of short, subdued applause from each of the religious men flanking in a semi circle on each side of the Head of the Sanhedrin.

Gamaliel yawned wide, despite the early afternoon hour. Everyone, except for Caiaphas, Annas and James, waited with a calm sense of patience for Gamaliel to compose himself. Gamaliel rubbed at his wrinkled eyes, before continuing on in a narcoleptic rumble, "We will commence this meeting after approaching The Most High for his blessing."

Obedient Pharisees and Sadducees bowed their heads low, letting their phylactery boxes hang and dangle away from their foreheads. A few others fell to their knees in a dramatic display, holding their hands out wide, faces titled up towards the ceiling.

A bald, ageless stenographer sat cross legged at the foot of Gamaliel's throne, ready to record every word into symbols on animal skin parchment. A small clay pot of lampblack ink sat next to him and a fresh dipped reed pen hovered in anticipation for dictation over the page.

Then, Gamaliel's gravel-gargling, weathered voice rumbled dull and lifeless throughout the chamber, bouncing off of the Hewn Stone walls, traveling in and out of earshot, "Most High God, we humbly come before you to thank you for what has been provided today and ask that you bless this meeting of the Greater Sanhedrin. Make our decisions wise and our judgements swift. Amen."

All of the men mumbled in concurring unison, "Amen." This was followed by the sloughing white noise shifting of their holy garments, as they all took their seats.

Immediately, Caiaphas stood, claiming ownership of this gathering. Nasi, feeling uncomfortable from being rushed, grumbled, "Rabbi, Joseph ben Caiaphas, you have called us here for what purpose?"

The High Priest of the Year, tall and sharp as a javelin, dove into the subject at hand, “It has come to be known that Jesus of Nazareth…has raised Lazarus of Bethany from the dead.”

The statement hung for a few solid seconds in a recoil of shock before a moral member with a thick, white cotton beard, named Nicodemus stood and said, “What? Impossible! He has been dead, what, three days now!?”

“Four,” Av Beit Din corrected in a strong growl.

“Practically five,” Caiaphas added, high and shrill.

A younger member named Joseph of Arimathea, took the floor meekly and prompted his peers, “If what you say is, indeed, true, then this ‘man’, Jesus of Nazareth, possesses much greater power than any of us here.” Caiaphas squinted his dark eyes down to a pair of suspicious slits. The adolescent member kept on, “Greater than all of us combined, for that matter!”

“Where would you say this ‘power’ comes from, Joseph of Arimathea?” Av Beit Din challenged, leaning forward, his grey, wispy beard brushed the tops of his knees. “Could it be that he possesses this ‘power’ through an alliance with demons?”

This caused the entire Chamber of Hewn Stone to erupt into a clamoring circus of overlapping opinions. Arguments and insults were hurled across the Chamber at one another without impunity. Some, like the young, ambitious James, were bullishly pushing the claim that Jesus’ power to resurrect life was being supplied by means of demonic forces. Others, like Nicodemus and Joseph of Arimathea, were trying, in a delicate way, to suggest the possibility of this power coming from a Divine source.

CLACK! CLACK! CLACK! CLACK! CLACK!

The piercing, manic smacking together of the femur bones cut all of these arguments off, like when a *Maakeleth* (a sharp, ritualistic blade), removes the head of a pure, sacrificial dove. Silence hung as solid as liquid. Weighing down, pressing on the bickering members long after the echo of the clacking finished bouncing off of the walls.

The Av Beit Din, held the two large bones in a confrontational posture, gripping the bright white bones in each gnarly hand. He then broke the hanging silence by saying in a gruff voice, “What are we accomplishing here?”

No one chose to answer this. Caiaphas smirked at the redirection he saw his father-in-law making.

Suddenly, a younger member of the Sanhedrin, known as Stephen, stood and obstinately offered, "What are we to do? Here is this man performing many signs. If we let him go on like this, everyone will believe in him! The Romans will see that we are divided and come to take away both our Temple and our nation!"

Caiaphas saw his moment and attacked, spitting venom, "You know nothing at all!" Stephen looked like an adolescent, scared rodent caught in the gaze of a viper. "You do not realize that it is better for *you* that this one man dies for the people than that the whole nation perishes."

Nasi and Ab Beit Din nodded their old heads in approval, knowing that this is what Caiaphas had prophesied earlier in the year; *that Jesus would die for the Jewish nation, and not only for the nation but for the scattered children of God, to bring them together and make them one.*

Av Beit Din corroborated this point by saying, "Brothers, don't you see that if Jesus of Nazareth incites an uprising by way of parading around these 'miracles' to the majority, who are the most common, the Roman elite will view us as disjointed? Divided. Our power will be taken." The Chamber of Hewn Stone bubbled in a demuring echoing murmur, then quieted. "Roman rule will then seize our beloved Jerusalem from us!"

A threatening sense of dread for fear they lose their positions of power, caused a murky evil to enter most of their hearts. Nicodemus and Joseph of Arimathea gathered a few fellow sympathizers and left the chamber in disgust at the utter lack of God in the modern Sanhedrin. However, for the rest, from that time on, they all joined in a campaign of conspiracy to trap and kill the *Messiah*.

viii

Mary, Martha and Phillip ate until they couldn't eat anymore. In between bites they weighed their minimal options and constructed a simple plan to try to make contact with Jesus and his twelve. They decided that their only viable path of action forward was sending word in the three directions that didn't lead to Jerusalem and hope for a speedy response. It wasn't much, but it was all they had. So, three rock doves were prepared with a succinct message attached to all three of their legs, which said, *Something is wrong. Come quickly. Martha.* The messenger birds were then cast off, bearing the hefty weight of a desperate prayer to the North, South, and East.

By this time, it was steadily creeping towards night. After sending the messenger birds away, their thoughts turned back towards Mary's room and what was being harbored behind the locked door. Lazarus, or whatever it was becoming was a mind-bending topic that they had avoided up until now. It was strange. Almost as though their minds were attempting to reject the stark reality of their situation. This same line of reasoning subscribed to the weak belief that if you didn't believe in the horrible thing, then the horrible thing didn't exist. An argument that instantly crumbled when challenged by the simple, cruel truth that eventually everything had to bend to the non-negotiable laws of reality.

While cutting across the atrium, Martha noticed a bright waxing gibbous moon, unmasked by any cloud cover and traveling high overhead. Stars clustered around it and filled the twilight canopy, like glittering salt scattered across a cold slab of dark slate. A fountain was bubbling in tranquil, quiet solitude. Oh, how she just wished she could sit for a while and enjoy this peaceful, serene setting, while hoping that...what? That Lazarus was alright now? Sitting properly and waiting for them in Mary's room? Fully cognizant and restored back to his normal self?

Martha prayed that her hope stayed intact and wouldn't be wasted on something that could never be. She was hoping against hope that the miracle of her brother's resurrection wasn't in fact turning out to be like what Caleb had called it, "an abomination". Also she held hope that Lazarus wasn't suffering. That, maybe, it took a day or so for their brother to be the way he was before. After all, he was dead for four days. That's a long time to go without any spark of brain activity.

They found themselves now down towards the end of the corridor standing in front of Mary's locked door. A definite, fetid smell was creeping around the edges, and from underneath the door. Phillip was holding his nose with one hand and a small, sleek oil lamp that cast only a bit of light for the trio in the other. Martha put her ear up to the door, listening for sounds of rustling or moans or growls on the other side.

Silence was the only thing she could hear coming through the wooden door and she pulled away. Looking at the other two, Martha swiveled her head from left to right. *Nothing.* This didn't do anything but keep them all clueless as to the situation inside.

Once again, Mary produced the long, iron key from the inner pocket of her robe. She paused momentarily with the tip of the key almost touching the mouth of the lock. "What do we do if he's worse than when we left?" Mary asked in an innocent voice.

Neither Martha, nor Phillip were able to give an acceptable answer to this hypothetical line of questioning. Phillip just shrugged his big shoulders. Martha however put her hand over Mary's hand holding the key, and gave her an answer that wasn't really an answer, "We'll have to cross that bridge when we come to it."

Mary nodded, not fully reassured. She tried to uplift her older sister, "Well, whatever the outcome, he's still our brother. Right?"

Even though she found this statement difficult to corroborate, Martha agreed. Nodding her head up and down silently. Her demeanor could be considered somewhat dubious, seeing as how she had drawn up her bottom lip into a deep frown.

Without any further hesitation, Mary plunged the key into the lock and turned it, activating the clunking mechanics within.

Putting their bodies into it and forcefully pushing the door inward released a powerful, juicy, dead stench that barreled out into the corridor, causing both ladies to wretch, almost losing the food they had just stuffed themselves on. Likewise, Phillip cringed away from the threshold, taking some of the precious light from the little oil lamp with him.

Luckily the initial bout of nausea passed and no one blew chunks in the corridor. With a trepid step they entered the dark, rancid room. As soon as their eyes had adjusted to the consummate darkness of the room they all sought out the mound of pillows that they had last seen Lazarus buried underneath. To their morbid surprise the pillows were strewn about the area where it had laid, leaving an empty pocket of an imprint where its frail body had once been.

Upon realizing Lazarus' absence their heads swiveled all about on their necks. Eyes darting this way and that. Searching all over the room and growing more frantic the longer they couldn't find him. That's when Mary noticed the large storage chest that she had used to conceal the comings and goings of countless, random lovers. It was pulled all of the way from the wall, exposing Lazarus' means of escape from Mary's locked room.

Martha and Phillip were staring at the little tunnel now, too. Puzzled, Phillip was sternly looking at the small opening that an adult could've easily crawled through. "What is that?" he asked.

It didn't even occur to Mary to be embarrassed about her secret entrance to her bed chamber being put on display for Phillip to cast his eyes and judgment upon. Without answering Phillip's question she kneeled down to crawl through, being followed promptly by Martha. Phillip had no other alternative but to go in after the sisters through the little, chiseled passage.

Outside, in the cool, fresh air of the night, Phillip emerged from the stifling rankness of Mary's room, on all fours. When he stood with the small oil lamp he noticed the sisters holding one another, standing a little ways away from him, stuck in complete paralyzing fear. As Phillip approached the sisters, he came to notice small, random chunks of bloody white and brown fur decorating the ground by their feet. These were a few sparse remnants from two older goats that had been their domestic pets for almost a decade. They had been ripped to shreds. The bulk of what remained of the decimated carcasses lay a few cubits away. Now that the scene was illuminated by Phillip's lamp they could see that both goats had been picked almost to cleanliness down to the bones, tendons and cartilage. Shock held all three of them firmly in place. Mary and Phillip were on the verge of full blown hyperventilating. Martha, as was usual for her, held her breath.

What could've done something like this? Martha wondered, but felt an inkling like she already knew a definitive answer to this question. Deep down she knew that she knew. She just wasn't even remotely close to admitting it to herself.

That's when their initial shock was shattered by the unmistakable siren sound of a woman's pained, terrified screaming in the distance. To the East. Maybe an avenue or two over from where they stood, as the crow flies. In the direction of the Mount of Olives and, by extension, their family's tomb nestled comfortably therein.

Upon hearing the scream, Mary broke her transfixed eye contact from what had up until recently been their two former pet goats. Moving fluidly she kicked open the bottom portion of the fence, so that they could all slip out through the slim panel of fencing. A tight fit for someone of Phillip's size and stature. After a moment's struggle, Phillip managed to wiggle through. Then the trio broke into an instantaneous sprint towards the source of the hysterical screaming.

Their frantic, racing route took them down an alley and wrapped around the street. Suddenly they were in the mix of a crowd of other people that consisted of mostly citizens of Bethany and a few alerted soldiers that had happened to be on patrol in the proximity. This led them all to an increasingly agitated throng amassed outside a gated courtyard. Behind that, a large house loomed big and imposing against the many torches that were being carried by most of those assembled. In a comical comparison to the surrounding bonfire of torches, Phillip held his teeny oil lamp, not even aware that he still had a tight grip on it.

"My son! My son!!" was being shrieked over and over again by a woman's voice on the other side of a locked wooden gate.

A shattered man's voice now joined her pained cries with its own heart-wrenching bellowing, "It's taken my boy! NO!!! IT HAS TAKEN MY CHILD!!"

Soldiers were beating upon the gate with the side of gauntleted fists, demanding that it be opened. Some people could be heard shouting above the banging, *"Look up there!"* and *"What in God's name is that?!"* They were all pointing up with extended index fingers towards the edge of the house at a dim, barely discernable figure. A curled over human-like shape stood as still as a stone for a second. Soft edges from the moonlight gave its silhouette a vague outline. With an inhuman howl it sprung from the roof of the house onto another, adjoining roof. Then another. Heading further East.

Some of the spectators, including our trio, broke away from the throng and chased after the creature. Their pursuit didn't last for very long. From rooftop to rooftop they tracked the shapeless monster, until it sprang away out of sight and was gone. Traveling on foot, by avenue and alley proved to be not as direct, or as speedy as traveling by supernatural bounding across rooftops.

Martha noted which direction the thing was heading. Once again, as the crow flies, it would be heading for the vicinity of their family tomb. The previous night's events leading up to this very moment played out in her mind. Thinking about Lazarus, struggling to come out of the tomb. Moving and sounding unnatural. The burn on its face from contact with a beam of direct sunlight. The demonic multiple voiced howl that followed. Also, the lack of inhaling and exhaling. Not to mention, the dead, mutilated goats in her yard. And the familiar howl heard once again from the rooftop. All of these factors piled on top of one another and crowded out every other sensible thought in her head.

Random diehard pursuers traipsed after the night creature, their necks craned to look up to the rooftops for any further signs of movement. Aloud they were speculating to each other about what could've possibly taken the young boy and hurdled across the tops of the houses at such nimble speed. They were wondering what the meaty, putrid smell that hung, suspended in the air could've oozed from. Pondering as to what could voice such a blood-curdling howl. Confusion, despair and fear rested across every face of the present investigating community.

Martha, Mary and Phillip, watched their neighbors, along with a couple of the soldiers, turn in circles while searching earnestly overhead, beyond the eaves.

Martha loudly exhaled a breath she had been holding, drawing the attention of her sister and Phillip. Together, they all exchanged a look between one another that suggested they knew something that no one else did. In an inconspicuous manner, they began to back away from the strangers, as they all chased after nothing further down the street, the trail getting colder by the second. Their fellow neighbor's panicked babbling trailed off and away from them, leaving the distant wailing of the grieving mother and father somewhere behind.

The three of them took to the lesser known alleys once again. Purposefully, swinging a wide route around this time to avoid the potential of running into the crowd with their torches and fear guiding them. Besides, all three of them felt certainty guiding their own intuition as to the true identity of the monstrous creature parading across the rooftops at inhuman speeds. Yowling like a rabid jaguar in many haunting voices. Holding a child in its clutches.

ix

The Mount of Olives awaited them tonight with sinister, swirling wisps of low clinging fog laying thick and gelatinous over every square handbreadth of the landscape. Trees seemed to sprout up right out of this opaque, luminescent soup. It twirled in dense, lazy ringlets around their ankles as they traversed through the grove with extreme caution.

The waxing gibbous moon's ascent had been minimal by the time they could finally make out the vague impression of the family tomb poking up at the far end of the courtyard. With the meager light that existed the tomb resembled something like a stout, rocky island rising out of a milky white lake's surface. Phillip's tiny oil lamp was proving to do very little in the way of brightening this wild endeavor.

As they crept up to the stone archway and the small courtyard beyond, they all felt a strange, foreboding sense of dread. Like something wicked waited in the air for them on the other side of the threshold. When they passed into the small, rectangular courtyard, they noticed an indescribable sense of a harmful, faceless force bearing down on them. Their skin began to crawl with the feeling of hundreds of invisible mandibles biting all over. An unexplainable burn went in their lungs with each breath and stung like citric acid at the corners of their eyes.

Mary broke the silence they had been coveting by whispering, while wiping at her irritated skin, "What is the meaning of this? Why does the air feel this way?"

Neither Martha nor Phillip could provide a credible answer to her questions, which were obviously their questions as well.

Near to hysterics, Mary continued to ask, "Martha, what could this mean, if he did, in fact take the child and come back here?"

Martha turned and stared large, serious eyes back at her sister. Tight lipped. Her lack of an answer scared Mary more than filling her head with any number of fantastical scenarios and horrific images. It was usual for Martha to always have a common sense answer or a remedy. That was part of her duty in carrying the mantle of an older, wiser big sister. The fact that the best she could come up with was nothing was truly harrowing.

Phillip opened his mouth and coughed upon the harsh, fizzy-feeling air, then began to offer some encouraging words, “Mary, I’m sure-” but he faltered in his speech as he stumbled over something laying on the stone path beneath the fog. By his quick reflexes though, he was able to catch his footing. Otherwise he would’ve fallen flat on his face. Once he was steadied, Phillip spun around and waved his free hand through the mist he had just passed through to see what he had tripped over. He pointed the oil lamp into the open, clear patches in the fog he created. This revealed a flash of something tan and red beneath the pale, low lying clouds. At first Phillip thought it was a short branch, so he reached down to pick it up and throw it off the path, but then he saw the small rigored fingers curled up into a tiny claw. Upon closer investigation, Phillip, Martha and Mary came to the petrifying realization that it was the severed, partial forearm of a young child. The tear line looked rough, with a snapped radius and ulna bone jutting out profanely. All three recoiled away from the lone, maimed body part, sucking in the cool night air through their exposed teeth.

While Phillip and Mary continued to examine the bodiless forearm, Martha stepped away, walking slowly through the fog to the tomb entrance. The entrance was once again covered over by the massive tombstone. A single dark, wet handprint glistened crimson and tacky on the face of the tombstone in the moonlight.

Could Lazarus have moved this alone? Martha wondered internally. Her eyes burned and her skin felt like it was begging to be scratched off.

“Martha?” Mary called breathlessly, rising up from the gory severed forearm.

“Sshhh,” Martha cut back sharply, while extending her shaky hand to touch the bloodied stone.

That’s when the stone rolled open a few handbreadths, being manipulated from the inside. This revealed a slim crescent of pure darkness and released an aged, rotten aroma. An echoing steady, rhythmic crunching could be heard, loud and crisp, coming from inside the antechamber. A stunned, speechless Mary and Phillip came up beside Martha to stare with huge, unblinking, frightened eyes into the occupied tomb.

“Why...are...you here?” the voices asked, sounding like detuned harp strings being strummed by a leprous stump. The sound of the voice could've been associated with their living brother, but it was also accompanied by more. It was a torn, ruined vocal overlapped by another slightly different vocal, and another. Giving the impression that more than one Lazarus was speaking.

"Lazarus?" Martha asked in a timid way, leaning forward in an awkward attempt to see into the pitch black interior of the tomb. Unable to believe it was really her resurrected brother in there, she asked. "Is it really you?"

Martha took a tiny step forward with her delicate hand extended out, and the crunching from within the tomb stopped with a sudden abruptness. Lazarus' voices erupted from the concealing darkness of the crypt, "COME NO CLOSER!!!"

Startled into swift action, Martha scrambled back into the waiting, embracing arms of Mary and Phillip. Contorted looks of absolute terror transformed all three of their faces. Mary shouted out random, incoherent, reactionary blasts of grief and fright into the ether of the night air. Phillip's little lamp flickered weakly against the all consuming darkness.

Inside the crypt, the crunching sounds resumed. As though casual, the voices from the tomb resumed answering her previous question in between chews, "As for...your question...to my being...Lazarus...the answer...is yes...and...also, no." This drew a perplexed silence from all three. Lazarus continued unabated, "This body...still...appears to be...what was once...your brother. But, now...it...is...so...much more."

"What? What do you mean?" Martha blurted out. Finally exhaling after holding a breath back in her tightening lungs.

Without a pause, Lazarus' multiple labored voices answered her back, "Something...that...shouldn't be." After these words, Martha thought she heard something that could've passed for a sinister chuckle bubble from the inky interior of the tomb.

Mary stepped forward now and wailed into the pitch blackness of the tomb, "But why are you back **here** Lazarus? Why aren't you home with us, you family?!"

"This…is…my home…now," was Lazarus' simple reply. The wet chewing sounds continued uninterrupted for a few moments. A gentle wind gusted across the courtyard, swirling the mist around their calves and causing the flame on the little oil lamp to dance a frantic jig.

"What can we do for you?" Martha broached as diplomatically as possible.

"Nothing," Lazarus answered. "Forget...I'm here."

"How do you expect us to do that?!" Mary screamed. "Now that we have you back, it's not really you? 'Something that shouldn't be?'" She sniffed back hard on a stream of clear snot, then continued on while marching up towards the tomb entrance, "We don't understand! How can we forget?!!"

Suddenly the rotten arm of Lazarus shot out from the darkness of the tomb, holding the removed head of a young boy by its slick, brown, bloody hair. The boy's face had been partially gnawed on one side, revealing a stark white cheekbone, upper jaw, a few baby molars and an empty orbital socket. The bottom jaw was also not attached.

"My God!!" Phillip shouted out loud. Martha remained hovering close to him. Both of their faces were barely lit by the small dancing flame in his hands.

Mary gasped aloud and stopped in her approach to get closer to the tomb. Her eyes were slightly crossed and pinned to the face of what used to be a ten year old boy, maybe. Beyond that, up past the protruding, stagnant stretch of arm that used to belong to her brother, was a vague outline of a sunken, bearded face. A solitary pale, lifeless eye was peeking around the edge of the stone and blazing at her above a gristled strip of blackened, charred skin. The blood drenched mouth worked up and down, metrically chewing on remnants of the male child.

Suddenly, the moderate wind died down and many voices filled the small courtyard, "I am...your brother...no...longer." Following a few rounds of the sickening chewing sounds, it commanded them to, "Leave...me be." It now pulled the mutilated child's head back in, and closed the tombstone, to continue its atrocious meal in peace and privacy.

Martha began to protest in her default, reprimanding older sister tone, "Lazarus, you can't expec-"

The enormous tombstone was flung to the side with ease. "LEAVE...ME...ALONE!!!" Lazarus' voices exploded from the pitch black tomb entrance, spraying blood from its mouth out to where they stood. Splattering their feet. Pushing the fog out away from the tomb's entrance in a fat arc, revealing the blood on their feet and the lone limb that once was attached to the boy. The scream made their eardrums tremble, causing their hands to fly up to the sides of their heads. The impact of the words felt as though they were punched right into their chests. Hard enough to blow out the flame on Phillip's oil lamp.

Martha and Phillip gritted their teeth and squinted their eyes against this assault. Mary, however, with hands clasped over her ears and eyes squeezed shut, returned defiantly, "NO, LAZARUS! WE LOVE Y-"

Lazarus lurched out into the moonlight, cutting off Mary's brief, defiant diatribe. Its hideous, naked body was illuminated pale and grey, with dark purple splotches that were as black as the inside of its tomb at the very center. With every movement Lazarus cracked and snapped, a side effect of being locked in rigor for four days. Blood was smeared up its forearms and down the front of itself in a shameless application. It still clutched the half eaten, severed head in its hand, but there was a little less of the head now than there was when previously seen.

By a sheer instinctual reflex they turned and ran. They ran and ran as fast as they could. They ran well past the point of their legs and lungs burning. True fear is what propelled them further and further until they were just outside of Bethany, where they trudged to a sloppy stop, at last. Then, they collapsed beside one another in a heap.

X

Back at the house, Phillip and the sisters let themselves back in through Mary's secret entrance. The thrashed goats still lay lifeless, gummy and glistening in the moonlight on their side of the fence. Now, knowing it was Lazarus that had torn them apart with its teeth and hands, Martha couldn't even bear to look at them.

The rock that had been used to conceal the low entrance to Mary's solo, non-profit brothel was still rolled aside (not that anyone would've messed with it). They crawled through one by one past the storage chest. Mary pulled the rock in over the hole in the wall, reminding herself of Lazarus moving the huge stone aside in its own tomb. She shivered, thinking of

Lazarus' pale eyes and the child's blood smeared all down the front of its torso.

After crawling on all fours into her room, Phillip and Martha helped Mary to her feet. Then they helped her push the hefty storage chest back against the wall. The room still held a distinct, gamey putrescence. Mary looked at where Lazarus' body had last laid and, in that moment, she wanted to set the pile of soft, velvety tufted pillows on fire.

Martha pushed open the window, holding a swath of fabric from her headwrap in a bunched fist underneath her nose. Phillip coughed and gagged in protest to the saliva flooding his mouth in preparation for vomit.

They were all still in collective shock from the shared encounter and had barely spoken to one another since leaving the family tomb. The three of them wandered about the room, tidying up, lighting candles and just moving around to avoid speaking about what they had seen.

"I need some wine," Mary announced to the room.

Martha chose this moment to speak on something that had been bouncing around in her mind since collapsing just outside of Bethany, "Wasn't there a rumor that Jesus also resurrected a young child that had died?"

Phillip slowed his fanning of the foul air in the room out of the open window with a medium, satin, fuchsia colored pillow and looked over at Martha. "Yes," he said, intrigued. Ceasing his fanning entirely. "A young girl. I think she was about eleven or twelve years old."

"Jairus' daughter," Mary said uninterested. "I'm going to call for wine, maybe some fruit. Do either of you want anything?"

Martha looked at her younger sister in surprise, "Mary, it's very late." Mary looked around disoriented. "The whole house is asleep," Martha explained to her like she was telling a child why they couldn't fly.

Not to be assuaged, Mary shook her head and walked towards her door. "In that case I'm going to the kitchen," she announced over her shoulder. "I'll be right back."

She was out of the door before Martha could utter another word of discouragement. Martha turned back to Phillip, who was sticking his head all of the way out of the window, breathing in deep through his nose and out through pursed lips. His eyes were squeezed shut as he concentrated on keeping his food down in his stomach.

"Jairus," Martha repeated out loud. The name rang a vaguely familiar note in her memory.

"Capernaum," Philip said in a monotone. His head still stuck out the window. Eyes pinched shut.

"What, Phillip?" Martha asked, genuinely not hearing him.

Phillip coughed a couple of times, spit, and then craned his face back around to look at her in the room. "Capernaum," he said again. "Where Jairus lives with his daughter." He popped his head back out of the window, where he could take great gulpfuls of the cool night air.

Martha paced the room back and forth, holding her breath and tapping her lips. Her mind was a jumbled up puzzle swept away in a fierce, sweeping typhoon. There were only minuscule, perceptible bits and pieces of the full picture flying around in her mind. Just trying to make any viable sense of what was known to her now, was far beyond what she is capable of. Martha wished for Jesus to be there. She was sure he would know what to do. Wouldn't he?

Martha was a fidgety, antsy ball of restlessness. She looked up and asked Phillip, "How fast could you get there?"

Looking green and queasy, Phillip drew his head back in through the window and asked her back, "To Capernaum?"

Martha nodded, *Yes.*

Phillip's eyes rolled up to the ceiling in careful thought, while he calculated the distance. "A thousand furlongs? I'd say, oh, roughly five days or so by foot."

"What about by horse?" Martha pressed urgently.

"Four days," Phillip answered. Shrugging, he added, "Maybe three."

Mary returned now to the room with a crooked smile on her face. She carried a bowl of figs, a pitcher of wine and three cups on a platter. A bleary quality now hung about her eyes, like she had already taken the liberty of imbibing a cup or two of wine before coming back to join them.

"Aneeone care fohr ah cup ovv wine?" Mary asked in a jovial tone. "Ur zum figz?"

"None for Phillip," Martha answered. "He has to leave."

"I do?" Phillip asked, stunned, at the same time that Mary asked, "He duz?"

Martha was nodding up and down in absentminded agreement, while tapping emphatically at her lips. "Yes," she answered them both.

"Whure izzee going at thizzour?" Mary asked thickly, followed by a long sip from one of the cups from the tray. Tilting her head back to accommodate the volume of liquid being consumed.

"Capernaum," Martha replied.

"Capernaum?" Mary and Phillip echoed.

"Yes," answered Martha again. She approached Phillip now, looking up into his handsome face. "I need you to go to Capernaum to seek out Jairus. I need you to find out what has become of his daughter that the Messiah is rumored to have resurrected." Phillip was nodding now in agreement with the plan that was formulating. Martha added, almost to herself, "Hopefully the little girl isn't afflicted like our poor Lazarus."

"Zhe wuzn't ded foor fur dayz," Mary slurred out.

"That's true," Martha agreed. She grabbed Phillip by his garments, up by his collarbones and emphasized, "Phillip, I need you to leave right away with our fastest horse. I need you to do this for me. And, please, be discreet."

Phillip grabbed the back of Martha's head and kissed her with obvious pent up intensity above her right eyebrow. Really, he wanted to smush her lips with his, to the point of making it painful. "It will be done," Phillip told her, gazing deep into her eyes. He squeezed her body hard in a bear hug that suffocated her a little, then let her go and spun around to exit in search of the stables. Stopping by a half drunk Mary to hug her, kiss her on the cheek, wipe his lips afterwards and grab a handful of figs before walking out the door. Setting out on a mission to see if the Resurrection miracle had, indeed, worked as intended before.

xi

The following day started late, again. Mary and, by total amazement, Martha had finished the large pitcher of wine in no time at all, while talking into the very early morning. The next pitcher emptied at a slower pace, plus Martha passed out before tapping into much of it. So Mary polished off her sister's portion for her, pushing her own troubled conscience deep into an alcohol induced coma.

Late morning light now blazed in through the lone window that had been left open from the previous night. Unadulterated sunlight slashed in a bright, single ray across the sister's covered bodies. The warm daylight was advancing with the steady rotation of the Earth up towards their comatose, slack faces. Mary snored without a shred of shame. Laid out on her back, mouth wide open, inhaling rough, irregular drags through her sinuses and exhaling out a raucous, guttural note through her mouth. By funny juxtaposition, Martha accompanied her sister's solo symphony with her own mild snoring.

However, at the moment, some commotion was building outside of Mary's room. Voices, rising in their sense of urgency, could be heard bubbling in stressed conversation around the corner from the open window.

Half asleep, drifting in and out of consciousness, Martha could only catch cloudy snippets of the exterior voices' conversation. A high, reedy voice floated into her ears, asking, “You say you found them like this?” Followed by a soft, older woman's voice which answered back meekly, saying, “Yes, my Lord.” Then, after another timeless moment spent snoozing, Martha heard the brusque voice of an older man demand, “Where are the *ladies* of the house now?”

Sunlight dappled, like abrasive pins on Martha's eyelids and she sat up quickly. Much too quickly. Her head screamed and pounded in angry, painful protest. She winced in regret as she became aware of the true pain of the hangover she felt. Her fig-stained fingers came up and rubbed in deliberate small circles at her temples. A tiny, whiny groan simmered in her throat. In her mouth, it was an awful, pasty, stale-wine essenced hole that stuck to her tongue as she rolled it around in disfavor. Imbibing like she had last night, was not a habit that she often practiced; that sort of disgusting behavior belonged to her sister. And for good reason.

How does she live like this? Martha weakly puzzled to herself.

Martha could hear the rise of mumbling voices above her sister's ripping snores. They were coming closer down the corridor. She looked down and shook Mary by the shoulder, whispering a terrible morning breath into her face, "Mary, wake up." The heavy snoring faltered, but picked back up right away. Martha shook Mary more with more force. "Wake up!" Martha persisted, with her efforts successful in stopping the snoring altogether.

Mary's eyelids fluttered and she stretched her arms over her head, groaning out loud. "Mmmmmmmmmmmmm. What time is it?" She asked. Smacking her sticky mouth, while picking pugnaciously at a prominent, crusty eye booger.

"Someone's coming!" Martha hissed. The voices were now almost outside the door.

That same high, piercing voice could now be heard saying, "I don't care if they are still asleep, woman. The hour is nearly noon."

"What?" Mary asked while yawning, stretching it out, *Whhaaaaaatt?*

Heavy knocking rattled the latch on Mary's door. That high voice, which Martha recognized now as belonging to none other than Joseph ben Caiaphas, called out from the other side of the door, "Mary? Martha? Open the door!"

Martha leapt up and called back out, "One moment!" She scurried about the room, first to close the window. Then she lunged over and placed the cups back on the tray in an orderly manner. From there she gathered up the soiled pillows that had been piled into the corner for washing later and tossed them into the oversized storage chest. Both sisters flinched when the lid to the chest was allowed to slam shut in her hastiness.

"Come now *ladies,* we've much to discuss," the High Priest taunted from the corridor.

A stern woman's voice, which Martha knew for Hannah's no nonsense tone, could be heard saying in harsh disagreement, "My Lords, if you will please come to the great room, I will have Martha and Mary join you as soon as it is possible."

"Nonsense!" Caiaphas chided the old woman and knocked hard again. "Mary? Martha?" He called. "Come now! Open the door."

"One moment, please," Martha called out in a mocking, melodious sing-song tone, while looking around the room. She took an extra moment to make doubly sure that nothing was out in the open that could be considered suspicious to the Holy Men.

Mary had only gotten to her feet and splashed her face with old, but refreshing basin water. She even scooped some up into her mouth and swished it around before spitting it back out. Martha rolled her sticky tongue around in her mouth and looked on enviously, wishing she had thought to do the same.

Instead, Martha brushed her hair back with her fingers and pulled her shawl over her head. She approached the door and put her hand tentatively on the latch. Before opening it, she glanced over to Mary, who gave her a tiny nod of approval, saying *Go ahead, open it. I'm ready.*

Impatient knocking burst again, but Martha opened the door, interrupting the frantic rapping. There stood Joseph ben Caiaphas, of course, with his hand raised mid knock. He was flanked by his old, rotund father-in-law Annas and two Roman soldiers, consisting of a battle-worn Tribune accompanied by a virgin-faced Praefecti. Just the very top of little, old Hannah's covered head could be seen peeking over the backs of the four imposing men.

"Good morning, High Priest," Martha muttered as Caiaphas and his entourage pushed past her into Mary's room. Hannah came in no further than the threshold.

"Hardly," Caiaphas replied, sauntering over closer to Mary. "It is, after all, only noon, in case you were wondering," he continued with obvious disdain coating his every word and gesture. He leaned in and took two quick sniffs of her hair. A look of disgust turning the corners of his wrinkled mouth down in a loathing grimace.

Annas directed a question at Martha, "What can you tell us about what happened to your goats?"

Mary stiffened, but Martha feigned cool ignorance and asked, "My goats? Nothing. Why? Has something happened?"

Caiaphas snorted out of his hooked nose, in disbelief.

Annas filled them in, treating the situation as if they didn't know, "Something, or someone, has killed them."

"Killed them?" Martha echoed, shaking her head from side to side in an act of disbelieving horror.

“Not just killed, my dear. They’ve been wholly torn apart,” Caiaphas stated as a matter of fact as he toured about the room. Investigating. With a couple skeletal fingers he nudged a bowl with two lonely figs across the platter. Then he sniffed in suspicion at the remnants of one of the cups. In response to the reek of wine, Caiaphas winced and set the purple rim stained cup back down upon the platter with a small, explosive clatter.

“What could’ve done such a thing?” Mary asked, now playing along in ignorance with Martha.

“What indeed, Mary,” Caiaphas shot back. “I don't suppose you’ve heard about the young child that was taken last night either, not far from here?”

Both women shook their heads *No.*

“Tsalav is gone as well, Martha,” Hannah called over the men’s shoulders from the doorway.

Caiaphas glanced over at the servant, then back to Martha, and asked, “Who’s Tsalav?”

“One of our horses,” Martha admitted.

Caiaphas dark eyes looked back into Hannah’s old, colorless ones and demanded, “Was there any blood or signs of foul play around the house stables?”

“No, my Lord,” Hannah stated.

Becoming terse, Caiaphas stared hard at the sisters and asked, “You know nothing of this as well, I take it?”

Both shook their heads in solemn, innocent, meekness. Again answering, *No.*

The High Priest began to peruse the room and continued, “It stands to reason that whatever tore apart your goats last night, and possibly took your horse, is the same thing that took the neighbor child last night. Do you disagree?”

Fighting through her screaming hangover, Martha did her best to appear dumbfounded and answered Caiaphas’ question with a question of her own, “Well, did anyone see this phantom that you speak of?”

Caiaphas breathed out through his nose in a furious gesture of tenuously contained anger. Annas took over while his son-in-law turned and regained control of himself, “Some eyewitnesses described a dark figure jumping across the rooftops.”

Martha waited for more details, hoping beyond hope that they weren’t recognized last night and reported as being there too, but that was it. She responded by saying as aloof as possible around a thick, dry tongue, "Huh. Seems vague."

Caiaphas spun back around and questioned in disbelief, "So, you've no idea as to what possibly took your horse and tore apart two of your goats last night?"

The sisters corroborated in partisan silence to this.

Caiaphas kept on, "And you've no clue as to the child that was snatched nearby or what could've snatched him up?"

"My Lord, we have just awoken upon your arrival," Mary offered, trying to come off as innocent as a lamb.

"Is that so?" Caiaphas asked back. Anger caused a slight tremor to shake his voice. "Late in the day for two-" he flicked his dark eyes like darts at Martha- "reputable ladies like yourselves to be sleeping. Is this not a busy household?"

"It is My Lord Caiaphas," Martha said in agreement, stepping forward, trying to stifle his visible brimming rage. "It is late and a very busy house. To be honest, our lives have been in absolute turmoil since our poor brother's passing."

"Yes, your brother," Caiaphas replied, seizing upon the segue. "Since your horse, your goats and the neighbor child are a mystery to you, let's try this one…" He leaned in close to the two sisters, close enough that they could smell traces of the Abottoir and some of the pungent ritual incense wafting off of him, "...did Jesus raise your brother Lazarus from the dead night before last?"

Both sisters stood with mouths hung agape, totally floored. Caiaphas, Annas and the attending soldiers seemed to rise up before the sisters and become an impenetrable wall.

"Who told you that?" Martha croaked. Her mouth had been completely sucked dry of all available moisture and she felt punched in the gut by the question. Her mind raced as to who was there that night.

Who would go straight to Caiaphas? Martha fretted in fearful anxiousness.

"Is it true?" Annas barked.

The sisters stalled and looked down at the floor. Mary mumbled something too low to be heard by the interrogators, but still drew a pinch through her robe by her older sister. The High Priest and his father-in-law leaned in intrusively.

"What was that Mary?" Caiaphas interrogated.

Martha took initiative and answered for Mary, "Yes it's true."

Caiaphas' charcoal colored eyes widened to the size of hard boiled eggs and he stepped in closer to Martha, staring his dark, molten daggers into the back of her skull. He placed both hands on her shoulders and dug his fingers in, like massive eagle talons. Fuming, he asked in an oily and calm, yet furious tone, "And by whose power does he command the dead to live again?"

In her naturally defiant way, Mary wedged between her sister and the High Priest. She breathed a wine tainted cloud of morning breath in his face, "He is the Messiah. His power comes from his Father, the Most High God."

Caiaphas recoiled from her breath and the word, *Messiah.* While covering his hawkish nose with the back of his hand, he spoke with tangible vitriol humming behind his words, "Did you know there are rumors that Jesus has resurrected before your brother? Twice. For instance, there was an account of a young man in a small village called Nain, who they say went insane soon after being brought back to life." He let that sink in for a second, then continued, "Another tells of the resurrection of a young girl. The daughter of a synagogue official named Jairus."

"What has become of her since?" Martha asked. A little too eager. She couldn't help but think of Phillip currently en route to Capernaum.

"Sadly, all we have are rumors that have traveled here from Capernaum and Nain. Nothing concrete," Caiaphas admitted.

Martha, becoming annoyed, asked him, "What are these 'rumors' conveying?"

"They speak of animal mutilations," Annas spoke in a deep baritone, counting off on gnarled fingers. "Nocturnal slumber. A hunger for flesh. Viable eyewitnesses claiming the child was scorched by exposure to the sun."

Caiaphas had meandered over by the storage chest, sniffing at the air surrounding it. Then he did a subtle sniff at himself. Wondering if he was only smelling the Abottoir on his robes, or something else.

"But it's only rumors," Martha retorted.

"Rumors don't spring from the ground," Caiaphas came back, as if explaining down to a child for the hundredth time.

Neither sister could answer back to this. Which led Caiaphas to continue by probing, "Where is your brother now *ladies*?" Silence was the sister's answer at first. "Hhmmm?" Caiaphas pressed.

"He's meditating in the wilderness, my Lord," Martha lied, kind of. This time, it was Mary's breath that caught in her throat.

Annas and Caiaphas squinted their eyes, already casting negative judgement to her claim.

Martha embellished upon the lie, "Seeing the other side of the veil has...changed him."

"Changed him how?" Caiaphas seethed.

Mary stepped in and said, "Just his perspective. That's what she meant." A quick, tense moment passed. Mary rearranged her words, "His perspective on life is deeper now that he has experienced death." In reluctance she added, "My Lord."

The High Priest slithered around the sisters and said, "Did you know that when the body dies, the soul exits the body? And when your *Messiah* raises these soulless bodies, it is said they are raised as empty vessels?"

Mary and Martha kept silent, instead of giving away anything that could be interpreted as information, as the High Priest circled back around in front of them.

Caiaphas then said, "These empty vessels are then subject to be possessed. Inhabited by demons. Hhmmm? Did you know that? That your Jesus of Nazareth commands sway over death by means of conspiring with demons?"

"That's a lie!" Martha spat out.

"Is it now?" Caiaphas asked while lunging in and almost touching Martha's nose with his own hooked beak. His fierce, smoldering coal eyes bore into her bloodshot ones. "We shall see."

The interrogators and the attending soldiers' imposing presence seemed to recede a little bit. They only had rumors and speculation at the moment, nothing more. Their limits to interrogation and intimidation had been met for the time being.

Annas asked, "When do you expect your brother to return?"

Martha shrugged and offered an ambiguous answer, "I suppose when he's finished meditating."

"BAH!!" Caiaphas shouted in frustration. He snatched up a cup off of the platter and threw it against the wall, shattering the clay drinkware. This left a purple impact spatter with cascading tentacle trails running down the wall. He was staring down upon the sisters with a boiling volcano of rage shaking within him. Frustrated and without any further recourse, Caiaphas yelled, “This is utterly pointless!” He then stormed out of the room, past the little, old servant Hannah, followed by the older Tribune and the much younger Praefecti.

Martha held onto an anxious, sticky breath behind her lips. SThe sister’s shared shock from the sudden break in Caiaphas’ pompous demeanor hung heavy in the room long after he had left.

Annas shuffled in closer. His old, withered looking, spotted hands protruded from his fine robes and draped out limply before him. He said, “We desire to meet with your brother and bear witness to the alleged ‘miracle’ as soon as he returns from this so-called ‘meditation’ he’s doing.”

“Alright,” Mary agreed. She felt a compelling desire to defend the lie about Lazarus wandering in the wilderness aimless and meditating. But, on second thought, she chose to remain silent.

“Before the end of the week,” Annas grumbled, scooting past them and heading for the door.

“But, what if he hasn’t returned by then?” Mary called after him, but his aged backside was slipping around the corner and out of sight without any answer back.

Hannah glared at his back as he shuffled down the corridor, following in the same way out angered son-in-law and the soldiers had taken. Martha blew out in a great, toxic gust from her mouth, releasing the breath she had been holding onto since she had last spoken. Mary lunged for one of the surviving cups upon the platter and emptied the remaining contents. Then, she poured what was left from the pitcher and tipped back a long draught.

Oh Mary, Martha thought. But, she didn’t dwell on her pity for her sister for long.

They had gotten rid of the Holy Men, for now. That was a blessed relief, no doubt, but Caiaphas and his goons would be back. They would be much more relentless next time.

In the meantime, Martha felt soiled from head to toe and wanted more than anything to bathe. Thoroughly. But, before that, there was still the matter of dealing with the disposal of the goat carcasses. They had been left outside, exposed to the elements all night and morning. Martha gave Mary a considerate hug and told her she would see her later for dinner.

“But, whut about breckfizz?” Mary asked. Her purple tongue was swiftly thickening from her disgraceful wine consumption.

Martha gathered Hannah at the door and left her sister upending the cup over her open, upturned mouth. She wanted to return back into the room and hold her sister. Tell her there are other ways to deal with the stress and pain. But, instead she turned and took Hannah with her.

On her way down the corridor, en route to deal with the mess of the mutilated goats, Martha couldn't help but feel a terrible sense of hopeless restlessness. Like, now what was she supposed to do? Go about her daily life? Act like everything was fine? Was she supposed to remain suspended in a paranoid limbo? Was she just supposed to sit around and wait for the certainty of something terrible or for the unexpectedly wonderful to happen next?

xii

Foregoing a much needed washing, Martha gave instruction and parted ways with Hannah in the corridor. Following this, she proceeded past a small vestibule with potted plants, a concrete bench, and a small water feature trickling away with birds and insects fluttering all about. Through the adjoining archway and around the corner, it led into the area behind Mary's room, where the goats had once been penned.

Here, she found Caleb grasping the sticky hind legs of one of the goat carcasses along with a silent male house servant, who had taken the front legs. They plopped the rigid animal corpse onto a large, plain burlap tarp without a hint of emotion. Turning, both men went to retrieve the second goat. That's when Caleb caught sight of Martha watching him in the brash light of high noon. He took note of the purple tint to her lips and the bleary way her eyes would shift in focus. She worked her tongue around her own mouth, looking dehydrated and clearly hungover.

Caleb dipped his head in a slight, solemn acknowledgment towards her, tickling the tip of his wispy beard to his own chest, before returning to fetch the second carcass. Then placing it atop the first. In revered silence they took the corners of the tarp and joined them together in the center, wrapping up the mutilated goats to be disposed of properly, underneath the observance of the Sacred Law.

The attending male servants took away the crude, macabre package. Caleb, with his hands, forearms and random spots on his clothing covered in dried, tacky goat blood, wandered towards Martha. His intent was set on the nearby well behind her, to draw up a bucket of water to clean himself. He managed to mutter in a meek way to her, "Good day, Martha," as he passed by.

"Good day, Caleb," she answered back, noticing his standoffish demeanor. But she chose to dismiss it since he was, after all, covered in goat blood.

He was drawing up the bucket by the rope when Martha said from close behind, "Thank you for your help," referring to the corpse clean up.

"It wasn't a problem," he replied with a cold succinctness to his tone, while he gave his hands and arms a vigorous washing in the bucket. With his back still to her, he asked, "You don't know what happened to them or to your horse that's missing?"

"No, um, no," she stammered in the lie, her mind feeling pained and sluggish. "Phillip has Tsalav."

Caleb asked over his shoulder, "The horse? Phillip has it? Why?"

Martha squinted at his over eager, inquisitive nature. "He's gone to Capernaum." She caught herself before she told more.

"Why?" Caleb asked again without turning around, still scrubbing at the stubborn, pink residue of the goat's blood.

"Just on a business errand, as a favor to me," she lied, kind of.

"You don't know what killed your goats?" He asked in a brash way. "What were you doing last night?"

"Mary and I were-," she caught herself before she told any more of the truth about last night, "-we were, um, celebrating our brother's return."

Caleb spun around, reddish water still dripping from his hands, "So, how is he?" He asked, looking around past her, as though Lazarus were there, hiding in the house somewhere. Eavesdropping on them. "Where is he?"

"He's gone," Martha responded, in a facile way of repeating the lie from earlier, "Meditating, in the wilderness."

"Is that right?" He asked, sensing a lack of truth. His memory wasn't so bad that he didn't remember chunks of Lazarus' dead flesh falling off and floating down the Kidron. He repeated his first question, "And, how is he?"

Martha's eyebrows furrowed, "He's fine," she lied, her voice rising significantly higher, "He's just reintegrating and getting accustomed from being dead to being alive again. You know."

"I see," Caleb said, returning back to the bucket of bloody water. "And how are you doing amidst all of this?"

Martha put a hand to her pounding head and lied again, "I'm fine, Caleb."

Caleb didn't answer back. Instead, he finished up his scrubbing and cast the water from his hands in a few aggressive flicks, before snatching up the bucket. Then he fanned the bloodied water over the area where the corpses had been. "That's good," Caleb then said in a voice almost too low to hear as he lowered the wooden, banded bucket back down in the well.

He continued on, "Did you hear about the child that was taken, not far from here?"

Martha nodded with caution and said, "Yes."

"Do you think that what killed your goats could've taken the neighbor child as well?" Caleb asked point blank.

Martha shrugged and frowned, "I don't have the slightest idea what did either of those horrid things."

Caleb harrumphed. "It just seems strange that your brother is brought back and now there are animals either missing or ripped apart, plus, a child has been abducted," he challenged.

Martha said nothing. She only frowned and held her breath, with her arms crossed in front of her. Her hungry, hungover mind was trying to understand what it was that Caleb was getting at.

Caleb spelled it out further, "It just all feels very coincidental, don't you think?" He began to count off on blood stained, damp fingers, "The goats are yours. The neighbor is yours. The brother is yours."

Martha became irritated with her childhood friend now. "What are you trying to insinuate Caleb?" Her voice was rising, "That…what? My brother, Lazarus, killed my goats and took the child?"

Caleb crossed his arms in opposing confrontation. He stared at her defiantly and sprang his eyebrows up, like a pretentious prick. All of his body language condescended to her and said, *Bingo! You figured it out!!*

"Get out," Martha growled low.

"Come again?" Caleb said, leaning in with his arms still crossed.

"Get Out!" Martha screamed now, beginning to march towards Caleb, forcing him into retreat. "You're no better than that...that snake! Caiaphas!! WAIT!"

Martha felt sick, but swallowed back the figs and wine trying to come up. She glared at her "childhood friend", and questioned, "Is that it? Are you in league with Caiaphas? Did you run off and tell him about Lazarus' resurrection?"

"What?" Caleb tried to lie. "Martha, don't be ridiculous!"

"I don't believe you!" Martha shouted, hurting her own head.

"Martha, I only meant-" he started.

"I know what you meant, Caleb!" She interrupted him. "You think that my brother's a monster!"

"I didn't say that," he argued back.

"I heard you," she hissed. "When he came out of his tomb, you called him an 'abomination'! Your words! Not mine!!"

"That's not what I meant," he tried again in a feeble attempt to calm her. They were coming into the great room and beyond that the front door.

"Then what did you mean?" she challenged angrily.

"I-" he started.

"I don't want to hear your excuse," she interrupted again. "My brother is alive and instead of being happy for me, you and your confidant, Caiaphas, accuse him! And me!!"

"Martha, I-" he tried again.

"Stop!" she commanded. They were at the front door. "Leave now, Caleb! You have said enough!!"

He lowered his head and shook it side to side while chuckling only in his chest. He brought his eyes up to hers and said, "I didn't mean to upset you Martha."

"Well you have," Martha came back in a brusque, slicing tone. "Now leave, before you say anything else stupid."

"Where is he Martha?" Caleb persisted.

"I told you," Martha insisted.

"I don't believe you," Caleb divulged honestly. "Why isn't he here? Meditating? In the wilderness? You expect me to believe that?"

Martha's bloodshot eyes had enlarged to considerable red rimmed saucers the longer Caleb kept on. Her face had darkened to a lush violet as blood rushed to her pounding brain and she clung onto her breath.

"Well?" Caleb asked her further.

Martha held her breath and remained like a stone. Retreating inward.

Caleb came up closer to Martha and, lowering his voice down to a confiding tone, he said, "Martha, I'm trying to help you."

Now, it was her turn to divulge her own bit of honesty and she exhaled out the air she had been holding in a gust of terrible breath, "I don't believe you."

"Martha, where is he?" Caleb asked again.

"Leave, Caleb," Martha demanded.

"Is he back at his tomb?" Caleb guessed correctly. Unexpectedly.

Somehow, Martha's eyes enlarged even more, but she repeated louder, "Leave now, Caleb!" Adding in a lower tone, "And don't come back to my house again."

Caleb scoffed to himself, hands on hips while nodding up and down. Without any further argument he opened the front door, releasing the familiar squeak, muttering on his way out, "Good day, Martha."

Martha, didn't give him the satisfaction of a reply. Instead, she just slammed the door behind him, spun around and put all of her weight against it. There she squeezed her eyes shut tight. Her head felt like it had been kicked by a mutated donkey. Inside her throat, it was as dry as a whistling desert wind.

That's when Mary entered the room, none the wiser of what had just transpired. Her mood was inappropriate and joyful. She asked, giggling, "Whut wuzz all tha yulling about?"

Then she hiccupped loudly.

xiii

Caiaphas and Annas stood with their small entourage across the street from Lazarus' house after their fruitless meeting with the sisters. The High Priest was still breathing in heavy exhalations through his large nostrils. There was no describing the pure, glowing anger that he felt towards Mary and Martha, for their sheer audacity to stonewall him.

Didn't they know they were putting the whole entire nation of Judea in jeopardy for this **Messiah** *of theirs?* The High Priest fumed to himself.

The uprisings. The extremist factions that would break off and incur violence when their arguments fell flat. These sisters saw none of it. None of the "unfortunate" groups that contained the diseased, the cast off and the poor that flowed in a nonstop current through the Temple every single day. No, that didn't matter to the wealthy sisters. They had everything they could ever want, even their stupid dead brother back from the dead, by all impossibilities!

If any of it is even true, a voice in Caiaphas speculated.

Annas' low scrape of a voice snatched Caiaphas out of his mantra-like seething, "What do you say my son?"

"I don't believe them," Caiaphas replied matter-of-factly.

"Well, of course," Annas said. "What do you want to do about them though?"

Caiaphas ran a spindly hand irritably over mouth. "The only thing we can do is watch them and wait for them to slip up," he grumbled.

"I will see to it," said Annas.

"As for Jesus of Nazareth," Caiaphas continued, "Instead of trying to catch him, maybe we **make** him come to us."

Annas perked up as much as a hunched over, decrepit old man of his age could perk up. "How do we do that?" Annas asked. He was already smiling through a partial set of teeth, just for the sake of the sheer joy that he experienced when at practice of his favorite pastime of scheming.

Caiaphas tapped at his wrinkled, thin lips in methodical contemplation.

Meanwhile, the street bustled with an excessive amount of people in the early afternoon. Wagons, carrying goods, pulled by mules, passed by in a series of rickety creaks and squeaks. Random citizens and vendors kept a constant stream of yelling and haggling conversations that flowed from one to another, past one another and over one another. Animals brayed and bleated, sounding very much like the people. Children laughed and cried in their parent's arms. It all blended into a hypnotic, babbling, cacophonous white noise river.

"I've got it!" Caiaphas announced. Excited, Annas leaned in away from the Roman soldier escorts standing guard. Caiaphas wrapped his thin, branch of an arm around his Father-in-law and drew him in for some juicy conspiracy. He whispered his outline of a plan of sending messengers to the North, East and South carrying a decoy message from Lazarus' sisters, detailing a tragedy of some sort. Maybe involving Lazarus falling ill again or something, the finer points could be ironed out later.

Annas chuckled and kept saying, "It will be done," at certain points in the plan. It was the best they had to go with right now, but time was running short. The week of Passover celebration was bearing down on them. That would bring out the zealots, the radicals and the true believers. Jesus would be practically invincible behind those combined numbers.

They were finishing up discussing the broad strokes of the plan to lure Jesus back to Bethany, when they saw Caleb, ejected out of the front door of Martha's house onto the busy street, looking red in the face and lost. With an anger set in his eyes, he glanced up and down the boulevard, hoping to spot some familiar faces.

Annas whistled through a gap where a tooth should've been. A piercing note that cut high above every other sound on the street. Caleb's head snapped over in the direction the whistle had come from and caught sight of his co-conspirators. He waded and weaved his way with some difficulty through the cross traffic of the flowing crowd to Annas and Caiaphas.

When he finally made it to them, Caiaphas asked, "Well?"

Caleb shrugged his shoulders. His breathing was a little labored and he answered, "She didn't tell me anything."

"Nothing at all?" Caiaphas prodded.

Caleb shook his head from side to side, "She claims to know nothing about the goats or the neighbor kid."

"What about their brother, Lazarus?" Annas asked from down by his shoulder.

"Nothing," Caleb said again. "Martha says he's 'meditating in the wilderness'."

Caiaphas grumbled something to the effect that Martha had told him the same.

Annas asked Caleb, "What of the missing horse?"

"Tsalav?" Caleb asked back. "Yes, uh, actually, she did mention that our friend, Phillip took him."

Caiaphas pushed his father-in-law aside by the face, and grabbed Caleb by the collar. "Where?" He demanded through gritted teeth.

"C-c-capernaum, my Lord," Caleb stuttered. "She said he went as a favor on business."

Caiaphas released him by tossing him away. Realizing there was possibly another lie there. Capernaum was, after all, home to Jairus and his daughter, who had received the same treatment given to Lazarus, albeit Jairus' daughter hadn't been dead for four days before receiving her resurrecting.

"Well, she's not keeping her lies consistent," Caiaphas murmured to himself.

"My Lord?" Caleb inquired, not fully hearing him.

"Nevermind," Caiaphas said with audible impatience, "You have done well." He then produced a small pouch of silver and handed it to Caleb's outstretched fingers.

"Since you were able to prove yourself slightly more valuable to me today, I have another task for you," Caiaphas enticed.

Eager, especially when it came to more coin, Caleb stood tall at attention and responded, "High Priest Caiaphas, whatever you require, I will not disappoint you."

"We'll see about that," Caiaphas said.

xiv

That evening, Caleb headed East to the Mount of Olives, with an accomplice named John. A rotund, swarthy thief, who was always reliable for a dirty job at any hour. John carried a tall, thick walking stick that had a length of simple rawhide cord wrapped around the grip. Dirty jokes, stale anecdotes, and elaborate schemes flowed from the thief in a constant stream for the first leg of their journey. The magnitude of John's brazen sense of humor seemed to wane and set along with the sun, though.

Dusk had almost completed its cycle. The day had cooled and darkened in its transformation to night. Mature, knotty olive trees already loomed like threatening, wretched giants in the dim light cast by their combined set of weak oil lamps.

Hours had transpired since Caleb's altercation with Martha and his meeting in the street afterwards with Caiaphas, in which time his resolve against this so-called resurrection and all who supported it had only strengthened. Plus, to be honest, it was his insatiable hunger for more silver that was the main driver of this foolhardy endeavor. After splitting the previous full reward of fifty shekels three ways and paying off some preexisting debt, his portion of the remaining silver seemed puny and felt light in his pocket. Sure, the payment he had just received from The High Priest for his intel regarding Phillip taking Tsalav and going to Capernaum was nice. But, the fact of the matter was that Caleb was greedy, and between his existing mountain of debt, coupled with his unusual personal appetites the amount of silver he was currently carrying wouldn't last him very long.

"What are we looking for, my friend?" his companion John asked, breaking into Caleb's calculated thinking.

"We are looking for a man," Caleb answered in vague terms. "I already told you this."

"Yes, you did," John agreed. "You did also say we'll be rewarded for information regarding this 'man' by your High Priest?"

"Yes," Caleb replied, already feeling a twinge of being annoyed.

"Forty shekels for us to split? That's what you said," John nagged.

"Did I say forty?" Caleb asked. Greed persuaded him to lie to John further by saying, "That must've been because there were three of us that we received such a large amount."

John looked instantly disenchanted. "That's not what you said," he responded petulantly, a frown deepening on his face.

Caleb put an arm around him, confiding to him, "Hey, John, thirty shekels of silver is still good money for a night of just gathering some measly information."

John grumbled something.

Caleb continued, "Come on. I'll split it right down the middle with you. Fifteen shekels a piece. Here," and Caleb reached inside his robe to produce the small satchel of silver. John could hear the faint *clink* of precious metal rubbing against precious metal within the little bag. John licked his cracked lips and came closer as Caleb reached inside, pulling out a small handful of fine minted silver coins. "Consider this a down payment," and he poured some of the coins into John's open hands.

Gladly, John accepted, and he shoved the coins down into his grubby pocket, patting at it in blind affection afterwards.

"And let me tell you," Caleb confided, lowering his voice, "If we go further than instructed and were to capture this man, then bring him in to the High Priest for direct questioning, I'm positive our reward would be monumentally more stupendous!"

John balked. "You want to capture this man?"

"Yes," Caleb said. He could see visible worry on John's dark, bearded face in the waning evening light. "Don't fret, my friend. This man we seek is very weak and feeble. I have seen this much with my own eyes." He then brandished a handbreadth of reflective, shiny blade that was sheathed into a worn scabbard within his robe, saying with a grin, "Plus, I'm sure he can be coerced with this."

"How much?" John asked, slowing down his walking pace.

"The man? Incredibly weak!" He responded, misunderstanding the direction of John's line of questioning. "One of us could easily overpower-"

"Not that," John cut in, silencing Caleb. "How much silver to apprehend him, possibly by force," he nodded to Caleb's concealed sword at his hip, "and bring him all the way to the Temple, to this Priest of yours?"

"Oh," responded Caleb, realizing John's line of questioning, and also that his accomplice's greed might even outweigh his own. "I don't know. Maybe a talent," he blurted out. (1 talent = 34-45kg)

"A talent!?" John repeated, stunned.

"Well, hold on. Don't quote me on that," Caleb tried to back pedal, holding up both hands. But it was too late. John's rapacious appetite for lovely, cold silver to join the lovely, warm silver in his pocket had been whetted and thoroughly stoked.

They continued walking on for a few moments in the cooling night, listening to the random sounds coming from the trees and beyond. Thousands of shekels were already being spent in hundreds of lavish ways within their limited imaginations. Both were sharing the same dreams of drowning in cascades of random women, good food and endless drink. Maybe even, trying their luck and casting lots to increase their mounds of silver into mountains of silver.

John broke into Caleb's walking daydream by asking, "So, what did this 'man' do that warrants a reward of a talent for his capture?" Caleb opened his mouth to correct, but not before John caught himself and added, "Possibly a talent. Yes, I know."

"He died," Caleb stated. John cocked his head, puzzled. Caleb clarified, "And now he lives again."

John blinked, as what was just uttered became understood. Realization dawned upon his face and confusion twisted his features, as he spat out, "What?! Impossible!"

Caleb shook his head in emphasis, and said, "No, I have witnessed his resurrecting with my own eyes. Two nights prior, by the hand of Jesus of Nazareth. At the very place we're going right now."

"Where's that?" John asked. A tentative quality hung onto the short question. Like he didn't really want to ask it because he was already afraid of what the answer could be.

"Lazarus' family tomb," Caleb told him.

John walked a couple of steps before asking, "What makes you think he came back to the tomb two days after arising from it?"

"Well he's not at home with his sisters, where he should be!" Caleb almost yelled.

John kept quiet. Not really knowing how to respond to that.

Caleb kept trying to explain, "Listen, John, you should've seen him when he...he," Caleb's mind flashed to a memory of the pale chunks of rotten flesh being gently carried down the current of the Kidron. Caleb shook his head to clear it, "Look, he was dead for four days. He's not what he once was." His voice dropped and he muttered to himself, "I know an abomination when I see one. I don't care what Martha says."

"What are you saying?" John asked in scared disbelief. "That he's some kind of...what...a ghoul?"

"Well, yes. Sort of. Now that there are dead goats and a child missing!" Caleb ranted without context. "Calling him a ghoul would be rather fitting."

"What do you mean?" John asked, genuinely not understanding. "I thought you said he was weak and feeble!" He now, completely halted in his tracks.

"He is," Caleb assured John, trying to nudge the stubborn man along. "If he did, in fact, do what is being alleged, he did it to two old goats and a young child." John still resisted. "Come now, John." Caleb clapped him on the back and pulled him in. "Listen. We are two strong men against this 'ghoul'. He doesn't stand a chance against the likes of us."

It took a little more coaxing, plus offering John the lion's share of sixty percent, instead of fifty of the reward for Lazarus' capture. More money certainly helped to incentivize his reluctant motivation to return. John now felt the allure, once again, of the siren's call of silver. Bags and bags of it. He agreed to the new terms and they pushed on.

The night had progressed steadily to achieve its full potential of darkness. Their lamps barely penetrated into the gloom that surrounded them. Low boughs of the olive trees hovered, sometimes resembling monster claws overhead. Black trunks stood in the near distance, like shadow sentinels, just off the path. Jerusalem Scops-owls were heard hooting eerily from unseen perches. The terrain now felt not so much like an olive tree grove, but more like a haunted forest of mangled, ancient statues holding their arms out and over them. Reaching for them with long, twisted limbs.

Before long they came to the quaint courtyard clearing of Lazarus' family tomb. The tomb itself sat on the far side of the courtyard, looking unobtrusive, quiet and, to be honest, quite dead. A stone archway marked the entrance and they passed through it without apprehension, into an inexplicable ambient climate. It was the same three sets of mature olive trees flanking the short pathway from the courtyard entrance up to the tombstone. However, now, there was a feeling of a physical pulling down upon their collars and hands. A pushing down on their heads and shoulders. Scratchy, skittering feet and claws ran all over their skin, even beneath their clothes. Their eyes and lungs burned, as though they had stepped into a harmful, chemical cloud. Beyond the distant hooting and their own labored breathing, strange ethereal whispers passed by their ears, like ghosts telling secrets.

Upon coming closer, Caleb squinted in skepticism when he saw the giant tombstone had been rolled back in place. Just the same as it was when he had come upon it two nights ago, before he helped roll it aside. How could he forget the rank, deceased smell that was released when they did so?

Caleb unsheathed his sword, making it sing in the empty clearing, *Fwing.* Paranoia and apprehension rose, like high tide within himself. In reaction to Caleb taking out his short sword, John held his walking staff in front of his own person, with both hands, in a posture of frightened defense.

"What? What is it?!" John screeched.

"Nothing," replied Caleb, slowly approaching the sealed entrance. "Just something strange."

"S-s-strange?" John repeated in a jittery cadence, spinning a one-eighty to look behind them. His staff remained held horizontal in front of his body. "Th-this entire p-p-p-place is-s-s s-strange."

"Yes," said Caleb, ignoring his scared cohort. "I was one amongst the men who removed this stone the night before last."

John didn't respond. Instead, he just kept his eyes squinted down to cut slits against the sting he felt at the corners. In the overbearing dark, John scratched and slapped at his skin. Causing the small lamp hanging off of his hip to shake and bounce all about.

"It wasn't without a fair degree of difficulty," Caleb said in a soft, wondering tone, almost to himself. His swordless hand came up and touched the rough, circular stone with shaky fingertips. Through the gloom and the acrid sting upon his sight, he noticed the shape of a reddish handprint staining the face of the stone. A detail that didn't exist the last time he was here.

"D-do you think s-someone h-h-helped him replace it for s-s-some reason?" John offered, still nervous. He was walking backwards in tiny steps towards where Caleb was studying the tombstone. On high alert. Straining his burning eyes to adjust and pierce through the heavy gloom.

“I’m not sure,” Caleb muttered, not really paying attention to what he was answering. He came around the side of the stone that was three handbreadths thick, at least. Upon sheathing his sword, Caleb tried to put his shoulder with some force behind it against the massive, chiseled stone. Caleb pushed and strained, leaning the entire weight of his body against its curved, rough edge. Sandals slipping and sliding on the Earth, in spite of his best efforts to even budge the stone.

After a couple serious attempts, Caleb came away from the side of the stone, sucking in great gulps of the tainted air into his irritated lungs. Tiny droplets of sweat sprouted on his forehead and glinted like diamonds in the moonlight.

John backed over in proximity to Caleb while the latter was catching his breath in scorching lungfuls. His itchy hands were braced upon his prickly knees. As his fiery breath began to slow, Caleb looked up, caught sight of John’s trusty, thick, rigid walking stick and, all of a sudden, snatched it from his accomplice’s hands.

“What are you doing?” John demanded.

Without answering, Caleb plunged the base of the staff down into the ground at the base of the stone in order to leverage it out of the way. He pulled down upon the top of the staff, bending it a little. These efforts didn’t budge the tombstone even one little fraction of a fingerbreadth.

Caleb let up and looked over at John. Breathing hard in and out, Caleb asked, but it came out sounding more like a demand, “Give me a...hand, will you?”

Startled into action, John hopped up once where he stood and came over to Caleb. They each grabbed onto the rawhide wrapped portion of the staff and began to pull down together. Bending the good, strong Acacia staff further. Pulling and bouncing down with increasing force. Bending...Bending...Bending, until...*CRACK!* The staff splintered and angled, causing Caleb with John’s assistance, to pull the broken top half down right into his own forehead. This consequence of physics sent him tumbling and taking out John’s legs from underneath him.

They both laid for a moment, groaning in pain. Taking a while to recover. Caleb’s searing eyes were squeezed shut. His nettlesome palm was placed tenderly on a spot where he could already feel a knot swelling up in the center of his forehead. Sprouting tears cooled the irritated sting at the corner of his eyes. When Caleb opened them, he saw there were multiple images of the tombstone floating around each other, like the view from inside a kaleidoscope. Unbudged. Still blocking the entrance, immobile as a mountain.

"DAMN IT!!" Caleb shouted, getting up and kicking the broken staff away into the dirt.

John wandered over and, with an air of nostalgia, he picked up his broken walking stick. His heart was infuriated and saddened that now this endeavor was costing him more than just time and effort. The thief made a private promise to himself to push for sixty-five percent now. Maybe, even seventy, once they were headed back to the Temple with their bounty.

Tenderly holding onto the broken remnant of his staff, he asked, "Well, n-n-now what C-Caleb?"

Caleb stood erect with his arms crossed and his back to the entrance of the tomb. Thinking about their next possible option, while pulling down in angry little tugs upon his patchy beard. He opened his mouth to suggest that maybe they could come back with at least two more men to move the stone. Caleb knew this suggestion would be met unfavorably by John; the prospect of cutting into their large percentages by splitting up the pie into more slices was not an ideal prospect for either of these two avaricious men. Not to mention the crushing disappointment that Caleb would feel when he returned to Caiaphas empty handed. That would absolutely affect the overall payout. No! Whatever they were going to do, it had to be tonight!

But, before Caleb could say anything, the massive, immovable stone rolled to the side. By all evidence, on its own accord. Scraping quick and easy, leaving the small void of the dark rectangle of the tomb entrance exposed. Allowing an invisible barrel of rank decay and clouds of interested flies to roll right out over the trespassers.

All sounds, besides their panicked breathing, ceased. The moment hung framed in time, virtually crystallized for Caleb and John. They couldn't tear their stinging eyes from the tomb's ominous, infinitely deep opening.

John gripped his broken piece of Acacia, his knuckles white and locked. His huge, prickling eyes kept darting between Caleb and the void in spasmodic, rapid flicks. He whimpered while hyperventilating. "C-C-Caleb? W-wha-"

All of a sudden, out of the tomb's pure black darkness, leapt the sallow, naked corpse of Lazarus. Flying through the night air, horribly spread eagle. From its blood-stained mouth came a startling, blood curdling, demonic shriek. Lazarus landed on top of John, snapping his broken walking stick completely in two. With rigored, powerful hands he held John down by the shoulders, exuding a putrid, deceased essence into his face.

John screamed, "MY GOD!!"

Lazarus put its decayed finger on John's quivering lips affably and vocalized in a horrid, legion of strummed voices, "No…God, John." It then bared its hideous set of decaying teeth in a wide rictus grin, beneath a slash of charred flesh and a sunken pair of dead, colorless eyes.

Caleb called out, "Lazarus!" and drew his short sword again, *FWING!!* This drew Lazarus' murderous attention up and away from the scummy thief.

John seized upon this temporary distraction and plunged one of the halves of his broken walking stick deep into Lazarus' side beneath the ribs. A fatal puncture for any living mortal. However, this crude, inflicted wound only produced a small dribble of black blood that oozed out in lazy trickles.

Lazarus responded by howling like a hellish banshee and lunging forward, sinking its brown, splitting teeth deep into John's neck. Completely ripping out his trachea and sending arterial spray across the entire tomb courtyard, as well as Caleb's feet and ankles.

John reached out toward Caleb with a shaking, pleading hand and tried to scream, but only gurgled. Lazarus dragged John back into the tomb in the same manner as when a lion drags away freshly killed prey with its teeth by the throat. The ghoul had to move awkwardly due to the snapped half of Acacia wood still jutting from its side.

Without any thought, Caleb turned and sprinted back up the path that led them here. Sword and lamp were still clenched tightly in each hand. Wild eyes, from what he'd just seen, were in a frantic search of the dark ahead. Peering helplessly through the soupy gloom that ran over the path and in between the sentinel olive tree trunks. In between delirious bouts of panting and moaning he would scream out, "HEEELLP!!"

As Caleb ran beneath the flanking olive trees, he could hear the crescendo of cracking of branches and the rustling of leaves approaching. Rising, like a horrific tidal wave behind him. Caleb chanced a glance over his shoulder and could only see many looming olive tree boughs whipping chaotically behind him. He tried to will his burning legs to pick up his already breakneck pace against the resistant, bogging down atmosphere of this place.

In times like this survival certainly could prove to be a powerful motivator. Unfortunately the human body could also sometimes be weak. In this most important, life or death moment, Caleb was proving to be weak. All too soon he began to tire. An ache developed and pinged with a dull stab in his side. Still gripping the hilt of his useless weapon, he dug a fist into his oblique, pushing against the throbbing ache. He leaned against an ancient olive tree trunk to catch his breath for a few precious seconds.

The beast-like, maniacal activity in the branches behind and overhead was advancing fast. It was true: there was NO rest for the wicked.

With a groaning whimper, Caleb pushed off of the knotted trunk of an olive tree. Desperate, he trudged along the path, sucking in huge intakes of the night air and exhaling out in either a constricted wheeze or a whimper. His sword hand dug hard into the throbbing pang in his side. His lamp hand hung straight down, limp, letting the flame of his lamp nearly brush the ground.

The loud snap of a mature branch breaking overhead made Caleb jerk his neck upwards just in time to see Lazarus dropping down upon him. Gangrenous cadaver claws preceded splotchy, pallid arms that led to milky, dead eyes, which blazed above a blood drenched, bearded maw. Many voices erupted out of that maw all at once in a terrifying chorus of terror. Lazarus landed on top of Caleb with a litheness that belied its haggard appearance. Upon pinning him to the ground though, Lazarus received Caleb's blunt blade, all up to the hilt. It went through and through its oblique on the side opposite of the one that had been punctured by poor John's splintered staff half. Drawing only another tiny, slow dribble of gelatinous, black blood.

Lazarus stood up in a stooped posture over the petrified body of Caleb and removed the sword from its own side in one single, slow continuous glide. *FFFFWWWIIIIIINNNNNGGGG!!* The blade emerged smeared sludgy black and glistening. Milky eyes stared down through Caleb, out of focus and furious. The slash of scorched flesh across its face from the beam of sunlight had scabbed over, but now it was cracking and bled a tiny bit of black plasma. Its lips were pulled back away from teeth that had visible bits of John's neck meat stuck in between them.

In a maladroit attempt, Caleb tried to slink away on his elbows and heels. But, he didn't get very far before Lazarus sprung up into the air, holding the short sword high in both hands. It was screeching in all of its octaves during its descent. Upon landing Lazarus sunk the blade, all of the way up to the hilt, through Caleb's navel, past his spine and into the packed Earth of the downtrodden path. Pinning Caleb in place.

Caleb cried out in excruciating pain. Flagrant gushes of blood spurted from his mouth and his fatal wound. He tried, with shaking hands, to grasp at the sword hilt sticking out of him. It was slick with the mixture of Lazarus' cold, congealed blood and his own hot, fresh brand.

Lazarus stood and watched Caleb's struggle. Stuck and twitching. The greedy human was clueless as to how to even begin to solve the predicament that he found himself in. Like a moth that has had its vital wings removed, only to be shown a cruel, enticing beacon of light afterward.

"LAZARUS! PLEASE!" Caleb screamed and more blood came up out of his mouth, flowing down each corner.

"Lazarus...now?" remarked Lazarus, as it took to circling Caleb. "I thought...to you...I was...Abomination."

Caleb's words, from the night of Lazarus' resurrection, recalled to haunt him, made him cry harder, "Please Lazarus, I meant nothing!" Caleb screamed. He coughed up copious amounts of blood and was getting hard to understand.

Lazarus dropped to all fours and came around close to Caleb's cheek, Then, he hungrily began to lap up at the blood dribbling down from Caleb's mouth into his thin beard. Sticking out a dead, grey tongue, Lazarus voraciously licked at the steady dribble of fresh, hot blood. Caleb tried to turn away, but had nowhere to go, so instead he could only hopelessly moan and plead against this fate.

Something cast a fleeting flicker in the gibbous moonlight and caught Lazarus attention while it was tasting. It came away from Caleb's face and reached down into his robe, pulling out a small leather satchel by its drawstring. It opened the satchel out of curiosity and poured out a couple of the silver coins in the palm of its dead hand, where they sizzled. Shocking Lazarus into an instant painful outcry and dropping the money to the ground beside Caleb. This left trails of smoke lifting from precisely branded, burned indentations of Tiberius Caesar Augustus' likeness on

Lazarus' palm, as though the coins were made of molten metal and its flesh was nothing more than supple wax.

"C-caiaphas," Caleb whimpered, coughing up more blood.

"What?!" Lazarus asked through pained, gritted teeth.

"The High Puh-p," he started before coughing and writhing in pain against being staked in the ground. Once he regained some of his breath, he continued, straining, "The H-h-high Priest, C-c-c-caiaphas."

"Yes?" Lazarus asked.

After another bout of painful coughing and moaning, Caleb went on, "H-he s-s-seeks to f-f-find you."

"Why?" Lazarus seethed.

He drew in shaky breaths through bloodied teeth. "H-h-he s-seeks to k-k-k-kill the M-messiah f-f-for r-resurrecting you." Caleb groaned out loud while grasping at the sword hilt sticking out of his midsection. Then, in a surprising move, Caleb smiled and looked right into Lazarus dead eyes, saying, "He k-k-knows wh-what y-y-you r-really are!"

Lazarus had heard enough of Caleb's final pontificating. In an exertion of minimal effort, it twisted Caleb's head off of his neck, with both of its hands. *"GAHK!!!"* was the last sound Caleb made, before becoming two pieces and spraying a violent gush of blood from his neck. Lazarus held the removed, dripping head in its hands, looking at the final agonized, terrified expression for a reflective moment, before throwing it overhand far over the tops of the trees and out of sight into the distance.

The night was once again peaceful and calm. Random, nocturnal animal and melodious insect sounds returned to the ear. In a methodical manner, Lazarus turned and removed the sword pinning down the headless body, *FFFFWWWIIIIIINNNNNGGGG.* It brought the blade up to its mouth and stuck out its rotten tongue. Running it up and down the blade. Slurping up blood and dirt, before tossing it into the trees, which produced a metallic clanging, silencing the night critters momentarily.

Lazarus bent down and scooped up the warm, headless body of Caleb. Hefting it up and over its cold, naked shoulder, like a lifeless sack of grain. Blood gushed from Caleb's neck and stomach wound down Lazarus' back and chest. Grey, pale mottled skin remained smooth and unresponsive to the enveloping chill. Bare feet and toes cursed with rigor, crushed fallen olive fruit along the path in the short walking trudge back to the tomb.

To its Home.

Its Cradle.
To gorge itself.

XV

"Where is that fool?" Caiaphas said aloud to no one in particular.

It was early morning. Dark purple and lavender gave way to the brightening orange announcement of another imminent sunrise. Roosters crowed and animals chattered busily in the nearby streets. Voices were building in volume behind the animal chatter, adding to the early, ambient discordant babble. All en route to the Temple, most likely.

The house of his father-in-law, Annas, was in close proximity to Jerusalem's Temple, their main place of business. It was a large two story monstrosity, surrounding a gorgeous, spacious atrium in its center. Fountains trickled idly. Graceful prinia, masked shrike and sunbirds flitted in happy existence across the courtyard, as bees danced and bobbed in the air around opening blooms.

Caiaphas stood with his arms crossed, tapping his foot, grimacing and squinting into the sunrise now cresting above the horizon. Caleb was supposed to be back before sunrise with information regarding Lazarus. Now, it was after sunrise, and still, no sign of Caleb.

After sending Caleb on his errand the previous afternoon, Caiaphas and Annas had been busy late into the evening.

Their first order of business was to send the young, ambitious Pharisee, James, along with an accompanying Tribune and Praefecti, to Capernaum. See what business Martha's Phillip was up to there. Question the locals, even Jairus himself if he had to. Report back without delay.

Second, there was the matter of trying to sway some of the more sympathetic members of the Sanhedrin through various means of persuasion to warm to the thought of killing Jesus. Some members responded with more favor if, say, monetary compensation was brought into the equation. Others warmed more to the lengthy advancement and empowerment of their own religious powers. Even a moderate number of Holy Men had egregious, moral offenses and were ripe for blackmail. Not particularly a great look in the public eye, which makes these methods very effective as leverage against some of his fellow Priests. Nearly every member had their vice or pressure points in one way or another. Some, though, like Nicodemus and Joseph of Arimathea, along with their small caucus, were lost causes. To Caiaphas, it was an inconvenience to deal with these so-called "peers" of his. In his mind, their wishy-washy indecisiveness was proof that the confident voice of God had **never** spoken to any of them.

Third, there were just the normal priestly duties of the Temple to attend to. Overseeing sacrificial rituals, collecting money from those selling Temple necessities, and mingling with the Roman elite, so as not to fade from their favor.

"Still no sign of your confidant?" Annas spoke behind his son-in-law, startling him a bit, as he was lost in his own train of thought.

Caiaphas turned to Annas. A sour look upon his face. "No." He walked towards the old man and stared down into him. "We must leave. At once."

Annas suffered a moderate fit of coughing until he spat out some early morning thick batter into a nearby bush. Once he could speak again, he asked in a hoarse voice, "Where to son?"

"The wilderness, to the East. To the Mount of Olives. We will do our own investigating," Caiaphas answered. Rubbing at his weathered face, speaking through his fingers. "We'll see if Caleb even went out to look for Lazarus last night, or if he just took his measly shekels and ran."

Annas was nodding in solidarity with his son-in-law. He knew the importance of restricting the knowledge of a possible, successful resurrection from the people. There had already been many, lengthy shared discussions between Caiaphas, himself and some select Sanhedrin of the fallout that would result in chaos on all sides. Rome would see the people of Judaea as divided and in need of solid leadership. They would then usurp total control from the religious leaders and enact authoritarian rule over all. The Temple would be obsolete. All of the prominent positions of power that they had fought so hard to attain and retain in the Temple would be of no more use to them than a jar of sand in the desert.

"When?" Annas asked gruffly, while spinning his arthritic pinky finger in his overly hairy ear, then removing it and gazing in sleepy investigation at the grotesque yellowish mass on the tip.

"Immediately," Caiaphas answered back. "Come Father, we must head for the Temple first."

"Why?" Annas inquired, now picking at the abundance of crusty substance that riddled the corners of both of his eyes and yawning. His questions were beginning to irk his son-in-law.

"We're not going alone," Caiaphas replied in a cryptic tone. "Get ready."

Annas yawned wide again, revealing an inner look at his cavernous, black toothed, white tongued mouth. He coughed some more and scratched aggressively in between his butt cheeks. "Who is going with us?"

All in all irritated, Caiaphas bit his tongue and stormed away, without answering his Father-in-law's last question.

xvi

By late morning, Caiaphas and Annas, along with a small entourage of Roman soldiers, were following the meandering dirt path that led through the olive groves. Happy birds chirped and zoomed all over the place. Bees and other insects floated by in random criss crossing lines. A soft, fragrant breeze, that was a pleasant mixture of olive blossom and jasmine flower, rousted the boughs of the trees into a dreamy sway, to and fro above their heads. The temperature was warm, but not hot. Altogether, it would've been a serene scene, had it not been for the incessant clanking and clunking of the armored soldiers atop their armored mounts.

Annas and Caiaphas, however, rode in silence on the backs of two mules a good distance behind the Roman soldiers. Scanning the path winding before them and all through the thick grove of tree trunks proved fruitless though. Even though Caiaphas didn't appear to blink while searching their surroundings for any movement or sound. Even though he sniffed at the air for any suspicious aromas. There was nothing interesting or alarming for a long while during their search.

Until they clip-clopped upon an unnerving scene. Up above them a mature, splintered olive tree branch dangled, nearly broken off of the tree itself. In the pathway, in front of them, was a small gash in the Earth, with a reddish maroon substance soaked into the dirt around it. A few loose silver shekels and a satchel lay in the dirt beside the stain. Just above that, was a large cone shaped spray of more reddish maroon coloring, staining the pathway. Some of the deeper points still appeared viscid in places.

The company of soldiers dismounted and approached with significant caution. They dispersed themselves into the grove, scouting and establishing a perimeter, while a first year Praefecti stayed close by tethering up the horses.

Annas had slipped off of his own donkey and was leading it along by the bridle, gigging at it to walk along. When he came closer, he leaned down first and picked up the shekels. "Caleb's?" Annas asked, holding up the coins in his gnarled fingers.

Caiaphas shrugged and answered, "Possibly."

Before continuing, Annas put the jingling coins in the satchel, then put the satchel in his pocket. After that he reached down and touched his fingers to the sticky, ruddy dirt on the path. A few moments were afforded towards the examination of the substance that stuck to the pads of his fingertips. Annas rubbed it in methodical circles and tested the consistency. He sniffed at the reddish stuff and recognized it right away for its particular irony aroma. Caiaphas' father-in-law confirmed, "Blood."

Leaning over his shoulder, but still astride his mule, Caiaphas inquired, "An animal's?"

Annas squinted. Sniffed again, then stuck out his pale tongue and tasted the dirty blood. "Could be," he said, rolling his tongue around his mouth. The old Priest regarded the size of the dried up puddle and added, "That's quite a lot of blood, though. It would've been a big animal."

Caiaphas digested this evidence. He felt goose pimples starting to raise on his arms and tiny hairs standing up on the back of his neck. Dread played in quiet, sinister solitude in the back of his mind. Murky images of possible scenarios that had played out here. Terrible things that had sunk to the bottom and he couldn't see from the surface.

Soldiers were clanking and clacking in the distance, glinting at random spots through the tree trunks. Patrolling three hundred and sixty degrees around, establishing a solid perimeter. Scaring away every animal within earshot of their discordant march.

Annas traced the edges of the precise slit in the dirt path with his old, twig-like fingers. Allowing his crooked digits the slightest brush and tickling the surface. Bushy, grey brows furrowed together, almost connecting in the center. "What made this?" Annas asked aloud. Caiaphas looked at the blood crusted opening in the dirt. Then, to the broken branch up above. Back down to where Annas was grazing the path with his fingertips. Trying to piece together a plausible string of events to fit the scene that lay before him. His thin, nonexistent lips were pinched together in quiet consternation.

"High Priest, Caiaphas?" A deep voice inquired, breaking Caiaphas' concentration.

Caiaphas looked up in irritation and saw a Tribune named Marcus walking towards him, holding a dirty, short sword in both open palms. "We found this close by," Marcus said and he offered the sword, hilt first, over to Caiaphas.

Caiaphas snatched the weapon from Marcus and restituted a meager thanks. Marcus saluted and wandered back into the grove to continue the search. Caiaphas turned the sword over and over slowly in his hands. Studying the filthy, smeared appearance of the blade. Stained with the same dark reddish maroon blood that painted the ground before them.

"Give that here," Annas said to his son-in-law and grabbed the sword out of his hands. He took it by the hilt and, with the blade pointed down, slid the sword into place in the gash of the path. It went all the way in until it stopped with a little over two handbreadths of blade and the hilt left sticking straight up out of the ground.

They both took a sharp inhale when the puzzle piece fit into place. A variation of possible, ranging events then began to cycle out in imaginary ghostly echoes. Caleb attacked. Caleb attacking. Caleb is not involved at all.

But, before an opinion on what could've happened could be voiced, a commotion arose from deeper in the groves. Caiaphas and Annas took off in the direction of the sound, leading their stubborn steeds by the bridle through the sparse maze of tree trunks. Following the yelling all the way to its source where a couple of young Roman soldiers stood, pale faced, wide eyed and pointing shaky swords and spears up into the tree limbs.

"What could've done such a thing?" one of the soldiers was saying, tears were quivering in his eyes. The other, younger soldier, retched and hacked dryly over a fresh puddle of his own puke.

Caiaphas followed their weapon tips in the direction they pointed and searched the limb line. At first, seeing nothing. It took only a moment, but he saw it right as his father-in-law clutched at his shoulder and shouted while pointing up at it, "Look!" It was a disembodied head resting up amidst the leaves. Half pecked and missing an eye. Mouth agape. Tongue missing as well. But, Caiaphas would know that scraggly, wispy beard anywhere.

"Caleb," Caiaphas breathed and brought a bejeweled hand to his mouth to stifle a bit of nausea building at the back of his throat.

Annas squinted and said, "My God, you're right!" He allowed himself a mirthless chuckle and, void of empathy, kept on talking, "I guess, now we know he didn't run away with his silver." And he jingled the coins comically in his pocket.

Caiaphas failed to see the humor in what they were looking at, and spoke in a grave, somber tone, "Death comes for us all." He looked back in the direction of where the sword had fit into the ground. Then he brought his gaze back to the tree. "Caleb faced a horrific ending. Let's pray we don't face the same."

The two youthful soldiers, upon overhearing Caiaphas grim words, took off running back towards the youngest Praefecti and the tethered horses. Before Caiaphas could begin to wonder where they were off to, Marcus called from even further down the path, "High Priest, Caiaphas! High Priest, Annas! Come quick!"

Both Priests moved as fast as possible with their mules through the grove, back to the path, and trotted the rest of the way. In their haste to get to Marcus, they failed to notice a consistent, incognito trail of blood drops on the path, camouflaged amongst the black olive fruit that had fallen from the trees. The patterned path led them to Marcus, standing outside the entrance of a small courtyard, with his arms crossed in front of his chest. A stern, spooked look was chiseled upon his face. "It's....uh....it's a lot of blood," he warned. He glanced up in wary fear at the stone archway and added, "This place doesn't feel right."

Even after hearing these words, the two Priests tried to pull at the bridles in their stubborn mule's mouths. Thinking they were going to somehow wrestle the animals into the courtyard. However, the mules resisted and refused to budge at all.

While Annas grunted and pulled against the physical protests of his mount, he asked Marcus with an inappropriate smirk through his bushy, grey beard, "Did you see the severed head?"

Marcus' stern, sick look became one of shock. "What? No!" Turning to Caiaphas, he intoned, "What exactly are we out here looking for, High Priest?"

Caiaphas took over the conversation, sounding bored, saying, "Yes, your two young...soldiers, if you want to call them that, found the severed head in the trees." A broad smile spread across Marcus' face. There was an obvious, inflated sense of pride swelling in his chest for the new blood coming up in the ranks, underneath his tutelage. Caiaphas continued on, extra dry, "Then, they ran away."

"Ran...ran away?" Marcus repeated in a disbelieving, deflated tone.

"Yes," Caiaphas. "I believe one might have been vomiting. The other was definitely crying. Both were for certain shaking."

"Is that a fact?" Marcus challenged.

"It is," Caiaphas snapped back. "Let me tell you, the next time you put the lives of two prominent High Priests in jeopardy, by supplying young, inexperienced soldiers, I will take it up with Pontius Pilate directly."

Marcus looked past them, over their shoulders, in the direction that they had come. A look of worry and disappointment furrowed his brows. Anger was also there, but not for his fellow soldiers. No, his anger bubbled for his current situation. Finding himself stuck here in this dirty, foreign land, on this fool's errand for these pompous Holy Men, who were now trying to threaten him.

He managed to grind his teeth and apologize, "My deepest apologies," adding, "This was only supposed to be a routine expedition. I was unaware I needed to bring battle ready, hardened veterans for this venture."

Before Caiaphas could counter what he took as a snide remark, Marcus pushed past him, muttering, "I will see to it that they are harshly reprimanded." Marcus never broke his determined stride, although he was hilarious in his clanking armor as he made his way back down the pathway towards the young insubordinates and the younger Praefecti attending the horses.

Annas and Caiaphas exchanged annoyed expressions between one another. Caiaphas shook his head in silent disbelief.

They made to enter the sun dappled courtyard, but their mules continued to hold up their stubborn resistance. Pulling against them and braying as the High Priests fought to drag them further along. They spent the next few moments exerted in a sweaty, futile effort against the donkeys, before finally giving up. After steadying their breath, they chose to tie their asses to a nearby tree and proceed into the courtyard on foot.

A heavy, oppressive feeling that both Priests recognized as a pure demonic force, came over them the instant they passed the threshold. As though the archway into the courtyard acted as a portal to evil. There was no denying the harsh sting and burn in their eyes and lungs, nor the creepy, irritating tingle teeming all over their skin.

Caiaphas prayed aloud for both of them, “God, protect us in this wicked place as we strive to bring glory to your name. Amen.”

“Amen,” Annas grumbled.

Slow and steady, they went about and investigated the scene. It was, indeed, “a lot of blood” as Marcus had stated. Blood coated a sizable swath of the limestone pathway of the courtyard to the right of the tomb’s entrance. Blood led away in an obvious drag pattern up to the tomb’s threshold, appearing as if passing through into the chamber beyond. Nearby, laid a splintered polished portion of acacia wood, two cubits in length. A smell of death hovered in the atmosphere, upon every breath, and behind that a thick, palpable demonic presence lingered like a looming gargoyle.

“This place feels evil,” Annas said. “Can you feel it?”

Caiaphas could most certainly corroborate to something unholy in their presence, although he didn’t respond. Instead, he came up close to the large circular tombstone and placed his long digits upon the cool rock’s face. He spent a little time investigating the brownish red hand print stained on the face of the stone. Then he moved to inspecting all around the tombstone for a breach point. The smell of squishy decay pervaded in generous wafts around its chiseled edges. Flies buzzed about happily in these conditions. He noted the presence of fresh disturbance in the dirt behind the stone, up against the small structure, as if it had been rolled aside, recently. Altogether seeming more recent than two nights before, when the alleged resurrecting transpired.

Jesus with his twelve most likely moved it aside with ease, thought Caiaphas. He was trying to envision them all standing here on the night of the resurrection. Caleb and the twelve apostles. Mary and Martha were most likely present too.

Annas sidled up closer to him, holding the broken bottom half of polished acacia in his hands. He cleared his throat and said, "Found this. Looks like the attack continued here."

"Or this is where it started," Caiaphas retorted.

"What do you think, son? Robbers?" Annas asked.

Caiaphas shook his head, slowly swiveling from side to side, "No. Robbers would've just incapacitated and taken what they wanted." The High Priest's dark eyes danced over the large, garish bloodstain, "This...brutality isn't for monetary gain."

Turning back, Caiaphas tapped with his big toe at the small angle of peaked dirt by the base of the massive tombstone. In a silly personal trial, he placed his shoulder against the curved edge of the stone and nudged. It was a ridiculous trial.The stone was just as immovable as he had thought it would be.

Annas had been watching him the whole time, amused. "You didn't really think you were going to move that?" Annas asked, a smile twitching on his lips.

Caiaphas shot him an angered look from two black molten pools. It was swift and temporary though. His momentary fury cooled as he became aware of the distant clip-clopping sound of horses and the accompanying comical clanking of lorica segmentata armor approaching from the pathway.

Horses were heard screaming just outside the courtyard in protest of coming any closer in vicinity to the tomb. When Caiaphas and Annas sauntered over to the edge of the tomb's courtyard, they saw Marcus, with his Praefecti, pulling down upon their horses reigns, against their fuming protestations. After a few moments of struggling they emerged victorious and managed to get the horses back by the restrained mules. Tying them to their own nearby olive trees. Then taking a few moments to calm them with a pat and a soothing word, before nimbly stepping over to where Caiaphas and Annas stood.

"Where are the others?" Caiaphas asked. His arms crossed in a tight weave in front of his chest. Already confrontational.

"Gone," Marcus admitted, shoulders slumped beneath his armor in a posture of defeat.

"Gone?" Annas repeated, sounding surprised, but not really. He seemed to be enjoying the conundrum that the Tribune now found himself in.

"Yes," Marcus went on, "Took the other Praefecti, Aquinas with them."

"And three horses," his own Praefecti chimed in. Proud and smiling at himself for being a good helper.

Marcus appeared to suffer within, but quickly shifted his embarrassment into a trembling smile. He placed his hand upon the Praefecti's shoulder, squeezed and said, "Thank you, Darius." Turning back to the High Priests, he reiterated, "Yes, and three horses."

Caiaphas worked his mouth toward an onslaught of insults, but Marcus cut him off before he could slice him to ribbons verbally, "I take full accountability for their hasty, foolish actions, High Priest, and will humbly resign my position of command upon our return to Jerusalem."

Marcus stood in stoic resignation, awaiting an onslaught of a poison laced, insult riddled tirade from the younger of the two High Priests. Wincing in anticipation of the inevitable, veritable verbal barrage of spears, arrows and catapults. None of which came.

Annas stood by. Hunched over, grinning in broad approval beneath his beard. Savoring every slamming second in joyful eagerness for his son-in-law to dress down this so-called "commanding officer", who was quite clearly inept. Just to see the Romans in any kind of unforced disarray, however trivial, solidified the Sanhedrin's right to power and prominence of the law in the region. But, the seconds slipped into a vacuum of uncomfortable silence.

Instead, Caiaphas pointed a curled, twig of a finger at the spear that poor, young Darius held and said in a shrill voice much too abrasive for the regular calm of the canopy, "Bring that spear, boy!"

Spinning a one eighty, Caiaphas marched back to the tomb entrance, skirting the large, dried stain of blood on the courtyard stones. Young, helpless Darius, looked over at his commanding officer, who nodded in consent, giving him silent encouragement to follow Caiaphas.

The four men, two soldiers and two Priests, found themselves in the courtyard, a place that could be likened to a spiritual sewer. Darius coughed and rubbed his irritated eyes. They had all gathered around the ridiculous mass of the tombstone. The smell of decay seeped out in sickening, curling tendrils around the outer edge of the stone, and swirled to assimilation in the warm afternoon weather.

Caiaphas snatched the spear from Darius' hands and addressed Marcus by saying, "What kind of wood is this spear made from?"

Marcus fumbled for the answer, "Uh...the spear...uh, is...uh-"

"Ash wood," Darius answered with an endearing, youthful meekness, while rubbing his upper arms in soothing caresses due to the prickly, evil presence that seemed to bite and dance on the air.

"Pfffft," Caiaphas balked and studied the Roman infantry issued spear he now held. Annas chuckled in entertained disdain at a near silent, low, rhythmic rumble.

"Why?" Marcus inquired, clueless.

"Well, we have to try," Caiaphas said, ignoring and waving off Marcus' question. Then, he took the spear and stabbed the bottom of the shaft into the ground at the base of the stone. Looking up, he commanded all of them, "Help me!"

One by one, they all grasped around the top of the spear and together they pulled down. This broke the spear immediately, without budging the stone in the slightest. Smacking Annas right in his phylactery box and sending the other three sprawling. Frustrated beyond the necessity for any attempt at decorum, Caiaphas jumped up, yanked the broken spear from the base of the stone and hurled the splintered, angled weapon into the grove. "BAH!!" The spear came to a rough landing after ricocheting and clattering off a few tree trunks first.

Darius ventured, "It's ash wood, High Priest." As if that explained everything. Caiaphas stood frozen. Stunned and speechless. Darius clarified, "It's soft."

Caiaphas opened his mouth to dismantle the young, maybe sixteen year old, Praefecti. Marcus, however interjected, saving young Darius, by asking in tired exasperation while rubbing at the back of his neck, "Why are we trying to break into the tomb, Caiaphas?"

"What did you call me?" Caiaphas asked in pure disbelief, turning towards the Tribune.

"Oh...um...High Priest," Marcus corrected himself. "Sorry."

"You should be," Caiaphas retorted back. "Tell me, Tribune, what landed you to this inauspicious detail? Surely, there's more glory to be had in leading as a Centurion than following around two old Holy Men, looking for another man around the Mount of Olives."

Marcus didn't speak. Couldn't speak. Caiaphas had even used the derogatory term of "Holy Men" in self deprecating reference to Annas and himself. How much longer would Marcus have to suffer the ridiculousness and insults of this pompous fool and his decrepit, creep of a father?

"Was it something immoral or deceitful?" Caiaphas prodded more. "Come now, don't be bashful. I can offer you some of God's forgiveness."

Marcus opened his mouth, and choked out, "It was…"

"Yes," Caiaphas coaxed, drawing out the single word in an elongated entreaty.

"It was my mistake," Marcus offered with astuteness, clearing his throat afterwards.

Annas, who had been preoccupied rubbing hard at his forehead, looking every now and then to see if he was bleeding, was openly giggling at the Tribune squirm. His shoulders were bobbing up and down in generous, bullish laughter.

Marcus asked again, "What are we looking for Cai-" Caiaphas eyes widened, "High Priest? What's in the tomb?"

Caiaphas answered him with the most vague answer possible, "We're looking for a man." Leaving this answer hanging in ether as being sufficient enough.

Marcus scanned the courtyard and asked, "A man?"

"Yes," Caiaphas answered back.

"A man that did all of this?" Marcus inquired further, gesturing to the carnage of the courtyard and the grove beyond.

"We don't know that," Caiaphas answered back.

"D-did the head belong to s-someone you knew?" Darius asked, surprising the High Priest.

Caiaphas regarded him from a shrewd disposition and answered his question with another question, "What are you getting at boy?"

"N-n-nothing High Priest Caiaphas," Darius stammered. "We're j-just out here f-f-for a good r-reason, I g-guess."

"Look," Marcus took over, "he's scared. I'm sure we all are. You say you're looking for a man. Well, did the head in the tree belong to the man you're looking for?" After a second he added as an afterthought, "High Priest."

"No, Tribune," Caiaphas answered back in a snarky tone. "I don't know who that head in the tree belonged to," he lied. He felt Annas glance up at him apprehensively from the corner of his eye.

"So, we're still looking for *your* man?" Marcus asked.

"Yes," Caiaphas answered sharply and clipped.

Marcus hesitated, then asked, "Did the man we're looking for do this?"

"No!" Caiaphas said, although he wasn't sure. But, he still said it and cast it off as if the very notion was absurd.

The monumental weight of the oppressive evil force of this place felt like extra gravity, pulling them down, physically as well as spiritually. Darius was subconsciously dancing from foot to foot, eager to get as far away from here as fast as humanly possible.

Marcus had one more question for the High Priest, Caiaphas, "Do you think your man is in the tomb?"

Annas spoke up now in his deep, grumbling timber, "We're not here to assume anything, Tribune. We are simply acquiring the facts of what we have stumbled upon."

Caiaphas broke in now, by saying in a rising, screeching tone, "You know, soldier, by your line of questioning, it would seem you are trying to implicate two prominent High Priests in a way as to be tied to this horrible tragedy."

Marcus took offense at being referred to as a "soldier". But, he also remembered his initial charge to maintain order with the local people. Especially the religious elites. He was still, after all, a foreigner in a foreign land, which meant he had to abide by their customs and ways. "My apologies," he started through gritted teeth. "No implication meant. I'm very sorry to have offended the both of you."

Annas smiled a broad yellowed grin in deep satisfaction. As a part of Caiaphas' relentless derision, he snorted back into the back of his throat and spit at the ground by Marcus' feet. The Tribune froze in place, eyes bulging in shock. His Praefecti, stared in horrified revulsion at the viscous glob splatter on the limestone, appearing to be frozen as well.

Caiaphas leaned in close, causing Marcus to flinch. The High Priest then said in a low, intimidating tone, “Don’t mistake us for being as low as you Romans.” He got right up on Marcus’ ear and growled, “For all we know, a filthy foreigner, like you, could’ve done this.” Caiaphas pulled back with his eyebrows raised and pinching his phylactery box just off center of his forehead. Challenging and being condescending to Marcus simultaneously.

Marcus’ gaze tilted towards the ground, like a reprimanded puppy. He muttered slowly, “Yes, High Priest.”

“What was that?” asked Caiaphas, cupping a hand around his ear, placing it in close proximity to the Tribune's mouth, even though he’d plainly heard what he said just fine.

Perturbed, Marcus repeated louder, “Yes, High Priest.”

Annas was in a blatant fit of chortling at how puny his son-in-law was making this decorated officer look. In front of a young, impressionable set of eyes and ears, no less. The predicament of the Roman officer was truly satisfying and delicious to the older High Priest.

“That’s what we thought,” Caiaphas said, ending any further discussion on the matter.

The day seemed to be waning and slipping away from them. A changing of colors was becoming perceptible through the flickering of the leaves. A coolness was now carried on the decaying breeze. Nightfall would be upon them soon.

Annas asked, “What now?”

Caiaphas answered, “Now? I would imagine we’d report these findings to the Temple,” he regarded Marcus, “and, of course, the Roman Governor, Pontius Pilate, at once.”

Darius, the young Praefecti, appeared visibly relieved at the mere mention of leaving. A small smile curled up one side of his lip and he spun around to go untie the horses, without any orders given.

“What about the head?” Marcus asked, ignoring the young Praefecti’s loss of decorum. “Shouldn’t we-”

“I think the birds and wildlife will take care of the rest,” Caiaphas offered in a cold way. Showing off a pure calloused heart. Marcus and Darius appeared horrified by this lack of empathy. Addressing the aghast look upon both of the Roman’s faces, Caiaphas added, “There wasn’t much left of it anyway.”

“Oh God,” Marcus gasped.

"Oh? And which one of your 'gods' are you referring to? Jupiter? Mercury?" Caiaphas taunted him.

Marcus didn't engage with either High Priest anymore. It would only result in more insults. More personal taunts. More professional criticism. More needling. Wisely, he chose to spin on his heel and follow Darius to the set of tethered, still skittish horses.

Caiaphas and his father-in-law exchanged amused looks between one another, before leaving the bloodied courtyard and making for their own tethered mounts.

A gust of wind rose up and tousled the olive tree boughs. Creating enough white noise and distraction, that no one noticed the tombstone on the crypt move aside just a little, revealing a small opening of darkness that no one saw either. Beyond that, there was a pale eye that no one spotted glaring at their four backs. Not one of the party heard the grinding of split, bloodstained teeth coming from within the tomb. Or perceived the rigid fingers gripping onto the edge of the tombstone. For certain, no one caught a variety of voices enunciating the name, "Caiaphas." Surely, not one of the soldiers or Priests discerned a smile that cracked dead lips and exposed a set of rotting teeth, as the stone rolled closed once again.

Until nightfall.

xvii

Martha and Mary sat at their looms. Sweating. Moving in a mechanical way. Just moving, to keep moving, so as not to let their minds drift to, what was now, a dark secret kept between each other. They had tried to keep busy over the last couple of days, avoiding real conversation or any solid eye contact with anyone in the house. The house itself harbored an edgy, constant buzz after the recent discovery of the mutilated goats and the neighborhood child abduction.

Servants and visitors would bring up tidbits of news and rumors to the ladies of the house. *Did you hear? More animals were found torn apart nearby.* Or *A local woman is missing. Blood was found at her house.* And stories like, *Another child was taken. A girl this time.*

Even Hannah, who had been privy to the sister's interrogation by the High Priest's, asked on more than one occasion about Lazarus directly. Had they heard from him recently? Seen him? Talked to him? Was he alright? Was he going to come to the house to see her? After all, she had been there to help raise him.

How long were they supposed to keep up this charade? Mary began to wonder.

She did love her brother and would do anything to have him back the way that he was. Not what he was now. If there were any way for Jesus, or God, to fix Lazarus, she would not hesitate to pay any price imaginable. But, she had already begun the process of saying goodbye to the brother she once knew. She wasn't looking forward to having to start the whole process over again, if nothing could be done by God's power to right the wrong that was now her brother's existence. This whole nightmare situation was hijacking her mind. Her only escape could be found in lust and drink, both of which she was now drowning herself in.

Martha, however, held fast to hope. Wonderful, enigmatic hope. It was really all she had to hold fast to. If she didn't, at least, have hope, coupled with faith that through Him anything is possible, her outlook would be mighty bleak. She would most definitely be finding herself trying to numb her senses through drink and flesh, like her weaker sister. No. She had to be an immovable example of sobriety, dedication, strength, and fortitude to her younger sister by holding fast to something virtuous, like hope.

The constant movement of the loom work gave the sewing room an almost...tropical feeling. Humidity draped over the sisters like a blanket smothering all around, even with two windows thrown wide open for a cross breeze.

Mary wiped at some sweat on her clammy forehead and arose from her wonky, befuddled weavework, breaking Martha's concentration on her own tight, precise pattern of zigzagging stripes. The younger sister began to stomp about the room. Sloppy and irritable. Weaving in her gait while anxiously wringing her hands together. Her loud breathing was coming in and out. Shallow and rapid.

"Ah hate thizz," Mary announced thickly to the stifling, warm room.

Martha remained silent, breaking eye contact with her sister, and returning to the calming, therapeutic work of her loom.

Mary, edging on hysteria and slightly drunk, continued, "Wur jus zauppozed to whait? Foor whut?"

Martha, while keeping consistent motion, ignored her sister's obvious inebriation and calmly answered, "We're waiting for word from either Jesus or Phillip, sister."

Mary countered with an inflamed tone, "Ow cen you be zo calm? Oor brutherr izz ah monzter!"

"Lower your voice sister," Martha's voice was firm in its command. She flicked a fierce set of brown eyes up at Mary, without breaking from the rhythm of her pattern. Droplets of sweat decorated Martha's forehead and bare forearms.

Mary stomped over to Martha and shoved her own face into hers. Gritting her mauve stained teeth together, Mary growled a reeking, stale grape breath into her older sister's cheek, "Wee shudove left im in thu tooomb! Why dint we yeave im ded in tha toooommmmb!?"

Upon being assaulted, Martha broke from her pattern and shoved Mary away from her, by placing her hand square on her sister's damp face and pushing it away as hard as she could. Mary stumbled backward, bumped and tumbled into her own loom, with a half finished, abandoned, abnormal pattern upon it. Her bloodshot eyes shot half focused daggers at her older sister. Anger boiled within Martha, as well, but she managed a look of pure boredom before deciding to not physically engage her tipsy sister anymore and returning to the safety of her weaving.

Martha, while her hands returned to working at a blurring pace, admonished, "The problem with you, dear sister, besides drinking wine for breakfast, is your amount of faith." Then, as an afterthought, she added a correction, "Or your complete lack of it."

Mary could've ripped her sister's hair out, like when they were children, right then and there. She would've, had it not been for the sound of footsteps approaching from down the hall. Mary spun and sat back down to her loom, red faced. Perspiring in profuse, poisoned secretion. Acting at being just an innocent, know nothing preoccupied at fixing her warbly weavework.

A quick knock preceded the door opening sans invitation. Hannah entered, frail and stern with her wrinkled old hands clasped at her waist. She gave the barest form of a curtsy to the ladies seated at their looms, before saying, "Good afternoon, Martha," then, as an afterthought, she looked over and added, "Mary."

Martha dipped her head. She half expected another exhaustive diatribe about nearby murders or animal mutilations. Or another collection of questions about Lazarus to dodge. Apprehensively, she asked, "What is it, Hannah?" Then she held her breath.

Hannah held her position by the door and said, "A messenger pigeon has arrived."

The sister's collective gasp seemed to suck what little air there was out of the room.

Martha blurted out, "What does the message say?"

"I don't know," Hannah answered with a tiny, smug curl playing upon her lips.

Mary blew a strand of hair out of her face and asked with a definite lilt to her speech, "Whooz it frum?"

The curl of Hannah's smile became more pronounced. Most certainly, the old woman, for some reason, was enjoying this. "I don't know," Hannah answered again.

Mary and Martha sprung up from their matching, small three legged stools. They raced out of the door, forcing Hannah aside when they pushed past her little old, bony body.

The hallway was populated by both servant and guest, trying to catch the attention of either sister. Some tried to facilitate the start of a conversation, but the sisters didn't break or slow in their stride and rudely brushed by all of them without a word of explanation.

At the end of the corridor, there was a wooden ladder leading up to a hatch that let out onto the roof. Mary went up first, missing a step and almost falling during the short ascending climb. Once Mary was up on the roof, Martha followed, into the blinding sunlight. Stepping onto the roof brought a welcomed whoosh of warm, fresh air. Bright afternoon daylight disoriented both of them for a moment until their pupils adjusted. Mary pressed a hand to her forehead and another to her stomach. Martha held her breath and warily watched her sister, to make sure Mary wasn't going to vomit.

When Martha was pretty sure that Mary wasn't going yack, she walked over to the cone shaped, stone dovecote. She searched the cubbies one by one until she found the dove of interest, with the note still attached to its leg.

Hannah is worthless, Martha thought to herself. *Or, maybe she's just being cruel not to bring the note down after seeing that it had arrived.*

Whatever. She couldn't get hung up on psychoanalyzing the old woman right now. That was just a distraction that required more energy and patience that she just did not have.

As she reached in, Martha blew a tickling, rogue strand of hair aside from her face and delicately removed the pigeon. Taking even more care to remove the small rolled bit of papyrus from its leg. She unfurled the tiny note and read it in silence, moving her lips with the words.

Mary wandered over to her and asked, "Whoozit frumm?"

"Jesus," Martha answered.

Mary waited. "Aaaand? Whud duzit zay?" She asked Martha.

Martha sighed and read the note in a robotic verbatim, "Coming to you. Trust in the Lord."

Mary snatched the note from Martha with a nimble hand that belied her reeking intoxication. To study the note, she closed one bleary, bloodshot eye, so as to help the letters stop from drifting on the strip of papyrus. The younger, drunk sister took some time reading the seven words in two short sentences over and over again, as if trying to decipher a secret code within the simple message.

Mary's eyebrows furrowed together and she slurred out, "Truzt? Truzt? Weeve ahlruddy dun that ahnd look whur it'z gaht uzz!"

Grabbing back the scrawled message from Mary's nonreflexive, numb fingertips, Martha admonished her younger sibling, "Temper your blasphemy sister!"

"You tempur yur own," Mary shot back, not really making sense with this quip. It was a drunk thing to say. She had hunched herself over and wore an obstinate grimace on her pretty face.

Martha rolled her eyes at Mary's immaturity. But, she didn't have the energy or patience for this bickering with her sister either. Especially her **drunk** sister. Instead of fighting more, Martha brushed Mary off, went to the roof hatch, and called down the ladder for anyone. Someone answered from below in prompt time. Martha requested a reed pen, a clay pot of lampblack ink, three short pieces of cord and three strips of papyrus.

Within a matter of moments, the writing items were handed up to Martha. She thanked whomever it was and brought the supplies over by the dovecote. She popped the cork on the little clay jar of ink, dipped the pen in the black liquid and proceeded to write three identical messages, all reading, *Go to tomb first. Help Lazarus.* It was cryptic, but to the point.

While she was scribbling out two more identical notes, she glanced up and caught Mary taking a pull off a leather flask that she had stashed on herself. Face tilted up towards the sky, eyes closed in sweet oblivion. Martha chose not to say anything meaningful and returned her focus to the messages, citing that anything meaningful said wouldn't resonate with her sister, especially with the state of mind she was in.

Without looking up from scrawling, Martha asked Mary, "Will you hand me a bird please?"

Mary broke from her spell, dropping the flask quickly back down her sleeve, like she was being crafty before being caught. Then, with movement much too rapid and sloppy, she yanked a random, cooing dove out of the nearest hole. She trudged over to Martha and handed her the upset, flapping bird.

Gently, Martha took the bird and tucked it under her arm, reassuring it. Bouncing it. Petting it with light, little strokes to calm it down, until it began to coo again.

As Martha gingerly affixed the note to the dove's leg, she looked up to her drunk sister and intoned, "Two more, please."

While Mary retrieved two more doves in the same manner that she had grabbed the first, Martha, facing North, released the pigeon carrying the first important message. After securing two more important messages to two more pigeons, Martha cast them off to the South and East.

Both sisters watched the last bird get smaller and smaller, until it disappeared into the darkening horizon.

Mary asked with a pronounced slur, "Dooyu thingk it wull reach im?"

As was her habit, Martha held her breath. Watching the last bird fly away, becoming a mere speck in the sky. She blew out of her mouth and answered with a solemn truth, "I hope so."

The younger sister's eyes were closed. She was weaving back and forth, like she was spinning in her mind. Martha knew what was going to happen next and it still took her by surprise. Sure enough, within the next few moments, without warning, Mary scurried over to the edge of the roof and proceeded to puke purple slime over the edge. Leaving an unsightly, bruised streak running down the side of their sand colored house.

Oh Mary, Martha thought to herself with a justified mixture of pity and contempt. Although, she still came over by her wretching, baby sister and held her hair back, so that she wouldn't get anymore purple puke in it.

xviii

Caiaphas hated this. Being questioned. Annas, Marcus, Darius, and himself had been sitting in front of Gamaliel, along with a few choice others of the Sanhedrin, in the dim, torch lit, stifling Chamber of Hewn Stones for the last lost bit of time. They had been recounting their discoveries in the Mount of Olives, during this very day's afternoon. The bearded, bejeweled Priests listened in polite astonishment to the story laid out before them until its conclusion, only peppering a few obvious questions in at certain points.

Sweat appeared in tiny, clear beads and ran in tiny rivulets upon everyone in the chamber. The increasing warmth of the season was held and on glistening display within these stone walls. Marcus, in particular, adorned in his heavy armor and underneath the scrutinizing gaze of the holy members upon the dais, was perspiring the most offensively amongst them. His face was a complete red sheen of saturated skin and his close cropped officer's hairstyle was plastered down to his skull. Sweat dripped in regular patters upon the scales of his *lorica segmentata.*

"And we are certain that the identity of the victim is unknown?" Gamaliel grumbled, immediately breaking into a wet, phlegmy session of coughing. Doubled over with his long, wispy beard almost touching the floor, his saturated gargling and hacking commanded the attention of the entire

Chamber. At last, the ancient Priest dislodged whatever was in his throat and gave it a hearty chew before swallowing it back down. Causing everyone else in the room to gag in reflex.

Caiaphas waited with polite forbearance for enough silence to answer. His gangly hands were clasped, calm and righteous, in his lap. A pious, half smile barely curved his narrow lips. Once Gamaliel's violent coughing had died down, Caiaphas answered, "Yes, Nasi. No one of recognition."

Darius spoke up then, accusing in a rapid stutter, "Th-that's n-n-not true."

"What is this now?" Gamaliel asked, rising up in his seat. Opening and closing his old maw, making a loud, moist smacking sound.

Caiaphas, at first, went wide eyed with surprise. He shot a menacing look down towards the side of Darius and Marcus, who were staring straight ahead towards the dias. Then, he relaxed and scoffed, "I have no idea what this *Praefecti* could possibly be referring to, Nasi. If we may continue-"

"Qu-quintus and-d-d G-gaius s-s-said you s-said the n-n-name 'C-C-Caleb' when-n you s-s-saw th-the h-head in the b-b-branches," Darius fired off. Marcus was swiveling his beet red face, like a fish's tail. Back and forth. Cycling between the High Priests, the small fraction of the Sanhedrin, and brave, stupid little Darius.

Caiaphas winced, just a fraction, at the mention of the name of his shadow cohort. He was trying to dodge anything possibly tying him to Caleb's horrific demise. He needed to steer the conversation in a much different direction. Despite being shook for the tiniest of moments, he managed to regain his composure in an instant.

"Who is this Quintus and-" Gamaliel asked, his ancient eyes looking at Darius for verification on the name and pronunciation, to which, Darius nodded an enthusiastic affirmative, "-and Gaius?"

"Deserters! That's what they are, Nasi!" Annas growled. His own eyes glared and burned into the port side of the Roman's faces.

Gamaliel raised an inquisitive bushy eyebrow. Some of the awake members of the dias leaned forward in interest, as well.

Caiaphas waved his hand in a dismissive brushing off of the previous accusation as tripe. "Another set of soldiers that had accompanied us," he confessed, while sounding bored. "They found the head."

"And they claim you said the name 'Caleb' upon seeing the head?" Nicodemus asked, marking the first contribution he'd had during this emergency session.

Without humor, Caiaphas chortled and mocked, “These *children* that were parading as soldiers were highly unqualified for the simplest task that was assigned to them.”

“That’s a lie!” Marcus declared, now turning his full attention to the High Priest of the Year.

“Watch yourself Roman,” Annas warned.

“Oh, it’s a lie is it?” Caiaphas now turned and challenged Marcus directly. “I believe those sniveling whelps you call soldiers would’ve said anything to get back home to the safety of their mother’s bosom!"

Marcus and Darius stood up now in defiance to this rebuttal. Passionate, aggressive youth bubbled in violent radiation beneath their neckline. Turning them even redder above the neckline. Their white eyes looked extra large and bulbous.

Both the High Priests and the soldiers then erupted into criss-crossing streams of garbled, incoherent arguments between all four of them. Diplomacy and foreign relations were all but damned for them now and Marcus couldn’t stop thinking about it being Caiaphas’ head stuck up in the branches.

CLACK! CLACK! CLACK!

Gamaliel stood holding the pair of large oxen femur bones. After the echo from them smacking together stopped bouncing off of the walls, the only sound was the harsh, constant scribbling of the attending scribe. Jotting down as much detail as he could on the parchment.

With a strong reluctance, Marcus and Darius had returned to their seats, sitting straight back. Sweating more than ever. On the inside, Marcus was cursing at himself for losing his temper.

Gamaliel had set aside the bones and returned to his own seat at the center of the dias. “There will be no personal insults or physical attacks tolerated within these sacred chambers, underneath the eyes of God,” Gamaliel huffed, then coughed a long symphonic, wet gargle that sounded like he should’ve spit it out. Instead, he worked the glob around in his mouth, rolling over his teeth. Chewing and studying the consistency, before swallowing it back down again.

Members on the dias were unabashed in their disgust, as well as those being questioned. Some were rolling their own tongues over their own teeth, imagining an awful, phlegmy slime coating their own mouths.

Realizing himself, Gamaliel grumbled, “Excuse me,” then held out a large hand, with fabulous, sparkling rings on three of the five fingers, “Proceed High Priest Caiaphas.”

“There’s not much more to tell, wise Nasi,” Caiaphas began in fake meekness. Oily once again. “We came upon the wicked scene we’d laid out for you previously and now we are reporting the treachery back to you, the **only** ones holding rightful jurisdiction in this land.”

He’d said this last part with emphasis, that was, in particular, pointed right at the Roman soldiers. Annas wheezed a subtle chuckle into his golden ringed fist at the obvious jab.

Not to be contained, Caiaphas stood up from his seat and continued, “If I might add, wise Nasi, that I am truly baffled and disappointed by governor Pilate’s decision to send grossly inexperienced soldiers to act as protective guard for two such notable High Priests into the wilderness.”

Annas seconded this by saying, “Yes, exceptionally poor judgement by the *governor.*”

Darius, full of hot, spunky, angry emotions, made to get up again, but Marcus gripped his hand, pinning him down to his arm rest and glaring at him with strenuous, protuberant eyes. This kept the young Praefecti glued to his seat and muzzled. No doubt, later on they would both receive a stern dissertation on being reserved in their behavior. After all, this wasn’t Rome.

“You may take audience with the governor over such matters,” Gamaliel limply waved away Caiaphas’ concern. “It is Passover week, after all. You must see him anyway to get the Breastplate and the Ephod in preparation for the holy week.”

A stab of disappointment poked at Caiaphas’ ego. Having to go and retrieve what was rightfully a relic of the Rabbinic Jewish culture, was extremely degrading. Why the governor was ever allowed to take possession of such an avowed piece of the Temple and their heritage was a true mystery to the High Priest, along with his father-in-law and many others.

Caiaphas grinned through his chagrin and nodded, while choking out, “Yes, Nasi.”

“Delightful,” Gamaliel grumbled. Then he continued by suggesting, “The Mount of Olives, in broad daylight, is normally not so treacherous as to need the escort of an armored guard.”

"Yes," agreed Nicodemus, perking up and leaning in. Tips of his elbows coming off of the armrests. Grinning behind his pure white beard. "What were you expecting to find out there that required the strength of four armored Roman soldiers carrying swords and spears?"

Caiaphas smiled a rictus grin, showing alot of yellowed teeth and held his hands out, palms up. Through an act, he was trying to convey a perfectly innocent figure of humble vulnerability. "My brothers," he started with slick oil coming out of his pipes, "We are all aware of the recent, vicious attacks in Bethany. They are not entirely surprising, to be sure. Quite common, in fact, for a persistent evil to exist within a city this size." He had waltzed over by the soldiers and leaned down to say, "By that measure, it must be a veritable hellhole in Rome."

The High Priest of the Year then winked a paper thin, crinkly eyelid at Marcus, drawing the officer's burning loathing in such a way as to be repulsive and infuriating. Marcus bit his lip, hard enough to taste irony blood, to remove his mind from his present anger.

Caiaphas spun, flourishing his pricey robes and addressed the dias with solemnity once again, "We just thought it much wiser to proceed with caution. Better to have it and not need it than need it and not have it, Nasi." He bowed, deep and dramatic, with arms splayed wide. His long, hooked beak of a nose nearly touched the stone floor in this flattering gesture of utmost fealty.

Nasi smiled. Taking the bait, with some of the wrinkles flattening out, softening on his forehead and in between his overgrown grey eyebrows. He coughed for a brief spell. Smiled once again, a very old smile, and asked, "So, you presume that the scene you discovered earlier this day, and the recent attacks in Bethany are...what? Connected?"

Caiaphas pondered for a moment. Long, spindly fingers placed strategically at his lips. "That is very possible, now that you mention it," he remarked, as if he hadn't thought of that possibility before. "Your wisdom is truly a gift from God.." Feeding the old goat's pompous, ravenous flattery even more.

Gamaliel smacked his lips together, trying to generate more hydration in his sticky mouth. He then stated, "You did the right thing."

This produced a syncopated set of groans from the two Romans and Nicodemus on the dais.

The old Nasi ignored their verbal disdain, by asking Caiaphas, "You will be sure to share anything further you find out about these...uh...attacks?"

Warm and as slick as freshly pressed olive oil, Caiaphas purred, "It would be my pleasure, Nasi."

The warm, grandfatherly smile that was upon Gamaliel's face, now relaxed into a mask of indifference, as he shifted in his carved seat to face Marcus and Darius. He continued now by pointing a segmented, gnarly finger at the Romans. His voice sounding huge and grave, resonating trapped within these walls, "Report what has transpired this day to Pilate, and Pilate alone. Facts only. I'll have none of these malicious rumors designed to incite animosity between our nations."

Nasi allowed the gravity of these statements to bounce off the Hewn Stones and repeat themselves in redundancy to the Roman soldier's ears, while the scribe dipped his long feathered quill into a small clay jar of ink. Scratching down the symbols onto the papyrus in a flurry of quickness.

"Do you both understand?" Gamaliel asked them, leaning forward. His long grey beard draped over his knees, like the dangling branches of a weeping willow.

Marcus and Darius nodded a resentful affirmative in unison. Marcus' face was completely soaked with a cascading sheen of sweat. He looked weary and sallow. Darius, on the other hand, looked terrified.

"Good," Gamaliel announced, pleased. "If there is nothing else, we shall adjourn this meeting."

"Excellent," Caiaphas said. Interlocking his long, thin fingers, he then laid it on extra thick, "We are truly blessed to have the wisdom of the Sanhedrin guiding us in these times when we are lost."

"Amen," Annas concurred, completing the charade.

Gamaliel then chose one of the random senior members of the Sanhedrin to lead them out of the meeting in "the privilege of prayer". A man that seemed at least a dozen years older than Gamaliel himself barely stood up, and with some difficulty, proceeded to drone a prayer wistfully with his head bowed.

To Marcus, this was dragging on much longer than was necessary. He already had known how this was going to play out while he was riding, mostly silent, next to Darius, all the way back to the Temple. He knew he would be walking into an unfavorable, biased room, full of judgmental Jews, the moment he had entered the Chamber. Marcus just wanted to be told that he was wrong, so he could get his stupid slap on the wrist and get out of this ungodly, sweltering room.

Lost in his thoughts Marcus didn't hear the "Amen" that came at the end of their speaking to God. He just realized everyone was beginning to mill about, talking low, or gathering scrolls. He looked to his left in time to see the backsides of Caiaphas and Annas making for the door. By the flickering torches he caught sight of Darius on his right, at his shoulder, still looking terrified.

"Let's go," Marcus commanded and Darius smiled.

Their armor announced their departure, but before they were out of the Chamber. Gamaliel called to them, "Romans!"

Marcus and Darius stopped abruptly in their tracks. Feeling a disappointing weight pushing down on them from being so close to the exit, but having to turn around now and indulge this old Jewish Holy Man.

Once Gamaliel was within normal conversing distance, he reiterated his earlier point, "Remember what I said," he then began to count each talking point on his fingers, "For Pilate's ears only. Facts only. No gossip. No rumors." Holding up four fanning, glittering, jewel encrusted fingers, he questioned, "Understand?"

They both nodded a silent affirmation. Darius was wholly speechless. Paralyzed by being submerged into this strange, backwards land. Marcus couldn't talk for fear of screaming what he really thought of all of these dense Hebrews instead.

"Good," Gamaliel said, satisfied by the outcome of the meeting.He waved them off as one would a troublesome gadfly. He smacked his floppy lips together in his sickening way, then broke into a violent fit of gushy coughing that followed Marcus and Darius, in their clunking haste, all the way out of the Chamber of Hewn Stones.

xix

It was early afternoon when Phillip trotted into the main, bustling drag of Capernaum. Solid, colorful cloth was draped over a whole cornucopia of makeshift stands. These varying kiosks flanking both sides of the dusty, dry Boulevard, were selling everything from salted fish to indigo dye to specialty knives. Voices caught up in the heated battle of haggling, or calling out their wares loudly, or offering the temporary service of a lady, could be heard overlapping one another in a one of a kind symphonic cacophony.

The day had been warm since late in the morning. Tsalav and Phillip were fried. His water was all but depleted and his stomach had been grumbling since he'd awoken early this morning. Phillip's steps were labored after he dismounted and trudged up to the first vendor he noticed in the marketplace. The proprietor was a towering, greasy man with multiple golden hooped rings woven into his beard, who looked as though he regularly bathed in a pool of olive oil. He was presently engaged in some serious haggling with a random, unsavory patron over some measly scraps of lamb.

The vendor's eyes flicked over to Phillip, while salty words flew out of his gross, spittle flinging mouth. "If you don't have good coin to spend, I suggest you get the Hell away from my cart, you filthy beggar!"

Phillip regarded the pitiful beggar, with a sense of sorrow welling up within him. He wished for a little bit of power, like Jesus' power. The skill the Lord possessed to be able to lift the lowest dwellers from their deepest pits, was something Phillip could only badly imitate by trying to emulate. Plus, he was in no frame of mind to engage with the caliber of lunatic that was willing to fight over gristled lamb scraps.

A tattered, dirty plain robe concealed most of the mendicant's waifish appearance. Filthy, near black, feet jutted out of the bottom of the robe, with toenails that were overgrown, jagged, and yellowed. An old woman's head protruded out of the top of the filthy robe, with an even filthier tangled mass of grey hair sprouting atop a truly ugly face. One milky eye and one dark brown eye seemed to look straight through him, as her toothless gob worked frenetically at producing something cogent to say back to the large, imposing vendor.

Instead, in an appalling display of indecency, the demented vagabond ripped open the crusty robe she wore, revealing her sun burnt, wrinkled, naked body. Her impoverished breasts dangled hideously on each side of her belly button. She possessed a dazzling white puff of pubic hair that rested in quiet anger below that, between a sinewy pair of thighs. A toothless mouth above all of this was cackling like a maniac.

Tsalav pulled away instinctively, tossing his head and shrieking in adamant condemnation of the disgusting sight. Both men at the stand averted their eyes by throwing up their hands, palms out, and turning away repulsed. The large, imposing vendor yelled out in a reflex for survival, "Please God, No!"

While they were turned away from her, the old vagabond grabbed whatever she could from the vendor's cart and proceeded to run away, clutching the viscous lamb parts to her floppy chest. Still cackling. Robe drawn back, barely clinging to her depleted shoulders in her frantic haste. She weaved this way and that through the other disgusted afternoon shoppers along the thoroughfare, while holding onto the slippery, bloody bits of mutton.

With a furious grunt, the vendor slammed his massive, hairy hand down onto the tabletop of his meager establishment, extracting another small whinny from Tsalav behind Phillip. He stared with blazing eyes at the vacant area where the parts of lamb and his profit used to be. His breath was measured, being drawn in and out in wrathful lungfuls through his flaring nostrils. The oppressive afternoon heat seemed to be absorbed and radiated through his murderous rage.

Phillip dared to clear his throat in a small, subtle cue to the vendor that he was still there. The proprietor's angry eyes snapped up to Phillip's and he muttered through gritted teeth, "What the Hell do you want?"

Ignoring the brunt aside to any motivated pleasantries between them both, Phillip followed the precedent set by answering, "I seek the house of Jairus."

The large man exhaled long and loud through his nose. He slowly crossed his oily, burly arms over his great, heaving chest and commanded Phillip to, "Buy something."

"What was that?" Phillip balked, not sure he heard him correctly over the constant chatter and din of the surrounding market.

Hinging on his hips, the giant man leaned in closer. His expression never faltered. His arms remained locked across himself. "Buy something, stranger. Then you'll get your directions."

At first, Phillip scoffed at the notion. However, after a few uncomfortable moments, Phillip could see this man wasn't kidding or one to be trifled with, (unless, of course, you were a crazy old woman absent of any hindering scruples). Phillip had some money on him, but he had to take into consideration his return trip to Bethany, as well. He was forced to peruse over an unidentifiable assortment of fly riddled meats, fruits and nuts. He ended up purchasing a Mina (1.25lbs) of dates and a couple of red apples for Tsalav.

Upon completion of the sale, the large, hairy man laid out a brief travel route for Phillip and, in so many words, told him to hit the road. Subdued, after stowing the fruit, Phillip still thanked the man meekly and clicked out of the side of his mouth for Tsalav to follow.

Phillip spent the next span of time weaving through the strange, dusty streets and boulevards. Capernaum was a much larger settlement than Bethany. A couple of times he feared that he had missed a pivotal turn or gotten turned around somehow. Dust clouded streets, beige stone buildings, unfamiliar landmarks and pained, dirty faces all began to look eerily similar to one another. He began to become increasingly aware of how lost he must appear to be.

"You look lost," a fragile, wheezing voice stated matter-of-factly.

Phillip's eyes darted down by his feet and saw there another dirty beggar. This one looked so tiny, hidden and dark within colorless fold upon fold of fabric, that at first Phillip thought it was an unfortunate child.

"Yes,uh," Phillip answered, kind of chuckling in an embarrassed way at his getting disoriented. "I am looking for the house of Jairus."

A skinny, filthy arm shot out from the folds with a palm held open. Phillip rolled his eyes in pure frustration. He turned and rummaged in his pack. After a moment, he turned again and dropped two leptons (the smallest and least valuable copper coin in circulation in 1st century Judea) into the beggar's palm.

plink, plink.

The beggar regarded the meager currency, frowning, and continued to hold out his extended hand. Not begging anymore. Demanding.

Phillip angrily turned again and quickly produced a shekel this time, dropping it heavily on top of the small, copper coins.

Plonk!

The hand returned with the coins to the darkness within the robe. "Follow this street north. Make your second right. Fourth house on the left."

Philip was already walking. He tossed a courteous token, "Thanks," over his shoulder. So far, he didn't like Capernaum.

He reached into his pack and pulled out a small handful of dates, popping a couple into his mouth, chewing with voracious aplomb. Tsalav shook his head in protest, causing Phillip to chuckle while he dug one of the apples out of his pack for the horse. They both walked and ate. Strangers in a strange city.

Within a matter of minutes, according to the beggar's directions, they had finally arrived at a massive peacock of a house. Overly large. Ornate and gaudy.

Phillip banged on the thick wooden door with the side of his fist and waited patiently. After a few moments, when no one answered, Phillip banged on the door again. Longer and louder this time.

Following a short, thirsty length of time, a small hatch swung open on the door, revealing an old, but statuesque woman's face.

"Yes?" She inquired in a melodious voice. "May I help you?"

"Good afternoon," Phillip started. "Um, I am seeking an audience with Jairus."

She squinted suspiciously. "What is this in regards to?" She asked.

"I have a few, um, uh, questions about his, uh, daughter," Phillip said as innocently as he could manage on the most sensitive of subjects.

The woman cursed an incoherent curse and slammed the little hatch as hard as she could.

Phillip was not particularly stunned by the reaction. However, right away, he began to rap on the door again with the side of his fist, shouting against the seam of the hatch, "Please! Madam! I need your help!"

Tsalav was becoming skittish. Spooked from Phillip's current antics at Jairus' door.

Phillip persisted. Banging harder. Shouting louder, "Jesus resurrected my friend! Please! He's not who he once was!!"

He kept banging on the hatch. Harder, if only for a brief time. The little hatch swung open again. This time it was a man's face framed by the rest of the poplar door. A middle aged bronze face, sagging and dour, but with a fierce sizzle burning in the eyes. "What di' you zay about Jezuz?" the man choked out.

"Jairus?" Phillip asked.

"Yes, I am Jairus," Jairus said.

Phillip put his road worn face up near his and spoke low, now, "Sir, I must speak with you about your daughter. About her 'resurrection'."

"Why?" Jairus croaked painfully. The definite scent of grape fermentation wafted out at Phillip and reminded him of Mary, back home in Bethany.

"Jesus has resurrected again," Phillip confessed. "Lazarus, my friend. He's...It's…We are in dire need of answers."

Jairus cast his gaze downward. A tear fell silently from his cheek above his beard line. Phillip couldn't see what he was looking down at, but it was a long time before Jairus asked in a thick voice, "How long ago wuz thiz?"

"Three, going on four days," Phillip answered without hesitation.

"How many are dead?" Jairus asked hoarsely, now squeezing his eyes shut, letting more tears fall.

Phillip's blood ran cold at the question. He spoke without much thought in a monotone, trying not to feel anything, "Two goats and a child," he confided. "That was before I left, though," he added. "There could be more now."

Without another word, the hatch closed gently and a locking mechanism could be heard releasing with an audible *Clank!-Clunk!* The large door then creaked open, allowing Phillip and Tsalav to enter into the home of Jairus.

XX

Jairus was not exactly gracious in his welcoming of the traveler and his horse. He had Tsalav brought to the stables to be attended to in necessity only. No excessive pampering allowed. Then, Jairus had Samantha, the older woman who had first answered Phillip's incessant knocking, settle Phillip into a cramped set of servant's quarters. There was a fresh basin of cool, clean lavender-infused water on a sturdy table for washing and a polished bronze mirror hung over the top of it. There was also a narrow single hay bed and a small, modest side table with an oil lamp sitting on top of it occupying the room. Above the bed, and out of the lone window, was a view of late afternoon dappled rolling hills leading down to an enchanting, sparkling Sea of Kineret.

Once Samantha was satisfied that Phillip was self contained for the night and took her leave of the guest room, Phillip stripped down out of his days old, ripe rags, to just his undergarments. He then took to the basin of fragrant water with bottled up avidity. Using his vigorous fervor to scrub with the provided sea sponge at his road-worn hands first. Then, extending the washing to his forearms and up above his elbows. Dipping the sponge again and working it all over the top of his head, his face, neck, shoulders, and chest. Now hitting the pungent armpits. He then scrubbed with the gradually darkening water at each leg from high up on the thigh down to the toes of each foot. Last, but not least, he stepped out of his undergarments, took the remainder of the murky water and dabbed adventurously at his nether regions. He looked out of the window again fondly, wishing he could just go and submerge his entire body in the cool waters of the Sea.

A fresh, standard robe had been supplied for him, while his current clothing would be taken to be washed and hung out to dry for his departure the following day. He dried off, wrapped clean undergarments around himself and slipped on the coarse robe. Before leaving to meet his host for dinner, along with some much needed answers (hopefully), he checked his reflection in the polished bronze mirror and tried to comb his damp, wayward hair, like a clumsy barbarian with his dumb, stout fingers.

When he was content that he was somewhat presentable, he retrieved the oil lamp and lit it with his flint. Making sure it was burning nice and bright before stepping out into a set of dim, alien corridors that he had passed through in a blur when he was guided to the room earlier.

Upon closing the door behind him, he was faced with the choice of left or right. He was already turned around and couldn't remember which way he had been led in from. With a steady trickle of trepidation, he reluctantly turned to his right. After a number of steps, just when he was about to turn around and go back the other way, he was met by the wonderful aromas of meat cooked in fragrant spices. His stomach jumped and quickened his legs through the rest of the hallway until it opened up to a large, pleasantly lit great room.

Thick wooden Aleppo pine beams dominated the room and drew one's gaze upwards instantly. Phillip spent some time studying the weave of the woodwork that appeared both bulky and intricate at once. Beneath the beams sat a colossal rectangular table, polished to a glimmering, mirror finish. The surface of the table reflected dozens of soft, fuzzy orbs of light back at the surrounding array of burning oil lamps and sconces surrounding the room. In the center of the table stood a magnificent marbled statue of two colossal Barbus Longiceps (carp) majestically breaching from a splash of water. Mouths open, eyes bulging. Entwined around one another, like a strand of DNA.

Phillip's own mouth was agape, mimicking the fish statue, as he shuffled further into the magnificent great room. Staring all around, he didn't notice a moderately inebriated Jairus lounging with a staunch, sober Samantha standing at attention beside him. Both host and hostess had been watching him stumble into the room from behind the statue centerpiece.

While looking up and walking, not paying attention to where he was going, Phillip bumped into a medium sized vase, nearly knocking it over. It would've shattered upon the floor for sure had he not reached out and caught the lip of the vase. He stood it back upright, steadying it. Bringing it to where it was resting before.

That's when his eyes shifted and landed on Jairus and Samantha. Before them, occupying a mere fraction of the huge, circular table, was a decent spread of platters containing steaming dishes of lamb and fish. There were also smaller plates of assorted fruit, nuts, rice, hummus and unleavened bread. Pitchers of water, tea and wine sat by a couple of goblets. A place had been set for Phillip. He grinned sheepishly at his clumsiness being on display and spectated. Neither Jairus nor Samantha smiled back at him.

Jairus instead said, "I zee yoove cleened up. I truzt your room izz zatizfactoury?"

"Yes, thank you Lord Jairus," Phillip responded, sounding grateful.

"Your clothes are being washed and dried," Samantha offered. "They'll be ready for your departure by morning."

"Thank you, ma'am," Phillip replied.

Jairus was keenly studying Phillip as he was standing before them. While looking his strange houseguest up and down, Jairus was rolling the rim of the base of his wine goblet in tiny circles on the tabletop. Jairus asked, "Whure are you frumm?" He gestured deliberately for Phillip to sit.

"A small village southeast of here, called Bethany," Phillip answered back honestly, taking his place at the table.

"Hhhoow fah away izz thut?" Jairus pressed, being candid about not knowing.

"Close to seven hundred furlongs," Phillip answered, keeping his hands locked in his lap, despite feeling close to ravenous.

Jairus sipped a long methodical, contemplating sip from his ornate, jeweled goblet.

Samantha inquired further from her perch at Jairus' shoulder, "By Jerusalem?"

"Yes," Phillip said. He was now feeling the definite stabbing, needle-like barbs of scrutiny being leveled against him. His skin prickled from the metaphorical assault.

"Whut are you hupping to lyearn by coming ere?" Jairus asked. He finally tore from a loaf of bread and began to fill his plate from the platters spread out before them.

Phillip, happily, followed his host's lead. Filling his own plate and relishing all of the flavors together with gusto. In between bites he said, "I am hoping to learn anything you can tell me?"

Jairus picked idly at his plate. Uninterested in the delicious food. He drank instead. Another long, deep draught, before lowering his gaudy cup, burping bombastically and saying, "Thure izz no ope."

Phillip stopped chewing for the moment. A chunk of hummus slathered meat jutting out offensively from his lips. “Excuse me?” Phillip mumbled around a mouth full of food.

“Mah angul,” Jairus said and then began to sob while hunched over his full plate of food. “Abigail, mah angul.”

Phillip chewed while wiping his hands on his loaner robe and placed a comforting hand on Jairus shoulder. “It’s going to be alright,” Phillip offered weakly.

“Mah zweet angul, mah angul,” Jairus kept repeating over and over again. Stringing the words together without punctuation. Like he was reciting a slurring, meditative mantra.

Samantha rubbed his back in soothing circles.

“Mah angul. Mah angul. Ah can’t rememburr her az mah angul,” Jairus now garbled. “Ah can unly recull her az an unholee demon!” His words, although mushy, became angry and strained. He looked up into Phillip’s face with red rimmed, tortured eyes. Slamming down his goblet and sloshing the contests, Jairus stood. He gripped Phillip by the scruff of the loaned robe and screamed a repugnant, fermented grape essence into his face, “He turned mah angul into a demon!”

“Who did? Jesus?” Phillip asked from a place of innocence.

Jairus released his grip on him by tossing him back to his seat. With a guttural scream he took his arm and swept his full, uneaten plate of food off the magnificent table, making a terrible clatter and mess.

Samantha restrained her master from any further outbursts by wrapping her arms around him, while whispering and cooing in his ear. She took her finger and thumb, rubbing his ear lobe between them. Shushing her master with calm words and touch. Refilling his cup, near to the brim.

Jairus had buried his extra dour face into his hands. His shoulders shaking up and down, racked by his jerky sobs. He could barely be understood when he pleaded a watery, “Why?”

Samantha tried to shush him, as she rubbed his back trying to pacify the broken man.

Jairus snapped his head up from his hands and asked Phillip through piercing, bleary eyes, “Why did he make mah angul a demon? Fur followerz? Fur power?"

Phillip’s heart pounded as though he were terrified. His mouth hung open again, while he shook his head from side to side, utterly baffled at the line of questioning. Jairus was not coping with his daughter's death well in the slightest. Phillip became aware of a massive lump of pity developing in his throat for the poor, grieving father.

That's when Jairus took the side of his fist and slammed it on the large table, causing the cups and plates to rattle loudly. "You're ere on hizz behalf, aren't you?" Jairus now accused. He pointed a wavering finger directly at Phillip, "You're ere tu take mah Abigail, aren't you?"

Phillip was flabbergasted. He tried to protest against these accusations, while shaking his head vehemently, *NO!* He denied Jairus' claim, "No, my Lord Jairus."

Unexpectedly, Jairus began to chuckle, "You're too late, though. Mah Abby iz an angul again." He was smiling broadly through painful tears. "Zhe wull never be a devil for yur Mezziah." He began to cackle, sounding insane, holding his arms out wide to his sides and pointing his erupting, misplaced mirth up towards the impressive ceiling. "Never!!"

Phillip, stunned, tried to explain to Jairus, "Forgive me Lord Jairus, but I am not here for-"

"Bah!" Jairus cut him off abruptly, waving off his explanations as one would an annoying fly. "How cun enywun believe in an ahgent of tha devil?" His words were becoming even more sluggish and thick. Sticky and slurred. As though they were becoming stuck together on his tongue.

Samantha caught Phillip's eyes with her own fierce expression. She was trying to telepathically demand Phillip's silence.

Jairus had now seized a decanter of dark, purple wine and brought it to his lips, like a nihilistic alcoholic would do. Bypassing the goblet altogether. The poor man just wanted to drown in all of the alcohol until he was numb. Or dead.

Samantha clapped her hands together with a quick double *smacksmack!* and called out for the assistance of a couple of servants, "Leah! Miriam!" She quietly approached Jairus from behind, placing both hands on each shoulder. Then she leaned down and whispered something influential in his ear causing him to begrudgingly rise from the table. Two younger, demure ladies entered the great room, their heads bowed and their hands clasped modestly at their waists. Jairus squinted and frowned suspicious slits at Phillip before allowing himself to be guided away by the two younger female servants, while still holding firmly onto the decanter.

Once he had left the room, Samantha spun to face Phillip. "You must forgive Lord Jairus," she said. "He's never been the same since-" She trailed off.

Phillip stood now and looked down into her pretty, older face, "Look, whatever has happened here, is happening now. Where I live." He thought of Martha. "To someone that I love."

"That someone isn't who you remember them as," Samantha stated without emotion.

He knew she was referring to Lazarus. A friend to him that had once felt closer than a cousin. He knew she was most likely right in her counsel, but his heart was not willing to accept and adhere to it yet.

"I'm not giving up," Phillip retorted in stubbornness.

Sounding exhausted, Samantha sighed. This entire household seemed to be holding on tenuously to any shred of normalcy that was left. She seemed like she was the only one keeping the house operating on a business as usual basis. Since the patriarch of the household had descended into being a total delirious drunk.

In a swift motion, Samantha snatched up a lit oil lamp and directed Phillip to, "Follow me." She began to take long strides out of the room. "There's something you must see."

Phillip grabbed his own provided oil lamp and followed her out of the house. Into the night.

xxi

A clear, star filled sky awaited them. A bright, almost full moon provided enough clear sight, to where they didn't really need their lamps to see where they were going. Lukewarm air gave delicate kisses all over their exposed skin. A subtle hint of sea scent mixed with jasmine blossoms sweetened every breath.

Phillip caught some movement to their right and held his lamp aloft. In doing so, he brought illumination upon a random dark skinned servant girl in the act of draping his clean, dripping wet striped robe over a thick, sturdy clothesline. He smiled and waved a friendly salute to her. She didn't react as though she saw him at all.

Maybe she didn't see me, Phillip thought. But, a solid feeling in his gut told him he didn't believe that.

Returning his attention back to the path, he saw Samantha a good distance ahead of him, waiting by the stables. She turned towards him, patiently holding her lamp low.

When Phillip got within a close enough range of her, she turned away and kept walking. Leading him around the quiet, dimly illuminated stables. From there, she led the way up a gentle, sloping hillside.

He double timed his steps to come up side by side with her. When he was keeping even with her pace, she said, "Your clothes should be dry by dawn. I trust you'll make your presence in the morning brief."

"Yes, ma'am," he said.

Samantha continued, "Please forgive my bluntness, but your being here is pouring salt in fresh wounds."

"I understand," Philip said. "That was not my intention by coming here."

"You won't get the answers you're seeking," Samantha uttered. "There is no hope for your loved one."

"Why-" Phillip started, but tripped over a protruding rock. Upon regaining his footing, he continued as if nothing happened, "Why do you say that? Through God all things are possible."

She let a quick, cynical explosion of laughter burst out of her. "You truly don't know anything." She quickened her pace now, pulling ahead of him. "I could never conceive a child. Abby was like my own." She paused for a moment, then carried on, raising her voice in conviction to talk back louder over her shoulder, "We thought it was a miracle at first. Our dear Abigail, being returned to us after being taken so suddenly. So early. We were overjoyed."

The mild slope they had been on had changed up into a moderate incline now. Somewhere a seabird screeched in the night. There was a pleasant sea breeze that lifted up and circulated all around them. Causing the small flames on their lamps to whip and dance in a frenzy.

"It wasn't long after Jesus and his followers left until she began to show signs that she wasn't our little Abby anymore," Samantha continued. She looked back over her shoulder at him for a split second, before turning back around and continuing upward. "Her skin would burn in direct sunlight. She sounded like a wild animal. We tried to send for Jesus, but he never returned a word." Samantha now breathed in heavy gusts in and out through her nostrils, bracing herself for the next part. "She left the house that very night. Animal corpses became a regular discovery every morning. Then, one by one children began to disappear."

"Where did she go?" Phillip asked.

"An isolated cave nearby," Samantha answered, her voice becoming broken and watery. "She would sleep during the day and come out to hunt at night. It was weeks before we found her. A group of men, including Jairus, followed her when she abducted one of the neighborhood children."

Her voice became constricted and thickened as her lachrymose emotions took her over. "Jairus said there were bones all over that cave! He said when they found her, she was naked and decaying! Covered with blood spread all down the front of herself."

They topped the peak of the hill they had been climbing. She wiped at the tears and snot that flowed uninhibited from her much aggrieved face. "It's hard to think of our sweet angel in such a way," she confessed in a warbly, breaking voice.

"What was done with her?" Phillip asked, realizing he was scared of what the answer might be.

She gazed down at the ground before them and lowered her meager light from the oil lamp. This revealed a crude black "X" scorched into the peak of the hillside. "The men," she began, before her voice broke and having to compose herself again. "The men staked her to the ground at her wrists and ankles. She writhed against her restraints and screamed horrible curses in a voice that wasn't her own. Tried to bite at her own father." She paused again, sniffling loudly and wiping at the mess of her face. "Morning came. The sun came with it and turned our poor, beautiful angel into nothing but ashes!"

Then she fell to her knees at the edge of the burnt earth outline. She kissed and touched at the mark, where the head would've been, with a heartbreaking, fresh pathos. Samantha wept in an explicit, unreserved, reckless way, that brought free flowing tears to Phillip's eyes as well.

"Oh, Abby! I love you my angel!" Samantha wailed from the face of the hillside while Phillip held her and attempted to console her. She let him, for a little while, until her hitching and sniffing were somewhat back under control. When she pushed away from Phillip, she swiped once at each of her puffed up eyes. Then she said with her voice sure and steady once again, "Like, I told you, 'there is no hope'."

xxii

Phillip laid in the bed. Wide awake. After sleeping on the road for days, the low quality hay mattress was as soft as what he imagined a cloud would be. The pillow cushioned his head as one would hold a delicate egg. Cool seaside air flowed all around him. His belly was nice and full.

But, his mind raced at a breakneck pace. His thoughts kept returning to Mary and Martha. Back in Bethany. Asleep in their beds at this very moment. Also, at this very moment, Lazarus, their brother that wasn't their brother anymore could be prowling around the city in their vicinity.

He knows about the opening behind the chest, Phillip kept ruminating over and over.

Phillip entertained thoughts of Lazarus burning to ash in a bath of sunlight. Leaving a glistening, black, body-shaped, smoldering stain upon the Earth. He had seen what had happened when a split second of exposure to a sliver of midday sunlight flashed across Lazarus' face. It burned a slash into Lazarus' face in an instant is what it did. What could change the physiology of dead matter to make it react like that to the rays of the sun?

These thoughts then spun into a swirling dervish of strategic scheming. Would he apply the same formula as Jairus had with his daughter, Abigail? If so, how many men would it require? He had seen, after all, Lazarus move the immense tombstone effortlessly the night they had confronted him. Who would help him after knowing what he knows? For that matter, who could he trust to know what he knew now?

He began to believe what Samantha had said earlier. *There is no hope.* Whatever Lazarus was to whomever before-a brother or a friend- now, he was transformed into a night walking, murderous monster. Just a horrible mistake, born from a miraculous gesture of power. The Resurrection. But, was it really Christ's gift to give? Was it really just an empty vessel created only to be occupied by an insatiable evil? An unexplainable phenomenon, replete with inhuman physical traits. Like a demon given a door, unknowingly, into the body of a human cadaver. Or like a puppeteer leading around a corpse as he would a marionette.

Giving up on sleep, despite it being well before dawn, he whipped the thin linen sheets off of himself. Being the courteous guest that he was, he folded his bedsheets, neatly placing everything at the head of the bed. He lit the oil lamp and tiptoed out of the door, into the hallway.

After shutting the door as quietly as he could, he turned right and followed the familiar path out through the great room with the massive table and the grandiose fish statue centerpiece. The room still held the rich smell of garlic, meat and vegetables in the air.

He slipped out of the large house into a late night that was much cooler than earlier, when he had stepped out with Samantha. A short trot from the door brought him to the clothesline, where his robe still hung, heavy and damp. Left with no other choice, he set down the oil lamp, ripped his loaner robe from over his head and slung it over the line as neatly as he could. Goosebumps prickled out on his newly exposed flesh. With dread, but operating on sheer will, he grabbed his frosty robe, wrung out as much of the freezing, cold water as he could and cloaked himself in it. Mentally, he had tried to brace himself for the extreme, biting discomfort, but he was still caught off guard by the shock of the frigid, wet fabric against his naked skin.

Without dwelling on his newfound distress for long, he scuttled over to the stables. There was a stable master's quarters located to his left. The door was left ajar a fat handbreadth. Silence and nothing more resonated from beyond the threshold. Phillip felt like the placement of his every step and the slight shifting of his damp robe was greatly amplified as he crept down a center aisle. On both sides there were pale, yellow bails of hay stacked beside stable doors.

Phillip clicked out of the side of his mouth as loud as he dared in this deathly quiet structure. His clicking caused a few of the presiding horses and mules to shift in disturbed consternation in the midst of their slumbered stances. After checking every other stable, he came to the end of the aisle.

Tsalav greeted Phillip with a familiar shake of his head and a loud, boisterous exhalation through his floppy horse lips. Phillip shushed at him as he unlocked the small paddock, leading Tsalav out. He kept patting his neck, showing accustomed reassurance.

Successful in the extraction, he guided Tsalav out of the stables, into the night. He walked the horse down a straight path around the monstrosity of a house, making a beeline for the front gate.

"Thank you," Samantha said, startling Phillip into near cardiac arrest.

He jumped about a cubit high. "Good God!" he exclaimed. His shaking hand raised to hover over his pounding heart.

Samantha smiled, tickled by his reaction. She was leaning against an exterior stone wall of the house. Arms crossed beneath her ample breasts. Phillip could positively make out the barest, amused curl of her lip in the generous, luminous moonlight. "Sorry," she offered, even though she wasn't really. "I appreciate you making yourself scarce so early in the morning."

"No problem," he whispered hoarsely. "I appreciate all of your hospitality." He took a couple steps in her direction. "I apologize for leaving like this, but I cannot rest. I must get back."

She raised an eyebrow, then assured him, "I understand. Believe me."

There wasn't much left to say. So Phillip said, "Well, thanks again. Bye."

He turned to leave, leading Tsalav to the exterior gate. *CLIPCLOPCLIPCLOP.*

Samantha called out to him, "Phillip."

He spun at the utterance of his name in the early morning air. "Yes, ma'am," he responded. Guarded. Teeth chattering.

She closed the distance between them, while clutching her shawl around herself tighter. In a conspiratorial tone, she urgently whispered, "You must kill it."

Phillip drew back, but said nothing. He wasn't positive that he'd heard what she'd said correctly.

Samantha was now within his personal space, looking up into his horrified face. Her beseeching eyes and face were still considerably puffy from earlier. In response to her encroachment, Tsalav tried to pull away against Phillip's hold on him. At this close of a distance, Phillip could smell a slight notion of fermentation on her breath.

"Whatever it was to you before, it's not that anymore. Do you understand?" Samantha didn't wait for him to answer her back. Instead, she continued, "You must kill it. No hesitation. Or be prepared to face the fatal consequences."

He could see the acute torment upon her face, even in the waning glow of the setting moonlight. "Samantha," he started softly, "that can't be the only answer."

She clutched his wet robe lapels, making them squelch a few drops of soapy water from the fibers. "It **is** the only answer. To doubt that fact is to invite the scourge right to your front door."

Phillip tried to assuage her, by saying her name again, "Samantha-"

"No Phillip," she cut him off. "You don't get it. It will kill everything. Everyone." She was becoming more unhinged with each spoken word. "Promise me you'll do what needs to be done."

He tried in his calming deep timber again, "Samantha, I-"

"Promise me," she urged as she pulled him down by his damp robe around his neck. This caused Tsalav to become more skittish and dance in place.

With manly tenderness, Phillip reached up and took her hands in his, engulfing both of her tiny, delicate mitts in his enormous, calloused grip. He looked into her wide, saturated, puffy eyes and said, "Alright. It will be done as you say. I promise."

She relaxed a smidge, but little did she know he was only trying to appease her violent solution. Truly, his only motivation now, was to get out of the gate, and, by extension, Capernaum. Days of dusty, agonizing travel lay before him and he hadn't slept a wink. In all honesty, though, he still held strong to the belief that Jesus, through the power of his Father, Almighty God, would have a divine solution to fix the problem with Lazarus back home in Bethany.

She released her grip, and stepped away from him, but still regarded him with suspicion. Like one would regard a wounded dog, baring its dull fangs.

"I promise," he repeated, with more conviction. Near pleading.

She wrapped her shawl tighter around herself. Her lips pressed together, making her older, yet beautiful face tighten into a stern, emotionless mask. "Go. And may God go with you."

"Thank you, ma'am," Phillip rumbled.

He held open his arms for a touch of welcomed warmth before leaving, and, instead of going to him, she turned. Without a glance backwards, she walked back into the pitch black shadow of the massive, morose house. Leaving him alone with Tsalav. Cold, scared and confused.

"Samantha?" Phillip called out, once. He waited with an ear cocked in the direction she'd wandered off to. After a few moments, when no answer returned, he steered Tsalav around and quietly left the house of Jairus.

As he navigated his way in the direction of southwest, and out of Capernaum for good, the sky portside began to lighten. Dawn was approaching in its steady, usual fashion. The sun would be high and hot before too long.

Three days and I'll be back in Bethany, Phillip thought to himself. He was optimistic. His thoughts, however, kept coming back to Martha. And Mary. And the secret entrance to the house that Lazarus knew about. He urged Tsalav into a vigorous trot, clip-clopping past the littered clumps of slumbering vagabonds. Some raising their sleepy, filthy, turban-wrapped heads as he passed.

By the time he was back on the main road, he had kicked Tsalav up into a galloping speed. The tiniest tip of blinding yellow sun had broken over the Eastern horizon. There was this itching pinch at the back of his mind, telling Phillip that even though he had only just started on his journey home, he was already running out of time.

However, he was lucky, due to his insomnia. Since he had been unable to sleep, he had managed to make it out of the city and well past where James ben Jonah, Caiaphas' copper bearded lackey, along with a couple of Roman soldiers slept beneath thin cloaks by a smoldering campfire. Not far off the main road.

xxiii

He awoke to a shrill squeal from an exerted horse galloping by. His eyes snapped open, along with one of his Roman traveling companions. The third member of their group, still slept hard. Sucking in through his nose and blowing out in deep guffaws through his open mouth. Eyes rolling busily behind closed eyelids in blissful slumber.

James propped himself up in his elbows and became acclimated towards the fact that he was awake in small increments. The sun progressed and ushered the dawn towards becoming day. James licked his lips and coughed, suddenly becoming aware of a stinging need to pee. He arose and stretched his arms over his head with a great groan. Then, stepped away from where he had laid on the ground and used a rock as a pillow. Choosing to pee behind a large bush of Jerusalem Sage.

While James relieved himself he thought about how stupid this errand was in comparison to doing something worthwhile. Something more important. Something like hunting down that meddlesome Jesus of Nazareth. But, he had to appease Caiaphas in these remedial, little tasks if he was to ever hope to be considered for High Priest of Jerusalem. James had already spent countless hours imagining the day when he would assume the title of High Priest and how he would wield the power that accompanies the position as one would a new tambourine.

He finished up and shook himself off.

When he returned to their campsite his grizzled, battle-hardened Tribune, Julius, was returning from his morning constitutional, as well. Silvanus, however, Julius' Praefectus levis amaturae, was still snuggled up tight in his cloak, tucked up in the fetal position. Eyes closed. Smiling. Snoring in great, big rips.

Julius scowled down at Silvanus, still enveloped in sweet repose. The Tribune then stomped over and kicked him directly in his protruding buttocks. "Get up you lazy ass," Julius growled, hovering over his Praefectus levis amaturae, as Silvanus shot up in shock. The poor kid was looking up into his Tribune's face in horror, like he had been awoken to a nightmare.

Then the pain set in from the kick of an angrily driven Roman issue boot and he winced, while beginning to rub at the assaulted area. "Yes, my Lord," Silvanus grumbled in a groggy, thick voice.

"What was that?" Julius challenged, hungry for confrontation.

Louder now, Silvanus answered full throated, "Yes, my Lord Julius!"

Julius squinted, then instructed him, "Get up and help me with the horses…and the Holy Man's camel."

"Yes, my Lord Julius!" came the overly jubilant, enthusiastic salute again and Silvanus was up on his feet trotting after Julius to where their steeds were tethered. There was a slight, but visible hiccup to his gait until he caught up to his mentor. He rubbed soothingly at his kicked buttocks, in between preparing the horse for himself and the camel for their charge.

James had watched all of this, while nonchalantly taking a stick and stirring the ashes of their perspired fire in an attempt to drudge up any remaining buried, hot embers. Or at least turn over some heated dirt, just to break the morning frost. The days were getting warmer, but the mornings still had a bite to them.

After a few moments of trying to warm his hands against a mildly warm fire bed, the two soldiers returned and asked if he was ready to embark. He stood, brushed his hands together and nodded in silent approval.

By midday they were off of their horses (and camel) leading them through the tangled, bustling streets of Capernaum. Guided by directions that they paid for by means of coercion, they looped down alleys, crossed boulevards and appeared totally lost until they were standing in front of a large, thick, solid wooden gate.

James signaled a quick nod with his head, urging Julius on. To which, Julius took a gauntleted fist and pounded on the side of the entryway. Their camel and horses snorted and pranced about anxiously in response to the banging. After a few unanswered moments, Julius banged again.

No answer.

Before the third knock, however, a small door in the large gate swung open with a little squeak. Within was a tired, but beautiful older woman's face. Her eyes were rimmed red and puffy, but she studied them with some misgivings. Her medium plush lips were turned down at the corners in a resting frown.

She asked in a bored, melancholy way, “Can I help you gentlemen?"

James stepped up, touching his phylactery box, attempting to draw her attention to his relic denoting his station of importance. Although, from her side of the gate, through the little cubby, she didn’t seem impressed in the slightest.

“Forgive our intrusion my Lady,” James started in a diplomatic tone. “We have traveled far.” He brought his face closer to her face through the little door. “May we find refreshment within your house?”

“Just state your business, if you don’t mind,” the lady responded tiredly. “We are not accepting any visitors.”

“Is this the home of Jairus?” James asked.

She slanted her gaze at the trio of strangers and raised an eyebrow suspiciously, “It is. Who are you?”

“I am a Priest from Jerusalem looking for a man that might have come by here,” James gave her the honest answer.

For the most fleeting of moments, the older woman’s eyes enlarged, as if she had been pinched. James noticed this slip and pounced, “Judging by your reaction, I’m guessing he did come by. You gave him lodging?”

She didn’t speak. She didn’t have to. He was doing all of the talking.

“Why would you say you’re not accepting visitors,” James continued as if puzzling out a real conundrum of a riddle, “when you just housed one last night?”

The woman rolled her eyes and said, “Good day *gentlemen.*”

She just made to close the little door and James lurched forward, plunging his jeweled hands into the opening, forcing the little door wide open. His face and fingers filled the entire rectangle of space. He had little diamonds of froth at the corners of his mouth that expanded when he opened wide to speak, “Did this visitor ask about Jairus’ daughter? That’s what he came for wasn’t it?” She had dropped back from the gate. A terrified look was upon her face. “What did you tell him? By the authority of the Temple of Jerusalem and God I command you to tell me!”

Beyond the older woman, James could see others, stable boys and house maidens, coming out of their respective buildings. Abandoning their duties to come see what the commotion was all about.

James’ eyes now bounced all over the property and something occurred to him. “Wait,” he said, “is he still here?”

"No!" The woman shouted simply. Two larger men were now swiftly approaching the gate with swords drawn, calling down for James to *Back Away!* Upon seeing them and their intent, James pulled away from the gate, easing his hands up in a vulnerable, yet disingenuous gesture of surrender. Julius and Silvanus flanked him on either side with their own swords unsheathed and at the ready.

The gate swung open and multiple men barreled out brandishing their own weapons. They all stopped short of James, Julius and Silvanus. The oldest looking amongst them shouted in a loud, booming voice, "Explain yourself, stranger!"

James stood pious like in between the Romans, adjusting the plethora of rings on his fingers so that they were all pointing straight up and out. He spoke softly now, the rabid spittle drying in the corners of his mouth, "A simple misunderstanding gentlemen. The woman-"

"Samantha!" One of the younger, shaky men corrected him.

"Right, Samantha," James adhered, sounding kind of peeved, before continuing on, "Well, Samantha was being reluctant to give straight answers to an official Priest of the Temple of Jerusalem about a recent visitor here."

The oldest amongst them didn't shout, this time, but he still spoke so loud, "That doesn't carry a drop of water around here, Priest." He began to chuckle obstreperously, inciting all of the younger men around him to join in the raucous mirth. He added between fits of giggles, "You're a long ways away from your jurisdiction, Holy Man."

James smiled warmly and elucidated, "My dear stupid Gentiles, don't you know?" They all stopped laughing in sync, faces going slack at the insult. "That I am a direct agent of the Most High God, and there is no jurisdiction limitation that a slack jawed, mother-humping Gentile like you can put upon the Most High."

That was the final straw for the older man. He bellowed out a frightening war cry, while raising his sword high above his head. Women shrieked. Julius and Silvanus crouched, bracing for a physical combat engagement. Horses squealed. The camel brayed. Men shouted. The oldest amongst them made to charge at the trio of strangers, when a slurred, but powerful voice cut through the chaos, "Ephraim! Stend down!!"

The scene came to a screeching halt entirely. There, stumbling up to the gate, wrapped up loose in a luxurious robe with visible greenish purple dried vomit on the sleeve, and holding on tight to a quarter-full, sloshing decanter of wine, was Jairus. His hair shot this way and that, in all different directions. The whites of his eyes appeared yellowed. His lips were tinted a dark purple.There was a unique air of disorientation and shrewdness about him. Still the Lord of the house, but now he was reduced to just a sad man on a lonely path to self destruction.

"Well. Well. Lord Jairus," James exclaimed with glee. "You are certainly looking the worse for wear."

"Zhut yur poizunuz mouth, znake," Jairus slurred, then burped. "Yoo have dizdurbed uzz enuff!"

With that last rebuke, Jairus threw his vessel of wine in the direction of the newcomers, his aim falling pitifully short and to the right. The decanter exploded upon impact, shattering colored glass and wine across the dirt laden boulevard, leaving a mauve stain that looked like a large, fresh, scabbed over wound.

Jairus lost his tenuous sense of balance and almost fell flat on his face had it not been for Ephraim, along with a few others there to catch and support their master.

James chuckled at the sad state that he now found Jairus to be in. Stumbling. Bumbling. Living inside a husk. Animating a daughter-less body that wanted to feel nothing. Samantha and a few of the surrounding maidens rushed to steady their shameful Master as he continued to totter about angrily.

"Tell me, *Lord* Jairus," James called over, with a disgusting smirk laying surreptitiously beneath his copper beard, "How is dear little Abigail faring since her miraculous visit from *The Messiah*?" Absolute silence filled the street at the sheer audacity of the question posed, which stole almost everyone's breath. James capitalized upon the collective shock and extended the insult, "Made a full recovery I presume?"

Multiple men and even a couple of the women, including Samantha, made to advance upon the vile, unwelcome trio. Jairus himself, wailed and fell on his knees to the ground, ripping open his tunic at his chest in extreme grief.

"You bastard!" Ephraim thundered above the din of rageful voices. "You're not worthy to speak her name!!"

Silvanus and Julius had already mounted their steeds at the sight of an overpowering mob forming. All three of their mounts danced and spun around nervously from the rising cacophonous rabble advancing. Silvanus held James' camel as steady as possible, while James was laughing out loud and he swung his leg over, mounting it. Once he was seated, the two Roman soldiers kicked their own mounts into escape.

Meanwhile, through an insufferable grin, James said to the small mob, "Thank you for your time and for telling me what I needed to know. May God be with you!" He jabbed his camel with his heels, causing it to grunt loudly, then bolt.

The throng of Jairus' household rose up and threw swords, knives, stones, pitchforks, chunks of crumbling masonry and buckets at his shrinking backside. A rapidly dwindling target. Some of the smaller pieces connected with him and the camel, but not enough to cause anything close to serious injury. He had escaped the angry mob and caught up with his Roman guards in a short manner of time.

Both of the Romans looked wholly incensed from his peripheral vision on his right side. They didn't appear happy with him or his choice to incite and antagonize violence when they were so grossly outnumbered. Julius barked at him, "Hey! What the fuck was that about?!" James rode through the streets of Capernaum, strident in ignoring them. "Hey! I'm talking to you Holy Man!"

James didn't seem to register, let alone care about their shared animosity. He'd gotten what he'd set out for. Quick answers, with minimal questioning and no one had to die. He kicked his camel harder into a faster gallop, leading the two armored buffoons out of the city. He kept it that way for a while, leading them both by a fair distance. It was now a race against one man back to Bethany and, little did James know, the horrors that awaited them all there.

"It's always going to be sour grapes with you boy, until you make it right with **Jesus**." - Puscifer, Sour Grapes

Part III: Regurgitation

i

Caiaphas sat like an impatient child. Shifting from one buttcheek to the other, unable to get comfortable in the ornate, golden padded chair that had been provided. His robes felt much too heavy for the temperature of where he now found himself. Like he was engulfed in the steam clouds of a Turkish bath.

It felt like this endeavor had been undertaken ages ago. Caiaphas had been led to a hot, shadowy chamber by an olive skinned boy of no more than fifteen. The boy was wearing a pure white tunic that was much too high on the leg and tight in the chest, tied at the waist with a thin cord of rawhide. In a reserved tone, the shy child quietly asked the High Priest to wait, gesturing with an unsure, timid hand to the chair. As Caiaphas sat, the boy bolted. Sprinting much too fast back the way they had come, like he was late for something of the utmost importance. The High Priest saw the flaps of the young boy's tunic lifting and showing the bottom portion of his buttocks. Caiaphas turned away from the sight, grimacing. Burning bile arose in his throat at the thought of what Pilate made that boy do behind closed doors. He banished the image away the instant it entered his mind. Totally disgusted by the utter shameless lewdness of a certain culture subscribed to by a certain few Roman elite.

Caiaphas been placed in a seating area amidst a forest of monolithic columns, dimly lit by a scarce amount of torches and large, evenly spaced squares of glowing coals mounding right up out of the floor. Up above, the column's lofty tops disappeared into the ethereal, pure darkness of the ceiling. Before him there was another gaudy, ornate chair of the same type, with a small useless, oddly shaped, although, nonetheless beautifully crafted hand table placed next to it. Firelight glinted in mute globs upon the golden filigree and dark wood grain of both furniture pieces. Many quiet echoes bounced and reverberated within the vast chamber, making it very unnerving to sit within it. All alone.

Pontius Pilate liked to play these stupid little games, so that he was in control from the beginning. He sets the time to meet. Caiaphas, The High Priest, does this foreigner a courtesy by arriving punctually, so as to not be obnoxious and keep **him** waiting. Now Pontius was late. Not to mention Caiaphas was really thirsty. As was normal, a guest would be offered a refreshment upon arrival. It was common practice by Jewish custom. But, these Romans operated like cutthroat dogs at nearly every encounter, disparaging basic etiquette for the sake of leveraging sway.

So now Pontius, whenever he chose to finally arrive, would arrive calm. Collected. Ready for a robust debate. Whereas, on the other hand, Caiaphas would be flustered, angered, uncomfortable, hot and thirsty. In short, not thinking straight. That was how Pilate achieved dominance before even speaking a word. Certainly, it had something to do with how he got to this point in his life. Living like a deviant king in the opulence of Herod's Palace.

God help me, it's downright stifling in here! Caiaphas thought as sweat rolled freely down past his tiny box of scripture and through his eyebrows. Stinging at the corners of his eyes, like vinegar and lemon juice, reminding him of a symptom of the wicked presence in the tomb's courtyard. Yes sir, with each passing, wasted moment in this baking, dark expansive venue Caiaphas was stuck in, the priestly garb was feeling thicker and heavier.

Comically, for a silly, vanishing moment, he wished he had a white, short tunic, like the one the young boy that had escorted him in here had been wearing. He entertained, for another silly, fleeting moment, all of the various nether regions of his own that a welcomed breeze would touch, if he was, in fact, adorned in a tiny, revealing smock.

His eyes stung from another rivulet of streaming sweat flowing right plumb into his sclera. He squeezed his eyes shut and rubbed at the closed lids with a tender set of creepy fingers.

While nursing the sting away, he noticed many sets of echoing steps that were louder than the other random, previous passing footsteps. Like a giant caterpillar, with hundreds of feet, getting closer to where he sat, sweating and rubbing at his stinging eyes. The distinctive audible swish of silk, linen and wool fabrics could be heard as well as the footsteps. It sounded like a decent entourage approaching. Caiaphas' eyes snapped open, just as the melodious sing-song, sultry voice of Pontius Pilate kicked off their dialog, "Well! Well! High Priest, Joseph ben Caiaphas! This is certainly splendid surprise."

Pontius drifted past him and took his seat with a flourishing spin of his flamboyant color choices. He was trailed closely by an entourage of glistening servants carrying palm fronds for fanning, a single table, as well as many platters of food and copious vessels of drink.

"Yes, Governor," Caiaphas answered back in deference. "It is good to see you," he lied.

"Mmmmmmm," Pontius mused. His portly hand had been placed upon the small useless table that had been stationed next to his chair. Pale, jeweled fingers danced and drummed in excited anticipation for his mandatory unspoken tribute. Defined as a kiss upon the ring.

Caiaphas stared back at him in obstinance, feigning ignorance for the moment. Dripping sweat. Drawing out his disdain for this degrading act of obeisance. Pontius held a smug, satisfied, lazy smile upon his face. The Roman elite flicked his eyes and nodded his head, hinting towards his hand awaiting its kiss on the table. Pilate wasn't going to entertain any further discussion with Caiaphas, until the High Priest swallowed his God given pride, forced down his delusions of grandeur and kissed the nasty ring.

Against his will, Caiaphas stood. Despite the oppressive heat of the room, he remained standing, frozen in place. Excited from the anticipation, Pontius wiggled his fingers upon the table, making random clacking sounds on the wood with his many rings. Caiaphas shuffled over to Pilate and the table, upon which his greedy, impatient hand waited. On his corpulent index finger was a particularly large gold ring with the likeness of Caesar inlaid. Caiaphas knelt, looking at the side profile of the Emperor before leaning down to brush his pinched lips as lightly as possible upon the ring.

Uncontrollable, ample droplets of sweat fell and splattered on the table, as well as the hand and wrist of Pilate. In delighted response, Pilate's fingers danced with childish excitement and the minimal contact that Caiaphas had been vying for was egregiously violated. Multiple fingers on Pontius' kissed hand extended and twiddled in their giddiness, touching Caiaphas all around his mouth and chin.

Caiaphas arose, repulsed. Spitting and wiping at his lower face with his sleeve as he returned to his seat. Pilate giggled heartily at his guest's discomfort resulting in his own personal satisfaction. Meanwhile, the table had been set. Two young, impassive boys in skimpy dress, took their palm fronds and began to fan in Pilate's direction alone. Other faceless young boys in skimpy white tunics, same as the boy who had led him in, scattered in various directions. Buttcheeks were on display **everywhere**! Pilate giggled again. Caiaphas' skin crawled. The High Priest felt as though snakes and spiders and creepy crawly things were swarming all around him.

Once Caiaphas was somewhat settled again, Pilate asked in his foreign broken tongue, "Now, to what we owe this visit from Jerusalem's most distinguished High Priest of Year?"

Caiaphas had a suspicious feeling, as though he were being mocked, but still answered cautiously, "First, Governor, let me thank you for seeing me on such short notice." Pilate waved away the formality while he sipped greedily from a goblet and plucked some grapes off of a beautiful, large vined bunch. "Second, we are approaching the week of Passover."

Pilate appeared very bored by yawning ostentatiously behind a soft, uncalloused hand, "Yes, so we are."

Caiaphas pressed his thin lips together, forming a horizontal minus symbol in his face. Then, the High Priest pushed further with his request, "As you may, or may not, know, The High Priest, me," he emphasized with a rangy hand upon his own breast, "has many duties during this consecrated week."

"Yes, yes," Pontius remarked in a condescending tone, seeming more interested in the state of his manicure, than hearing what Caiaphas' duties were or what he was angling towards. "Very interesting."

Sweating buckets and suffocating bit by bit, Caiaphas was becoming ever more irritated by this powerful Roman's theatrics. Yet, he swiped at his dripping face and chose to respond diplomatically, trying to add a little dollop of oil to his reedy voice, "Well, my Lord, you have the Ephod and

The Breastplate of Judgement with the Urim and Thummim in your possession."

Pilate simply stared at Caiaphas with a blank expression. Blinking. Looking as if Caiaphas had just begun to articulate in a foreign language. The Governor's exotic foreigner eyes, penciled in a kohl eyeliner, drifted away from whatever the High Priest was saying and landed to lust on one of his scantily clad servant boys.

Following a few silent, awkward moments, Caiaphas continued by raising his voice a little and hinting at the obvious, "PER Our tradition, I am required by Mosaic Law to don these holy garments you *covet* for the duration of this sacred week of the-"

"Covet?" Pilate interrupted. Echoing this odious word back to Caiaphas. Visibly affronted, the Governor had taken particular offense to the word and the implication that came with it. Caiaphas knew he would snag Pilate's attention by accusing him of it. "No, no, no little Joseph, you misunderstand. I am merely storing for you for safekeeping."

Little Joseph? Caiaphas fumed on the inside.

The High Priest managed to force a strained grin. He had to keep things diplomatic with this Gentile scum. He donned his oily affect, "A misunderstanding I'm sure. But, the time has come and I must have them."

Pilate finished off the contents of his goblet, giggled and then confessed, "I must admit, I'm not sure where they are."

"What?!" Caiaphas exploded. He felt his face redden as his anger soared.

That was when Pilate erupted in boisterous, uproarious laughter. He rolled from side to side in his chair, knocking over the hand table and coming close to falling to the floor. He hyperventilated in spasms of fitful glee while Caiaphas stared at him writhing from something obscure, yet, apparently hilarious.

Once Pilate's fits had calmed back down to random giggles, he confessed again, "I'm joking with you."

"What?!" Caiaphas repeated with even more edge to his tone.

This brought on another round of raucous laughter from the Governor, during which time a young, half naked boy appeared at Caiaphas' side with the Ephod neatly folded and cradled in his arms. The jeweled Breastplate of Judgement sitting atop. Caiaphas took the holy garments from the boy gently, trying to catch a glimpse of his downturned eyes in the dimness.

At one point, the boy did look up and into the High Priest's pitch dark eyes. What Caiaphas saw there was nothing. Vacancy. Removal of one's self from one's reality. A soul had been crushed behind the boy's eyes and now the body (the husk) was carting around what remained. The boy drifted over by where Pilate was sitting, wiping away mirthful tears. The bottom portion of his backside was peeking out beneath his tunic. Revealed for all to see. Caiaphas shut his stinging eyes and turned away before seeing anything more that he didn't want to see.

Emotionless, the boy had stationed himself by his master's side. Pilate's laughter had trickled down to random, sporadic titters. He slapped the boy hard on his exposed behind, making a sound reminiscent of a whip crack that echoed, weaving in and out of the columns of the chamber. "I trust this is everything you require for your 'holy week'," Pontius Pilate said, seeming particularly sarcastic about the holy descriptive. Rolling his R's in his broken dialect.

Caiaphas felt for the Urim and Thummim amongst the garments. At first, nothing. He rummaged more. Dug deeper, until he felt the two, significant flat stones by the heart of the Breastplate. "Yes, my Lord," Caiaphas answered with a feeling of relief washing over him. "Everything's accounted for." He rose to depart. The urgency to leave this smaller scale version of Sodom and Gomorrah was stronger than ever.

Concerned, Pilate asked, "You are leaving?"

"Yes," he confessed while backing away slowly, a handbreadth at a time, clutching what he had come for to his chest. "There are...uh...other...um...priestly duties I must attend to. Busy week and all."

"No, no, no little Joseph," Pilate insisted. He then urged him to stay and drink. Eat. He even pulled the boy at his side close to him and asked him what would be so terrible about *not* being High Priest for just one day.

Caiaphas felt vomit rise up in the back of his throat and declined once more as graciously as he could. Spiders and snakes swarmed and hissed in his mind. He tried not to hurry out of this dark, sweltering, pedophilic pit too quickly as to be insulting, but nevertheless, his steps increased in pace until he was running out into the fresh air and sunshine. Bursting out of the Praetorium of Pontius Pilate, as though he were breaking the surface of quicksand, after being pulled under and held near to the point of finally taking that first gritty inhale.

Evening was advancing steadily. Night would be upon Bethany soon and with it, now, came a foreboding sense of dread. Like being caught in a violent electrical thunder storm and wondering where the next strike of lightning would touch down.

Caiaphas had the tools he needed now. Only he could stop this madness that Jesus had brought upon the poor people of Bethany. It was up to him to restore the order. By hook or crook, in God's name it would be done.

ii

Martha raced about in a dizzying frenzy from room to room, except for Mary's. Tidying tables that had already been tidied. Fluffing already fluffed pillows. Wiping down surfaces that were already wiped down. Adjusting vases a handbreadth over one way, then fingerbreadth by fingerbreadth back the other way, until they were right back to their original places on tables and ledges. There seemed to be too much to do in so little time, even though she consciously knew that she was just following behind housemaids and servants, undoing or redoing what had already been done.

She would pass familiar servants in the corridors in her haste from one room to the next. These servant girls, who were once like nieces to Martha, would now see her coming and station themselves with their backs pressed up against the wall, heads dipped down in subservience. They would circumspectly look up at her passing by, like the pinging, wild woman that she was portraying herself as lately.

But, really, how should she be reacting to the daily news of nightly abductions and murders, while knowing damn well who the suspect was? She could be numb, drunk, sequestered in her room and intentionally aloof like her sister, Mary. Or she could be like all of the men in her life right now and just **not** around.

She prayed while stalking for rogue clutter or disarray from room to room. First of all, she prayed that there was something that could be done for her brother. Amen. Secondly, she prayed that Jesus would arrive soon and safely with his twelve. Amen. Lastly, she prayed that Phillip was alright and almost back home to Bethany with a good report, or even just a positive minor detail, from Capernaum. She would welcome even the slimmest shred of something hopeful right now. Double Amen.

Now that the rooms, except for Mary's, had been visited multiple times and turned over for any speck of dust, Martha decided to go check the dovecote once more before night fell and took any remaining light of day with it. This would make any message that she would prefer to keep a secret to herself, difficult to read.

As she passed by Mary's door on her route to the ladder up to the roof, she heard muffled laughter. Instinctually, as a protective older sister, she silently smushed her ear to her younger sister's door. At first she heard nothing. She plugged her other ear with her pinky and pressed in even harder against the door. Immediately, from the other side of the door, Martha heard a man's voice loudly moan, followed up by her sister shushing, coupled with her unmistakable inebriated snort and giggle. The man that had moaned, was now deeply sighing and breathing heavily. There was a sonorous chuckle and a matching voice that purred, "Too quick, my honeypot."

Mary's drunken drawl could be heard saying, "Nut to werrry. We haave aaaallll night, lurver." After that, there was a loud slap and the male voice whimpered.

Oh Mary, Martha thought for a few sad reflective moments. She took her pinky finger out of her ear and pulled away from the door, wiping her yellowed, soiled finger subconsciously upon her own robes. Before she knew it, her legs had picked back up to the pace she had previously been keeping.

But, after turning the corner that would lead her straight down towards the ladder, she ran right into Hannah, doing her nightly ritualistic duty of lighting the lamps in the hallway. Her face looked all the more lined and haggard in the flickering light of the torch she held in her hand. It made Martha self conscious of how her own sleep deprived, tear depleted face must look in the same flickering light.

"Good evening to you Martha," Hannah spoke, sounding even more deadpan than usual.

"Good evening Hannah," Martha replied.

"How are you?" Hannah asked, sounding as if she didn't care what the answer was.

Likewise, Martha didn't feel like giving her much of an answer in return, but she was cordial in her response, "Fine, and yourself?"

"Curious," Hannah fired back, ready.

Martha really didn't have time for this. She could feel the sky getting darker by the second outside. She imagined every time her heart beat, outside it shifted to a deeper, darker hue of evening sky. In her mind, she wanted to question her servant, Hannah's curiosity, but realized she was habitually holding her breath, once again. Her eyes glanced past Hannah and saw the dark, symmetrical outline of the ladder to the roof at the end of the hall. Its vertical and horizontal shadows danced and shifted upon the wall behind it.

Hannah continued, "I'm curious as to whether your brother will be attending our Passover feast."

"I'm not sure," Martha responded tiredly.

"I see,""Hannah said, as if she expected such an answer. "May I ask you something?"

No! Martha screamed on the inside.

"Of course Hannah," Martha tenderly answered on the exterior.

"Have you seen him?" Hannah asked in plain terms. "Lazarus?"

Martha was holding her breath again and shaking her head from side to side in a slow swiveling.

"No?" Hannah asked in an attempt to confirm.

"No," Martha exhaled out. "Not since the day after his resurrection."

Old Hannah stared at Martha sternly. "You don't find that strange at all?" Hannah asked. Her gaze never broke amidst the ever changing contours of her face from the firelight dancing in her hand.

"To be honest," Martha leaned forward in a confident manner, "I find the whole thing strange." She sighed in a flippant, wistful way and continued, "It is both strange and wonderful what the Lord has the power to do. Isn't it?"

Hannah had been around long enough to recognize the sense that she was being brushed off like a pestering gadfly. The old Lady pressed, "It is also peculiar, you might say, that these nightly horrors in Bethany we are only recently experiencing, began **after** your brother was miraculously resurrected."

The hallway was beginning to feel cramped, like the walls and the ceiling above were closing in around herself and Hannah. Squeezing them uncomfortably closer together within the confines of the corridor. It might have been the darkening towards night outside or the torch in Hannah's hand siphoning all of the available oxygen between them both. Either way, Martha had to tamp down the overwhelming urge to push past her nosy, antique servant and make a run for the ladder to the roof.

"What are you saying?" Martha asked her. Challenging Hannah to come out and say that she thought Lazarus was a murderer who was totally capable of all of the recent atrocities in their little city. Forcing her into the uncomfortable position of standing by her wild conviction.

In obstinance, Hannah planted her free hand on her old lady hip and asked her a question back, "Is he really in the wilderness meditating?"

"Yes," Martha lied. Maybe. Who knows what he was doing in the crypt all day. She was only mostly sure as to his nocturnal rituals of late.

"How are you so sure?" Hannah continued. "You said you haven't seen him since just after his resurrection. That's what you just said." The old lady pointed a crooked finger up at her face.

"I just am sure, Hannah," Martha said, beginning to adopt a stern, bossy, yet still annoyed tone. Hannah took her turn to lean in conspiratorially, with her flame flickering in wild reaction to the breath between them both. She spoke matter-of-factly to Martha, "Well, unfortunately, I believe that he's not in the wilderness meditating, as you say."

"Oh?" Martha snuck in the quick query.

Hannah went on as if Martha hadn't interrupted, "Personally, I believe he has something to do with all of this terrible carnage in Bethany lately." She shrugged and added cynically, "Sorry to say so, but **we** all think the same."

Martha felt as if her own once vibrant, warm house was now transformed into a cold, sinister pit of writhing vipers. She shook her head somberly. Exhausted from the constant barrage on all fronts. Her soul desperately craved relief. Lasting, plentiful relief. Knowing relief wouldn't come in the way she desired, she sighed, then calmly questioned her servant, Hannah, "Hannah have you ever been dead?"

Hannah, for a moment, was speechless. Stunned by the question, not entirely sure she heard it correct, she asked, "What was that?"

"Have you ever been dead?" Martha inquired again, then attacked with even more aggressive questioning, "For four days? Hhmmm? Have you ever been dead for four days and then resurrected?"

"Martha," Hannah broached the lady of the house, trying to calm the younger woman's rising fury. The historical old servant held her hands up in defenseless prostration.

"No!" Martha shouted now. Feeling unable to stop herself. "Out of all of the times that you or someone that you've known has been dead for four days, then resurrected, how did you or that someone act afterwards? Hhmmm?!"

"Martha, my Lady," Hannah tried in a soothing manner again.

"Shut up!" Martha seethed behind gritted teeth. Elderly Hannah was stunned. Wide eyed and speechless. She had never seen Martha like this before, not even when she was a child. Martha's eyes blazed hotter than the torch Hannah held, like two roiling, smoldering embers stuck into a tanned haggard pit of a face. The Lady of the House had positioned herself like a coiled snake, warning of the imminent strike. She continued, "Do you think any of this is easy?"

Hannah, wisely, chose silence as her answer to this posed question.

Regardless, Martha didn't even give her a chance to answer, "Between the coming Passover! Mary's slovenliness! Lazarus! Caiaphas snooping around!" Martha was shouting out the perpetrators of her distress in bursts in between short pauses. "Now you!"

Hannah responded by embracing Martha. Wrapping her up in her arms and shushing the furious, hysterical woman. Martha clawed at her and beat at the small, aged woman with the sides of her fists, while saying things like, *Let me go* or *Have you lost your mind?* Hannah withstood the physical abuse and continued to soothe her. Even humming a melody from Matha's childhood. Hannah kept this up until Matha began to calm down from her fit. Until she was only weakly protesting against Hannah's suppression. To Hannah, it was a nostalgic moment that drudged up memories of soothing a crying, young Martha with a skinned knee.

Before they knew it, they were two familial-like women holding each other and crying in the hallway.

Hannah whispered into Martha's ear, "We don't have to host the Passover feast, Martha."

Martha pushed away from her servant and looked at her with confused, sopping wet eyes.

"If it's too much," Hannah added in an almost lifting tone of a question to soften the suggestion.

Martha wiped tears away from both of her eyes irritably. She seemed angry. Not at Hannah, though. More like she was angry with herself for giving into being emotional and vulnerable, even if it was for just a short moment. She had to maintain a stoic atmosphere amongst these walls.

"No," Martha said simply, shaking her head side to side in short little, adamant jerks.

"No?" Hannah echoed.

"That's right, no," Martha replied. "We will continue preparing for the Passover feast as planned."

Hannah began to protest, "But-"

Martha quickly cut her off by brushing past her, making way for the ladder. She murmured clinically as she passed by, "Thank you for your concern, Hannah."

After a few strides, Martha heard Hannah softly call to her, "Martha?"

Martha didn't falter in her advance towards the ladder. She was merely four or five cubits away from the roof access. Her hand was already eagerly outstretched for the rungs.

"We don't believe you," Martha heard Hannah state from behind her. She stopped and turned around in the hallway to tell her servant to get back to her duties, when she found that she was the only one there. Had she imagined Hannah saying that they didn't believe her?

She had no more time to dwell on the matter and she climbed up the ladder, out into the evening. It was now, almost completely night. A small tinge of pink and purple still illuminated from the West. She rushed over to the dovecote and searched amongst the cooing pigeons within. A thorough search of all of the birds, both of their legs and all of their pigeon holes three times with the rest of the dwindling light, turned up zilch.

Oh, Jesus, where are you, she thought. Her mind rested on Jesus for a moment. But, inadvertently, her mind switched from thoughts surrounding the Lord, to thoughts enveloping Phillip. She felt an ache and found that she yearned for his presence. For his burly arms to be wrapped tightly around her. From memory, her mind could conjure up his scent, causing her heart and, naturally, her groin to ache. Here, in this moment, on the rooftop, with no word from the Lord or Phillip, standing above the pit of vipers that used to be her home, she never felt more alone.

Night had fully fallen. She imagined Lazarus awakening, chalky eyes glowing in the darkness, moving aside his tombstone and stepping out into his element. There would be more murder tonight. She was sure of that, at least. Her only hope was that it was too far away to reach the ear of her staff before a day or two had passed. She just needed more time.

iii

Mary curled her toes and squealed in glorious delight. The muggy room spun intensely as she writhed in her throes of excessive ecstasy and drink. They had been going at it for what seemed like hours. Her, pleasuring him for a bit, then him returning the pleasure. Then, both pleasuring concurrently. Back and forth reciprocal favors traded at will, with periodic breaks for refreshments over an unknown length of time had brought them to this point. Exhausted, but driven beyond human exertion in the pursuit of lust. Sweet, elusive lust held their appetites trapped in voracious captivity.

At the moment, his face was placed snugly between her sweaty, quaking legs. His purple, wine stained tongue flicked wildly, tracing a short, capricious path from her clitoris to her anus. Simultaneously, his deep voice rumbled like a tremor against her sensitive vagina, making her want to clench and expand at the same time. Her knees, however, were held up near her shoulders by his muscular forearms pressed against her slick hamstrings, leaving his fingers to tickle the inside of her knees and thighs delicately, which was a sweet juxtaposition to his energetic, aggressive form of cunnilingus.

Likewise, she spun, caressed and tweaked her own nipples to heighten the seemingly immeasurable, eclipsing crest of pleasure that she rode like a seasoned sea nymph. Her eyes rolled up in her cycling head and her moans reverberated within her own ears. She bucked her hips against his laboring mouth in hearty rhythmic union. At one point, one of her hands meandered down away from her breast, grasped him by his thick bushel of hair and pressed him harder into her insatiable organ.

Both of these thoroughly inebriated individuals were so caught up in sexual rapture, that they didn't even notice that a third party had entered the room. Neither one had heard the harsh scrape of the large storage chest being pushed open beyond the sound of their own animalistic moans and grunts. Or that the flowers in various vases about the room drooped, wilted and blackened rapidly in the presence of this new arrival. Nor were they aware of the rancid smell of decay that had wafted into the room like a cornucopic bouquet of rotted meat.

Mary's closed eyes parted barely and she thought she caught a flashing glimpse of a pale, hunched over, grinning phantom standing just slightly off from the foot of the bed. But, when her eyes snapped fully open and she pushed herself up on her elbows, interrupting the wonderful cunnilingus, the grinning figure that once was there, had now vanished.

From down between her legs, her lover rumbled, "What's the matter, my honeypot?"

Her head was spinning from the excessive amount of wine and rapture. She placed a hand on her forehead for a brief moment and brushed it off as a silly symptom of, "Tu musch wine." She then kissed him deeply on his moist, fragrant lips, seized him by his bushel of hair again and shoved him down, commanding him to, "Keep eating."

All of a sudden, many unexpected voices joined the conversation in a strummed unison, by announcing, "Shame."

Before either Mary or her male lover knew what was really happening, Lazarus had pulled the lover up by his mane of hair from his position in between Mary's legs. Lazarus was as stark naked as they both were. Mary was screaming maniacally and attempting to cover her breasts and vagina, while scooting up to the head of the bed. Her lover kicked uncontrollably in the air as Lazarus lifted him off the ground. Some of the hairs ripping from the roots on his ascent. He held on with both hands to the rigid, branch of a decayed arm that dangled him a couple handbreadths over the floor.

Lazarus, the impervious ghoul, then placed his free hand on the shoulder of Mary's lover. Lazarus took a long, exaggerated lick of the flesh on the side of the lover's neck, allowing its colorless eyes to flutter and roll up inside his skull. The struggling of the victim, coupled with Mary's terrified shrieks weren't enough to deter fate. Bypassing any further ado, Lazarus bit into his victim's sun-beaten neck with his large, splitting, brown teeth, tearing out a huge chunk of tanned flesh with visceral meat. This sent a hot fan of blood spray across the room, along with splattering Mary's naked body and screaming face.

Her lover roared in pain and horror, then glugged, while beating in utter futility at the ghoul. The victim was appearing weaker from each exerted effort. Lazarus, still holding its new meal aloft, beamed with a glistening, smeared crimson grin plastered across its face. It began to back towards the secret entrance of the room in a way so fluidly, that it seemed as if it were sliding instead of stepping. The room was now fully ripe and blossoming with the strong metallic smell of blood, alot of it, and the unmistakable odor of absolute death. Mary was caught gagging in between screams, as she was breathing in great gasps of the foul air.

Dull, frantic banging started to rattle Mary's locked door on its hinges. Muffled, shouting voices could be heard past Mary's manic screaming and the strong beating on the door. These outside voices demanded that she *Open the door at once!* This was followed by a succession of singular, louder bangs, as if they were trying to break the door down.

Finally, one of the larger servants, by the name of Jacob, busted through the locked and wedged door with his shoulder. Martha and basically the whole population of the house followed by trying to squeeze through the open doorway all at once behind the human battering ram. They entered just in time to see Lazarus slink out of the secret tunnel behind the storage chest, dragging his freshest, bleeding victim out with him. The last thing being seen were the nude, bloodied, weakly kicking legs and feet of Mary's lover being hauled out of the small portal to the exterior of the house.

"Oh my God!" Martha exclaimed in horror.

"What in God's name was that?!" Many were shouting, along with proclamations of, "It's the devil itself!" Then, all as one, the population ran outside to follow it to where the tunnel let out behind Mary's room. Where the two goats had been discovered, what seemed like ages ago.

Martha stayed behind with Mary who was shaking and still screaming sporadically. When she wasn't screaming, she was muttering over and over again, "ItwasLazarusItwasLazarusItwasLazarus."

Martha meanwhile inspected her sister from head to toe, making sure none of the blood covering Mary was from any suffered wound of her own. Over the next few mechanical, silent and surreal moments, she helped clean and dress her younger sister. Martha then gingerly guided a near catatonic Mary to the bed. There she held Mary's head in her lap while stroking her damp hair gently and humming a random, soothing tune.

"Don't worry," Martha whispered. "Jesus will fix this."

The corners of Mary's mouth turned down and she looked at her older sister out of the edge of her partially closed hazel eye. Without a hint of a slur to her voice, she replied pessimistically, "No, he won't." Then she closed her eyes again, brought her head up a handbreadth and then slammed it down once, as if to make Martha's lap contour by force to the shape of her head.

Martha, still whispering, but sounding shocked and on the cusp of reprimanding, said, "Mary! We must trust in the Lord. We must have faith that through Him all things are possible."

The younger sister laid with her arms crossed underneath her covered breasts and her eyes squeezed closed. She replied soberly, "Shut up. Through Him we have blood on our hands."

Martha gasped. The big secret they had left unspoken between each other, had now been spoken. Lately, when Martha experienced random, lucid moments on the matter, she'd been practicing stuffing it down and denying the fact of their complacency in their "brother's" nightly mayhem. She had held some shred of hope that Mary had been keeping herself too numb and preoccupied with debauchery to notice their guilt by lack of action. Martha also held fast to her own hope for her brother, that, each day, seemed to be slipping through her fingers. Like she was trying to grip oil in her fist.

Martha sent up a quick prayer for strength and patience. Then tried again, "Mary, we have to be strong in the Lord."

"We have to kill it," Mary stated as a matter of truth. Her words, when delivered, were as bereft of emotion as possible.

Hearing it out loud from Mary actually shocked Martha and she launched into a rushed, raspy whispered explanation about why they couldn't. Shouldn't. Wouldn't do anything of the sort to their baby brother.

"We must hold fast to faith, Mary," Martha beseeched her sister. Her sister stayed silent. "There is still something good inside of him. I believe it. I mean, after all, he didn't hurt you. Right?"

Still no response. "Mary?" Martha intoned, leaning over her sister.

There was no reply from Mary. Martha looked down closer at her sister and saw her face had relaxed. Her jaw was slightly shifted. For the most part, her sister's grimace had faded. There was a gentle, deep rise and fall of restful breathing. Behind the thin veil of her shadowed eyelids, Mary's eyes rapidly flicked back and forth.

After sitting this way for a little while, Martha became lulled into a comfortable thought pattern, cycling between Phillip and Jesus and Phillip and Lazarus and Phillip. And Phillip. Mary's light, charming snores began to deepen and take on a labored, more throaty characteristic. Her brows pinched together and her eyes flickered back and forth in slumbering consternation, like two stones floating loosely beneath the surface, at the whims of the current, near the scrummy edge of a lonely pond.

After a little while like this, the young, dumb, larger manservant, Jacob, that had broken down the door earlier, and the venerable Hannah entered. Their entry made Martha aware that she had been holding her breath for some time. They stood in front of The Lady of the House with their hands clasped at their waists and soberly briefed her on what had transpired outside.

Jacob said in a low voice, "The beast took to the rooftops. We lost it not long after." When no one spoke right away, he added, "It's an awful, fast thing."

Martha recalled her first sight of her transformed brother, speeding across the rooftops, wondering what on Earth could move that quickly while holding an injured, maybe already dead, pre-adolescent child. This time though, Lazarus was carrying an injured, maybe just almost dead, full grown man. Still, he was capable of zooming across the skyline of Bethany at a breakneck pace. Its strength, be it bestowed by way of demon possession or not, was truly impressive.

Hannah kept quiet and stared unblinking rage at Martha.

Other servant girls entered the destroyed room and began to bustle about with buckets of water from the well, cleaning up all of the liberal dashes of blood splattered from floor to ceiling. Stripping the room of all douched fabrics. Opening the window to let the cool night air in and as much of the pungent air out as possible. With some difficulty, two of the small servant girls pushed the large chest back into its place against the wall. Wine goblets, emptied decanters, half eaten platters of food, and ash littered incense dispensers were cleared away in a mesmerizing display of efficiency.

Jacob was still droning on about what they could do to pursue it, or what they could do to reinforce the house's defenses against intruders.*Starting with sealing up that hole behind that storage chest there.* He seemed to be talking all on his own. Deftly answering his own posed questions.

Hannah, still glared with unflinching disdain for Martha, who sat cross legged and drained to empty now that her adrenaline had ebbed away. Humming an innocent tune. Running her delicate fingers through her younger sister's dark hair in a soothing, meditative way. Hoping, praying in her mind for the Lord to show up soon. Pining in her heart and soul and loins for Phillip to be there.

Martha imagined, for a moment, that it was her head resting on Phillip's lap. Looking up into his deep brown eyes, while he stroked hypnotic traces along her hairline with his big, bulky fingers. Martha allowed herself to stay stuck in this daydream until-

"-finish up by hiring a private armed guard to patrol at night," Jacob was saying. "What do you think, my Lady?"

The room seemed emptier, now. All of the bustling housemaids had departed, leaving in their stead a litany of freshly scrubbed surfaces and the pervasive odor of lemon and vinegar. More than a hint of the ghastly aroma of tonight's event in that very room still remained, despite the maids liberal dousing. It would be days before that scent of decay was gone.

Martha nodded up and down a slow, silent agreement. Not entirely sure as to what she was agreeing to. Her cognition hurried to catch up with where the conversation was at on... what?...increasing the security of the home?

"So that's a yes?" Big Jacob broached delicately while picking at his fingers in a fidgety manner. "To all?"

"Yes," Martha answered with more conviction, even though she still wasn't fully sure as to what she was agreeing to. But, Jacob had a good heart and she knew it was all aimed towards keeping everyone safe. He most certainly seemed overjoyed that she had agreed, without any push back, to all of his suggestions...whatever they may be.

Hannah, however, stepped forward, clutching her apron with little hard, white stone like knuckles. Her ancillary face had reddened to a near crimson hue, making the whites of her eyes and teeth all the more pronounced, as if they were almost glowing. The lines had become significantly more pronounced all along her pinched lips. "What of the Passover, Martha?" Hannah asked through a clenched jaw. "Tis only a couple of days away. All of the preparations have been made." She paused for a weighty moment, breathing laboriously in and out of her nose, allowing time for her next question to land heavily with a double meaning, "Do you still want to continue on the same course that you are on?"

Martha sensed something strange in Hannah's tone and wording, but paid no mind. She permitted the snide spice in her head maid's tone to roll on over and past her like a small wave overhead. She replied thoroughly exhausted, or maybe just exasperated, or both, "Yes, Hannah. Everything will continue as planned."

A quick flash of fury contorted Hannah's features before she spun around and stomped out of the room. She ripped the door open and left it completely ajar upon her exit. Martha seemed to not notice Hannah's obvious utter distaste for her decision.

Jacob, however, had clearly noticed the slight uncomfortable squabble between the two women. He shuffled forward in tiny incremental fingerbreadths and broached Martha with trepidation behind his tremored voice, "My Lady?"

Martha sharply inhaled some of the lemony, vinegar-laden, foul air through her nose as if being awoken from near dozing. She smiled warm and almost motherly at the younger, big man, "Yes, Jacob?"

"If there is nothing else, I'll wish you goodnight," Jacob said timidly. His steps began to reverse him towards the door in small, little shuffling advancements.

"Yes," Martha confirmed and then yawned wide. Wide enough to make an audible *Crack,* which sounded loud in the empty room. Her eyes watered. Bleary tears distorted the room and the hulking frame of Jacob as he edged closer to the open door. "Goodnight Jacob," she heard herself say with a thick tongue.

As she leaned back against the pillow, with Mary's head in her lap, drooling and lightly snoring, she could hear Jacob's voice from a distance, fading and saying something about *Getting started right away* and *Not to worry.* But the rest of whatever he was saying all became muffled and lost to the eternal, dark sleep that now took her like a thief in the night. Or, maybe more apt, like a brotherly ghoul slipping away into the night with a fresh, new victim.

iv

Tiny white clusters of flowers, by the billions, speckled the myriad of branches in the thousands of Jerusalem olive trees. Their fragrance was subtle, yet still attracted birds and bees by innumerable droves. The shaded canopies of the grove were absolutely humming with sweet buzzing, fluttering life.

A hidden sun had already reached and passed beyond its zenith in the daily scheduled azimuth. Up above the treetops, the day was warm and, to be sure, blindingly bright. Here, beneath the teeming boughs, it was much cooler and could've been mistaken for late afternoon, nearing dusk.

Jesus and his twelve treaded confidently across the Mount of Olives, towards the site of Lazarus' family tomb. Starting with the Lord leading the group and, of course, faithful, fervent Peter at his side. John behind them, with Andrew and James (Son of Zebedee). Following behind these three were Philip and Bartholomew, walking the path silently. Then Matthew, Thomas, James (Son of Alphaeus). Closely trailing next was Thaddaeus and Simon the Zealot. Then, even further behind all of these, traipsing along with a nasty scowl on his face and his arms crossed obstinately, was Judas Iscariot.

They all walked along, not altogether quiet. Beyond the thirteen pairs of sandals crunching on the path, they listened to God's work at play in its musical craft all around in nature. A cool breeze ruffled the tree boughs noisily. Birds sang sweet tunes and the bees provided a low frequency drone. Meanwhile, beneath it all, Jesus and Peter were involved in a low conversation between one another.

"Any man is capable of betrayal," Jesus was saying, "Although, it is only a selfless man that is capable of loyalty."

"My Lord," Peter began with concern in his voice. He then asked, "Are you saying that one of us will betray you?"

"I said **any** man is capable, Peter," Jesus responded calmly. "For who can know what truly is in that man's heart, but the Most High God and that man alone?"

"But, Lord," Peter beseeched, "My heart *is* pure."

Jesus smiled comforting and warm at his troubled apostle. The Lord placed a consoling hand upon Peter's shoulder covered by his smelly, rough spun robe. "All men are born into sin, my dear Peter. Including yourself, your nature is prone to sin." Peter's facial expression went from anxious hopefulness, to bleak disappointment in the blink of an eye. "All men have the inherent evil of the first parents, Adam and Eve, inscribed upon their hearts at birth."

"Not my heart, Lord," Peter disputed louder. "There is no evil inscribed upon my heart."

The others following behind them broke from their monotonous focus on the *Crunch-Crunch* of their collective footsteps and began to take notice of the worrisome conversation up ahead. One by one, down the line, they all closed the distance between themselves and The Messiah, to see what had prompted the rise in Peter's voice.

All, except Judas. He still hovered far away from the rest of the group. Arms crossed in defiance, eyes dead in their sockets and his mouth turned down dramatically at the corners. The gait of his tread seemed as though he were being tugged along against his will. Almost as if he were leaning away and resisting against a force or something stronger that was pulling him along. Like there was an invisible rope tied around his waist.

Jesus went on to tell most of them, "Truly I tell you that the hearts of men can be likened to that of the jackal." The Lord was speaking as though from far away. Loud enough for most of them to hear his words, but in a tone as if he were pontificating alone. "Seen how a family of jackals will descend upon a carcass and still manage to fight one another viciously as they pick the bones clean of the rotting meat."

Voices of the encroaching, circling apostles now began to bark and yip in valid concern, "My Lord?"-"What do you speak of?"-"Jackals, Messiah?"

As if a dense black cloud passed over the face of the sun, the sky above the canopy overhead then darkened by many considerable shades, causing a further nervous stir amongst most of the men. All around them the atmosphere took on a strange, fuzzy, humming quality. A tinny ringing in all of their ears caused further panic amongst them. They pressed their Lord for further explanation on this and of his metaphor.

Jesus' expression had become as dour and dark as the dusky sky up above as he continued, "It's only then, once the skeleton is revealed, that you realize the carcass they've been picking from is just that of another jackal."

"My Lord!" Multiple men, now upset, pushed in closer. Tripping over themselves and each other to reach their leader. "What do you speak of? Betrayal? Jackals?"

Peter barked back at his crowding spiritual brothers, "Quiet!"

However, the apostles weren't quiet. They kept picking and gnawing. Nipping and yapping.They were beginning to take on vague characteristics similar to the pack of wild jackals spoken of in the parable. Near to snarling and biting for favorable position in the Lord's eyes.

John now pleaded from behind Peter's shoulder, "My Lord, are you saying one of us will betray you?"

Bartholomew's deep resonant voice overlapped John's question with questions of his own, "Which one? Who?"

The surrounding apostles then broke into an indecipherable, garbled opera of finger pointing accusations and soul saving exonerations. Proclamations of unbreakable devotion were yipped and barked from one and all. Whistleblowing confessions of the sins of their apostle brothers were bandied about recklessly. Promises were ready to be signed in blood. Any terms for bargaining and negotiating were on the table.

Judas, who was still sour and not engaging as the others were, trailing well behind the group, then heard Jesus' voice, clear as a bell, right in his ear. As close, as if he were standing right next to him, *"Is it you?"*

Meanwhile, the ringing in the apostles' ears disappeared, the atmosphere around them returned to normal and the sky had brightened back to early afternoon.

Jesus had brightened as well and was speaking in a soft, reassuring tone to the others. Trying to calm down the pack, he said, "My dear apostles, I merely stated that man is born with the capacity for betrayal." This abruptly quieted their loud scavenging for exoneration down to a couple grumbling attempts to interrupt. "Through faith in me and My Heavenly Father however, a man can achieve a pure heart. He will not be like the rest of the scavenging jackals roaming about."

They all could see a break in the thick grove up ahead. Jesus was finishing up his point, "You see, my dear apostles, the man, through his well applied faith in the Most High God, will find himself elevated in thought and action. Abandoning his base desires, leaving them to the simple beasts."

There wasn't much time for the twelve to digest the lesson of the jackal parable, though. They were all halted dead in their tracks. The olive grove had fully receded and opened up to a familiar limestone encrusted courtyard. The happy, buzzing bees and flitting, chirping birds were not to be found in this place, anymore. They had come to the entry of the courtyard and there was a true corporeal evil emanating outward from the, otherwise, serene place of rest on the just on the inside.

Jesus was the first to cross beneath the stone archway, past the threshold into the courtyard. He was immediately followed closely by Peter. Then, one by one, with trepidation most of the rest entered the incredibly minatory area. An unspoken fear had gripped them all in a cold clutch by the Adam's Apple and the testicles.

To the apostles, it seemed as though each of their mortal bodies had become weighted down entirely. As though, the moment they entered this space, gravity began to pull down upon them in a more intense fashion. Also, the atmosphere had dimmed considerably. Not as if it were darker, like earlier, but more like every vibrant color from before was now left stripped and devoid of vibrancy. Like the daytime had been washed in a depressing sepia. An ominous, tainted quality clung to the air and was noticeably tangible on the back of the tongue. A wave of nausea steadily crept over most of the men as they stumbled closer to the tomb's entrance.

Pallid white headed, brown feathered mangy griffon vultures with stained red beaks were perched and scattered around the periphery of the scene. They groaned metallically and flapped their large, impressive wings irritably at the presence of their queasy new arrivals. Random, sporadic shifting from foot to foot, added to the display of the bird's uneasiness.

Judas, however, was obedient to his fear. He remained planted firmly in place. Arms crossed in a defensive posture. A fearful scowl screwed his features up into a mask of hateful disdain. He remained decidedly guarded, just outside the low stone wall and arched entryway, at the edge of the grove.

It wasn't long before some of the men walking behind Jesus noticed little piled clusters of random white bones shoved up against the interior courtyard wall. A few of the apostles pointed and shouted, "Look!" upon seeing ghastly, white skulls smiling eternal grins at them from blackened, emptied sockets. Stacks of these cleaned, human bones were heaped up against the gnarled, knotty trunks of the courtyard's mature olive trees. It almost seemed as if some attempted haphazard care had been taken in trying to tidy up the gruesome, macabre collection of shellacked human remains.

It was then that some others became aware of the large, dark congealed stain on the limestone pathway leading the courtyard. The color was infinitely black with a bland, matte sheen. Peter was kneeling down, brushing his fingertips, so as to study the mysterious stain closer. Matthew knelt down beside his spiritual brother and asked him, "What is it Peter?"

"Blood," Peter said. He scanned the circumference of the stain. "An ample amount of it too."

Some of the surrounding apostles within earshot asked excitedly all at once, "What is that?"-"Blood?"-"Are you sure?"

After seeing the amount of bones and blood, out in the open, some of the men turned and hurriedly retreated to a safer spot back over by Judas, beneath the courtyard archway. This now left it to where they were almost split into two equal groups. Seven within the courtyard. Six outside.

The enormous circular stone had been rolled back to fully eclipse the tomb's small entrance, just as they had found it upon their last arrival, in the middle of the night. As they closed the distance, the rancid smell of old decay floated out and drowned every inhaled lungful. Peter retched involuntarily. Some of the nearby apostles, in reflex, covered their mouths and noses with the dirty sleeves of their filthy rough spun robes.

Jesus stoically approached the thick, massive stone. More than a few fat, buzzing flies hovered and touched down on all of the wonderful, soiled surfaces. He sent up a brief, but intense, interior prayer up to his Heavenly Father, then placed his hand upon the tombstone's rough exterior. After a long thoughtful moment, he put his ear to the face of the stone and listened intently. Some of the apostles held their breath during the lengthy suspense.

Time stretched out into an infinity of stasis. Conjuring up thoughts of images of elongated, drawn out grains of sand slowly drifting down, like dreamy, weightless angel feathers descending within the boundaries of a gargantuan hourglass.

Through the microscopic pores of the cool tombstone, Jesus felt what could be described as the excretion of burning, hot slime. Like acidic, thick honey seeping out past hard, cold apertures. An evil, unseen toxin that oozed and cursed this entire burial ground.

Jesus pulled away from the stone, feeling a scathing, throbbing pain where his hands and face had touched. A sensation on the side of his face, where it pressed against the stone, like it was now blistering and bubbling up.

"Lazarus?!" He called out boldly, while rubbing his healing, cooling hands together and applying a bit of his God-given power to his own cheek, temple and ear.

Just the surrounding griffon vultures hissed, flapped their wings and groaned in response to Jesus' call. Uncomfortably shifting their dingy, hulking, aviary bodies from foot to foot, while watching the group of humans watching them. Their pale, bald heads seemed to hover in a magical, levitating way. Supported on long, phallic-like curved necks, flicking sharply this way and that, from angle to angle. Multiple pairs of pure, black beaded eyes focused intensely on the newcomers. Maybe the vultures were guarding their treasure trove of picked clean bones. Maybe the birds were making sure that none of these interlopers were there to steal any of their hoarded cache.

"Lazarus?!" Jesus called again, slapping his open palm on the face of the stone. Following another lengthy period of silence, Jesus turned to the others and shrugged. "Come," Jesus instructed. "Let's get this open."

It was then, at that very moment, that the immense stone rolled cautiously, in a slow, subtle move to the side. Fingerbreadth by fingerbreadth. Only coming open enough to expose a small pie of the internal absolute darkness of the tomb on the top and bottom. Silence, flies and putrefaction exuded in a big wafting barrel of a wave out from the entrance. The bordering vultures flapped and hissed. A couple of the mangy buzzards floated down weightless from their lofty perches and laid claim to some of the bigger piles of bones to stand over. Spreading their impressive wingspan wide, as though they were guarding their chosen pile explicitly from what they knew was concealed in the darkness. Or, maybe a better way of phrasing it would be, from what came out of the darkness at night.

Everyone outside of the tomb had become crystallized in place. Time stood painfully still as they all were coming to the realization of the stone rolling aside with ease. Being maneuvered from within by something powerful and hidden. This summoned more images of feathery, buoyant grains of sand, cascading down in a sepia tinted hourglass. Long stretched out bits of time hovering in mid decent, like dust motes dancing as angels would in the air.

Jesus had spun around at the sound of the stone scraping on stone and the vulture's strange hissing. He now crept forward circumspectly. Waving away at some of the annoying flies. "Lazarus?" The Lord called out. They all stared from their travel-worn, dirty, bearded faces into the small, infinitely black space. Anxiously waiting and hoping for...nothing. For most of the twelve, their breath was caught. Subconsciously held captive in their lungs, just as Martha herself would do in such a situation.

"La-" Jesus started again, but was immediately cut off by the sound of many strained voices harmonizing and ringing out from the blank nothingness beyond the threshold, "Why..are you...here...Son of...God?!"

Long, shocked moments passed without an answer. Then, Jesus spoke, querying, "Lazarus? Is that you?" When no answer was given, Jesus continued, "Lazarus, your sisters grow worried." His pained brown eyes surveyed the huge bloodstain and piles of bones littering the courtyard. "We are all greatly concerned for your soul, brother."

"Soul?" The hellish chorus mused. "Yes...this...vessel once...housed a soul."

"Once?" Peter repeated, puzzled. Unsure that he had heard the numerous strummed vocal cords from within the tomb correctly.

"Yes," Lazarus continued. The vocal cords being manipulated, coupled with the echo from within the chamber, made it very difficult to understand. It said something to the effect of, "Very much...like...how The…Son…of God…became...living...upon birth...to life, so too, I...came to...live...in this…body upon...birth...from death."

Jesus took a miniature step closer to the entrance. Interrupting Lazarus' discourse. "Why not come out here, Lazarus," The Lord invited. "So that we may speak on such matters face to face?"

"No," was the blunt, instant answer from the interior darkness.

"Why not?" Jesus asked again. He would try to lure him with a honeyed statement. "It would be good to see your face again, my brother."

"NNNNNOOOOOO!!!!!" Lazarus howled from the void. Loud enough to make the men as far back as where Judas stood cover their ears in reflex from the piercing decibels. The surrounding buzzards hopped around as well, greatly disturbed. Flapping their wings wide and hissing returned threats in answer to the demonic scream.

Jesus spoke in a calm tone to his volatile creation within the tomb, "I can sense your reluctance to come out, Lazarus. I want to know why."

"Too...painful," came the low reply from Lazarus.

"Painful?" Jesus asked, suspicious. "How so?"

There was the sharp, echoing din of something reticulated and hard smacking something harder and more solid on the inside of the tomb. It was a stripped bare spinal cord clattering upon the bloodsoaked stone floor, but no one outside of the crypt knew that. This was followed by the many voices, sounding as though they were coming from the bottom of a well and speaking in candid terms, "The light...The warmth."

"Daylight?" Jesus ventured. He glanced up above to the Heavens. "The daylight is painful for you?"

Inside the tomb's antechamber Lazarus softly touched where its face had been burned. "The…light burns."

"Demonic!" Judas shouted from back beyond the courtyard, only to be stifled by an invisible force seizing his own vocal cords. His mouth and tongue kept enunciating the words, *The body is possessed*-and-*It is an empty vessel!* but his voice had been stolen away entirely. Peter, who was still hovering close by The Lord's side, turned and glared at his fellow apostle, Judas.

"What if I come in and talk to you?" Jesus asked. "Would you allow me in so that I may, at the very least, check on your well being, brother?"

A short pause of contemplation, then, the overlapping voices from the bottom of the well, strummed a short answer, "No." Its reply was followed by the stone being gently rolled back into its fully closed position.

Jesus marched forward through the flies and the deathly stench. With his right palm he slapped the face of the stone over and over, "Lazarus, don't do this! Don't shut me out!!" He paused for a slim moment. Getting frustrated Jesus slapped some more, and added, "Lazarus, I need you!"

They all waited. After a long, hanging moment, Peter spoke to Jesus' back, "My Lord, he's not what he once was."

Jesus ignored Peter and rapidly slapped his palm against the face of the stone again, making a sound like small thunder claps, rippling and echoing in this small space of the courtyard. He boomed, "LAZARUS!!!"

The enormous tombstone rolled all of the way open in one swift motion, causing Jesus to back into the safety net of Peter and Matthew's awaiting embrace. From out of the solid dark opening was thrown a half-chewed-on femur bone of a human. It came to a meaty, slapping landing right at Jesus' sandals, which caused himself and his apostles to leap back two full cubits. The meat on the bone was greyish and bloodless, yet, it still sent the surrounding vultures into a ravenous frenzy. The feathered fiends all swooped down and attacked the discarded bone with voracious enthusiasm. Squawking, hissing and fighting amongst one another over the crude morsel. Just like the jackals in the parable.

From the pocket of Peter and Matthew's arms, Jesus bunched his hands up into fists. Digging his fingernails into his calloused palms and proclaiming in a bold, stentorian voice, "LAZARUS! BY THE POWER OF THE MOST HIGH GOD, I COMMAND YOU TO COME OUT!!"

A sinister chuckle oozed out of the darkness, "Stupid words...*Michael.* Your Father...speaks...directly to...us."

It was obvious to Jesus that the demon had seen his spirit and recognized it as the Archangel that it had shared Heaven with eons ago, before it was cast out.

However, for the divided dozen, shock and confusion flowed through their minds like blurred rushing river rapids. The most perplexed amongst them was Peter. He wondered in his subconscious, *What was that name? Michael?*

In a tone dripping with malevolence, Lazarus taunted, "Your...Most…High Father is... most…unhappy...with you."

Deep beyond the tomb's threshold, a vague outline of a hunched, ashen body was barely decipherable among the darkness. Faint contours of a naked man's diminished body stood out a shade of black lighter than the rest of the interior of the tomb. It appeared that Lazarus was holding something, but they couldn't make out what it was. Something shapeless and bulky extending down from its right hand. Maybe another half eaten femur bone?

Jesus stepped away from his close, faithful apostles that remained in the courtyard and came right up to the dark, rectangular portal of the tomb. His fierce stare pierced through the thick, shifting clouds of flies and rancid stink into the infinite blackness. Those brown eyes of his burned with a godly, electric intensity.

Lazarus, within the antechamber, was still finding copious amounts of amusement and chortling at the expense of Jesus and his twelve, "You came...here...for nothing. Now…Leave!!"

Jesus tapped into his great power and passed into a realm alternate to the physical. The spirit realm. Jesus lit up his whole entire being, from head to sandal, like a fiery beacon to be seen from hundreds of furlongs away. As bright as the sun. As bright as the very face of God himself. Shining so brilliantly as to cause an instant blinding to mortal human eyes. However, the mortal human eyes of the apostles were still stuck in the physical realm. Those in close proximity to the ignited Jesus Christ felt something like an invisible solid balloon of pressure, pushing and expanding outward from Jesus.

Along with Jesus' holy combustion of himself, he also adopted that sickening, fuzzy hum (which would've been familiar to Mary, from her reoccurring nightmare). The hum now emanated from The Lord and made the very air feel charged. Like it was magnetic for flesh. Fizzy. As though the molecules in the atmosphere were alive and stinging all over like tiny wasps. Again, to his closer followers in the courtyard, this sound and feeling of a humming, charging up of power, was only interpreted as an unexplainable tingling itch and a simple ringing in their ears.

These two spiritual changes of The Messiah were strictly visible and felt only by the demon that was using Lazarus' noncompliant, dead body like a costume. Upon seeing the holy fire donned and feeling the burn of the Heavenly, warm, biting hum, Lazarus shrieked. It held up a blood stained hand in helpless defense before turning and leaping away out of sight. The demon driving the body sent it down a set of stone stairs deeper into the pit of the crypt.

The Lord went to step inside of the antechamber of the tomb, to follow after Lazarus, only to be grasped by his sleeve from behind by his most fervent. Peter was looking into his face with much aggrieved worry. "My Lord, no!" Peter pleaded simply.

Jesus put his crackling, powerful hand on Peter's and reassured him, "My dear Peter, there is nothing to fear."

Peter felt his tight grip on Jesus' robes loosen involuntarily. There was a strong, unseen force prying open his fingers. Before he knew it, or could make an attempt to protest further, Jesus was slipping in and disappearing past the sackcloth veil of the black threshold.

Within the tomb, the smell was vomitous. The amount of flies and maggots inside the crypt was vulgar, although they kept their distance from Jesus and his emanating power. There were far more bones and skulls in here than what was laying out in the courtyard. Piles of viscous viscera in various stages of dehydration were randomly splattered and puddled across the floor, walls and ceiling. Large, congealed puddles of thick, jiggly blood covered the low spots of the foundation. The hum pulsating from Jesus, vibrated and rippled their surfaces in sickening visual disturbance. It appeared more like a saturated, functional, cannibalistic abattoir than a dry, dusty tomb of sweet repose.

Steps led further down to the catacombs and the older ancestors, long departed. Infinitely darker than the initial ground floor darkness. Just past the first few treads of barely perceptible steps, the dark was truly recondite in its depths.

From this deeper, abyssal void, Lazarus threatened. Growling in its many voices, "Stay...away."

Jesus took the first steps down. His sandals stuck annoyingly in some of the tacky blood on the stone steps, producing loud, echoing squishes and pasty ripping sounds. He amplified the brightness of his angelic firelight and the potency of his Heavenly hum as he descended.

Lazarus was squealing, "Stay away!" Jesus could hear the body of Lazarus flopping and slapping against the moist floors and walls in a frenzied, manic session. Like a large, air deprived, fish flipping about on the deck of a boat. "STAY AWAY!"

Jesus stepped off the last stair and put his travel-worn sandal down into a fingerbreadth deep puddle of bloody ick, touching the bottom of his foot into the cold, thick wetness. He paid it no mind and with his following steps, walked weightless on top of the congealed puddle. By the pure light pouring out of him, Jesus saw before him an aisle with ancient, sealed sarcophagus on each side. Behind these were slotted walls, loculus, with long extinguished torches and shrouded mounds of the forgotten remnants of ancestral skeletons. A slab of granite, used as a station for burial preparation, sat central to the large lower level of the crypt.

Jesus followed the abundantly violent thrashing and empty threats down to the end of the bloodsplattered aisle. There, behind the last sarcophagus on the left, in the darkest corner, crouched the grey, twitching, blood smeared cadaver of Lazarus. Its distended belly hung low enough to dip and smear into the jellied blood that covered the entire floor. Snarling and banging its head into the stone wall. Between each impact of its head with the wall, it screamed vile atrocities, "I'LL KILL YOU AND BATHE IN YOUR BLOOD!!" and, "I'LL KILL EVERYONE YOU KNOW!!" also "YOUR FATHER IS FURIOUS WITH YOU!!!"

The Lord, in all of his mighty, blinding glory, came up close on the thing that used to be his dear friend Lazarus, spun him to face the glory and forcefully commanded, "SILENCE! TELL ME YOUR NAME DEMON!!"

The body of Lazarus began to convulse and writhe. It started to hack obnoxiously, while doubled over, its spine protruding out in grotesque, shining nodules. Then, from out of its mouth fell clump after clump of sallow, rotting, undigested flesh. Its regurgitation of rancid, grey meat splashed and piled up in an ankle deep puddle of blood. The once distended, pregnant looking belly shrunk and had now sucked in nearly all of the way to its backbone.

"ENOUGH WITH YOUR SILLY PAGEANTRY!!" Jesus erupted, glowing brighter and hotter against the dead skin of Lazarus. To the evil spirit that inhabited the long deceased body, it felt like extreme scorching that went all the way past the decayed muscle to the bone. The holy fire seemed to penetrate deep into the pocketed marrow.

The body of Lazarus cowered and whimpered. Turning away from the celestial countenance of The Lord in all of his unimaginable glory. It was trying to claw its way further into the corner. Then it tried to slither into the very bottom, unsealed loculus, that had been carved into the stone wall centuries ago.

Jesus hovered in closer. Humming louder. Loud enough to rattle Lazarus' loose rotten teeth and pale eyes within their shrunken sockets. "TURN AND LOOK AT ME!"

The grey, blood-slimed body twitched and squealed. Its lower naked half stuck halfway out of the loculus. Its knees and shins slipped and slid in a bloody pool.

Jesus pressed up even closer to it. Shining brighter. Radiant, like a divine star pulled from the night sky and placed in this eternally dark pit. His eyeballs were only sclera, glowing completely white. His long, brown hair, beard and robes shifted and flowed with an effect as if He were underwater. "LOOK! AT! ME!!!" The Son of God thundered.

Lazarus quieted and squirmed back out of the slot. Crouching, with its pale gaze cast downward. It was growling low in multiple tones, partially from pain, mostly from anger. It kept rubbing at the burned, ashen slash across its face, feeling as though the singed mass was boiling beneath the blackened dead flesh.

The Lord visibly dimmed and the fuzzy hum subsided a little. Not enough to relieve the discomfort inflicted, but enough that it would listen to what Jesus had to say.

'Lazarus!" Jesus said sternly, "or whoever has captured your body and parades it around now, you will hear my words and abide by them! Do you understand?!"

Lazarus growled a gravelly threat in its throat. It held up a hand to block Jesus' blinding illumination and squinted through the jagged shadow its fingers cast. Cracked, rust stained teeth grit together and were bared in pure helpless hatred for being made to come to heal. Just like a rabid dog foaming at the mouth, having obedience involuntarily foisted upon it by means of being beaten with an unforgiving, decisive rod.

Jesus levitated a full handbreadth above a rippling puddle of blood. His hair and robes billowed all around him in ethereal dreaminess. "Even though I should destroy you right now, I need you temporarily," Jesus' voice rang loud and clear in the lower level crypt, although his lips never moved.

Suddenly, Lazarus attempted to leap at Jesus, with its claws and teeth at the ready to eviscerate. This resulted in The Lord cranking up the scorching brightness shining from him to a level that would rival that of the brightest star in the universe. Also, the hum emanating off of him grew to a deafening throttle that seemed to push off wave after wave of shredding, extreme heat against Lazarus' cold, decayed skin.

The body of Lazarus recoiled and whimpered, as a kicked mongrel would. It hunkered down low to the floor and tried to hide its face. If the body had possessed a tail, it would be firmly tucked up between its legs.

"DON'T TRY THAT AGAIN!" Jesus bellowed. Once more, without physically enunciating the words. Verbally attacking through a spiritual, telepathic power.

Satisfied that Lazarus would remain docile, Jesus, once again, lowered the light and the temperature radiating off of him. Lazarus quivered like an autumn leaf on a gusty day. Reduced from being a terrifying, monstrous abomination to a weak, pathetic abomination.

"Now, listen well," Jesus continued, powerful and sonorous. "In two days time, I will return to collect you. The miracle of your resurrection will be testified on that night."

Stunned into being stupefied, the demon swiveled the head of Lazarus on a rigored, cracking neck up towards the vision of Jesus floating above it. Jesus continued, smiling, "You will do this to bear witness before many."

"I will...not!" Lazarus argued back, even though the conviction behind its many voices felt flimsy. "I...will...kill you!"

Jesus recognized the empty threat for the nothing that it was and kept going, unphased, "The miracle of your resurrection shall serve as a testament to the power and compassion of The One True God."

"NO!!" Lazarus reacted

"SILENCE BEAST!" Jesus smote, reducing the fearsome animated corpse to a scared, groveling whelp. The holy fire surrounding The Lord absolutely raged. Making molten lava seem chilly by comparison. He was rising higher above the floor, humming to an extent where little bolts of cracking, energetic lightning jumped and jigged all over the outline of his being.

The beast groaned loudly and, despite the massive pain it felt, it shifted with difficulty and made as though it would try to lunge at Jesus once again.

"STAY DOWN!" Jesus' voice rang in the hollow chamber. Lazarus did. Its frail looking body shied away from the blazing holy power that Jesus produced. It appeared to be utterly exhausted from the excruciating pain and the hopeless struggle campaign it had been waging in futility against a being much more powerful than it could ever hope to be.

That powerful being, Jesus, now floating a good cubit above the bloodied floor, reiterated from earlier, "Two days!" Slowly, The Lord rotated about face and floated back past the flanking, ancient sarcophagus towards the stairs. He said one more thing before reaching the steps leading up, "Be ready to bear witness for The Most High."

He ascended and left the demon possessed body of Lazarus shaking in the dark, on its hands and knees in a sanguine pool. As he topped the rise of the last step, his sandal gently touched down on the desecrated stone floor of the ground level antechamber and he became just the human, Jesus of Nazareth once again.

Out beyond the rectangle of light, the day appeared blinding white, even though some time had elapsed. The air was a veritable perfume in comparison to the sludge he had just been immersed in. His twelve, all outside of the courtyard wall now (with Judas), crowded their faces in and around one another's. Peeking over shoulders and dancing anxiously from foot to foot. Awaiting Jesus' safe return.

Upon seeing The Messiah emerging safe and sound from the crypt, Peter instantly rushed back into the courtyard to him, followed by the rest, excluding Judas of course. The remaining eleven wrapped their Lord up in a collective, giant embrace that squeezed the fresh air out of his lungs and brought stars to the edge of his sight. When they released him, they flooded him with question after question, "My Lord! Are you alright?"-"Are you hurt?"-"Did you kill it, Jesus?"

He hurried them back out of the cursed courtyard and answered **none** of their questions. Instead, he walked ahead of them, calling over his shoulder, "I'm starving. Come! Let's make haste to the house of Simon the Leper."

While trailing behind, Peter noticed the one foot and sandal of Jesus being bloodied. "My Lord! You are bleeding?!"

This alerted some of the others who were also paying attention.

Peter had jogged to catch up with Jesus and match strides with him. Jesus dismissed Peter's claim that he was injured. Waving it off like it was one of the bees that, at the moment, buzzed joyfully overhead. Or, you could even say like a swath of flies that droned, joylessly down below. Take your pick.

"What happened down there, Lord?" Peter asked in a hushed tone that the others strained to, but couldn't hear.

"I talked with Lazarus," Jesus stated.

Peter insisted, "No, Rabbi. There's blood on your foot." Jesus tenderly tried to shush him. Peter added, "Why did Lazarus call you by the name Michael?"

Jesus laughed, forcing fake mirth and said, "Peter, you are by far my most fervent and most persistent jackal."

"What?" Peter asked. Flummoxed. Recalling the parable of betrayal from earlier.

Most of the rest of the twelve had caught up with them, squashing any more confidential questions from Peter. Chants for food were announced from all, as they traveled further and further away from the oppressive burial site, with its vultures and bones, back into the realm of the living.

Meanwhile, from the darkness of the antechamber of its lair, Lazarus stared hateful, pale burning coals at all thirteen of them. Jesus would drop his guard at some point and that's when it would take its chance to strike.

V

Over the Western Bank of Bethany a golden yolk of a sun dropped low in an eternal, blue cloudless sky. At its most boiled down, it was a giant burning star touching down and dipping past the edge of this hunk of orbiting rock steadily. Another beautiful, yet dreaded, sunset. Its arrival had come much, much sooner than expected.

It had been two and half days since Phillip, riding atop Tsalav, had galloped out of Capernaum. They now found themselves approaching the border of Bethany, blanketed in a thick coat of dirt and grime. Majorly starving and thoroughly dehydrated.

Their travel schedule, to which Phillip had adhered to rigorously, afforded neither him nor the horse much sleep; not as though Phillip could get viable sleep. His mind kept cycling constant images of the burned outline of little Abigail's body burned into the face of the hill. These images were paired with memories of Lazarus emerging from the tomb with the half-chewed head of a young boy in his grip. During the span of the trip, little kernels of doubt had begun to sprout in Phillip's mind. Challenging his faith on whether or not Jesus would be able to do anything at all for Mary and Martha's brother. Phillip also couldn't deny that, as the endless, monotonous landscape passed by hypnotically for the past two days, his heart ached in longing clenches when his thoughts drifted to those of his female, childhood friend. He would lavishly bask in these lingering daydreams of taking Martha and wrapping her up in his arms. Kissing her. Squeezing her. This would occasionally lead to his mind running away with him. Conjuring up uncomfortable, bloody, horrific thoughts, committed by her monster of a brother. Phillip's protective nature would urge him in a blasting, repetitive voice to kick Tsalav faster. *Get Home.* That same voice yelling at him, telling him Martha and Mary were in danger. *Get Home!* Sometimes that voice would be full of doom and gloom, telling him he might be too late. *GET HOME!!*

Through bleary, sand beaten eyes, Phillip saw the skyline of Bethany come dimly into view, like a mirage. Tsalav's poor, worn hooves clapped, like drunken rhythmic percussion on the hard packed, well traveled dirt road. To his right, the sun was sunk down halfway to its own equator. A once baby blue sky had begun to darken and shift into familiar evening hues. The warmth of the day was waning.

Phillip saw blobby stars beginning to blink fluidly at the edge of his vision. His cracked, dry lips were parted. Halitosis breath puffed out of him in fruity, metallic wheezing gusts and his tongue stuck to the roof of his mouth. Moving without thinking about it, he unslung his water skin and what little remained in it. He tipped it over, close to his mouth and drained the last few warm drops of dirty water from it.

Almost there, thought Phillip.

Phillip's head felt as light as a feather and his eyes wanted to roll all the way up in his head. He swooned and reeled, nearly falling off the back of Tsalav before catching himself by grabbing onto the hair of the horse's mane.

The rest of the ride consisted of small pockets of lucid moments, as Phillip drifted in and out of consciousness. Huge chunks of time and chronicling were lost between elongated blinks. To Phillip's mind, he would blink and when he opened his eyes, he saw the outskirts of Bethany...

...blink...

...they were clip clopping down a wide, dusty boulevard...

...blink...

...he was staring at the gate which led to Martha's stables...

...blink...

...a large, young man was asking him muddled questions that he couldn't understand...

...blink...

...Martha held his head in her lap. She was smiling and crying while holding a water skin to his lips. He felt like he was smiling back at her, because of the pain he was distantly aware of in his split, cracked lips. The cool water she administered poured into and all around his mouth. He took a couple uncomfortable, yet blessed gulps. Martha kissed him gently on his forehead, while saying *Thank you God* over and over again...

...blink...

When Phillip finally awoke, it was in a room he had never seen before. In a bed he had never slept on before. There were two medium sized four pane windows that let in a view of a vaguely familiar fountain on a vaguely familiar atrium. The sky beyond displayed hints of pink and purple, with a few visible stars cresting above in the darker hues.

He sat bolt upright and looked about the foreign room. His eyes landed on Martha asleep atop some pillows on the floor. He blurted out loud, waking her in the process, "It's almost sunset!"

Martha's eyes snapped open and fluttered. She worked her tongue in her mouth, rolling it over her teeth. Then she sat up and stretched her arms over her head. Yawning wide. Kind of giggling as she said, "No, it's morning. I'm glad you're awake."

Philip looked about the room bewildered. Bit by bit, he was coming to the realization of where he was. This had to be Martha's room. He was apparently laying in her bed. One of her pillows was shoved up between his legs and was being smushed up against his morning wood.

Feeling ultra awkward, he arose from the bed suddenly, which was a mistake. First off, because he was unaware that he had been stripped out of his dirty, traveled robes down to just his undergarment. Second, his strong morning erection was poking straight out. And third, his legs buckled, sending him sprawling to the floor where he slapped his face and torso hard upon the mosaic floor. *Uuugghhhh,* he groaned. All three factors greatly increased the previous awkwardness he felt.

Martha pulled her blanket tighter around her and leapt up to help him, saying, "Oh, Phillip. You poor thing." She rolled him over and he groaned some more. “Are you alright?” She asked, but Phillip could swear there was a touch of that giggle again in her voice.

Their eyes locked and they couldn’t deny something unspoken and solidifying being passed between them. An understanding that, while absent, they both became very cognizant of their dependent need for one another. Time became an insignificant thing, that only existed in the natural lightening up of the room. Phillip noticed that Martha was holding her breath, and he couldn’t help but find that nuance about her totally charming and endearing.

Phillip’s stomach suddenly rumbled. It was a hollow, angry sound that gave a perfect voice for something being neglected for so long. They both chuckled now in response to his bodily function awakening them from their gazing in a twitterpated way at one another.

Martha stated the obvious, “You must be starving.”

Phillip arose and snatched the bedspread from Martha’s bed, covering his protruding immodesty. “Yes, I am,” he said, looking around the room. “Where are my clothes?”

Martha, meanwhile, had stepped behind an intricately carved, paneled room divider. There she dressed herself while telling him from the other side, “Your clothes were very dirty...and they smelled really bad.” She pulled a simple, linen robe around her. “Since Jacob is about your size, he offered to lend you a set of garments. They are folded on the table over there.” Her delicate hand extended up above the top of the panels and pointed in their general direction. “Fresh undergarments too.”

“Jacob?” Phillip repeated the name in puzzlement. Maybe he felt an early itch of jealousy.

“Yes,” Martha confirmed. While pouring water into a basin for a quick wash, she chanced to take a quick peek around the side of the panel and blushed at the amount she saw of Phillip. “He’s the young man that held you up at the gate yesterday,” she offered. She emerged from behind the room divider, drying her face and rolling her eyes, while adding, “He’s taken it upon himself to initiate stricter security around here, ever since Lazarus attacked.”

Phillip gasped and erupted, “What!? Attacked!? Mary!”

“She’s fine, she’s fine. Everyone is fine.” Martha assured him. She had come up close to him and was looking up into his deep brown eyes.

"Well, what happened?" he asked, looking down into her face. His breath was terrible, but she didn't mind it.

Martha grabbed his hand and said, "Come. Let's get some food in your belly and we'll talk." They were already out of the room and walking down the hallway. She prompted, "I'm sure you have much to tell me as well about Capernaum."

"Yes," Phillip said without much enthusiasm. "Much to tell."

She stopped without warning and spun around to him. Looking up into his burly face again. "I do have one pressing question, though."

Phillip didn't say anything verbally. He just lifted his bushy eyebrows, inviting the question.

"Who's Abigail?" Martha asked, feeling her own itch of jealousy. Phillip dropped one eyebrow and left the other raised in suspicion. "You mentioned the name in your sleep," she went on to explain.

The big man looked at her in grave seriousness and concurred what she had said earlier, "Well, like you said, there is much for us to discuss."

So it was, for the next couple of hours, in low, conspiratorial tones, over early morning tea, unleavened bread with fruit and chickpea spreads, dates, apricots, along with a variety of nuts and seeds, they regaled one another with their tales of what had transpired over the last six days. Phillip's eyes grew increasingly wide with horror upon the spilling of the details of Lazarus coming in through the secret tunnel and abducting Mary's lover from her room. Right from in between her legs. While in the middle of performing cunnilingus.

When Martha digested what Phillip told her of Capernaum, Jairus, Samantha and, ultimately, Abigail, (or, more to the point, the burned outline on the hill that was Abigail) she said empathetically, "Oh, poor thing." She sighed and added, "If only Jesus had been there to help her."

With a smidge of caution, Phillip mentioned something that had been turning over and over in his mind, 'But, Martha, it was by Jesus that she became what she became."

"That doesn't mean he wouldn't be able to fix what was wrong," Martha retorted.

"But, why was something wrong with her resurrection?" Phillip demanded. "Why is there something wrong now with Lazarus?"

Martha scoffed, "Well, I can't answer that. I just know The Lord to be mysteriously powerful."

Phillip mulled on this, unsatisfied with her line of reasoning. He worked his mouth, searching for a diplomatic way to proceed, while flicking his tongue around his molars, picking out and nibbling on little remaining bits of breakfast. He chose his next words carefully. "The Lord is certainly powerful, to be sure." He paused, then went on, "However, does willful use of that power always result in something good?"

Martha's brow furrowed down as she tried to make sense of what Phillip was saying. She challenged him by asking, "What do you mean? That my brother being alive again isn't in some way...good?"

At this point, unexpectedly, Mary entered the room, seeming very groggy. It was obvious she was just waking up, even though the hour was nearing eleven. She half heartedly stifled a wide open, purplish yawn and spoke with a thick tongue, joining the conversation without emotion, "I dun't thingk it'z any gud."

Martha glared at her younger sister, as she stumbled over to Phillip and kissed him on both cheeks, without emotion, as a means of dutiful salutation. The sour, fruity essence of stale wine that wafted from Mary, was tangible from at least a couple of cubits away. Between her drooping, dark eyelids, rested aggravated sections of thoroughly bloodshot sclera. Not to mention, that her clothing had been draped about her in such a way that it left her hairy armpit and right breast completely exposed.

Once Phillip noticed Mary's wanton impropriety, and her obliviousness to it, he immediately covered her immodesty and asked, "Mary, what's wrong with you?"

Mary lolled limply against Phillip's manly mass and laughed a hoarse, ugly honk up into his face. He looked over to Martha, who was still at the table, peeking, albeit mortified, through her fingers.

Phillip turned back to Mary and searched for something alive behind her dead, unfocused eyes. "Mary?" His great, big hands held her steady by the shoulders, while her chuckles tapered off. He tried to jolt her with one stiff shake. "Mary?!"

Mary snickered and pushed off from him. Instead of answering him, she went to the table and grabbed a picked-at-platter of random nuts, fruits and meats, as well as a semi full pitcher of water. She turned with her snatched spoils and weaved towards the door. Before reaching it, she spun around haphazardly, nearly losing her balance and stated, while gesturing with the pitcher of water, "We ull ave blud on oer handz." She looked at Martha directly, tears shaking in her reddened eyes, before continuing, "Knowing whut we know and not zaying anything. Juz allowing more tu be killed!" Her voice was rising in hysteria.

Phillip and Martha tried to gently shush her. Their hands were raised up, palms facing out. They timidly approach Mary as one would approach an unpredictable wild animal that was snarling and baring its fangs.

Before they could reach her though, she laughed again as she had before. This time, though, with active tears in her eyes. Then, she turned and tottered out the way she had come in.

Phillip turned to Martha, who was still glaring out the doorway at her sister. There was anger behind that glare, and also some fear. Phillip could sympathize with both contrasting emotions, understanding that Martha was watching her only "living" sibling deteriorate mentally, physically and emotionally right before her eyes in real time. Phillip said her name in a comforting tone while reaching out to her, "Martha."

She, instead, walked a few steps in the same direction Mary had left, before turning around and telling him in a business-like tone, "I'm going to attend to Mary. She doesn't seem well."

Phillip barked out a single, cynical *Ha!* "Well she's traumatized and drunk."

Martha continued as if he hadn't laughed or said anything, "I'd suggest, that after picking up your clean clothes and leaving, that you pray for faith in the Lord. I'd say between you and my sister, there's almost no faith to be spoken for."

She slipped out quickly before he was able to argue against her accusations. Leaving him all alone in the quiet kitchen, wearing someone else's itchy clothes.

After a few confused, paralyzed moments, some servants came in. Silently they cleaned without a word, or a glance at him. Or at one another for that matter. The platters and dishes did all of the conversing instead. Once finished, they left just as silently as they had entered.

As Phillip stood there in the lonely, quiet room, he came to a hard realization. The house he was surrounded by certainly looked like the home he had left six days ago, filled with the people he loved. But, in reality, in the six days he was gone, it had become something else entirely. In six short days it had transformed into a forlorn fortress for the mostly dismal.

vi

Twelve different jewels, representing the twelve tribes of Israel after coming into their sacred covenant with The Almighty God, glittered and sparkled majestically when put into direct contact with the early afternoon light. Bright, unfiltered sunlight, which poured in through a panoramic set of large windows, glinted favorably off of the adorned opulence.

It was nearly a week before the actual Day of Preparation. Soon the marathon of rituals and festivities would begin. An eager, anxious electricity was palpable amongst all of the people. It could be felt while walking in the streets or crowding into the Temple. Everyone's mind was focused on the holy ritualistic holiday that so many looked forward to each and every year. Lamb's blood would be smeared on the front doors of houses that wished for the angel to pass over. Feasts would be held. Joy would try to be had. But, for Caiaphas, he was utilizing this holiday for another reason altogether.

The Ephod was tied snugly about his angular frame, and over that, he wore the heavy Breastplate of Judgement. The glorious wealth of the thing, that literally weighed heavy upon his shoulders, was so vast as to be incalculable. Priceless. A preserved holy relic from the ancient world of Moses and Aaron. Now that he was adorned in the powerful garb, Caiaphas didn't ever want to remove it. He imagined this is what an Emperor must feel like.

Annas circled him, like a vulture would a carcass, scrutinizing his son-in-law head to toe for any absent trinket of regalia. Adjusting, tucking and nitpicking.

Caiaphas certainly was decked out in luxurious layer upon layer of lavish, pure white silks. A flashy ring was worn upon every slender finger and glinting off the early afternoon sun. Ostentatious, golden jeweled necklaces hung like an exorbitant noose about his scrawny neck. This, along with the weight of a decadent, jeweled coronet balanced atop his head, caused his gaunt face to crane down and forward.

When Annas was satisfied that this was as good as they could do, he said, "There! You're pretty enough to be one of Pilate's little playthings!" An immediate, obnoxious guffaw burst from Annas at his own joke. There was a great deal of joy for him in teasing his son-in-law. His laughter went on for too long, with both hands placed upon his bouncing, round belly.

Caiaphas was not amused in the slightest at the jest. Admittedly, he was a little traumatized by what he had seen within Pilate's Praetorium that day. Worse, though he felt, were the things that were unseen in that place. Things that could only be conjured up in the imagination. When no visitors were around. Behind closed doors. In short, he really didn't want to talk about it ever again.

However, Annas' self-inflicted mirth was short lived. James was escorted in, skinnier than remembered, drying his freshly washed hands and forearms on his dusty robes. Looking travel worn and unkempt for the most part, although his eyes remained suspicious and fierce. He slithered his way to them both. Weaving between masterfully carved tables and lush sofas with limestone statues depicting expressionless, great men from ages past.

The High Priest spoke once James was close enough for a lower, imperceptible tone of conversation, "I'm glad to see you've returned unscathed, James ben Jonah."

James bowed and kissed a large jade jewel set in an ornate, filigree gold ring on Caiaphas' right index finger. He stood and answered, "Glad to see you as well. You look simply...regal, High Priest Caiaphas." In all honesty, though, instead of regal, James really wanted to describe his mentor as "stupid" or "ridiculous".

Caiaphas scoffed and waved away the forced adulation, even though, in secret, he thrived from receiving such comments. Even if they were disingenuous. "So, what did you learn in your jaunt to Capernaum?"

"Well besides the fact that Romans are nothing but dirty, shiftless pigs," James started, which extracted a fleeting titter from Annas, "I've learned that we are definitely in the midst of, shall we say, a *demonic* situation."

"I knew it!" Caiaphas beamed. "So, the girl?" He paused and looked to his Father-in-law, "What was her name?"

But, James answered instantly instead, "Abigail."

"Yes! Abigail," Caiaphas said, damn near salivating, repeating the three succinct syllables of her name slowly. "Her resurrection was an abomination as well I take it?"

"Yes. From what I gathered," James answered.

"What do you mean from what you gathered? You didn't question anyone directly?" Caiaphas demanded.

"I questioned people! Jairus directly!" James defended himself.

"And what did you ask Jairus directly?" Caiaphas challenged. Then he mockingly imitated James questioning Jairus, "Yeah, you don't know me, but I was just wondering, was your dead daughter possessed by a demon?"

Annas added, "I don't like that at all."

"Well, we-we-we were attacked, my Lord," James stammered.

"Bah!" Caiaphas exploded, throwing up both of his hands and turning away in furious anger.

Annas came up closer to James and confided, "This is not good. Not good at all."

James stepped away from the older man to beseech The High Priest, "My Lord, I inquired them about the girl, and just by their reaction alone, I could tell that her resurrection was *indeed* an abomination."

Caiaphas' heavily ringed hand swung around and clunked hard, making precise impact with James' cheekbone. The younger Priest's small phylactery box went flying from his head, skipping across the floor. The slap had split his sun and wind burned, paper thin skin. Dark blood began dribbling out of the gory gash, down and into his dirty, frizzy looking copper beard.

"YOU COULD TELL?!" Caiaphas screamed. "WE NEED ACTUAL PROOF AND NOW ALL WE'RE LEFT WITH IS YOU TRUSTING A FEELING?!!"

James knelt and bowed his head low to the marble floor. Blood and tears dripped individually onto the polished stone floor. He apologized to the bejeweled High Priest in a low, humble tone, "I have failed you. I'm sorry."

Caiaphas grumbled something unintelligible while rummaging aggressively in the front pockets of the Ephod. James, for the most part, kept his head bowed low, palms flat on the cool stone. For a split second he chanced a glance upward and saw Annas waddling over to his son-in-law before returning his gaze to the floor.

Once he held the two small, smooth stones in each hand, Caiaphas cleared his throat before asking James, "What is your name?"

James looked up again to see both older men staring down at him. Regarding him as one would regard a squashed bug. Pity, revulsion and anger mixed and intertwined across their features, like an unpleasant color of paint splattered pell-mell across a pair of wrinkled canvases.

"What?" James asked, confused.

Caiaphas repeated, "What is your name?"

"I don't understand," James said. "You know what my-"

Caiaphas cut him off sharply, "**What** is your name?"

"Answer him," Annas commanded gruffly.

"James ben Jonah," James answered in a moderately irritated tone.

In Caiaphas' right hand the Thummim warmed a considerable amount and softly thrummed in response to the correct answer being given. Its temperature increased all the way up to a hot tingle before subsiding back to its normal tepid, hard stone surface. (Just as the Urim had reacted in his left hand. Tepid, lifeless and hard.)

"Good," Caiaphas said. "Good. Now, tell me, did you just return from Capernaum?"

James snapped his head up from his prostrated position on the floor and challenged angrily, "What is this? You know I just returned."

Annas shuffled a couple of steps over to James and knelt down by him. In a blindingly quick moment, he grasped James' face by the lower jaw with a hand that felt like an eagle's claw digging sharp talons into his skin past his scraggly beard. Annas had turned James' face fully towards his. James saw that the older man's eyes were wide and fiery. Through clenched teeth he said, "Just answer the questions, son."

Annas, then forcefully directed James face away and upwards, towards Caiaphas. The tall, gaunt, shining High Priest stood stock still, awaiting the stupid answer to his stupid question. Both of his hands were concealed in the front pockets of the Ephod. The multicolored array of jewels on the front of the Breastplate of Judgement appeared as though they were illuminating at random, but that could've just been a trick of the natural light. Maybe.

"Yes," James relented. The one word answer was muffled by his face being smushed. A slimy string of drool leaked out of the side of his mouth and down onto Annas' hand. To which, Annas reacted in disgust, releasing his face with a little toss and wiping his soiled hand upon the back of James' robes. The old Priest's face expressed a deep, disgusted frown.

Again, for Caiaphas, the Thummim vibrated and heated up when the correct response was given. The Urim laid cool and dormant in his left hand.

"Good," Caiaphas purred. A satisfied slight curl touched his lips on the outer edge. He was nodding his head up and down in goading affirmation. "That's good, James." The gilded and much adorned High Priest began a leisurely saunter about the room. Keeping the pace of his steps slow and calculated, tracing the outline of an invisible semi circle. "Do you think you know better than I do?" Caiaphas asked.

James kept his head bowed and answered as meekly as he could manage. His voice lifted, almost turning his answer into a question, "No"

The Urim instantly began to buzz in Caiaphas' left hand and took on an icy chill. Freezing and vibrating. James was lying. Without another word, Caiaphas stepped over and kicked James in the side, sending him rolling over onto his back. The younger man laid, eyes squeezed shut, clutching at his injured side. He was coughing and sputtering and carrying on like a yiping, disciplined dog. Baying at the top of his lungs, "What did you do that for?"

"Silence, you lying scum!" Caiaphas words struck quick and precise, like a venomous snake bite. Paralyzing poor James with his mouth open in mid bellow. Caiaphas went on in a more subdued tone, "Since you have failed in your task, an adjustment to our plans must now be made." By this time, Annas' downturned frown had reversed upward into a malicious smirk. "Return to the Temple and make sacrificial offerings for your transgressions until we call upon you again."

James answered in a groan, "Yes, High Priest Caiaphas."

Caiaphas leaned down into his face and told him, "Now get out of my sight you lying worm!"

James scrambled to get to his feet, but jolted and yelped at the stab of pain where he had been kicked. It was possible a rib or two was cracked. Causing him to wince and whimper all the way out of the door he had come in through.

Annas asked Caiaphas, "So, what did you learn from that?"

Caiaphas thought about this for a long moment, then answered, "First, I've confirmed my suspicions about James' deceptive nature."

Annas nodded mutely, bobbing his great grey head up and down. He wasn't nodding in agreement. No, more like he was ruminating in wise contemplation. "Are you sure?" Annas asked point blank. "You know the stones can't be trusted if your heart is even the slightest bit compromised."

Caiaphas breathed in a sharp intake through his nose, "What are you saying about my heart?"

Annas didn't say anymore. He didn't have to. Deep down, Caiaphas knew his own intentions weren't neutral. He knew that his heart **hoped** to catch Jesus in a public lie. They both knew Urim and Thummim would be unreliable with these partisan desires in play. But what other choice did they have?

Caiaphas adjusted his coronet and puffed out his chest. "Regardless of what you think, we have no other choice," Caiaphas stated as a matter of fact. "We have the holy instruments."

"That will possibly be inaccurate in your hands," Annas threw in.

Caiaphas kept his debating going, raising up the volume of his reedy voice. "This is our only chance to corner him, father. Even if it holds the slimmest chance of success, we have to take that chance. For God's sake we could lose the Temple!"

Annas couldn't argue much with the fact that the Temple and their rule over the people was on the line. Plus, that it was better to try than to not try. With a grim reluctance, he nodded his assent before quietly returning to the tasks of primping Caiaphas and plotting for the upcoming confrontation with Jesus Christ.

vii

The very next day broke out in a trickle of disinclined joy amongst a large portion of the citizens of Bethany for the commencement of the week-long celebration of the Passover. Celebrations this year were much more mild by comparison to previous years. Overall positivity had cooled.

A morose, oppressive shadow hung like a menacing hand over the modestly sized community. It was at the back of everyone's mind. On the tip of everyone's tongue. No one felt safe during this time of year originally reserved for joyous celebration.

Throughout the warm day, village children kept busy playing silly games and jangling tambourines. Their innocent squeals of laughter echoed, sounding strangely out of place, throughout the thoroughfare. Equally loud, but less pleasant, brash merchants peddled their various goods. Soldiers and a variety of Holy Men-Pharisees and Sadducees alike-clogged the busy, dusty streets. A smattering of quiet veiled women here and there completed the demographic.

At the house of Martha and Mary, it was a veritable bustling beehive of activity as well. Servants rushed this way and that way through the entire house, carrying out various tasks in final preparation for the annual dinner. They were busy beating the buildup of dust from large woven rugs, rushing with arms full of fresh linens, or on their knees bent over, scrubbing at the floor with perfumed water from a wooden bucket.

Machboos, a traditional cuisine consisting of heavily spiced slow roasted goat, could be smelled permeating in every room of the house. Cardamom, cinnamon and turmeric could be tasted on the air itself. Yet, appetites among the house remained unwhetted. The gruesome memory of the two recently mutilated goats was still a fresh scar on everyone's mind.

So far, the day had passed swiftly in a furious, industrious blur of periodic checks on Mary, whom Matha had not seen since yesterday, or brief encounters in hallways regarding last minute, inordinate security measures and staff concerns about the finite expected number of guests. In between suffering some of these finer details, amidst the blur, Martha would sneak away to scour beneath the tucked, hidden legs of every dove within their dovecote on the roof for any new messages.

There had been no word from Phillip since Martha had left him standing with his mouth agape, dumbfounded, in Jacob's clothes, in her dining room yesterday, and it had been nothing but crickets from The Messiah for days now.

It would be nice to know if there were going to be more mouths to feed, at least, she thought, while her small, bare feet hurried her along the cool, damp floor. After all, anywhere Jesus went, there were twelve hungry mouths coming along with him.

After her last check on her sister, Mary, who was thoroughly passed out and ripping away on some loud, drunken snoring, a stealthy Martha weaved as quietly as possible through the hallways. She did all she could to avoid random pairs of eager eyes trying to meet hers along the way and mouths already parted in preparation for conversation.

Martha passed by an intersection of corridors and saw the lit up side profile of little, old Hannah down at the opposite end. She was talking sternly to two young servant girls. While her mouth was moving, no doubt chastising or giving commands to the poor girls, her eyes flicked up and caught Martha's eyes looking at her. When their gazes locked, Martha jumped slightly, spun around and scurried down the hallway, to the ladder leading up to the roof.

Once there, in the progressing, aging day, above the chaos below, she basked and luxuriated at maximum length in the solitude. Taking slow, measured steps from the access hatch over to the dovecote. Observing the minimal, wispy clouds streaked across the wonderful, eternal blue sky beyond. She wandered over to the edge and peered down at a constant stream of fellow citizens passing by. They were hurriedly scurrying in opposite directions of one another. She began to wonder which one would be an unsuspecting future victim for her brother. Imagining these strangers, adults and children alike, passing by with plenty of blood spilling from their eyes, ears, nose and mouth. Glistening, red chunks appearing to be torn from their exposed skin. Their deaths were already written and certified by her own complacent hand.

Your silence is their demise, she thought to herself.

Sickened by her uncontrollable flow of morose omens, she turned back to the softly cooing doves. Each one tucked snugly in their cote. Martha began to pick amongst them in a process of elimination, from top to bottom, one at a time pulling out a frantically flapping white bird to check its legs for a tiny rolled message. On the fourth dove pulled, she saw a little piece of parchment as soon as she flipped it over to inspect. Stunned at the reality of there actually being a note, she almost dropped the bird. With her hands shaking and her breath held, she gently removed the note, then returned the frazzled bird to its hidey-hole.

She unfurled the small strip and, to her surprise, it was from The Messiah! She raced through reading the words, not digesting their meaning, at first. Then she read it again. And again. And once more to make sure she wasn't imagining the words, much like the premonitions of blood and violence that she had just envisioned upon the random faces of her fellow neighbors.

The words succinctly said in Jesus' perfect script, *Expect us this evening, with Lazarus.*

As she poured over the note again and again, her mind spun and careened from one wild explanation to another. What did Jesus mean? Could The Lord have fixed what was wrong with her brother? Did her faith in hope prevail? Were her tortured, wishful prayers really being answered?

When she came to her senses again, she was back in the house, standing in the hallway, staring at the unfurled tiny note in her hands.

"Whut iz that you've gaht?" Mary's thick, sleepy voice startled Martha and, by instinct, Martha quickly hid the note behind her back. Thinking the voice could belong to Hannah, or one of her maids sent to spy.

Upon seeing her ragged sister, Martha produced the small piece of parchment and handed it over. Mary took it and read over it with lackluster enthusiasm at first. But, as she held the note and scanned the words again and again, allowing their meaning to penetrate into her understanding, her crusty eyes widened to huge, bloodshot saucers. Her purplish mouth hung apishly agape.

"What?" Mary asked, not directing her question at anything in particular. More like she was just exclaiming her confusion out loud.

"I think he's done it," Martha said, trying to corral her eagerness and keep her voice restrained to a whispering shout, "I think he's saved our brother!"

Mary looked at the tiny, rectangular note in her hands suspiciously, squinting her red rimmed eyes and running a tongue over her furry teeth inside her mouth. Then she flicked her gaze up to her older sister's near giddy face. Martha was practically hopping on her heels and wringing her hands together. Holding her breath. Mary, however, remained skeptical. To be honest, her head pounded and she wouldn't be able to think clearly on this until she had a drink or two.

Unfamiliar, distant voices could be heard rumbling and drifting through the halls of the house. Guests were starting to trickle in for the annual feast.

Martha's thoughts shifted to the seating arrangements that had already been established. She snatched the note from her sister's unsuspecting fingers and rushed off to rearrange the large dining room, last minute.

"Where are you going?" Mary weakly called after her. But, Martha was already down the hall and around the corner. Mary felt exhausted. Sludgy. Her older sister seemed to be operating at twice the speed she was.

Mary went to step and felt woozy in an instant. Without thinking, she put a hand against the nearby wall to brace herself. The dizziness intensified further, making her feel an uncomfortable fluttering in her stomach and tasting vinegar, like burning bile rising up at the back of her throat. She closed her eyes and waited for the horrible revolutions to relent.

"Are you coming?" Martha asked, peeking around the corner at the end of the hallway. Without waiting for an answer from her sister, Martha disappeared back around the corner and beckoned further, her voice fading, "Come on, Mary! Hurry!"

This is going to be a long, long evening, Mary thought in her head.

viii

It was a truly magnificent feast that stretched out across multiple tables and rooms, all leading to a spectacular great dining room. Prodigious Aleppo pine beams stretched from one wall to the other, with ornately carved chandeliers dropping down between them, giving off a comfortable amount of ambient illumination. Dried dates, golden raisins, apples, grapes and apricots sprung up in colorful, arranged towers on all of the tables. Among the festive towers, there were dozens of platters of hummus, baba ghanoush and flatbreads crammed in wherever they could fit. Elaborate bouquets of buttercup, hibiscus, poppy and lavender flowers graced every tabletop. Four slow roasted goat carcasses were showcased on the main table, intertwined and putting off an aroma that was both miasmic and delicious. Casks of wine seemed as though they were being continuously drained throughout the evening. A copious amount of flies buzzed about as though they were on the guest list.

There was a quartet of musicians playing sweet melodies upon a flute, a medium-sized harp, a double sided tambourine and a decent sized skin drum. Those who were assembled within earshot, subconsciously swayed and thrummed to the music that acted as a backdrop to their eating and conversations.

Both of the hosting sisters seemed markedly more exuberant and cheerful than they had been in the past few weeks. This was especially evident to Hannah and the rest of the staff, who had been receiving the brunt of the sister's anxiety riddled grief for weeks now.

Mary laughed and giggled as she danced away from one familiar group of faces to another. Mineral kohl shadowed her eyes. Rose hips brightened her cheekbones and her lips were already perpetually tinted violet, by means of her drinking habit. She was wrapped snugly in criss-crossed layer upon layer of sheer pastel silks, not leaving much to the imagination. (For the men that were really looking/leering, they could most certainly make out the subtle pigmentation difference between her natural skin and her nipples.) A cup, with sloshing contents, was always in her grasp. As a matter of fact, her own wine consumption might have been nearing that of an entire cask.

Martha sat high and regal at the center of the main table and engaged everyone happily. A fine modest robe of an indigo hue was draped about her voluptuous form in flattering contours. She wore a simple splash of kohl eyeshadow and rose hip rouge, elevating her classic beauty to stunning. Her attitude had transformed completely to a jovial calm, which was quite the shift from the depressed husk that she had been only a few hours ago. The internal increasing pessimistic nagging had subsided and been replaced with an anxious, albeit nervous, optimism.

Sometime after dusk, once bellies had been filled, amidst a joyful array of conversation and wine chugging, a golden, sparkling, veiled tall figure confidently entered the large dining room. This figure was headed for where Martha was seated and engaged in flippant dialog at the head table. The veiled figure was preceded by a similarly veiled, hunched over gargoyle of a man, carrying a comically tall, gnarled piece of almond wood, used as a walking stick. Both of these men were followed closely by two unveiled, expressionless Roman soldiers, brandishing long Pilum spears. The dissonance of many babbling voices slowly died down upon the entry of the newcomers. The quartet of musicians gradually let up on their melodic jamming as well.

Martha's attention drifted away from her present conversation towards the four unknown newcomers. From the other side of the decently illuminated room, she could see that the tallest amongst them sported a dazzling Breastplate with twelve different colored, sparkling jewels in the three rows of four upon his chest. These jewels would alight and glow with an inner luminance that cycled from gem to gem at random. Above his dark eyes, hung a small leather box, which Martha recognized plainly for what it was. Her eyes instantly flicked to the hunched over, older one and there, she spotted his phylactery box as well, swaying against his wrinkled, segmented forehead. No doubt it was Caiaphas, adorned like royalty, and his henchman of a Father-in-law, Annas. She'd identified them before the moment they reached up to one side, by their ears, and drew their solid black veils aside, revealing twisted smirks created by smug confidence.

With supreme gall, the new arrivals moseyed to the center of the great room, before the head table and the unwelcoming gaze of Martha, along with a solid number of guests flanking her on either side. Those gathered together for fellowship and celebration, in an irresolute way, allowed Caiaphas and his small company a wide circular berth. Affording them a considerable amount of floor space in order to hold an audience.

Once the initial blather in response to their uninvited presence had subsided, Caiaphas stepped forward and spoke in a loud voice that contained a decent modicum of slick oil, "Good evening. Most of you know me," he scanned the scared, glaring faces around the room, "For those of you that don't, I am Joseph ben Caiaphas, High Priest of The Temple of Jerusalem. A ranking member of both the prestigious Sanhedrin and Pharisees."

Mary sidled out from between a couple of dumbstruck guests, stumbled up to him and stuck her finger in his chest while slurring out, "You're gnot nvited izz whooo ***you*** ahre!" She brayed like an unattractive mule at her own joke. Snorting and giggling noxious wine fumes up into Caiaphas' face.

With a quickness like that of a viper, the old Priest, Annas, seized Mary's pointing hand and wrenched it up behind her back. Mary cried out in shocked, angry pain from being torqued and twisted by the old troll. The crowd collectively gasped in unison to her capture.

Martha stood and pounded upon the table once with the side of her small fist, making the plates and cups clatter, while she shouted for Annas to, "Let her go!"

All of a sudden, the stunned, surrounding crowd split open, creating a path. An ear splitting, metallic scraping could be heard growing in mounting crescendo. Out from the crowd Jacob emerged, roaring and dragging a large *Rhomphaia* (a long, broad sword). Along with him were two other larger, muscular compatriots, brandishing sharp, double-edged *Machairas* (short swords). Across from them, the two Roman soldiers, in return, deftly assumed battle posturing and leveled their spears at the three armed men.

"Unhand her!" Jacob exclaimed in a chivalrous growl. His white knuckles gripped the leather hilt of the barbaric sword he drug along with both hands. Allowing the chipped tip of the blade to drag heavy and scrape harshly across the tiled floor.

"Or what boy?" Annas challenged. He twisted Mary's arm up further behind her back. Mary tried to spin around and claw at his old face, her stained teeth were bared with furious intent. Annas pulled his face back in time to only have his veil clawed away. The old priest yanked her arm up further and she yowled out in extreme pain. Those gathered around gasped as one once again. Actual tears now welled and stood quivering in Mary's eyes.

Caiaphas' smile broadened as he soaked in the power he felt from the fear and pain inflicted. His dark eyes met Jacob's wide, scared ones. They stared at one another and he could see the spunk rising up in the young man. Caiaphas noticed Jacob's grip tighten on the hilt of the ridiculous sword. The High Priest permitted the suspenseful moment to hang and hang and hang, until it became absolutely unbearable.

Before the vexation could escalate itself any further into outright violence, Caiaphas placed his gangly hand upon his father-in-law's shoulder. Annas turned to his daughter's husband, who nodded just a little, up and down. *Let her go,* is what that nod intoned between them.

And Annas obliged. Releasing Mary. But, not before whispering an admonishment in her ear, with his nasty hot breath steaming upon her cheek, like sweltering excrement on a baked afternoon road, "Watch your mouth, whore."

Mary broke away and slid sideways between the tensed Roman soldiers. She ran a few steps towards Jacob and the main table behind him, but not before turning and glowering hatefully at the uninvited Holy Men. She was rubbing her injured shoulder with streaming tears flowing freely down each cheek. From an unknowable distance to her ears, she heard her sister calling her name from behind her. *Mary! Mary!*

Mary turned and saw Annas looking at her. Smiling. He pursed his lips and kissed the air, mocking her openly. Mary grimaced in disgust and spit a purple blob past the soldiers and spears, coming to land with a *splat!* onto the toes of Annas' left foot. The old Priest cried out with revulsion at the slime that slid between his toes, as he desperately tried to swipe his foot back and forth across the tiled floor.

Mary guffawed, buzzing laughter through her tears before slipping further past Jacob. Martha met her with her arms open and quickly inspected her for any substantial injuries. When she was satisfied that no permanent damage had been done to her baby sister, she spoke directly to Caiaphas, "What is it that you want? What is the point of this unwarranted persecution?"

With a repugnant conceit, Caiaphas responded, "Well, first, I would like to wish everyone a happy commencement of this holy week of remembrance." He took a long second to smile with fake warmth upon dozens of unreceptive, frowning faces. The jewels upon the Breastplate of Judgement were beginning to quicken in their random, strangely hypnotic flashing sequence.

Martha had to actively pull her eyes away from the flashing pattern of the jewels. She looked right into Caiaphas' cold, determined eyes and spoke defiantly, "Fine, you wished your-"

"Second!" Caiaphas interjected in a high stentorious voice, cutting through all other sounds like a sharpened razor. "I am seeking Jesus, his followers, or any information pertaining to where these perpetrators of the Law might be."

"For what purpose?" Jacob demanded recklessly. His eyes, however, were locked in sync with the magical, cycling illumination of the different colored jewels.

"We'll ask the questions, boy!" Annas answered.

Meanwhile, Caiaphas had slid his long, spindly hands into the front pockets of the Ephod. He had not broken visible contact with Martha's scared brown eyes. He asked her shrill and clear, "Where is Jesus of Nazareth, Martha?"

A crooked grin parted Martha's face. She cocked her head slightly to one side and answered him back, "Honestly, I do not know." Then she held her breath.

In Caiaphas' left hand the Urim shook and decreased in temperature, to where it felt like a vibrating ice cube. He smiled and inhaled greedily through his cavernous nostrils. Very satisfied at having caught her in a lie right away. The slick oil returned to his voice, contradicting the cold rot that bloomed behind his pupils, "That's not altogether true now is it, Martha?"

Answering back in an audacious manner, Martha scoffed and doubled down on her lie, "Pfffft! Yes it is!" After uttering this, though, she felt her face go crimson and the air go static in her throat, mid exhale. Mary was still nursing her tweaked shoulder, lightly whimpering and hanging like an anchor upon Martha's side.

In the front pocket, the Urim froze further in Caiaphas' palm, almost sticking to the skin, like a tongue stupidly applied to frost. A sinister chuckle bubbled up in his throat, inspiring Annas and the two soldiers to join in as well. Caiaphas spoke out loud with supreme confidence, "Stop lying woman! Spare your dignity in front of your guests!"

Martha held Mary tighter and kept trying to persist in her dishonesty, "I-I'm n-n-not-"

"What is this all about?!" A new, familiar timber of a certain deep, bellowing voice broke through Martha's weak stuttering. All attending heads swiveled toward the unidentified source of the question.

"Who said that?" Caiaphas demanded. Stretching his long, sinewy neck up to try and scan those assembled in the general direction from whence the voice came.

By the east entrance, the densely packed crowd began to stir like upset chickens in a compromised, fox-breached hen house. All assembled murmured in troubled turbulence. Annas and Caiaphas looked on with deep frowns creasing their features. The sisters, Martha and Mary, tried to peer through the bodies with some difficulty, only snatching quick, elusive glances of a passing thick, broad chest or of a fleeting grizzly, brown beard. By far Martha appeared more eager than her intoxicated younger sister.

Biting her lip anxiously. Nearly hopping up and down with giddy anticipation.

To her delight and relief, Phillip emerged from those gathered with the air of a prideful lion stepping out from the tall grass. He strode over to Martha, who was still holding Mary, and placed a warm, comforting hand on her shoulder. The sisters, both slid easily into his arms, as one would similarly slide with ease into a warm, enveloping bath. His earthy smell and the feel of his bulk beneath his robes, took Martha away for a fading moment from everything.

Like she was recreationally perusing an exotic marketplace filled with strange temptations, Martha, in those few seconds, with her face buried in Phillip's chest, meandered playfully from thoughts of gently kissing, all the way to deep, fulfilling penetration. Intense tingling arose in her breasts that were pressed against him and down in the region between her legs.

Caiaphas broke her from her trance with a short, shrill question, “Who are you? I recognize you.”

“My name is of no importance,” Phillip answered. “I asked *you* a question: ‘What is this all about?’”

This drew a sharp gasp from the crowd. A soft, little voice was then heard from somewhere amidst the sea of faces,”"His name is Phillip.”

Annas barked a laugh and yelled out to Phillip, standing with Mary and Martha, behind Jacob, “You must be a special kind of stupid!”

Shining like a glorious chalice from the surrounding torches and candlelight, Caiaphas spoke in a grating, pretentious tone, “Phillip, is it? That's right, I remember. You had the camel scat on your sandal!” The soldiers, Annas and a few of the people in the audience laughed. “Well, Phillip, I am here in search of blasphemers to God. Charlatans speaking lies for truth.” He squinted his eyes at Phillip, lowering his voice, “Confidants willing to hide such atrocious sinners. Or, worse yet, those willing to lie for the sake of sinners that would drag them all the way down to Sheol with them, Martha!”

Martha spun her face away from Phillip’s manly chest and glared hateful wishes at the High Priest. Holding her breath. Biting her tongue. Praying that by some unexplainable, magical means, Caiaphas and his cronies would just vanish.

Mary stared blankly in no particular direction. She leaned against Phillip for vertical support. Her mouth worked zealously at swallowing the saliva that kept welling up in her mouth, as though she were about to vomit.

Phillip held both sisters tight and propped his head up high in defiance. His jaw was set firm and locked. "There's no one here matching any of those you've described," Phillip said, enunciating loud and clear. 'We are all servants of the Most High God here, just like you.'

"Ha!" Caiaphas cynically squawked, even though the Thummim buzzed in response to the truth being uttered in the right front pocket. "You dare compare yourself to be an equal to a High Priest?"

Jacob now emphatically demanded that Caiaphas, "Leave! Leave us in peace for God's sake!"

"Why?" Caiaphas challenged while chortling at the same time. He eyed the entire room with palpable contempt. The jewels of the Breastplate shifted in illumination from the green emerald to the blue sapphire. "Your Messiah hasn't even arrived yet. The evening grows late, however your hostess, Martha, is still expecting more guests." His gaze flicked directly to Martha's incensed face. The blue sapphire dimmed out and the red ruby lit up for its turn. "Aren't you?"

Phillip spoke while Martha's breath stayed locked in her throat, "That is preposterous and we won't be-"

"Let ***her*** answer the question!" Annas roared, breaking something loose in the process. He coughed and dislodged a massive hunk of phlegm, which he then provincially spat upon the floor, hushing the great room into stunned, grossed out silence. A few flies were drawn to it and landed on the stinking, greenish glob. The little, annoying flying insects proceeded to vomit, then rub. Then taste.

Upon seeing the green, glistening gobbet sitting and still jiggling on the stone floor, Mary lurched in her diaphragm. Her hand flew up to cover her mouth and she ran from Phillip's side without warning. Martha called out her name-*Mary?*-with a concerned, doubtful lilt put upon the inflection.

"Where is she off to?" Annas growled.

"She's sick, you old, nasty goat!" Martha screamed at him. "Get out of my house!" Really, she intended *that* scream for all of them.

Jacob backed her up by adding in his most intimidating tone, "Yeah! You're not welcome here!"

"Stupid boy!" Caiaphas sneered through grubby, yellowed teeth. Likewise, the jewels switched in their illuminating pattern from the red ruby to a citrine topaz. "Holy Men of The Almighty God are welcome in every house. You honestly think that I, the High Priest, who alone is privy to the sanctum of the Holy of Holies, is not allowed gracious entry into every house in the land? Are you not aware of these elementary truths, you dumb young pup?"

Jacob worked his mouth, but up above, in his brain, it was void of a clever rebuttal to this line of logic. So, instead he filled the empty space by saying, "You're not welcome in this house, *snake!*"

Many in the room felt the slap of that last insulting word. Nearly every muscle present tensed up. Hackles were most definitely raised. Buttholes were puckered. Somewhere in the human soup there were young children crying.

Annas snarled and pointed his gnarled walking stick at Jacob, "Watch your words, boy. To affront a High Priest, is to affront God Almighty, himself!"

Just then, a baby faced manservant, named Levi, who had been one of those tasked with guarding the front door for the night, surprised everyone when he appeared at the east entrance, like a blessing for most and a curse for the rest. His eyes were wide with all of the attention magnetized towards him. Licking his lips and breathing , he naively interjected with a small grin upon his face, "The Lord...J-Jesus...approaches." His adolescent voice cracked on the utterance of the name.

As when a stone is thrown into a calm pond's surface, a stir rippled and roiled all throughout the room. Martha snapped her head up from Phillip's chest. She stood upon her tippy toes and tried to see above the field of taller heads in the way. Phillip put his big hands upon her waist and lifted her a full handbreadth off the floor. Her erogenous zones tingled once again, feeling his powerful hands and arms lifting her effortlessly. She stole a sinful, selfish moment and imagined herself as a malleable putty in his hands, being tossed around and contorted in all the pleasurable ways.

Meanwhile, Caiaphas and Annas had caught each other's attention. Their frowns swung upwards into sinister smiles. With the holy tools at his fingertips, the High Priest would most certainly catch Jesus in a lie. It was even possible that Lazarus hadn't even died to begin with. That this was all a lie. An elaborate ruse put into play by many conspiring actors in order to trick the mouth breathers into believing in the possibility of a so-called "resurrection". A truly complex, convoluted attempt at usurping **his** power and assuaging **his** believers away from Jerusalem's Temple.

The Devil is always seeking to topple you, so you must be unbreakable, The High Priest would constantly tell himself over and over in a kind of self soothing mantra. This same phrase now repeated itself, without punctuation, behind Caiaphas' eyeballs.

From beneath the wide stone archway of the east entrance, eleven apostles entered. Starting with John and Bartholomew, one by one, they stepped into uneventful, subdued fanfare. There was a long pause in their procession toward the end. Eventually, a pinched, sour-faced Judas Iscariot emerged. Arms crossed and the typical, petulant stomp to his step. However his eyes did alight for a split second upon seeing the High Priest, Caiaphas, bedecked in jewels and refineries. Standing tall like a peacock, preening in the center of all of this tumultuous chaos. While walking to where his spiritual brothers were standing, Judas would keep looking away from where he was going, to try to get Caiaphas' attention in a sneaky, covert way.

The eleven weaved through a pathway that had opened through the gathered guests, all the way to the main table. There, Phillip awaited with Martha. They greeted most of the apostles discreetly, nodding and whispering quick sentiments or questions. Kissing one another lightly on each cheek, per the traditional custom. Capacity in the great room had been reached and passed before the eleven had arrived. Now the overly stocked room felt seriously cramped. The very air surrounding them felt like that of the interior of a kiln, going in hot and stale as it was inhaled.

All eyes had left the apostles and were now locked on the arch way. Everyone, in anticipation, seemed to lean in closer, as if being drawn forward by an unseen magnetic pull. The moments passed by excruciatingly slow, like they had been dipped in tar and frozen. A troubled, droning murmur bubbled unbroken in everyone's throats. They shifted and scooted, pushing their numbers tighter against the wall, widening the circle in the center. Many climbed upon the tables, clattering plates and cups in the process. With less air space to flit around in, even the flies seemed thicker in numbers.

Peter then stepped in, keeping pace and continuously looking back at something else coming behind him. A sword, much in the style like the *Machaira*, was placed on dangerous display upon his hip. There was a muted sense of joy that could be felt while the ripple of his name fluttered from mouth to ear throughout the room, as though it was carried on butterfly wings. Or, for that matter, on a fly's wings.

Mary entered next. Smiling gauchely with tears still running down her cheeks, leaving smatterings of fresh, dark moisture spots to bloom and spread upon the bodice of her silks. In one arm, she cradled a small container of what some-including Martha-recognized to be a luxurious, highly expensive perfume derived from the nard plant. Her other arm was entangled with that of a hunched over, ragged, hooded stranger, completely smothered in colorless, ripped rags and garments, that looked like a random hodgepodge of dirty cloth thrown atop a diseased, shapeless mass.

The hooded, pale figure seemed to move in jerky, pained movements. Like it was being forced, in a way, to place one foot in front of the other. Rigored joints cracked and popped with every movement. Its tattered coverings were draped over it completely, concealing most of the details about its face and body. An ugly, low frequency growl could be heard, rumbling in an unnerving manner from its depths. The entire population of annoying flies became instantly attracted to the arrival of its presence.

On the ominous stranger's other side, Jesus walked in such a smooth way, that The Lord actually seemed to celestially glide. A tangible sense of power emanated from him, producing an intangible, unwavering, high ring in the ears, like an approaching wave of tinnitus. Building up far from shore. Never cresting. Never fully rolling in to crash upon the sand. The Lord's hand was positioned custodially upon the strange figure's shoulder, the way a handler would maintain control over a wild beast. It was hard not to notice the stranger leaning away from The Lord Jesus, favoring Mary's side, where she was heedlessly tossing up large, glistening dollops of the exorbitant perfume into the air.

This greatly upset some in attendance, loosening some complaints about the waste and the cost. Loud shouts of *Is she mad?* and *What is she doing?* or *Isn't that nard?* also, some cries alleging *She's drunk!*

But, it was Judas Iscariot that was the most vocal of all, saying, "What is the matter with this woman? That perfume is worth three hundred denarii! An entire year's worth of wages. It could've been sold to feed the hungry or poor!" This drew loud cheers of approval and applause. Also, some jeers were voiced for his unwarranted opinion.

Mary heard these conjoined voices of disdain, then answered by upending and pouring out the rest of the entire expensive bottle over both the stranger and Jesus' head. The perfume dripped all the way down to the Lord's sandaled feet and the floor. There, Mary dropped to her knees and began to anoint the Lord by taking her hair and rubbing the expensive perfume into the tops of Jesus' dusty feet. A large portion of voices erupted at her brazen impudence. Peter rushed back to help scurry along Mary, Jesus and the shrouded one, down through the aggravated throng, to the open area, where Caiaphas awaited, jewels ablaze. Smiling smugly.

Martha had peeled herself away from Phillip and was entering into the crudely cleared out circle as well. She crept tentatively towards the stranger hunched over between Mary and Jesus. Once she was close enough, she gently reached and lifted the hood on the stranger's robe just enough to see a wide open, staring pale eye. Scraggly, damp brown hair. Gaunt cheeks, sucked in against brown, rusted teeth. A nose that used to resemble the shape of her own and a telltale slash of blackened, charred skin.

It was him! It was her brother, Lazarus! Miraculously docile and not covered in blood. With mild apprehension, she slid her arms around him and hugged him tightly, emitting a gasp from almost everyone surrounding them. He felt so thin, like holding a bag of bones. Her nose caught the potent nard perfume, of course, but there was also the underlying grotesque stench of decay, coming from underneath his wraps. Buzzing flies swooped and landed busily all over her face, but she didn't appear to be bothered by them, other than swiping her hand past her face, periodically.

Martha was weeping and blubbering. Asking, "Is it really you, my brother? Have you come back to us?" She reached over with one arm and grabbed her younger sister. Drawing her into an embrace between the three of them. Siblings. Engulfed by a thick cloud of large, excited flies. Behind Martha's moments in elation, she subconsciously noticed that Mary's body was rigid. As rigid and uncomfortable as Lazarus' certainly was, like Mary was locked in partial rigor as well.

Martha pulled away from her indifferent siblings, wiped the tears-and the flies-away from her face and turned to Jesus. Overcome by a flurry of different emotions, from outside of her body, she saw herself wrapping her arms around The Messiah, feeling a vibrating heat radiating off of him. Feeling diminutive stinging all over her flesh. Hearing the distant, tinny ring and her voice expressing her eternal gratitude through an indecipherable whimpering, *You did it. You brought Lazarus back to us.* The Lord's free hand touched her lightly above the midpoint of her back, while his other hand stayed locked in place, gripping Lazarus' shrouded shoulder. Jesus smiled down at her and she could swear she heard his soothing voice in her head, saying, *Do not be afraid, Martha.*

Gracefully, the Lord turned her around and had her stand close to her complete set of siblings. Along with Peter, they, with Jacob, the extra guards and the eleven apostles, not to mention, Phillip, stood as a united front against the shining, glittering High Priest and his small squad of cohorts.

Caiaphas cleared his throat theatrically, drawing the attention back to himself and his reason for being here. "Well, wasn't that just...so touching," he spoke loud and clear with a high voice of screeching oil, mixed with a healthy undertone of venomous animosity. His sweaty hands were clasped mockingly by the side of his face. He uttered a swift, cordial, "Good evening to the newly arrived guests. We all know the faces of Jesus and his apostles, but we have not yet been introduced to this newcomer they bring with them." The gems of the Breastplate flashed from opaque, reddish Jasper to a brilliant, clear diamond. "Tell us your name, stranger."

It was a long pause before a strained voice, that sounded like many tongues flapping and overlapping one another, said, "I am he...who was...once known...as...Lazarus."

The crowd stirred uncomfortably and loudly murmured.

In Caiaphas left pocket the Urim shook and froze, indicating a *false* answer. This was confusing to The High Priest. He shook his head briefly and tried to consciously clear his heart of all of its reckless desire. He flung both of his sweaty hands into the front pockets of the Ephod and tried directing his biased heart towards being in a state of neutrality. Quickly, he sent up a wasted prayer for fairness in his Judgement to a nonexistent God through his worthless phylactery box. He then asked the shrouded figure to confirm, "Lazarus? Did you say Lazarus? Brother to Mary and Martha?"

Another long pause. "Yes," came the agonized set of voices again.

This time the Thummim buzzed and heated up in his right pocket, perplexing Caiaphas even further with a response indicating the truth had been spoken. Maybe his prayer had been answered. His mind stirred up the admonishment from his father-in-law earlier on a perpetuating loop, about the readings given from the stones being unreliable due to his reckless heart. The phantom voice of Annas' questioning in his mind over and over again, *Are you sure?*

The aqua colored beryl gemstone's cool illumination on the Breastplate faded and gave way to intense fiery, red carbuncle. Caiaphas pressed on, "Did you die?"

Jesus spoke to the question, his voice sounding far away and with a slight vibration, "He was raised from his tomb after-"

"The question wasn't intended for you, Jesus of Nazareth," Caiaphas cut off the Son of God, like a sharpened knife through tender Machboos. The random pattern of the sacred jewels lighting up on the Breastplate, now began to switch and flicker at a more rapid pace.

"This...body...has died," Lazarus answered through gritted teeth. A guttural rumble throttled menacingly in its chest and he jerked away from Jesus slightly, as if slapped. Martha felt her brother jolt. She turned and looked at him concerned, then took to rubbing his bony, emaciated forearm soothingly.

In the right pocket, the Thummim warmed and rattled agreeably. "How is it you've come to be among the living again?" The High Priest asked, oil upon his words. Annas looked up and winked in approval of the progress. Everyone in the great room was transfixed by watching the exchange between the massively jeweled Holy Man and the recently resurrected ghoul that they had once known as the man, Lazarus.

"Birth...from...death," Lazarus groaned.

"Huh?" Annas asked aloud.

This answer also flummoxed the stones in the front pockets of the Ephod, as they lay still. Just acting like they were no more than just stones, that could be sitting idly on a lakeshore, somewhere. Waiting to be picked up and skipped playfully across the calm surface.

Caiaphas confessed, "'Birth from death?' I don't understand."

From the blackened depths in the shroud, Lazarus voices explained, "Bloom...from wilt...warmth from...frost. Light...from dark. This life...you've...been given...is not by...accident."

The Thummim kicked into hot, buzzing life in Caiaphas front pocket.*True.* Pure sapphire faded and darker onyx took over, keeping tempo with the rhythmic shift of the gems on the Breastplate. The High Priest squinted his eyes suspiciously. His lips drew tight, into an unfavorably thin slit, lost in his gossamer beard.

Annas turned and looked, fearfully, with one eyebrow raised high, to his son-in-law, the one holding the holy stones. The old man was hoping for a vote of confidence in Caiaphas' eyes, yet, he saw none there. Instead, there was accelerating frustration pinching his son-in-law's brow together. Maybe a little fear was present in those dark eyes too.

A nervous muttering bubbled amongst the crowd. Even the Roman soldiers exchanged sideways glances at one another.

Some random man's voice, coming from the throng of onlookers, spoke up without invitation, "What is death like?"

There was a lengthy pause before the reply came from the black, baleful hole of the shroud, "For the...physical body...it is...nothing. You simply...cease. However...the soul...transcends." Lazarus made a gesture with a completely wrapped hand. Lifting it and its gaze upwards towards the ceiling. Then, it suddenly dropped both, and leveled its sight to Caiaphas. "Or...descends," Lazarus added cryptically.

The Thummim vibrated and heated up wildly, burning Caiaphas through the sturdy cloth of the Ephod. Sweat had broken out on his forehead and upper lip. His demeanor had shifted from that of a pompous peacock to more of an intimidated cobra being challenged by a brazen mongoose.

Mary, all of sudden, took a couple of unsteady steps away from her post at the fly infested side of her brother. Peter, caught sight of her movement and swiftly got ahold of her by the shoulders. The apostle turned her and guided her back to her brother's side. *Ah hhhaaavvve tu pee,* she was urgently slurring, while still clutching the emptied bottle of perfume to her lower belly. Martha reached over past her brother and touched her sister's arm. It was an attempt to calm and console, but fell massively short.

With a cough and a quick adjustment of the multicolored, flashing Breastplate, Caiaphas continued with his questioning, "What is the first thing you remember of your, so called 'Birth from death'?"

A low frequency imposing growl rose, trembled and quaked from Lazarus, in between Mary and Martha. This was followed by a sense that the very air surrounding The Messiah solidified and ballooned out, falsifying the physical feeling of pressure being pushed against those within a reasonable distance. The nearly imperceptible ringing sound, crescendoed to a definitive whine. Little pinches and stings nipped at everyone's skin. Lazarus loudly whelped just then, like a dog getting kicked in the side, and he shied away from Jesus.

Martha clasped her dead brother's fibrous forearm through the nearly diaphanous garment. She could feel serious pressure and intense warmth radiating off of Jesus. A deep shade of concern laid starkly across her face. In her gut, she sensed that there was something deeper at work going on here.

Annas, hunched over, with his arthritic claw grasping his gnarled walking stick. Caiaphas stood tall, exhibiting a glittering, flashing paragon of piousness. Both narrowed their gazes at Jesus and the wraith he brought dressed in rags. Both father and son-in-law shared a similar intrinsic musing about the interesting dynamic in the relationship they just witnessed between The Messiah and Lazarus.

Jacob, along with both of his guards, could feel an unexplainable, moderate pushing, as well, from the air behind them. Their attention was simultaneously torn between the invisible phenomena occurring to their backs and keeping the Roman soldiers at bay in a staring only, weapons unsheathed, motionless standoff.

Mary held the empty bottle loosely and low, down by her crotch. Her eyes were unfocused, hovering at half the lid. She was wavering in her stance, with Peter watching her closely. His taut hands were readily positioned on each side of her, in case of the sudden need to catch Mary and save her from herself.

The apostles and the surrounding crowd were stuck to the scene playing out before them. Most mouths hung agape. All knew they were witnessing some kind of miracle, or spiritual force in action.

Judas stood stock still. Arms crossed defensively. Sneering at the spectacle The Lord was so rashly commanding. *He has to be stopped,* this thought had been invading his mind more and more so recently. Sometimes repeating itself over and over, like it was right now.

The ballooning pressure finally subsided. Lazarus wobbled in its stance, before going almost completely slack in the legs and collapsing. Jesus kept his hand locked in an intransigent claw upon Lazarus' shoulder. By the elbow, Peter helped support Lazarus as well, taking the chance that Mary wouldn't pass out for the next few seconds.

"Well?" Caiaphas taunted with a splash of oil upon his tongue, giving his words a false feeling. Jewels flashing from opal to topaz to onyx. "We're waiting for your answer, Lazarus."

After a moment, Lazarus regained its balance and stood unassisted again. "The first thing...remembered...was...the voice of...*Michael*," Lazarus said through, what sounded like, wincing pain.

There's that name again. Michael, Peter thought to himself.

In active response, the Thummim, once more burned hotly and buzzed against Caiaphas skin. Everyone in the room became silenced by a unanimously held confusion at the unknown, spoken name. "What?" Caiaphas asked. He was not entirely sure he had heard what Lazarus had said correctly.

Peter was looking suspiciously between Lazarus and The Lord. He mumbled low, "You mean Jesus." It wasn't a question.

From the black hole of the shroud, the name *Je...sus* was repeated by the scraping of multiple voices, with a foreign inflection put upon the two short syllables. As though pronouncing the name for the first time **ever**. Lazarus then continued as if he never stopped, "Then...I went...up...the steps...into the...light."

Both stones shook in each pocket. Freezing on the left and burning on the right. Perplexed and frustrated, Caiaphas wiped a profuse amount of sweat from his face. Annas looked up at Caiaphas to spot an indication of how this was all going. From the furious flashing of the jeweled Breastplate and the intense expression upon his son-in-law's face, he could see it was not going well at all.

Surprisingly, in the crowded great room, among the low murmuring, a faint nuance of trickling liquid could be heard. Martha looked down and saw a puddle of urine spreading out around Mary's feet. Her younger sister swayed in place, eyes at half mast. A crooked smile upon her face. The perfume bottle was barely dangling from her fingertips. She was standing completely blackout drunk. In a series of swift motions, Phillip and Martha accosted Mary by each arm, causing her to drop the nearly empty perfume bottle. This allowed it to shatter upon the floor, where her fresh puddle of pee pooled. Mary was giggling awkwardly while being escorted, stumbling away. Touching random amused or concerned guest's faces with ham handed delicacy. Telling them in sloppy terms that she loved them. Tears still clinging moist and stubborn upon her own cheeks, like blobs of wintery snow atop a distant peak in early summer.

Upon Mary's merciful removal, Caiaphas scowled and muttered, *Pathetic* low, but not low enough to be completely unheard. His face twitched sporadically at the corners of his mouth. The oil was absent from his tone when he continued, "I see. You heard Jesus' voice and you went up the steps to the light." A slight nod of affirmation bobbed a few of the heads assembled before him. Caiaphas dark eyes blazed in his adorned skull like two smoldering coals. With a voice, piercing like that of a screech of the falcon, Caiaphas asked, "And, then what happened?"

"I...was taken...from the tomb...bathed...and...brought here," Lazarus stated bluntly, with minimal hesitation. It could feel the warning blast ready and radiating off of Jesus in small consistent waves against the left side. As though it was being held at knife point.

The Thummim gave off heated, thrumming waves as well, indicating *truth* had been uttered.

"But, you do not stay here?" Annas asked impatiently. "Where do you stay?"

A long, drawn out pause ratcheted up everyone's anticipation to where Annas felt compelled to redundancy by reiterating the questions. The old Priest opened his mouth with an audible sticky peeling, but before he could ask anything, Lazarus answered in a low, apprehensive growl, "No...I do not...stay...here." Lazarus looked above and around, regarding the old house, where this body used to live. "I...stay in...the wilderness."

The Urim chilled in response to *false* words uttered. Caiaphas struck at the chance, like a crocodile waiting at the Nile's edge for thirst to compel something-or someone-to come over for a drink, he snapped his jaws down, "False!" He sang happily. Then, he pressed to confirm what he already suspected to be true, "The tomb? Do you stay at your family's tomb?"

Another lengthy pause, before the simple confession, "Yes."

Many gasped at such a thing. Sleeping and living amidst the dead! No sane living being could fathom it.

The Thummim reacted in agreement. Caiaphas rushed and followed up, "Why on Earth would you stay in the tomb!?"

"It...calls...to me," Lazarus admitted. "Like a...cradle."

"A cradle?" Caiaphas repeated back with disgusted incredulity. Meanwhile, both stones changed temperature and vibrated by his lower belly. Frustration boiled and raged within him. His heart was obviously compromised, otherwise the stones would be more reliable. At least he now had a confession and ratified knowledge of where the creature slumbered.

James might have to pay Lazarus a visit with some Roman soldiers carrying long spears and sharp swords soon, Caiaphas thought privately.

Some with wine induced bravery in the crowded room, began to chant Jesus' name and rejoice at the living proof of a viable resurrection standing, conversing right before their very eyes. Subtle smiles mildly curled the lips beneath the bushy, dirty beards of most of the apostles. As was typical, Judas remained indignant and scowling.

Annas looked sideways up towards his son-in-law. He could feel the shift in the room against their presence. Emboldened, audible grumblings of animosity were being fired like warning shots towards his old ears. He noticed the Roman soldiers shifting nervously in front of him from foot to foot. Their open circle of floor space seemed to be shrinking as the encircling bodies started to press in imposingly.

Jesus remained stoically by Lazarus' side. His hand still gripped the restrained cadaver's shoulder in a dominant manner. The Lord's chestnut eyes had never left The High Priest, Caiaphas, standing before him. Challenging the power of God. Looking ridiculous in his garish garb and increasingly angered. Later, some would say it seemed like Jesus had stared straight through Caiaphas, as though he were locked in a powerfully hypnotic state.

Aggravated muttering changed quickly into angry pointed threats directed at the intruding Priests and the Roman soldiers. Calls began of *What is the point of this?* and *You've asked your questions, Holy Man. Now go!*

Caiaphas removed his hands from the pockets of the Ephod and shot them up in the air in an attempt at crowd control. "Silence!" he screeched at the top of his lungs. The Breastplate gemstones were lighting up and cycling through pattern after pattern at a dizzying speed.

Angered voices died down to a mere trickle of ruthless, childish tidbits of mudslinging. Martha had reappeared with Phillip by her side. Both of their faces appeared feverish and flushed. They each took their place by Jesus, Lazarus and Peter, right behind Jacob and his two fellow guards.

Caiaphas leveled his sweating brow and fiery gaze at Jesus. The High Priest's intense black eyes never left the serene veneer that Jesus portrayed when he directed his next question at Lazarus, "Tell us, Lazarus, what do you know of the recent violent abductions that, coincidentally, began after your...resurrection?"

Unanimously, the apostle's memories flashed back to the courtyard, littered with piles of bones. Shellacked human skulls, gleaming like little, craterous full moons. Blood on the Lord's sandal upon coming back out of the tomb.

Deep, sepulchral rumbling idled threateningly in Lazarus' throat. Imposing pressure, tepid warmth, increased pinpricks and a tinny ringing all increased in output from The Messiah. One of the beams above them cracked loudly, as lumber sometimes does when it is manipulated to the point of snapping.

Caiaphas continued to harp, "Where are they? What have you done with them?"

The deep, guttural growl coming from the inky pitch black hole in the shroud, grew exponentially in volume. Flies buzzed in and out of the face hole of the shroud, like bustling commerce at high noon at the marketplace. In answer, more warmth and pressure surged out powerfully, like invisible energy beams, from Jesus. This caused the sinister growl leaking from Lazarus to weaken momentarily.

The whole array of jewels across the front of the Breastplate flashed furiously, from color to color, when Caiaphas then talked down, condescendingly to Lazarus, "Or, maybe you can tell us what happened to your sister's goats." The High Priest followed this accusatory statement with an exaggerated, insulting wink towards Lazarus.

Visibly, the shrouded body of Lazarus began to shake. An unseen impact occurred and extended out from Jesus. Sweat had begun to bead and drip down The Lord's face. In the spiritual realm Jesus was on pure fire, holding Lazarus back from completing the desired sequence of his murderous rage.

Caiaphas then probed to a final breaking point, "Are you, Lazarus, in fact, commanded by the power of demons?"

Before Lazarus could react to the litany of accusations Caiaphas was piling up, a roar of angry disagreement erupted from the crowd. Cries of, *What are you saying Priest?* and, *That's going too far!* or, *Get him out of here!* were tossed from every which way.

Peter loudly objected to Caiaphas' last question, by proclaiming with both hands cupped around his mouth, "This is absurd!"

Ironically, Caiaphas felt the Thummim warm and buzz against his lower belly on the right side. *Truth.*

It wasn't long before a large chunk of juicy tomato was hurled at the unwelcome interrogators, hitting Caiaphas dead center in the chest, splattering all over the ornate scroll work and jewels of the Breastplate. Juices already soaking through to the Ephod beneath. The entire room froze for a moment after the messy impact that left seeds and slop plastered across the front of the High Priest.

Mortified, looking down at the mess, Caiaphas sputtered out apoplectic sentence fragments, "What?!...You can't...I'm the High-"

He was cut short, though, by the sudden torrent of food that then came raining down upon himself, Annas, and the two soldiers. They were pelted by half eaten bits of bread, covered in oil, gristly, cold hunks of goat meat, assorted, gnawed on fruits and handfuls of seasoned rice. Wine. So much wine. Plates and cups were not excluded from the foray. They landed and shattered sharply upon the Segmentata armor of the soldiers.

With their arms held up defensively over their heads, the High Priests scurried to the exit, running behind the protection of the armor and spears of the Roman soldiers. In their haste for egress, they were pursued by the encouraged, fortified guests all the way out of the house and into the street. Taunts and jokes were now flung at them instead of food. Once they were chased outside, in the streets, the door slammed shut on them. Leaving the Holy Men covered in food and shamed, with only a smidge more information than what they came with.

Annas picked at some random food slime tangled in his long, scraggly, grey beard. "Your heart was reckless," he said calmly. He slurped at some of the food and wine in his bristly mustache, then nibbled on the bits he got. "Obviously."

Caiaphas stomped away angrily. Annas caught up with him, leaving the Roman soldiers to trail behind them both as they were wiping remnants of the feast off of themselves.

Between spitting, Caiaphas leaned in and hissed into his father-in-law's ear, "We must kill Lazarus before anymore see what Jesus has done."

"Word will spread of this, fast," Annas agreed.

"Then we must be faster," Caiaphas hissed.

They turned a corner and quickened pace to get out of this city. Back to the safety and sanity of the Temple.

After a few wordless moments, Annas asked, "What about Jesus?"

The jewels on the Breastplate had slowed to a periodic blink. Caiaphas eyes squinted down into venomous slits, then he said with a sinister calm to his tone, "We must kill him too."

Forebodingly, the Thummim buzzed. *Truth.*

ix

The remainder of the night played out briefly at the house of Martha and Mary. The latter was presently laid out diagonally upon her bed. Still fully dressed in her sheer silks and sprawled out unabashedly. Noticeably damp in her crotch, down the inside of her thighs and calves, all the way to her ankles. Snoring sonorously. The former, Martha, stayed in the great room fraternizing with Phillip, The Lord, Lazarus, the apostles and the thinning roster of guests. She would keep touching her brother on the arm throughout the rest of the visit, like she had to keep confirming to herself he was really standing before her. Despite the multi-layered barrier of death thrown up between them.

Jesus, Lazarus and the apostles only stayed a little while longer. Some of the apostles had taken advantage of what remained from the feast and available wine. Jesus' physical body was becoming tired from restraining Lazarus, while answering a gamut of predictable, vanilla questions. Sometime before midnight, Jesus and Lazarus, along with the twelve, migrated to leave. One by one, from Jesus through most of the twelve, strong hugs and tender kisses of deep affection were traded. Judas, as usual, came up last and begrudged Martha with a cold, emotionless hug, coupled with some mumbled words of false appreciation.

Martha then turned and grabbed ahold of her brother's cracking, rigored body in a fierce embrace. From where he stood in the angelic, spirit realm, witnessing Martha hold the restrained, possessed body of her brother and whispering that she would *Come and visit him tomorrow,* was a bittersweet moment for Jesus. He knew what he must follow through with. Tonight. Posthaste.

Close to an hour later Jesus and company found themselves beneath a majestic, cold, waning crescent moon that hung bone white and weightless up in the cosmos. A few thick, nocturnal clouds blotted out whole sections of swirling galaxies and twinkling stars. Owls hooted curiously from various obscured branches, *Hoo-Hoo*. Asking like they were the unofficial gatekeepers of the olive grove, demanding identification from those who dared pass through their lands in the dead of night.

They all walked in silence beneath the canopy of olive trees once again and, hopefully, for the final time. A tiring Jesus led up the line with firm command and unwavering restraint still being imposed upon Lazarus, who remained a shrouded, growling, shuffling, consistently resisting, possessed cadaver. Peter followed closely with his sword unsheathed and at the ready in one hand. A burning torch, one of three carried amongst them, was gripped tightly in the other.

It wasn't long before the lunar-dappled, bone-riddled courtyard came into view. Its low stone walls squared off the existing dark with angles of darker edges. Agitated, bald griffon vultures flapped their wings from up on their perches. Squawking and hissing offensively in reaction to seeing the trespassing humans returning.

Past the courtyard threshold, that notion of an unseen, oppressive force, dragging down upon their collarbones and pushing down upon their heads, became prevalent once again. Demonic wickedness fizzled and nipped at their flesh. A wave of spinning nausea spread amongst the men. The pitch black, wide open entrance of Lazarus' cradle awaited them straight ahead. Steadily, they crept across the limestone, until they all stood just outside the tomb's hellish, repelling portal.

Jesus called over his shoulder in a marginally weakened voice, "John, I need you for a favor."

Without hesitation, John trotted up to him and answered, "Yes, my Lord. Are you alright? What do you need?"

"Take some of your brothers and clean up this mess, please," Jesus said, waving with his free hand in a vague gesture at the courtyard behind them.

Confused. Pinching his brows together, John asked for clarification, "Mess?"

"The bones, John," Jesus said bluntly and slipped into the horrible blackness of the tomb with Lazarus without another word.

Peter knew something of what the Lord had planned. He had sheathed his sword and now just held his torch aloft at the precipice of the tomb's antechamber. With a quick flick of his head he signaled to Matthew, Thomas and his brother, Andrew, *Come with me.*

At the same time, the rest of the apostles had dispersed and meandered throughout the courtyard. One by one and unanimously unenthusiastic, they started to gather up bones by the armload. From there they would then carry them out deep into the grove for some nocturnal critters to take. They really should've given the dead the respect they deserved with a proper burial, but obviously their present circumstances and just the sheer number of bones made that impossible.

Meanwhile, Peter and company entered deeper into the cradle. The horrific aroma further instigated the threat of a geyser of vomit that was already bubbling at the bottom of their throats. The single torch they carried provided meager light against the plague of flies and the all-encompassing darkness, yet they kept tightly tethered to it. Like four frightened, discombobulated moths. After a moment, when their senses had adjusted to the pitch black gloom and they realized the emptiness of the upper antechamber, they noticed an ominous set of stairs leading down to a deeper chamber reserved for the ancients.

"Come, Peter," Jesus' voice echoed, strained and hollow from the subterranean lower chamber.

Their footfalls quickened through the clouds of flying insects. Loudly, their sandals peeled from the congealed, sticky steps of tacky blood. The entire floor glistened and shifted from the torchlight they carried illuminating the sickening movement of trillions of fat maggots as they squirmed through the fibrous moisture. An indescribable stench of rotten meat, excrement and death clung stubbornly to each breath. They could taste it on their tongues. Andrew reflexively threw up some remnants of goat and bread chunks, coupled with wine and bile, near the bottom of the stairs. Matthew, Thomas and Peter gagged, while holding the sleeves of their robes tightly over their mouths and noses. They could've each sworn that the overwhelming, disgustingness of the mind-bending odor was actually crawling right into their eyeballs, ringing their ears into deafness, and seeping into their skin. Like the symptoms of what was experienced in the courtyard was exponentially heightened down here. At the birthplace of demonic evil.

Jesus watched the four of them struggle in their descent down the stairs. The Lord was beyond exhausted from hours of detaining the demon raging and thrashing within Lazarus' dead body. Beside The Messiah there was a large, rectangle slab of granite jutting up from the bloody, chunky soup covering most of the floor. Its surface gleamed dully in the light from the lone, flickering flame.

A random, uncontrollable thought passed through the racing, terrified mind of Peter, *Did Jesus walk down here in the dark?*

Lastly, Andrew joined them at the bottom of the steps. His face was twisted in terror and disgust like the rest of theirs. Squinting and wiping at his mouth. Behind his sleeve he rolled his tongue around the interior and spit the residual taste of vomit off to the side. He forgot about his emptied stomach, though, when he noticed the strain and the sweat on Jesus' face.

"Jesus-s?" Andrew asked shakily. "Are y-y-you alright?"

"Yes, yes," Jesus responded in a rush. "Come and help me, will you?" He sounded weary.

The four of them squished and squelched, as rapidly as possible, through the fermented visceral slop, to where Jesus hovered. An orgy of maggots squirmed and popped beneath their sandals. Once close to Jesus, they could see The Lord's hand was clenched. White knuckles visibly gripped into the collarbone and shoulder blade of the diminished body of what used to be his friend.

An unearthly, low rumble reverberated from the chest cavity of Lazarus, causing some of the surrounding deeper, congealed puddles to ripple in sickening disturbance upon their surfaces. The sight, of which, made Andrew nearly double over and puke again.

Muffled behind his sleeve, Matthew yelled, "What do you need us to do, Lord?!"

"I need all of you," Jesus stated. "Peter. Set down the torch, please."

Startled, Peter forgot he had even been holding it. It was such a puny amount of light in such a massively black space, like a tiny pinprick of light shining through a thick, black canvas. Lamely, he set it down on its side on the worn, carved lid of a sandstone sarcophagus close by.

"N-n-now what?!" Peter asked, his voice was definitely jittery with fear.

There were a few passing moments of the only sounds being the persistent, threatening growl coming from Lazarus, the lone crackle of the horizontal torch, the buzzing of billions of flies, the occasional random rodent squeak and a rogue *drip-drop* of something plunging into a viscous puddle somewhere in the tomb.

"Seize him!" Jesus commanded suddenly, clear as a bell from inside their minds.

It all happened in a series of movements too fast to be decipherable. For a split second, Lazarus' feet were straight up in the air and Jesus was slamming it hard into the slab, with his hand concavering Lazarus' sternum. Lazarus' hood had fallen back, revealing its pale, partially burned, raging, hideous face. It was arching its back, flailing and furiously snarling, like a wild animal. Lazarus kicked its blue veined, pale legs wildly. Despite their best efforts, Peter and Andrew were sent sprawling across the soiled foundation.

Matthew and Thomas held fast to Lazarus' arms while The Lord blasted it, in the spirit realm, with singeing shockwave after shockwave of electric, holy fire.

Peter and Andrew immediately got up, returning to the impossible task of holding Lazarus' flailing legs down. They were mostly covered in the smelly, slimy leftovers that coated the entire floor. A large swath of the byproduct of Lazarus' mayhem painted Peter up one side, all the way up to his hairline. The stuff looked thick and gelatinous. Happy maggots mingled in his beard. Scarlet droplets of the pudding-like plasma stubbornly clung to his eyebrows and eyelashes. Andrew had fared slightly better, with the jellied blood only smeared up his back, into his hair, and coating each hand, up to this wrist.

Jesus' voice rang out powerfully in the catacomb, "Come out, demon!"

Lazarus drove its heels and shoulder blades down into the slab, arching its human spine beyond what was naturally possible. A throat ripper of a scream sailed right out of Lazarus' grisly maw, allowing full view of all of the grey bits of old meat securely wedged between its browned, decayed teeth. ***"FUCK YOU, MICHAEL!!"*** It bucked and tried to pull either Thomas or Matthew in closer to it, in order to bite.

Good God, he's strong!! Matthew thought.

Jesus pushed Lazarus down again. Drawing upon more of the divine power from the Holy Spirit, Jesus drove the body forcefully into the unforgiving slab. Blasting, furnace-like heat into the demon within Lazarus. Ballooning, invisible pressure, incessant pinching and a static, whiny fuzz rolled out from the Lord in a strong wave in the physical realm. "In the name of The Almighty God, I command you to come out of this body, demon!!"

The convulsions performed by Lazarus worsened considerably. Maniacally strummed voices kept screaming, ***"FUCK YOU! FUCK YOU!! FUCK YOU!!!"*** Four strong, able bodied men could barely restrain the frail looking corpse, as it thrashed and wailed vehemently against their combined strength. It also didn't help that they were slipping and sliding in the blood of Lazarus' victims.

"Pray aloud, brothers!" Jesus ordered. When they didn't start to right away, Jesus said again, loudly within their skulls, "Pray!"

They began to pray to God from the Psalms. At first, low and shaky and out of sync, *"Even though I walk in the shadow of death, I will fear no evil."* Gradually, their voices solidified, gaining in strength and determination. *"FOR YOU ARE WITH ME; YOUR ROD AND YOUR STAFF, THEY COMFORT ME!!"*

In the weak light produced by the torch laid upon its side, they witnessed Lazarus twist itself and flounder against the slab. It started to tear at its own bicep, high up by the shoulder, with its gnashing, rotten teeth. The arm it tore at was the one being held by Thomas. Almost no blood, save for the barest sludgy trickle of nearly black blood, was produced by the self-inflicted wound. Lazarus then jerked its head to the opposite side of the bite and sprayed Matthew directly in his eyes with a mouthful of its own repugnant, bloody spittle.

Matthew, yelled in reactionary disgust, *Gahk!!* while letting go of Lazarus' arm and spinning away to rub aggressively at his splattered face with the roughspun sleeve of his robe. The black blood gunked his eyelashes together, partially blinding him.

Lazarus smiled, which looked terrible. Its mouth was smeared black with its own expired blood. ***"THOMAS!!"*** Lazarus' voices screeched and it lunged over with its newly freed arm to grab at the young apostle. Thomas shrieked and let go of him, allowing Lazarus the attempt to sit up on the slab.

Instantly, Jesus jumped on top of Lazarus. Both of The Lord's hands mashed its chest down into the unyielding slab further, breaking some of Lazarus' brittle ribs for sure. A colossal display of power blasted out from

The Lord, causing Lazarus to momentarily recede and whimper. "IN THE NAME OF GOD, I COMMAND YOU TO COME OUT OF HIM DEMON!!"

Matthew and Thomas had returned to their task. Each struggled to regain control of each of Lazarus' arms that were swinging all about haphazardly. In their heads, Jesus' voice boomed, *KEEP PRAYING BROTHERS!* They took up reciting the Psalms again, yelling the verses in sync with Peter and Andrew.

Jesus loomed over Lazarus' writhing corpse and seized it by the scruff of the collar, "LEAVE THIS BODY, DEMON!!"

Lazarus lurched its face forward on its pithy, skinny neck and tried to bite The Lord. This strike missed Jesus' nose by less than a quarter of a fingerbreadth. Its set of deadly incisors snapped together with an audibly loud *CLICK!*

To his angelic sight Jesus saw the face of the demon extend out further than the face of Lazarus. From his perception in the spiritual realm The Lord recognized the surfaced transparent aura of the evil spirit, resembling an old Gothic visage turned beastly and full of madness. An angel that used to reside in Heaven at one point. Jesus reflexively pulled back from the close strike and slapped the possessed corpse hard across the face, making a sound like a thundering whip crack in the cavernous space.

The attending apostles would later swear that The Messiah became at least four cubits tall at that moment. That his eyes shifted completely to all white. A wind came up from nowhere and whipped all around them, swirling The Lord's robe and hair as though he were totally submerged in water. They would say that they could've swore they heard the sharp crackle of sustained lightning in that moment. And, finally, they would relay that he spoke in an immensely lofty, god-like tone, "I COMMAND YOU IN THE NAME OF THE ALMIGHTY GOD TO LEAVE THE BODY OF LAZARUS NOW, BELIAL!!!"

Upon hearing the utterance of its ancient name, the demon within Lazarus screeched and caused the body to arch up once, intensely. Navel pointed up to the ceiling. From Lazarus' mouth, the demon, Belial, let loose an unearthly wail that occupied the entire audible spectrum and warbled all of their eardrums. This forced the apostles to let go of Lazarus' extremities and cover their ears. Then, after a few decibel-breaking, intense moments, the screaming stopped. Lazarus' body dropped in a decisive heap. Like a sack of grain, the corpse went slack and laid upon the granite slab lifelessly.

The four apostles watched and waited for the body to move. Expecting Lazarus' corpse to suddenly jump up. Or speak. Or twitch. Maybe even blink. Nothing happened though. It just laid there, motionless. Eyes, unfocused, pale and staring through the clouds of swarming flies to the ceiling.

Jesus' feet came down with a soft touch upon the grimy floor. In a gesture of benevolence, he brushed a shaky, quivering hand downward over his dead friend's face, closing Lazarus' eyelids for eternal rest. The Lord then lowered his head upon the makeshift altar, clasped his hands together over the body of his friend and wearily stated, "It is done. Thank you Heavenly Father. Please accept Lazarus into your bosom. Thank you God. Amen." When he turned around, his followers could see free flowing tears trickling down Jesus' cheeks into his tangled beard.

Following the short prayer, The Lord went to take a step away from the slab and nearly fell from the thorough exhaustion of the night. Thomas and Peter rushed forward and took one of The Lord's arms over each of their shoulders, supporting him to stand. Gingerly, they guided Jesus towards the stairs, leading up and out.

"Andrew?" Jesus called.

"Y-y-yes, my L-lord," Andrew answered shakily.

"Please make sure Lazarus is covered," Jesus said. "Now he can finally rest."

Andrew, with torch in hand, and Matthew, looked about the chamber for any semblance of cloth that would suffice for a death shroud. They pulled some fabric scraps off of some of the nearby dead ancestors, only to have them disintegrate to dust between their fingers. Eventually, Andrew just resigned himself to giving up his own soiled robe. Once down to just his undergarments, Matthew and himself draped the robe over Lazarus, covering his face entirely. Leaving his grey shins and feet sticking out, with rusty looking toenails.

Jesus, Peter and Thomas were halfway up the sticky steps. Their sandals created a strange, albeit sickening, syncopation as they assisted The Lord up and out. Quickly, Matthew and Andrew caught up with them. It felt as though they couldn't get out of this earthly Hell fast enough.

Once in the antechamber, they shuffled across the floor with the spent Messiah towards the entrance and the rest of their brother's eagerly awaiting beyond. Wisps of fresh air from the grove were noticeable to them now, and they rushed the last little bit of the way out of the cursed tomb.

Their brothers came to greet them, but immediately saw the blood upon them, not to mention Andrew in nothing but his skivvies. Rapid fire questions flew from nearly all of them, *What happened down there?-What is all over you?-What's wrong with Jesus?- Where is your robe?*

Judas spoke up as they were setting Jesus down by a tree that was previously surrounded by human bones, "Is Lazarus dead?"

Jesus ignored Judas Iscariot's question and weakly directed the rest of his apostles to roll the stone back, sealing off the tomb. They all bounded away eagerly setting to work at the task.

Judas knelt down and looked into Jesus' fatigued face. He hissed, "I heard you say 'come out demon' from out here. Is that what was in Lazarus?"

Again, instead of acknowledgement that he even heard the inquiry, Jesus pretended to be preoccupied with watching the other apostles industriously at work at rolling the stone back. He was breathing heavily and taking long blinks to rest his eyes.

Judas moved over to be directly in front of Jesus'. When Jesus partially opened his eyes, Judas hit him with a question, "Do you command demons, Lord?"

Exhausted and exasperated, Jesus finally indulged Judas and said, "My dear Judas, why do you continue to doubt after everything you've witnessed?"

"Hmmpphh!" Judas harrumphed and stood, just as his eleven "brothers" were coming back to join them after sealing the tomb. They were all gabbing like a bunch of excited hens to one another about what had just transpired down below.

A few surrounded and gathered up Jesus while still engaged in frightened, energetic conversation. The Lord's legs were wobbly and unsteady, so he was assisted upon the mantles of Peter and Andrew. Together, their clamoring voices faded away into the grove as they increased the distance between themselves and the tomb's courtyard with each step. For what was the last time.

X

Back down below in the epitome of darkness in the lower level of the tomb, everything was still. The men's voices on the other side of the returned tombstone had faded and then disappeared entirely, leaving only the vultures to trade a squawk or two, before piping down themselves. Flies incessantly buzzed. Rodents chirped and squeaked. An occasional hollow drip methodically filled a rancid puddle somewhere in the catacomb. Lazarus' body laid like a motionless stone upon the granite slab, cloaked with a sand colored, jellied-blood smeared, roughspun robe.

Void of purpose.

Void of a spirit.

Void of any signs of life.

Until...

...the big toe on Lazarus' right foot spasmed by twitching once. Twice. Toe knuckles popped loudly. The pair of eyelids beneath the roughspun robe began to flutter, revealing dead, shrunken eyeballs rolled over full white. A sudden jolt made the body flop, like a fish out of water, on the polished granite. This was followed by another jolt and another. And another. These actions were enough to send the robe covering the body of Lazarus tumbling to the floor, soiling the light colored fabric further. The body jumped again, looking like a puppet whose puppeteer was trying to untangle a knot in the connecting strings. All of the joints snapping and popping in a macabre concert.

Then it stopped. For a little while, the body did nothing more than a constant fluttering of the eyelids and a few spasms clicking fingers and toes randomly.

Somewhere in the tomb a rodent squeaked and Lazarus' eyes snapped open. The once pale eyes now physically darkened to an inky, absolute black. Sinister irises were nullified of any rim of sclera. The body sat up straight with the naked legs extended out on the slab. For a long time, the body remained motionless. Its newly pitched black eyes stared out blankly into the dark.

Void of any movement.
Void of any blinking.
Void of any consciousness.
Void of any appetite.
Until...

...its head turned to the side while the body remained facing forward. A carnivorous grin almost split its thin face into an uneven top and bottom half. It swung the body's legs off the slab and touched down onto the floor, making a syncopated *SNAP!* sound that exploded from the knees. The mild impact of the landing caused it to fall down to all fours in the glutinous scum on the floor.

It brought its fingers up to its face and ravenously tried to identify what it had fallen into. With shaking curiosity it stuck out its slug-like, pasty tongue and tasted greedily. Delighted, it began licking and sucking upon the hundreds of bloody maggots and slime that coated its fingers. When those were cleaned of the expired, juicy remnants, it slammed its face to the floor of the crypt and lapped up more of the soup hungrily from a thick, rancid puddle.

Upon reaching its fill to temporary satisfaction, it took some of the congealed blood from a puddle on the floor and slicked back the remaining hair on its head. Then, it then collected the sopping, blood soaked robe from where it laid on the floor by the slab. Standing upon unsure legs, it nimbly donned the soiled robe in a loose drape over its bony shoulders. The garment looked huge over its recently crushed chest.

Its first few steps were unbalanced, like those of an infant. Wobbly in the legs. Those initial steps took it in a direct path to the set of stairs leading up to the ground level antechamber. It seemed as though the absolute dark didn't affect its vision in the slightest.

The first couple of steps on the stairs were taken in cautious, cracking trepidation. After acquiring a sense of confidence with the skill of driving this cadaver, the new host made the body scoot up the rest of the flight. There, it stood staring with its wicked ebony eyes at the backside of the tombstone, which had been rolled back over the entrance.

With properly placed self assurity, it positioned its skeletal hands upon the heavy, porous stone. It couldn't feel anything, other than the attractive flutter of scrumptious life abuzz on the other side of the sealed barrier. An abundance of blood flow and life force flourished beyond the confines of this chamber, nurturing a singular, obsessive motive to the new demon within Lazarus: to devour every bit of it.

From exerting the most minimal of efforts, Lazarus rolled aside the stone, revealing a world teeming with wonderful, unassuming life. Its prime food source.

In the distance a waning crescent moon dipped, as it was well past its peak in its nightly cycle. It descended down to the Western horizon and smiled slim, white and lonely in the sky. Lazarus stood tall, with good posture and grinned back at the moon, terribly. The possessed corpse's own crescent of a smile glistened black and horrible from the threshold of its cradle. This was in stark contrast to the reciprocating white, lunar grin hanging up above in the heavens.

Once again it belonged to the night.

Once again the night belonged to it.

"Drinking the blood of **Jesus**. Drinking it right from his veins. Learning to swim in the ocean. Learning to prowl in his name."-Ministry, Psalm 69

Part IV: Retaliation

i

Early morning in the house of Martha and Mary was somewhat hectic, to say the least. Many bodies moved about busily to put the house back in regular working order, following the most eventful dinner. More dinners and guests were expected over the course of the Passover week, but nothing as grand as the induction of the celebratory week last night.

The shimmering tip of the sun was barely peeking over the Eastern horizon and the old battle-axe, Hannah, was already stalking about from room to room, on the proverbial warpath. In the dining room, she reprimanded a pair of young servant girls, on their hands and knees, vigorously scrubbing the floor, to, *Scrub the floor!* In the great room, a couple of men were actively moving one of the heavier, larger tables, to which Hannah scolded them to, *Get that table out of here!* Periodically, Hannah took a small trip to the wash basins and troughs outside, to check on the pair of dishwashers busy at work. The two would be energetically scouring the steadily depleting stacks of dirtied pots, cups, and plates next to them. Their forearms only emerged from the murky, silty, fly-dappled water long enough to stack the clean dish with the others and grab another dirty one to dunk. Hannah would then scream at them to, *Hurry up! Those dishes aren't going to clean themselves!!*

Martha, blissfully kept her distance from the tyrannical, bitter woman. Even though that meant retreating when she heard Hannah's stern, forceful way of giving orders coming from an adjacent room. On one such occasion, she abandoned her breakfast, leaving her half eaten plate of food on the table and still chewing her last bite, while scooting down the hallway, out to the stables. Far, far away from the cranky, old woman.

Really, all morning, Martha's mind had been divided up into two unequal parts. Thoughts of Phillip dominated and attacked her relentlessly, like a hive of bees threatened. Flying into her consciousness and stinging her right in her productivity, as she would catch herself trapped in stasis, daydreaming about his build. His smell. His reciprocal desire for her. When she managed to break herself away from these carnal thoughts, another strong, underlying voice was left, *Go to Lazarus*. It kept rotating around again and again, like an incantation her subconscious was metronomically trying to hammer into her. She had risen before the sun for this very reason, with a plan set in place for Mary and herself to depart as early as possible.

First, she had to visit the stables, in order to secure a couple of men, with horses, to escort Mary and herself to the family tomb. An empowered Jacob, on this new day, seemed overjoyed and was more than accommodating to Martha's request. At first the big lug insisted on supplying half a dozen armed guards, complete with armed steeds. But, after some hemhawing, half-hearted promises and persuasive convincing, Martha managed to talk Jacob's overprotective nature down to just providing a measly two guards and four horses.

Second, and more difficult by far, she had to prepare her severely hungover sister. So, after the stables she stopped by the kitchen to grab a tray topped with a pitcher of water, a simple clay cup and a small bunch of grapes. A few moments later, she found herself standing outside of Mary's door, holding the tray in one hand, knocking with a light sense of urgency with the other. After politely rapping upon the hard wood with her small knuckles she waited for a response, ***any*** response, to come from the other side of the door.

While she waited, a few bubbly, giggling servant girls, walking en route from one completed chore to another uncompleted one, turned the corner to head down the wide swath of corridor towards her. Upon seeing the "unstable" Lady of the House, the girls shied away and hugged tight against the opposite wall. Martha gave them a warm and motherly smile and a slight little bow of the head.

From a room close by, Hannah's voice erupted, loudly grating, "You call ***that*** clean?!" Upon hearing the familiar shriek of the rampaging shrew, the small group of girls jumped up in collective fear. Quickly, they managed a shortened version of a curtsy in mid-stride and then scurried past The Lady of the House.

Martha, once again, knocked on her sister's door, this time with a little more force and urgency placed upon her knuckles impacting the wood. A slovenly groan from the other side of the door was enough of an invitation for Martha to engage the latch and let herself in. Her sister was laid out in the same position Martha and Phillip had left her in last night. On her back. Spread eagle across her mattress. Still wrapped in her snug, sheer silks. Glistening wet from the waist down due to a recent bout of involuntary, blacked-out bedwetting. The dark kohl eyeshadow had run down, as well, and smeared her rouged up cheeks during her deep, alcohol-induced slumber, giving her a gaunt, almost afterlife appearance.

A hybrid aroma of fermented grape, bad breath and urine richly filled the room. This created an unpleasant fog that was a horrible combination of sweet, tinny and mealy, all at once.

Without wasting any time, Martha crossed the room, then placed the tray, with a clamorous clatter and scrape upon the table. She went to the window and threw it open, letting in fresh air and indirect morning sunshine. In this light, it was not difficult at all to notice the contrast of her sister's skin color to that of her nipples. Not to mention, the darker blotch of her bushy vagina, blatantly visible beneath the layers of soaked, violet silks.

Mary groaned in reaction to the invading light and sounds pouring in from the ajar window. She rolled over onto her side in extreme mental and physical discomfort. Then she lifted her top leg and farted long and loud. Ripping cheeks like she was all alone and sighing a loud, boisterous sigh for the blessed relief she felt in her bowels. She was denying to herself that anyone was in the room. Resisting the pressure to open her throbbing eyes. It was a slow process, but her mind became aware and treaded carefully into regretful cognition. Her head pounded in powerful double hammer hits in sync with her pulse. She wanted to scream in protest against the brightness on the vibrant display just on the other side of her charcoal painted eyelids. With her sensitive eyes still squeezed shut, Mary realized the uncomfortable dampness of her lower half and reached down with her fingertips to confirm that she was, indeed, a sick pig, lying in her own waste. Another long, compunctious groan escaped her upon touching her urine soaked crotch with her fingers, deepening the lines of her grimacing face further.

Despite the comical, fresh puff of flatulence from her sister, Martha didn't laugh. Instead, she said in an irritating, joyful sing-song voice, "Wake up sister. We must go visit our brother, Lazarus."

Mary's one eyelid parted open to the slimmest of squints. She spoke in a garbled fashion, without emotion, "What are you saying? Lazarus is no longer our brother."

Tsk, Tsk, Martha gently reprimanded, as she poured water from the pitcher into the basin. She spared the rest of what was left in the bottom for the cup. "Your words deceive your actions, sister. Only last night you saw him. You stood with our brother, next to Jesus."

"I did no such thing," Mary denied, as a matter of fact. She rolled her repugnant tongue around her parched, grotesque mouth.

"Yes, you did," Martha insisted. "That is, until you pissed on the floor in front of everyone."

This fact was obviously undeniable, since the proof was quite literally squishing between Mary's legs. Wisely, Mary chose silence as opposed to furthering this conversation. Her back was to Martha, but she could feel her sister's eyes drilling into her back, demanding her attention.

Martha clapped her hands together twice, in rapid succession, and tried again diplomatically, "Come, Mary. Let's not waste this day."

Mary blindly seized a goat's hair pillow and covered over her pounding head with it. Her voice was muffled from underneath it when she said, "What you're planning ***is*** a waste of the day."

Martha's voice rose then to bordering on anger, "This isn't up for discussion, sister. You're going." Her breath became locked in place, while she half expected a wild, violent outburst from her hungover sister.

Nothing violent in nature came, though. No slicing claws. No hurtful words meant to sever the jugular, in a metaphorical sense. No stiff, defensive body language. Just an exasperated sigh and a lesson in how to unsuccessfully ignore someone came from the younger sister.

"Mary," Martha sang. "Mary, come on. Let's try to be a whole family again."

Mary just waved her sister's persistence away with her one hand, as though Martha were an annoying mosquito in the night.

In one great tidal slap, the basin of shockingly cold water deluged down upon Mary, while she laid on her side on the bed. She shot up, aghast. The left side of her was completely drenched, just like her crotch. Bloodshot eyes were dumbfounded and furious. She saw Martha standing there, holding her breath and the empty basin sideways in one hand, nearly allowing the lip to touch the dirty stone floor. In a series of false starts and stops, Mary weakly sputtered out a stream of incomplete insults and fragments of questions and curses, directed at her older, only sister. *What?...You complete idiot...This is...I can't believe what a total bitch...How?...Why couldn't it have been you?....*

Before Mary's diatribe against her sister could advance any further, Martha dropped the thick basin to the floor, where it clattered symphonically. Then Martha sprung from the floor with a ridiculous warcry, flying through the tainted air, coming to a hard landing on top of Mary. Sitting atop of her sister, Martha began to try to wrestle Mary into submission. At first, Mary screamed, spit, bucked and fought against her older sister with more strength than she seemed capable of. Martha noticed, as they were pushing into her own face, smushing her own cheeks and lips, that her sister's hands stank like turned yogurt dip. However, it wasn't very long before Mary's fortitude and resolve against Martha's wish to drag her out to the family's tomb, for more tormenting disappointment and emotional pain, began to wane. The younger sister's strength was depleting expeditiously.

Neither sister, during their rough tousle, had noticed a growing, albeit small, number of house servants standing in the open doorway of the room. The group was frozen still with indecisiveness. Just blinking stupidly with mouths agape, watching the ladies of the house engaged in a brutal, one-sided physical altercation.

"What in God's name is all of this standing around about!?" Hannah's familiar shrill siren of a voice spoke vociferously from the corridor beyond the threshold.

Likewise, Mary and Martha stopped their fighting once they heard Hannah approaching. Within a matter of nanoseconds, Hannah was squeezing into the room past the gathered custodians and maids.

Hannah started with, "What is the mean-,"

The encased, mingled aroma of Mary's breath, farts and piss smacked her in the olfactory senses, like getting kicked in the face by the hind legs of a donkey. Hannah forgot what she was saying and staggered momentarily from the unexpected toxic whiff. Upon regaining her senses, she covered the lower half of her face with the sleeve of her robe and tried again, "What is the meaning of this?"

Martha sat atop her sister, her hair crazily frayed with some strands stuck to a sweaty face flushed to a dark vermillion. Cheeks puffing in and out, like a blowfish quickly inflating, then deflating. At Mary's neck, Martha's hands were clutching two fistfuls of the delicate layers of silks. Looking exactly like she had been interrupted whilst in the middle of throttling her younger, hungover sister.

"Martha attacked me!" Mary screamed, professionally playing at her born role of being the youngest. Always portraying the most wronged and the least favored, when, in reality, the truth was the complete opposite.

Martha had released her grip and unmounted her full straddling position over Mary. All eyes were trained upon the Lady of the House. She was smoothing out her robes and hair, when she responded by ordering those standing and gawking past Hannah to, "Clean up my sister and have her at the stables, ready to ride in one hour."

A few of the witnessing heads bowed, taking on the terrible task of bathing and dressing an unwilling, hungover adult.

Mary tried to sit up and stand, saying, "Wait! You can't-," But, for her, the room spun and her legs became weak, forcing her to sit her soggy bottom back down on the bed.

Martha held her breath before attempting a stealthy slip past Hannah and the advancing group of servants blocking the door. As she passed, Hannah placed a halting hand on Martha's upper arm. Martha sighed in an exasperated tone on the outside, but groaned miserably on the inside. Reluctant, Martha proceeded to suffer the thin lipped, hard nosed woman and looked up at her. Repulsed by the sight of Hannah's tired eyes ablaze, yellowed teeth gritting together, greying hair tightly managed into a compact braid, wrapped about her head, beneath a spotted and stained bonnet.

While some of the servants closed in to put hands on Mary for bathing, Hannah stood on tiptoe to get close to Martha's face and asked plainly, "Where are you off too?"

"You forget your place in this household, Hannah," Martha spoke low, underneath the dissonant cover of a weary Mary vocally struggling against five pairs of servant's hands. "Your tongue may wag too freely to be forgiven one day."

Hannah's eyes widened further, "What disrespect is this? I helped raise you from your adolescence."

"I don't care, Hannah," Martha interjected the matron. "I don't care, I don't care, I don't care." She repeated, trying not to sound like she was bordering on hysteria.

Hannah's mouth hung open, but Martha continued on, "Your claim to raising my siblings and myself for a **living**, and not out of a selfless, sacrificing love, doesn't give you unlimited access to my love and respect."

Hannah's mouth dropped even more. In the midst of her speechlessness, Martha said a quick, but angry, "Good day!" Then the Lady of the House turned and disappeared around the door frame, into the corridor beyond. Hannah stared after her, replaying the words over and over again. Coupling the slicing words with memories of braiding young Martha's hair. An alive, young Lazarus. A passing memory of a toddler aged Mary, tottering on unsteady, chubby legs.

"Excuse us, ma'am," a little voice broke Hannah out of her remembering.

Hannah, with fresh tears on her lined cheeks, turned and saw the small group of servants surrounding an older, sadder version of Mary than the one she was just recalling. Mary is still tottering, like her toddler days, on unsteady legs. Emotionless eyes, gothically streaked with black charcoal smeared all the way down her cheeks, to her jawline, were focused on nothing at all. A trickle of her thinned alcoholic's blood dribbled from her right nostril down to her violet tinted lips. She would stick her tongue out occasionally and lick at the flowing blood. It served as a tasty, visual remnant of her recent sibling tousle with Martha.

Hannah stepped aside to allow the clump of people to pass by her in their haste to the wash troughs. "Mary?" She called, reaching out in a helpless gesture.

A disheveled Mary stopped and looked over at Hannah, bleary eyed, but otherwise expressionless. Seeming to look through her from a hidden place deep within her two dark, nihilistic portals that served as her eyes. Actually, seeming to need to be more so supported by those holding her, rather than be restrained by them.

Mary tried to spit in Hannah's general direction, but the consistency of her saliva was excessively mucilaginous, and didn't travel any farther than her chin. There, it hung stubbornly. Jiggling offensively. Sporting a purplish tint.

Collectively, the five holding Mary, yanked her away and out of the room, like a yielding rag doll. "Bye Hannah," Mary called happily from beyond the threshold. Her inappropriate tone fading down the corridor.

Hannah was left standing in the hanging stench of Mary's room, stunned. Reeling in the absolute loss and dysfunction of the house she had worked for years to instill a sense of order in. A sense of safety. A culture of family. Now it felt as if that had all been stolen out from underneath her. Leaving just a hollow sense of misery and loneliness quietly echoing within its walls.

ii

Late morning in the Temple of Jerusalem, following the Sabbath after the inaugural day kicking off the week-long Passover celebration, was surprisingly inactive. Attendance was markedly more sparse than any previous year in recent memory. Pharisees and Sadducees alike, lined up in tight little solitary groups in the Court of Priests. Awaiting for the occasional temple attendee to ask for a simple prayer or incense. Maybe inquire about a dove or ram for the purpose of sacrificial offering. Or just a little holy advice. A meaningless blessing even.

Some of the older Holy Men stifled unsightly black, cavity-riddled yawns behind uncalloused, golden ringed fingers. Only a few dozen worshippers had shown so far, on a day when as many as five thousand had been counted in years before. Indeed, a slow start to a Holy week, set an unfavorable shadow of a precedent for the week, maybe more, ahead.

The spectacle of Caiaphas, bedecked in luxurious garb, with the Breastplate gemstones flashing a slow, mild pattern, and his short, squat father-in-law, Annas, entered in through the Nicanor Gate. Caiaphas, in the lead, wordlessly stomped on by his peers, heading in brisk strides for the direction of the Chamber of Hewn Stones. An air of stern determination, like visible, wavy lines rising from a stench, exuded from The High Priest. Caiaphas, despite his permanent scowl, was the epitome of bedazzling, catching and reflecting the sun by means of either adorned gold or jewel. Annas kept up as best as his old, shorter legs could, while toting around that nonsensical, towering walking stick.

Nicodemus leaned into Joseph of Arimathea, shook his shoulder and spoke in a clandestine tone, "Look, there!" The older Priest's crooked finger pointed across the The Place of Slaughtering, in the direction of the Chamber of the Hearth. There, peeking around a towering Corinthian column of The Holy Place, was James. From the looks of it, James was keeping tabs on Caiaphas' and where he was in conjunction with his own location within the Temple.

"I wonder what that young one is up to," Joseph mused, which was humorous, in a way, because Joseph was not much older than James.

Nicodemus hummed in amused contemplation, then commented, "It doesn't appear to be of a forthright nature, whatever it is."

James watched Caiaphas and Annas with intent as they stopped for a brief discussion with a pair of modestly adorned Sadducees. The young Priest was engrossed in the study of their gestures and body language. (At the moment, the group seemed to be moving on from the subject of how stupendous Caiaphas looked, to remarking on the strange, eerie emptiness of the Temple). Through keen observation, Nicodemus and Joseph noticed an discoloring injury on his left cheek, by the eye. They could also see James' lips moving just barely.

"He's trying to read their lips," Joseph blurted out louder than intended.

Clipping him off, Nicodemus whisper-shouted, "I know!" Then he snapped a rigid index finger to his stern, pinched lips, *Ssshhh!*

The small conversation between the Sadducee members finished up with embraces all around and customary kisses upon the cheeks. When the pairs broke, Caiaphas took a moment to scan the barren Court of Priests, causing James to tuck himself in hiding behind the massive column, just like a suspicious, distasteful person would do.

From a bird's view, the voyeuristic, scalene triangle consisting of Joseph and Nicodemus watching James; James watching Caiaphas and Annas; and The High Priest, with his troll of a Father-in-law scanning the court for James, held its shape a little longer. Until the top tip of the triangle, which was Caiaphas and Annas, broke away and continued on their previous path, into the Chamber of Hewn Stones.

James took the chance to peek around from his hiding spot. Rewarded with a view of the backs of Caiaphas and Annas disappearing into the Chamber. His eyes, however, never deviated until he was absolutely sure they were completely out of sight.

Once James was secure of where his abusive mentor was, he pulled his gaze away and looked leisurely about the court from his perch. Panning around, letting his eyes lead his head around to the point where he was looking directly at Joseph of Arimathea and Nicodemus looking directly back at him.

Nicodemus waved at him in a dainty, mocking way, sarcastically signaling *Gotcha!* Joseph held a modest chuckle behind a raised hand, confirming to James that they'd been watching him for a while.

A look of mortified horror widened James' eyes and twerked his bottom lip, as if he wanted to say something all the way across the Court of Priests to them. Sparing himself any further embarrassment, he chose to spin around and flee in great haste. He held a hand to his side as though nursing an injury there. In his hurry to disappear from their sight, he came close to tripping over his own feet and embarrassing himself further. His robes trailed out behind him, flowing on the wind from his own velocity, like a runaway bride's train. A modest set of luxurious, jangling necklaces and bracelets distantly announcing his abrupt exit all of the way out of the thick walls of the North Gate.

"He must be in trouble with the High Priest," Joseph said, stating the obvious. Looking to Nicodemus like one would to an all-knowing uncle.

"Yes," Nicodemus said in a reticent way, while he stroked his cotton white beard at the chin. Thinking out loud, he asked, "But why?"

An expression of being purely confused plastered itself upon Joseph's face in an innocent bearing, likened to when you ask a child about a broken vase and they truly don't know any details of the crime. Flummoxed, he shrugged his shoulders high, puffed out his cheeks and shook his head from side to side. *Beats me.*

Some Roman guards passed by in front of the Priests doing their contemplating. The foreigner's exotic eyes were locked on Joseph and Nicodemus. Maintaining Temple decorum, the Priests put their palms together at the chests, in a gesture of bestowing a blessing.

Nicodemus broke into his pitch, "God bless you, my sons. It is the week of Passover celebration, may I offer up a prayer for you?"

The guards kept walking in unsettling silence at the same slow pace, but never broke visual contact. Nicodemus continued, "Maybe an offering to the Most High?"

Joseph said, loud enough for all to hear, in Nicodemus' ear, "They're polytheistic."

Nicodemus ignored him. The ambition behind his persistence being: it was a slow day-hopefully, not a slow week. He had to make money for the Temple wherever he could. Even from one of these Gentiles. The older Priest kept on in his booming sales pitch, "Or how about a Sacrifice to God Almighty, showing gratitude for God's forgiveness and acceptance of one's own sinful nature?"

After this last prompt, the two younger, but, somehow still swarthy-looking guards stopped and turned back to Nicodemus. Upon seeing their battle scarred faces head on, Joseph became intimidated and took a half step closer towards the older Priest.

In a thick, broken accent, the guard on the right asked, "Sacrifice? Like virgin?" Then, they both, in unison, flashed sinister, dingy grins at Joseph and Nicodemus.

"Oh no!" Nicodemus replied, while nervously chuckling. "N-no, no, no. W-we...we just sac-sacrifice the an-an-animals h-here."

Both Joseph and Nicodemus held shaky expressions containing naive, goofy grins. Showing alot of teeth and forcing the corners of their mouths as far as they could, out to their ears. Trying to be both chummy and dismissive at the same time.

The two nasty guards turned away, chuckling amongst one another. Speaking confidentially, in their native language, then sounding off on a duet of great, honking peals of laughter. So great was their disruption in the holy Court of Priests, that a few of the nearby Pharisees approached them, saying something to the effect of, *Such disrespect won't be tolerated on this sanctified ground during this Holy week.* This was brushed off as nothing to be worried about by the guards, who immediately saw themselves out by way of the Nicanor Gate, to the Court of Women.

Joseph and Nicodemus relaxed a little, once the threatening, foreign guards left. The pair of Priests looked at one another. "Barbarians," Nicodemus said in a negative connotation. His hands had curled into fists and were planted firmly upon his hips. He was shaking his head, as a disapproving father would, from side to side.

"I'm just glad they're gone," Joseph confided. His light brown eyebrows came together in genuine concern, and he asked Nicodemus, "Do they really sacrifice virgins?"

"Ha!" Nicodemus barked out a quick laugh at the young man's question. He opened his mouth to pacify the younger Priest, but something over Joseph's shoulder caught Nicodemus' attention, making him lose his answer and his train of thought entirely.

Wait.

Not something.

Someone.

A surprising, baffling someone that hadn't set foot in the Temple since Jesus of Nazareth overturned the tables and made an enemy of himself to most of the Priesthood. Especially Caiaphas.

Joseph noticed Nicodemus looking past him with uncomfortable concern wrinkling his brow. The young Priest spun a one eighty and, without delay, locked in on one of the few men he thought he would never see within these walls again. Looking wildly out of place and frantically searching all about, the lost man wandered aimless. Eventually, he dropped his eyesight down to Joseph and Nicodemus and warmed slightly his demeanor when he noticed the two familiar faces.

He made a beeline for the both of them, where they stood, paralyzed by the reality of his very presence in the Court of Priests. They observed the totally unexpected newcomer as he declined offers for prayer and services from the pushy Priests gathered along the Slaughter Tables. They also observed him checking over his shoulder, at least, a half a dozen times, in a paranoid manner, before reaching them, at last.

"I didn't know where else to go," he said in a desperate plea.

They both huddled in towards him and Nicodemus asked, "What in God's name are you doing here?"

iii

The Chamber of Hewn Stones echoed annoyingly from every little step or movement or blink or breath within its impenetrable walls. With only two souls occupying its vast space at the present moment, the great, commodious depths of the chamber allowed any sound (no matter how minor) to bounce from one surface to another, to another, uninhibited. At the moment, the cacophony of sounds in the chamber were an overlapping pacing set of steps and a constant stream of grumblings churning out from The High Priest.

All of the committee chairs on the dias were empty, except for one. The center chair of most importance, which was usually reserved for the butt of Gamaliel, now supported the rump of Annas. The old Priest was smirking, despite their present situation. Finding the consternation that his son-in-law was currently feeling, pretty amusing.

"What in God's name is taking him so long?" Caiaphas asked of no one in particular. His sandals clapped upon the hard stone floor in rapid, pacing slaps. His jewels and adornments jangled with every step.

"Maybe you scared another one away," Annas suggested. But, really, he was just trying to goad Caiaphas on. "It appears your young students don't enjoy your aggressive methods of teaching."

Caiaphas ignored this, although he fumed all the more so after his father-in-law voiced his comments. James wasn't even tardy for their impromptu meeting. However, after last night's public embarrassment, Caiaphas was extremely impatient to get to eliminating every single one of these...**threats** to Jerusalem's theocratic order, and, more importantly, his place within that seminary establishment.

After a few more rounds of irritable pacing that was becoming more hostile and jangly with each agitated step, Caiaphas came to an abrupt halt in mid stomp. He had heard something beyond the sounds he himself was producing. Eager, he perked his ears up. Faintly, two sets of footsteps could be heard approaching past the fading echo of his previous erratic ambling.

"It's about time," Caiaphas said out loud to no one in particular. In an obsessive, compulsive way, he adjusted his robes, the Ephod, The Breastplate and all of the rings on fingers. Doing his own version of assuring his dominance before even seeing the sour face of his subordinate. While giving himself a speedy once over, he noticed a solitary pale, red rimmed tomato seed stubbornly stuck to the face of the emerald in the second row on the Breastplate. It was a pride-stinging, tiny trophy left over from last night's loss. A small, simple, derisive symbol of defeat, that had been missed by the initial scrub. Caiaphas took the discolored fingernail of his index finger and scraped it off. Also taking care to scratch off any dried splatter that surrounded where the seed had initially gone *SPLAT!*.

Annas shuffled a little ways up beside Caiaphas with his towering, walking stick evoking a sharp, echoing *CHONK!* upon every other step. It was comical to notice the comparison of Annas' covered head only reaching about the height of the top row of jewels on Caiaphas' Breastplate, compared to the old Priest's gnarled walking stick, which towered above Caiaphas' crowned head by a good half a cubit.

Together both Priest's positioned themselves as a forefront, as an alliance in demand for strict adherence to one's elders. Caiaphas, once again, planned on utilizing the Urim and Thummim on James, even though they proved somewhat unreliable last night. The two stones presently sat dormant and unimpressive in the front pockets of the Ephod. In Caiaphas' mind, he thought he only had access to these holy implements for the rest of the week, so, he might as well use them as much as he could, before having to hand them back over to that pervert, Pontius.

It wasn't much longer until the pair of footsteps entered the Chamber. The first set was attached to the misguided, difficult, young bleeding heart of Joseph of Arimathea, entering the Chamber morosely. In close proximity to Joseph in the lead, followed the second set of footsteps, belonging to...Judas Iscariot?

"Wh-what?" Annas stuttered. His grey wired maw was busy at work, kind of chuckling and hooting in disbelief. Bouncing his attention from his son-in-law to one of Jesus' apostles standing in front of them and back again.

Looking as though he hadn't slept in days, though still manic enough to be talkative, Judas marched up and delivered the same anxious line he had given earlier, in a slightly more urgent cadence, "I didn't know where else to go!"

On the Breastplate, the gemstones adopted a more active shifting pattern. From diamond to ruby. Now from ruby to amethyst. Fading into glowing.

Caiaphas was stunned and caught in a temporary, but instantaneous, surreal shift in reality. He couldn't believe his dark eyes were seeing, what could only be described as the divinely ordained prospect of one of Jesus' twelve apostles approaching him from the far side of the Chamber. Beyond Judas, Caiaphas witnessed Joseph, housing a pale, grim expression and backing out of the Chamber. The wheels in the High Priest's mind spun out of control, while he observed his own richly decorated hand extend out, allowing Judas to kneel and put his forehead with reluctance to the hard jewels protruding from his fingers. "Rise, Judas Iscariot," Caiaphas heard himself say.

Before standing and while still clutching onto Caiaphas' near rawboned, gem-laden hand, Judas looked up from his kneeling, penitent position and rambled out worriedly in a jumbled rush of words, "Heslosthismind!Hesoutofcontrol!"

Annas' gravelly voice and smack of the base of his walking stick upon the hard stone floor, *CHONK!!,* broke into, and cut off, Judas' pauseless speaking, "Calm down, son!"

Simultaneously, Caiaphas said, "Slow down." On his chest, a bright red carbuncle faded and gave way to gloomy onyx gleaming.

Judas nodded a jittery affirmation and tried to calmly exhale out through his parched lips. He was wringing his dirty hands together and still glancing every so often behind him, as though he were making sure he wasn't followed here. Shaky breaths continued to stutter in and out of his lungs in short, unequally distributed exhalations. His hands were balled up and rubbing at his wild, yet exhausted eyes.

Glittering off of the flickering torchlight and glowing outwardly from the divine power bestowed upon the holy garments he wore, Caiaphas shone like a pharos in a dark, desolate world. The High Priest applied a liberal amount of some super slick oil into his high voice when he asked his next question, "Now, tell us. Who's out of control?"

"Jesus," Judas minced no words. "Jesus of Nazareth."

Caiaphas felt, on the right side of his lower belly, the Thummim warm and trembling. *Truth.* A smile crept across both sides of his slim face, showcasing a set of incomplete chompers as yellow as egg yolks. "Why do you say that he's out of control?" Caiaphas purred, while stepping forward and placing a friendly hand on Judas'shoulder.

From there, Judas allowed himself to be guided over to the nearest seats on the dias. All three plopped their rears down. When Judas began talking, it was pure babbling and jumping all over the place. Between quick, flicking glances back towards the entrance of the Chamber, he told stories about Jesus commanding a demon named Legion to leave a banished man, in the Gentile country of Gadarenes, and enter a herd of swine. The swine, then, promptly stampeded themselves off of the edge of the nearest cliff. He spoke of the son of a widow, in the town of Nain, who had died and been resurrected by Jesus, only to immediately burn to ash in the sunlight. His loquacious prattling touched upon the already familiar tale of Capernaum, with Jairus' daughter, Abigail, and the tragedy that followed there. Altogether, it surrounded the main theme that plagued the forced, false joy surrounding Lazarus' recent resurrection. And now it all came culminating up to the point of Jesus casting out a demon from Lazarus, late after the dinner, at the family's tomb.

In the Ephod, during Judas' dissertation, the Thummim reacted more than the Urim did. It was, in all honesty, inconclusive whatever the stones were actually telling the user, in this case. So, the user, Caiaphas, ignored tempered caution and with a devil-may-care attitude, decided to abuse their gifts. Interpreting their meaning to match his own selfish desires and save his own skin. Both preserving his position and the power of the Temple in the eyes of the occupying Romans.

Annas leaned in and asked, "What can you tell us about Bethany and the abductions there? Is Lazarus to blame?"

For Caiaphas, this dredged up thoughts of blood on the ground. A nearby sword that was found and then fit perfectly into a slot in the blood soaked pathway. Caleb's severed head found up the branches of an olive tree.

Judas passed a trembling hand over his mouth and beard, before answering, "Oh yes! Absolutely!" After a brief, contemplative moment, he added, "There were bones all over the courtyard."

Animated once again, the Thummim buzzed and that was good enough proof for Caiaphas. *What a wonderful turn of events,* he thought and relished in the waterfall of facts, leisurely. He took this moment to thank Judas for coming to them with this information.

Judas thanked them back, for their time. "Well, enough is enough," he kept saying. "He's got to be stopped."

These comments caused the Urim to shake and freeze against Caiaphas' lower stomach, on the left side. He paid it no mind, though. Instead, he told Judas, "We can help you stop him." Judas brightened temporarily. "But, we'll need your help, as well…if this plan is to succeed."

Judas balked and cowardly asked, "Really?" Making it even worse by adding, "I was hoping you could just go get him."

What a scumbag! Caiaphas thought inwardly. Outwardly, he offered the "scumbag" a satchel of Tyrian shekels (30 pieces) and a brief summary of his plan. The former thief couldn't resist the offer of money added to this exchange. Once the money was placed in Judas cupped hands, Caiaphas spent the rest of their conversation posing light to hard demands on Judas' commitment to the conspiracy that they were about to engage in. After some torquing from both Caiaphas and Annas, on either side of Judas, the "scumbag" agreed and entered into a contract that would end with his untimely, though, warranted horror.

iv

Martha breathed in the air greedily. Sucking great inhalations through her nostrils. On the back of her tongue, she tasted the familiar musk of the horse she rode upon and the wisps of dirt kicked up by the horse's hooves trotting ahead of her. Her palate picked up notes of the gentle breeze flowing in careless swirls all around her, carrying the olfactory herald of blossoms, the bark and the leaves from the trees. There was also an unidentified twinge of something else that her sense of smell would catch hints of every so often. An offensive, stale alarm that would be assaulting one breath and nonexistent upon the next.

Astride trusty Tsalav, Martha quietly trailed not too far behind a trio of horses setting the pace ahead of her. Mounted atop the two outer horses were the two young guards provided by Jacob. Bouncing playfully in between the salivating guards, was her sister, Mary. At the moment, she was busy in shameless flirtation with both of the eager "men" pressing in on either side of her.

Mary was freshly scrubbed, smelling sweet and flowery, adding to the mingling cornucopia of aromas tingling Martha's nostrils downwind. Her giggling sounded fake and forced to Martha's experienced ears, but the young, dumb male ego was easily fooled by the tricks of a beautiful, wanton woman. There would be the occasional brushing, flirtatious touch across the shoulder, or a blatant placing of her hand upon one of the thighs of the young guards, sending their faces rocketing into a crimson blushing.

If Martha didn't know any better, she'd say that her sister was drunk again. Or, at least, swiftly on her way to getting her three sheets into the wind. The older woman shrewdly observed her younger sister swaying in the saddle, second guessing her lithe rocking from side to side for concerning teetering. Listening to Mary talk, Martha thought she picked up on the hint of a slight, but all too familiar slur to her sister's cadence. Martha's eyes squinted down into two suspicious slits and her breath stopped somewhere behind her tonsils.

Oh Mary, she thought in her frustrated, sad, yet, still maternal way towards her sister. But, mostly frustrated.

Before the nausea could build anymore from the sight of her sister fawning all over the two-let's just call them what they really were-boys, the grove thinned and opened up to the low stone walled courtyard. Beyond that, the sealed family's crypt came into view, foreboding and repellent. Mary's giggling and flirting, along with the boy's dumb attempts at conversing, tapered off to choked silence once their destination came into view.

An acute animal instinct within the horses caused them to resist and scream in protest well before reaching the courtyard threshold. The two in the front, one mounted by a guard and one mounted by Mary, reared up on their hind legs, coming so close to throwing one or both riders off. Tsalav balked at going any further as well, turning in looping, skittish circles, snorting and shaking his head in protest, causing his blonde mane to fling up in quick, flopping arcs from his neck. Clear snot and spittle flew from his muzzle, like sparkling crystals flying through the air.

Martha dismounted, as did the others. The older woman couldn't help but notice her sister wobble and almost fall when touching her feet down onto the pathway. This brought Martha close by to put a gentle, steadying hand upon Mary's elbow. The two sisters stood by, timidly waiting while the guards tethered the horses to the nearest trees. With a soft touch, the young men tried to pat the scared animals on the neck and tenderly talk to them in an endeavor to calm them. A few red Rome apples, distributed from a pack they had brought with them, served to pacify the horses for the time being.

Once the steeds were situated, the sisters and guards shuffled to the entrance and stood, four wide, shoulder to shoulder. Mary and Martha stood as the bookends, with the scared guards sandwiched in the middle, before the face of the stone archway. Altogether, the four of them could truthfully attest to feeling an oppressive, draining force coming from the atmosphere within the courtyard. It felt like it reached out for them with nasty tendrils, like small, deformed fingers, covered in feces.

As a group, they stood motionless for a little bit, until Martha mumbled just loud enough for them all to hear, "Come. There is nothing to fear." Then, she stepped away from the quartet, making it a trio, being the first to cross over into the courtyard.

She was followed next by the two young guards. They entered the courtyard with their swords drawn and and at the ready. The two boy-guards were shaking like scared, beaten puppies. Their behavior, similar to frightened children in the dark, contradicted their full grown, man sized bodies.

Mary took a liberal pull from an upended water skin. After draining a good amount of the contents, she wiped at her perpetually stained mouth with her linen sleeve. This left a faint violet stain on the fine fabric. Finally, she took a deep, stabilizing breath and followed the others in.

There was an onerous quality to the very environment they were surrounded in. It seemed scratchy in their lungs, burning to their eyes and crawling on their skin. The feeling of being pushed and pulled down was strong enough to lower their chins down towards their chests.

Two short rows of olive trees framed a narrow stone path leading up to the sealed doorway to the tomb. A reddish black stain caught the eye close up towards the crypt's entrance. The dark stain coruscated in the partial sunlight. On top of the burial structure, perched almost directly above the entrance, was a single vulture. Bald and ugly, with a long, bent neck, extending out of a gray tuft of filthy looking feathers rimming the collar bone. Its sharp beak was stained dark maroon from a lifetime of carcass scavenging. To put it in mild terms, the vulture's mood became severely agitated when it saw the four new visitors shuffling down the path towards where it roosted.

After what felt like the equivalent to a furlong, they finally reached the large, round stone. While the two guards stayed back by the first set of trees closest to them, with the blades of their swords catching the reflection of the sun occasionally, Mary followed Martha to where she stood in front of the thick limestone disc.

Martha was looking up above, near the pinnacle of the stone at the vulture craning its neck to look over and hiss down at her.

"Wha' an ugly creashure," Mary said in disgust as she walked up.

"Ignore it," Martha instructed as she dropped her attention back down to the stone. With the small set of knuckles on her dominant hand, she knocked upon the surface in a quick, staccato beat. She placed her ear up to the tombstone's porous face to listen for any signs of life. The stone sizzled on her face, but that could've been because it had been bathed in generous sunlight for hours.

There weren't any sounds of life within the tomb to hear. Unsure, Martha called for her brother through the thick stone, "Lazarus!" She then knocked on the sun warmed stone once more, hurting her delicate knuckles in the process this time. She put her ear to the burning stone again while rubbing at the throbbing pain, stinging in her knuckles.

"Whut d'you 'ere?" Mary slurred, acting like no one noticed.

Martha rotated a quarter turn and dubiously squinted at Mary.

"Wha'?" Mary asked, trying to come off as innocent.

Martha leaned in and sniffed within her sister's personal space, coming away with the unmistakable stink of wine souring in her nostrils. Consequently, she began to paw all over her sister, frisking her with both hands. "Where is it?" Martha asked angrily, while searching all over Mary, who was busy squirming away from her older sister's efforts.

"Whu're you doin'?!" Mary demanded.

The two guards meekly laughed from a distance at the two ladies grappling in front of them. Martha held Mary around the neck from behind while plunging her hand down the front of the robe and the sleeves. Searching for a sewn in pocket or some secret compartment.

"Ge' off me, you idjit!!" Mary screamed.

That's when Mary's water skin fell from her person in the midst of their scuffle. Both of the sisters saw the skin laying on the ground and dove for it, with both placing possession on it at the same instant. They each tugged on the water skin against the other. Teeth bared. Both women were sweaty and dirty, once again for the second time today.

Through a clenched set of gritting purple teeth, Mary kept repeating, "StopStopStopStopStopStop!!"

From their vantage point by the trees, the two young guards stared on with wide eyes firmly transfixed on the battling siblings. Jutting an elbow into the other's ribs, as if to say, *Get a load of that!*

At one point, Martha removed a hand from the tug of war and punched Mary in her right eye with her little, balled up left fist. Mary screamed. Then the younger sister released the water skin, and rolled over, moaning with both hands covering her freshly injured eye. The two eager guards came closer to assist, inciting the presiding vulture to squawk and hiss at them, while raising itself up to its tallest and flapping its mangy wings.

Triumphant, Martha stood and took a second to dust herself off. She afforded another second to blindly adjust her hair and garments back to somewhat normal. Five eyeballs, seven including the vulture's, watched her unstop the top and made to bring it to her nose for further inspection.

"Martha!" Mary protested. Desperation was twisting her countenance.

Martha stopped with the skin halfway to her face and looked at her younger sister. Stern, tired anger simmered upon her face. This was a moment that Martha was thoroughly aware that she was relishing in too much. All of the little details were becoming branded into her memory for later perusal. The bleary worry construing Mary's pretty features. The futile grasping for the skin as it was being moved closer to Martha's nose. The prevalent staining present on Mary's recessed lips and exposed teeth. The aura of pure, red rage lifting from Mary like quicksilver rising from eternally baked Egyptian summer sands.

Martha brought the water skin to her nose and sniffed its contents, confirming her suspicions. Wine. Mary had filled her **Goddamned** water skin with wine. Martha recoiled from the alcohol smell and dumped out the entirety of the purple contents on the ground, letting the liquid splatter and be absorbed at her feet.

"No!" Mary yelled and lunged for the last of the cascading stream of wine. Looking super pathetic, like an ultra alcoholic. Whimpering and sniveling on all fours, prostrated before the drying puddle.

Oh Mary, Martha thought. *How did you let yourself get like this?*

Tiredly, Martha asked her only sister, "Are you ever sober anymore?"

Without looking up at Martha, Mary answered with, "Yeou eren't my motha'!"

"You're impossible," Martha admitted and threw her hands at her, in a discarding, throwing away, gesture.

"No!" Mary screamed back. "You ore! Whut ahre we e'en doin' out 'ere?!"

"We're here to-" Martha began, but Mary cut her off. From her hands and knees she was looking up at her older sister, glowering down at her on the ground.

"Ah know, I know," Mary said while waving away whatever Martha was going to say with a flippant hand gesture. "Wee're ot here to vizzit our murderin' ded brather!"

"Shut your mouth!" Martha seethed.

In all seriousness, which didn't suit the young lad at all, one of the guards leaned in and asked Mary, "What did you say?"

Before answering the guard, from her low position, literally and figuratively, Mary looked over and saw a black set of wild, familiar shaped eyes staring at her from underneath the tombstone. During the sister's fighting, no one had noticed it had been rolled partially aside. Just enough to give a small view to the occupant on the inside of the outside.

Mary screamed when she saw the pair of inky, dark eyes and scrambled up to her unsteady feet. Once upright, she folded, like a defenseless damsel, into the bulky, tanned arms of one of the concerned young guards. In reaction, the tombstone grinded and rolled back to its original, closed position. The two guards were left looking about themselves scared and clueless, but on high alert. They were both demanding of Mary what it was that she had seen.

Without a need for explanation from Mary, Martha slapped on the stone covering the crypt. "Lazarus!" she called positively. "Lazarus, we've come to see you! Mary and I!"

The stone and Lazarus on the other side of it, remained silent. Other than some muffled feet slapping on the floor, there was nothing of interest to hear within. Martha heard the smacking footsteps fading in and out, like her brother was running to and from from the entrance in the black interior.

"Lazarus!" Martha called hopefully. Her hand slapped at the tombstone face. To her surprise, she was answered back by Lazarus imitating her own slapping by slapping back harder on the inner face of the tombstone.

"Mawtha, less leeve," Mary tried beseeching her sister, reaching out to her with a single hand from her nest. It was ridiculous, because she was trying to be genuinely sincere or serious, but her mushmouth made her come off as a total drunk, jackass.

Martha pointed her finger into her sister's face, "Shut up!" Then she resumed calling through the solid stone to Lazarus. This incited their brother, the occupant within the crypt, to galavant about the interior and slap hard upon the inner face of the tombstone. It also caused the vulture presiding above to screech and hiss. In so many words, telling them all to leave and never come back.

For a little while longer, Martha persisted in trying to assuage her brother to engage with them in her lame attempt at a visit. Calling her brother's name to the point where her voice began to crack and fail. Smacking the sun warmed limestone until both of her hands were stinging and pulsating. Ignoring the stupid, harmless bird hovering over the top of her. All with the same disheartening, weird results coming from the other side.

Mary and the guards then stepped out of the mysterious, burdensome courtyard, leaving Martha to persevere in her fruitless endeavor alone a little bit more. When the older woman gave up, at last, and trudged out of the courtyard to meet back up with the group, she was completely defeated and dejected. Head hung low.

"Mawtha," Mary tried, but Martha silenced her instantly with only the expression upon her face.

Meanwhile, the two guards had untethered the horses. With minimal talk between them, they assisted both women in mounting their horses before mounting their own. There was a thick, permeating fog of confusing disappointment cloaking and hanging over them as they all morosely trotted upon eager steeds for the ride home, which was spent blanketed in silence.

V

With the sun advancing outside through its daily routine quicker than usual, beginning its timely descent towards the West, the sense of losing time within Caiaphas was a veritable cauldron bubbling over. His mind swirled in a metaphorical hurricane, tossed about in an intense, debris riddled maelstrom. At length, his thoughts twirled in a whirlygig amidst the most fortuitous batch of unexpected, unrequited information from Judas Iscariot. Ultimately, compelling The High Priest to second guess at what was the next best course of action was for him to take.

At first, Joseph ben Caiaphas was playing around with the idea of sending his subordinate, James, into Bethany, to gather whatever information he could attain from those in attendance at Martha's dinner. Just something stupid, remedial and time consuming to keep the conceited whelp busy. However, since the moment the deal was struck with Judas, those plans had been altered significantly.

Earlier, after a slightly richer Judas departed the Chamber of Hewn Stones, Caiaphas had ordered Annas to summon James, *By any means necessary.* Annas was more than happy to leave the stuffy, dark confines of the Chamber, where he already spent a good portion of his daily duties.

In the meantime, Caiaphas kept at his incessant pacing and ruminating. He was anxiously fidgeting, tugging at his exorbitant garments, this way and that. Rotating the rings on each slender finger out of askew. With sightless fingers he adjusted the golden, flat hammered coronet sitting atop his pate. At a certain point in his frenzied waiting, his hands had subconsciously wormed their way into the front pockets of the Ephod. In each of his creepy, long fingers there rested the Urim and Thummim. Out of sheer curiosity, Caiaphas tested the stones against himself by saying out loud, "I want Jesus of Nazareth dead."

The Thummim buzzed into responsive heated life in his right hand, of course, signaling that a truth had been uttered.

The High Priest smiled sourly, taking a small delight in this result and cleared his throat before trying another solo prompt on the stones, "I am the greatest High Priest of all time." In a disappointing result, this caused the Urim to chill and shake in his left hand. False.

Stupid things, Caiaphas thought dismissively, letting both stones tumble back to the bottom of the pockets. With a mild bit of hemhawing, he decided he would utilize the holy devices during the rest of the Passover week, but he couldn't place his full faith in what the stones had been telling him. Either way, James was wrong no matter what the stones chose to convey about him.

"Where in the blazes is that no account?" Caiaphas erupted out loud to the uninhabited emptiness of the Chamber. A sparse amount of lit torches flickered and crackled in dim, mute isolation.

It wasn"t much longer before Caiaphas became aware of the approaching telltale *shuffle-CHONK!* combination of Annas' walking with his walking stick. Another set of normal sounding footfalls accompanied Annas all of the way into the Chamber.

James entered with an unhappy look upon his injured face. He held a hand to the side that Caiaphas had kicked, while taking big strides. His downcast eyes flicked up to Caiaphas' set of dark eyes glowering back at him as he crossed the span of the room. James' gaze lingered for a moment, when he noticed the slow blink and fade of the random gems across the Breastplate of Judgement. In a cordial way, he afforded the slightest bow of his head to his gilded master.

Impatient to end this already, Caiaphas prodded, "Where have you been?"

In a nonchalant, flippant tone, James touched at his bruised face and answered, "I have been in the Temple performing prayers, blessings and sacrifices."

On the left, the Urim froze and trembled. "You lie," Caiaphas accused, as Annas took his place at his side. "The Temple is practically empty!"

James, facing them both in this vast, cavernous space, smiled a smug, slight curling of the lips and shrugged his shoulders. Writing off this lie as one would write off being accused of taking the last piece of cake. In a totally brazen manner, as though denying guilt even though there are obvious crumbs all over his face.

Caiaphas stomped up into James' personal space and drew his arm across his body, looking like he was preparing to backhand the willful, arrogant cuss. James shied away and threw up both hands in a defensive posture, preparing for the expected strike.

However, with his arm drawn back to the maximum, and the gemstones flashing in a moderate pattern, The High Priest stopped himself from completing the violent action. Instead, Caiaphas untensed. Bringing his features to soften as much as possible. With a slight shake to his hand, he adjusted his phylactery box below the golden coronet, and spoke a single, echoing word, "No."

Surprised to hear a word, as opposed to feeling a hit, James reluctantly peeked from between the fingers of his raised palms. Within a cubit's distance, he saw Caiaphas standing before him with both fists clenched, breathing in aggressive bursts through his nostrils. There was a fast, blinking, mesmerizing pattern playing across his chest. Out of focus, in the background, hunched Annas, leaning upon his altitudinous staff. Even through the lens that was keeping Annas in a significant blur, James could see the older Priest's grim features drawing his face down low, to where the tip of his beard came close to grazing the floor.

As Caiaphas continued to speak through a clenched jaw, James dropped his guard and lowered his hands all the way down to his sides, "I have an important task for you," The High Priest announced.

"Yes, Rabbi," James answered. "How may I serve?"

Caiaphas stared at him over the dancing jewels, "I require you to grab some soldiers, strong ones. Maybe, I don't know," he looked back to his father-in-law, "What? Half a dozen?"

"Maybe eight," Annas suggested, as he began to step towards them, initiating that signature rhythm to his gait. *shuffle-CHONK!*

"Eight?" James asked incredulously. "What is this being planned for me?"

Caiaphas brushed it off, "You'll just need their might to move the tombstone."

"Tombstone?" James repeated.

Annas had joined up beside Caiaphas. "Yes," Caiaphas said, then went on to explain, "We need you to confirm the irrefutable, undeniable death of a man."

In a quick, irritable gesture, James ran a hand over his scraggly copper beard, then asked, "Let me guess…Lazarus? The man Jesus recently resurrected?"

"Yes," Annas answered this time. "We have received word that he is no longer walking among the living. We need this confirmed by someone we can trust."

Caiaphas jumped in, to lay out the entire plan of how to go about using the soldiers for moving the stone to the side, going into the crypt (don't forget a torch!), and just make sure that the body of Lazarus was no longer animated with further intentions of being a menace. Once the body was confirmed to be, in fact, fully deceased, put the stone back and return to report. Easy-peasy. Oh, and hurry, because it was getting late in the day. No sane man, no matter how strong, would want to be caught dead in that wicked place after hours.

Annas exhaled through compressed lips, *Pfffft!,* and added facetiously, "We're telling you, from the information we have just received, you'll only need the soldiers to move the stone." He raised his free hand up high, "It's massive!"

Caiaphas stepped forward, saying, "Just make sure the body is no longer alive. This is, by no means, a dangerous task." The High Priest came right up to James and placed his luxurious hands heavily upon the younger man's shoulders. James's left cheek puffed out offensively from being struck recently, Jewels from the Breastplate lit up both of their faces from a luminescent diamond glow. This then faded and shifted to a red incandescence alight beneath their chins. Caiaphas squeezed James' shoulder as to be threatening and admonished his disappointing lackey, "Do not fail me in this."

"Do not worry, Rabbi," James answered with a sure tone of confidence. "I won't."

In the left pocket of the Ephod, the Urim buzzed and frosted in response to the apparent falsity. Caiaphas fought the urge to roll his eyes from the amount of cynicism and contempt he felt for James.

Within Caiaphas' thoughts, there arose a clear voice, very much in a timber similar to his adversary, Jesus' voice, *Over my dead body, he'll never be High Priest.* But alas, Caiaphas was unaware that he wouldn't have to worry much longer about the thorn in his side, that James ben Jonah had most certainly been for far too long.

vi

Beneath a darkening canopy, underneath deepening amber skies, James sat upon a calm tempered, pale horse. Not exactly progressing at a brisk trot. Just James and the nameless horse, alone. He was currently amusing himself by drawing his voice up as high as he could manage and screeching to the birds and bees among the blossoms above in his best Caiaphas impersonation, "'Do not fail me in this!'" Then he added in his regular voice, "What a jackass!" This comment launched him into a tirade of fitful laughter that took him a while to tamper down.

Wiping tears from his eyes and rubbing at his sore face, James began a dialog with himself. First, by asking dubiously, "What in the world do I need eight soldiers for?" A couple of steps later, he continued, "To make sure a dead man is actually dead? No wonder Rome wants to take us over, when they see how wasteful we are with their resources."

With a chuckle and a tone conveying a mountain of misplaced confidence, James added to the uninhabited ether, "This is why there needs to be new blood finally recognized in the Temple." This was an obvious reference to himself as the "new blood". He continued, "The old men in those seats have become so out of touch and lazy." As though reasoning with someone who wasn't there, James kept going, "I mean, look at this! Making sure a dead man is dead? Ha! What a waste of time!!" He laughed without a hint of mirth this time and then rolled it into a resentful grumble, "My talents are being squandered on these stupid errands of his. We're chasing our own tails! When we should be enacting and enforcing the law against those that choose to break it." By saying this, he was obviously referring to what he considered were the main threats against the Temple, i.e., Jesus and his followers.

Continuing on down the path with a nonchalant attitude, James started to whistle a goofy tune to the hovering birds and bees that he trotted by. His mind, at one point, drifted away to what he was going to get up to following completion of this bogus errand. In all honesty, he was primarily using this unnecessary field trip as a reason to get away from that luxuriously bedecked buffoon, Caiaphas. Not to mention his trollish, henchman father-in-law, and, for that matter, the poorly managed, empty Temple withering in depressing decline. A ghost now of what was once a glorious beacon to The Almighty God.

However, before James' mind could drift too far away from the task at hand, the canopy opened up to a rose colored sky, nearing twilight. Three low, black vulture silhouettes turned in ominous circles overhead. Two short rows of mature trees lined an equally short limestone pathway, leading to one wide open crypt. The tombstone had already been rolled completely to the side, leaving a pure black small rectangle portraying a wholly uninviting entryway.

The calm horse he was riding upon stopped dead in the steady pace it had kept solidly since he had mounted it. They were roughly twenty cubits away, give or take, from the courtyard entrance. James clicked out of the side of his mouth and tried to gig the animal on. It shook its head, thrashing it in defiance a couple of times. *NO!*

"That's odd," James uttered aloud, cocking his head slightly to the side. Looking like a partial failure of a man, at the moment, lost in inquisitive, curious thought. He swung his leg over and dismounted the immovable steed. Taking a couple of steps to the front of the animal, James tried to pull it along by the soft rope bridle. Again, the horse embedded its hooves and pulled back from being moved one fingerbreadth further. It shook its head again. *NO!NO!NO!*

"Stupid animal," James muttered. What was he to do? The thing couldn't be budged forward. At all!

"Whatever," James said. It was only a short walk from here. With a little tracing-of-steps, the horse allowed itself to be led back the way they had come, to a nice, fat based olive tree. There, James lassoed the reins around the trunk and in a decent scaffold knot, tethering the pale horse.

The young, ambitious Priest walked the hundred, or so, paces the rest of the way to the unassuming courtyard entrance. At the threshold, James' pace ceased, very much like how the horse just did. A dark, icky force, which he couldn't-or wouldn't-admit to himself was actually there, seemed to reach out with multiple invisible tentacles. To a set of eyes from the angelic realm, they would've seen this dark, icky force as a pulsating, malignant gateway, with grotesque, bulbous tendrils reaching out and curling like obese, soiled fingers. Grasping in extreme desperation for the "new blood" that had come as an aloof, nescient offering.

Against an interior sane voice screaming at him to otherwise run away, James stepped in past the foreboding archway. It was an immediate feeling. A heavy pushing and pulling down upon him, like gravity became exponentially concentrated. Or like he was being ushered into an overly eager introduction to the host of Hades. Fresh nausea bubbled at the top of his guts. His eyes stung, like lemon juice had been squirted directly into them and his flesh became irritated, as if bitten by hundreds of tiny, horrible insects. Panic settled upon him like a blanket when he felt, with all assurity, that the air had been partially diluted, producing something that felt akin to burning and suffocating within his lungs, in concurrent time. Overall he interpreted the atmosphere as wicked.

Past the first set of trees, underneath the duress of these unexplainable conditions, and he felt as though he had walked a half a furlong. The soles of his sandals seemed to stick to the path, quite literally forcing him to peel his foot from the ground with each step.

"This has to be Jesus' doing," James said, convincing himself through clenched teeth. As he was struggling past the second set of trees, a thought occurred to James, "What exactly is *The Messiah* trying to hide with all of these deterrents set in place?"

Not yet even with the third set of trees and the presence of an ungodly stench almost knocked him back. A series of wet retches escaped his stomach, doubling him over. Splattering the pathway with a dark, meaty bile. Causing his stinging eyes to trickle water and his nose to generously leak. By taking the lapel of his robe and using it as a makeshift filter over his lower face, he wiped his face and managed to make the unbreathable air just barely breathable.

During the final stretch to the entrance, one of the three vultures screeched from not far overhead. James glanced up through his squinted eyes and saw their three mangy bodies circling above. In the depleting daylight, only a few of the details about their characteristics were visible. From the ground, James could see the trio of spiraling, featherless heads and necks extending out, like penises, from grey, crusty collars. Their normally brown feathers appeared solid black from this distance and the waning sunlight. Some random white spot on one of the vulture's legs was hard to distinguish from the rest of the underside. There was also the occasional glint of reflected sheen off a sinister talon, tucked underneath their bellies, connected to three sets of dirty, grey legs.

At last, upon reaching the entrance, James touched the massive, thick tombstone and gave a little nudge, just to test the movability of the thing. Without any surprise, it didn't move a hair's breadth from his puny might. If he was being honest with himself, he felt kind of silly for even attempting to singlehandedly budge it.

Looking in through the thick clouds of flies, James could see there was a minimal amount of ambient, natural light being permitted into the initial antechamber. An elongated, fuzzy-edged rectangle laid upon the floor, leaving the perimeter of the room unknown. But, what drew James' attention was an inauspicious portal, centered in the antechamber and a few of the top steps to a set of descending stairs. Ghostly outlines of pale red footprints pointed this way and that on the illuminated slab of floor. He gave a longing glance back towards the courtyard entrance, and, for the most meager of moments, entertained the idea of turning around, getting away from this cursed place and reporting back to Caiaphas that everything at the crypt was A-OK! Hunky-Dory!

No, his interior, aspiring voice rebuked. *What if there* ***is*** *something implicating Jesus here? What if* ***you*** *were the one to discover it and bring it before Gamaliel directly?*

Just the prospect of sticking it to Caiaphas and rubbing his face in it, was enough to push James past his better judgment, and further into the tomb. Within his mind, he talked to a god, thanking him for courage he didn't have; despite his instinct sounding alarm bells off. Within his mind the bells were blaring an internal message of self preservation. Telling him as though in red writing being scrawled on the wall to *GET OUT! GET OUT! GET OUT!*

Taking timid steps, he shuffled forward handbreadth by handbreadth, to the stairs leading down. Breathing shallow and fast, James frantically searched the small, surface level chamber, as far as his adjusting eyes could penetrate into the solid border of darkness that laid heavy, like cement, just outside of the edges of the shrinking rectangle. Flies abounded in plague level numbers in this space. He didn't dare leave his island pad of dwindling, fading light to try to scour beyond the boundary.

While telling himself in his mind, in his father's voice, that he was brave, James called out. "Lazarus?!" Deep inside he hoped that he wouldn't get an answer.

Outside, the circling vultures gave harsh calls to one another. A stiff breeze rustled leaves upon the branches of the courtyard trees, sounding like a miniature crowd applauding at some gladiator games. Beyond that, in the distance, James thought he heard a screech from the pale horse he had tethered. It screamed a high, grating horse scream, sounding ethereal and creepy, as though originating from another realm.

James shuffled forward in tiny increments. Looking like he was traversing a plank over a long drop. Little by little, James was feeling angry at himself, for being so stubborn and adamant against **every** word of advice or caution given by Caiaphas and Annas pertaining to this task. Especially on the matter of his refusal to bring a torch along. With evening departing and night coming at a steady approach, a torch would've really come in handy right about now.

Also, he wouldn't have minded the protective company of a Roman soldier or two, armed with some sharp swords and spears, as well. Those would be nice to have at this terrifying moment too.

He kept rotating the mantra of, *There's nothing to be afraid of,* in his mind.

Bringing his toes to the edge of the top step, James leaned down a little and strained his eyes, trying to peer down into what was down below. Absolutely nothing was visible past the fourth step, as though the stairs disappeared into a pool of lampblack ink. Somehow, there was a worse stench rising up from the depths of the crypt that brought fresh tears to James' eyes. Coupled with a dry heave or two, for good measure.

Feigning an amount of courage he, by no means, possessed, James wiped the bitter vomit remnants from his lips. Then, he called down into the void, loud and melodious, "Oh, Lazarus?! Anyone home?!!"

After a few gracious moments were spent allowing the dead to respond, James straightened and turned to leave. Already congratulating himself on another simple, yet, nerve wracking task accomplished.

Before James could complete the revolution and fully spin around on his heel, the enormous tombstone rolled shut, as though fifty men had manipulated it without any difficulty whatsoever. This was followed by the sound of settled joints cracking and a sticky scurrying that faded as it fluttered down to the catacombs.

"H-hello?" James called out past the buzzing of countless flies, muffled behind his lapel. "Hello? L-La-Lazarus-s?"

There was a harsh combination of a maniac's chuckle and a lunatic's cackle, equaling a demented giggle, that floated up like campfire embers and ash from the lower level. Accompanying the ghoulish glee from down below was more of those rapid, peeling footsteps. Altogether, sounding tremendously mischievous, hellish and scary.

James was left in complete darkness and a pure state of rapidly surging dread. Gagging on every quick inhale of the putrid air. Whimpering and lamenting with every short exhale. A plentiful quantity of flies landed on his exposed bits of skin, causing him to twitch and jitter and blink and spit. Some were trying to enter into his hyperventilating mouth and nose that was tucked behind his fine linen lapel.

Weird, yet familiar, clacking could be heard coming up from down below. An echoing sound reminiscent of two stones being hit against one another enough times in rapid succession to produce a spark.

With his free hand extended out in front of him, feeling blindly, James tried to walk towards the exit, where the slimmest sliver of late evening light tried to creep around the worn chiseled edges of the tombstone. His unsure, scraping steps and shaky breathing echoed hollowly in the enclosed space. The fine, golden spun tzitzit fringes at the base of the mantle of his robe dragged low and brushed intimately against the tacky, bloodied floor.

Stumbling forward he eventually came into contact with the cool, hard inner surface of the tombstone. With a wild phase of frantic energy, James tried to bang, slap, yell, shift and throw his whole body at the enormous, circular hunk of rock.

Amidst his raging hysteria, a soft, dancing glow bloomed from the catacombs below and caught his attention. Drawing his frightened gaze away from the only exit and pointing it back to the stairs, now leading down to a meager, solitary torchlight. Against the reasoning part of his brain, James took a couple of unbalanced steps towards the descending stairs. He raised himself up as high as he could on his tippy toes in a ridiculous attempt to gain a lofty vantage point. Doing this stupid maneuver in order to give himself a straight line of sight down into the unknown sublevel.

What am I doing?!What am I doing?!What am I doing?!! James' mortal mind raced.

When James redirected his attention back to the sealed entry, it brought his weak, human eyes into unsuspecting, locked contact with a set of bulging, black, unfocused eyes. These were set into a ghastly, hawkish face. Long, patchy hair on top was slicked back with an unknown goo. Below, there was a tangled, bearded grin, smeared with a ravenous, glistening vermillion. Even further, beneath these grisly features, stood tall a dead body, with a filthy robe draped like a damp rag over its bony shoulders. A concave chest with splintered bone poking out through the decayed skin was exposed in a roughspun robe that had been left wide open. Being naked otherwise, this revealed all manner of nastiness out in the open, down the front.

"L-La-L-L-La-," James managed to stutter out, before being shoved backwards with tremendous force and tumbling down the viscous stone stairs. Rolling and toppling, end over end, until he came to a hard final landing on the same injured side of his face. His entire body was splattered all up and down the one side with a gamy, gelatinous goo, teeming with squirming, corpulent maggots.

Seconds later, when he came to, his face was partially submerged in the unidentifiable, visceral ooze and covered by an enormous population of flies. That instant, he launched himself upright and wiped at his covered face with both sleeves. Spitting in profuse sessions. His head rang with a solid, unwavering, high pitched note, flooding out any other sound to his ears. He doubled over in savage, retching spasms from the realization that there were some squirming maggots and also, at least, eight dead flies in his mouth. Vomit-inducing as well was the continued inhaling of quick, clipped lungfuls of the rancid, meaty atmosphere, not to mention, also tasting some of the fingerbreadth deep puddle he had landed in. The involuntary reaction to the multi-sensory maladour drew his backbone upwards to the ceiling, yet, his stomach, by this time, had been emptied to completion. Only a thick, slimy, fly and maggot-dappled line of red tinged bile dangling wistfully from his bottom lip was produced from his strong, reactionary convulsions.

Gradually, his vision came back into focus, and the ringing in his ears subsided, but his cognition was still wandering, due to the minor concussion he had suffered. A lone torch crackled and flickered in this pit, reminding one of a certain metaphor regarding a canary in a coal mine.

Behind the whiny buzz of myriads of flies, a viscid, peeling of bare footsteps could be made out, advancing.

James couldn't see where the source of the steps was coming from. The single torch only provided a minimal amount of light against the immense darkness all around. It was as though he were stuck within a feeble globe of light, that was stuck within an overwhelmingly black, sinister void. He drew his *Maakeleth*, a long curved, razor sharp knife, mainly for use in services of the Temple Abattoir. In this case, it was a vital weapon, in a life or death scenario. Putting on a threatening demonstration, with the blade poking out from the pinky side, James took a couple of quick, audible slices through the air. *SNICK! SNICK!*

"Come on!!" James screamed. Had he found his bravery?

For a moment, the impending, tacky footfalls ceased. All that was left to hear was just the subtle *crackle-pop* of the torch flame, the incessant buzzing of millions of flies and James shallow, jittery breathing. James tried to strain his eyes to see past the thick, virulent fog of aerial insects and further into the unknown dark. His right arm was held up in defense across his body, with the sweaty hand holding the knife poised up by his left shoulder. Ready to strike.

Off to his left, James heard a single prodigious voice whisper his name. James screamed a berserk warcry while spinning towards the direction of the voice. He sliced left to right in a blind flurry, just hoping to connect his knife with something. Anything. By sheer force of numbers, he had to, at least, be killing hundreds, if not thousands of flies from his efforts.

Behind him now, James heard a monstrous, amused, imitation of a plucked string of a voice, chuckle and say, *"Not-over-there."*

With a one hundred and eighty degree spin that flourished his golden tzitzit tassels, James struck out with a singular blind ferocity. *SNICK!!* Missing a connecting blow from his *Maakeleth* with the intended target. The force exerted from his wasted strike came close to making him lose his balance and go tumbling to the moist floor.

In a quick, fluid motion, James regained his fighting stance and screamed out, "Come out and fight, devil!"

Close by, the sinister, precise voice spoke James' name again. It was strange though. The voice didn't sound like a normal voice, in the way that there was no breath projecting the syllables out. This voice sounded as if just the vocal cords were being manipulated manually. Like plucking a single harp string to produce a deep, resonating vibration.

Again, James spun and sliced towards the origin from where the voice came. Again, he missed by a miserable distance. He was beginning to feel like he was most certainly being toyed with by an unknown demon. A real cat and mouse situation, with James, being the proverbial mouse.

Sticky footsteps danced and pattered all around, just outside the sphere of paltry illumination. James backed up to the lone, lit torch ensconced on a wall of carved niches for dead relatives. He stood locked and ready.

"James," the demon's voice uttered the name, plain as day to the right.

This time, however, James didn't react to the demonic pronouncement of his name. His knife and reflexes remained primed for slicing.

"James," from his left this time. Louder.

James remained steadfast. His eyes darted all about. In a frenzy, he scanned the border of his limited semi circle of torchlight.

"JAAAAAMMMMEEEES!!!" The voice roared from all available directions.

"COME OUT YOU GODLESS THING!!" James roared back.

From off to James' left, Lazarus launched out of the darkness with a snarl and rust colored fingernails bared like claws. The base of Lazarus' filthy, confiscated robe rippled out behind him like a battle flag on a pole, caught in a bluster. Skinny, grey legs sprinted across the torch lit scummy, stone floor. Black, dead eyes without any emotion or consciousness were peeled wide open. There was an inhuman maniacal, murderous intent behind those eyes operating all of the switches and pulling all of the levers.

James braced himself and met Lazarus with a swipe of his large knife. Lazarus stopped short with the blade, only getting the tips of its pinky and ring finger shaved off on the left hand. Two little grey finger nubs went bouncing across the ground, like lots being cast. With a brief howl and a sidestep, Lazarus repositioned itself on James' right hand side. It took a nasty swipe, meant to take off James' head in one go. James ducked and countered by sticking his knife right into Lazarus' neck, producing a squelch, black blood and a shocked, inarticulate pluck from the dead vocal cords.

With a relieved sense of victory washing over him, James let his grip on the knife go. Leaving it lodged, with the wooden handle sticking straight out of the neck of Lazarus. A small, triumphant smile curled one side of James' scum smattered mouth.

"God be praised!" James shouted, looking up to the black ceiling. He lowered his eyes back down to Lazarus and declared victory by pointing at the possessed corpse and saying, "I got you, devil! I got you!"

Lazarus took one stumbling, wobbly step back. It grasped at the knife handle jutting out from the front of its neck with one hand and felt the tip of the *Maakeleth* blade poking out of the back with the other. It gargled a wet indecipherable phrase before falling to its knees.

James leaned in closely, while pointing at it with his finger and shamelessly gloated further, "I got you, you devil!!"

Then, in a movement too quick to be registered by the human brain, Lazarus removed the blade from its own neck and sliced across James' midsection, disemboweling him. Shocked, James stood paralyzed for a moment, feeling a hot sensation running down the front of him. His mind was trying to comprehend what had just happened. James' perspective tilted and he fell into Lazarus' cradling arms, which, in all actuality, felt like two lifeless, hoisting branches. From a lucid place outside of his body, he heard the *Maakeleth* clatter upon the floor. He was distantly aware that he was being carried. An excruciating pain began to radiate out from his lower abdomen and he groaned aloud.

Lazarus looked down with dead, doll-like, unfocused eyes at James and mimicked without a shred of sarcasm, *"I-got-you!"*

Horrified, but helpless, James screamed and beat in weak patters upon Lazarus, collapsed, splintered chest. His stomach shrieked in seering, protesting pain to every movement. Every breath. Flies flooded at the fresh wound as a greedy mob.

James was finally flopped down onto a hard, cold, granite slab that had most recently been used for an exorcism, but was primarily utilized for embalming and preparing a dead body for eternal rest. *Here is where I'm going to die!* He allowed the terrified thought to reverberate in his head. This became coupled with multiple remorseful reprimands against himself, asking, *Why didn't I bring the soldiers?! Why didn't I listen to Caiaphas?!!*

"Pride," Lazarus said in answer to James' internal thought with that deep, single note. *"New-blood."*

This horrified James all the more, but there wasn't much time to dwell upon the fact that a demon possessed, resurrected corpse was reading his thoughts. That corpse, that had once been known as Lazarus, was now circling, like the vultures outside. A murderous, rictus grin split its face into two. The new wound in its neck was dribbling out the barest bit of inky blood down to the collarbone. It scraped its fingernails upon the outer edge of the slab, making a screeching etch into the surface.

James was trying to cover his gaping wound with both hands in a desperate attempt to keep any more of his guts from spilling out. The little bit of light available dimmed as he began to fade in and out of mortal consciousness. His head lolled heavy on his weakening neck. His eyes rolled up in their sockets. He was bleeding out. Suffering from sanguination.

Lazarus slapped him across the face. Hard. Drawing a fresh trickle of blood from James' lip and nose, and also waking him up to the present moment. James brought his bloody hand up to touch his throbbing jaw with tenderness. That's when Lazarus plunged its hand into James' open cut, sending blinding blooms of pain scattering across James' field of vision. From what seemed like another dimension, James heard himself let loose a blood curdling scream, permitting dozens of flies to enter his mouth.

Through a bleary, blood stained lens, James saw Lazarus remove a loop of James' entrails and bite a section out. Then, while chewing with intense delight, Lazarus proceeded to wrap his neck loosely with another loop of James intestines. Revolution after revolution. Around and around, pulling more of the slick organ from the bleeding wound, like it was unwinding a rope from a reel.

Either from exsanguination, or pain, or both James lost consciousness with his own deafening screams and the buzzing of flies all around him, being the last things he heard in this mortal world.

vii

Tuesday morning. It was very early. The sun had just now begun to discolor the Eastern view with a discolored horizon. Up on the roof Martha was checking the doves in the dovecotes for any word, even though she knew it was much too soon. She had only sent off the urgent message yesterday afternoon, following her return from the tomb. A small note for Jesus, expressing her newfound concern for Lazarus, subsequent to their most recent, bizarre visit to the crypt. Frustrated with the lack of response she already expected to get, Martha still inspected every last bird. She took the last dove she checked and affixed another prepared short, succinct note to its leg. Facing the general direction of where she thought The Messiah might be, Martha let the bird loose. It flapped out of her hands in quick, spastic flutters before it caught the lift and drag it needed for successful flight.

Martha spun away from the dovecote, holding her breath, again. Turning only once in her short walk back to the ladder leading down, for the purpose of hopeful longing. To see if, by chance, the dove she had sent yesterday was returning, carrying reassuring words from Jesus. But, she only saw the speck of her recent attempt, flying away from her.

Once down the ladder and back in the gloomy corridor, she was met by Hannah, looking a supreme kind of haggard. The poor old woman looked as though she hadn't slept a wink in days. A light shade of blue from her shawl framed her face in effigy of anti-exuberance. Dark circles around each eye were greatly enunciated by the drooping bags that gave her whole face a weighted sag. From an open mouth, she vented sharp, metallic scented breaths into Martha's vicinity.

No good morning. No, how are you today? Hannah, instead probed Martha with a vague question, "Did you hear?"

Already tired of this conversation before it even got going, Martha kept her eye rolling to a restrained minimum and answered, "No, Hannah. Good morning to you, as well. What is the matter?"

Hannah pulled her light blue shawl tighter around her dwindling-with-age frame and clued Martha in, “More have been taken.”

“More what?” Martha asked, denying that somewhere in the back of her mind, she was afraid of what the answer might be.

“People,” Hannah blurted. “He’s taken more. Oh, I didn’t want to believe it when one of the girls told me yesterday morning, um, uh…” The old woman wrung her hands together in extreme consternation.

Martha could feel a “But” coming on, so she initiated it for Hannah with a drawn out inflection that lilted the word upwards, “But…”

“But, only just this morning has word been spreading around Bethany about another abduction,” Hannah laid bare.

Martha veered around Hannah and assumed a brisk walking pace down the hall, towards the kitchen. Hannah trailed upon her heels, regurgitating the rumors that had been swirling about. “It was a woman. A mother this time. The children saw him take her.”

“Who?” Martha asked in a clipped manner. Not noticing she was now holding her breath and quickening her steps even more.

Befuddled for a moment, Hannah answered her back, “Who? The children?”

“No,” Martha answered testily to Hannah’s denseness. “Who did the children see take their mother?”

Hannah didn’t answer. Almost as if she were trying to have Martha, on her own, reach the same conclusion they had all reached. It was obvious, she was implicating Lazarus. The suggestive silence radiated like a loud battle horn from Hannah and gave away her passive game to Martha.

As a means for diversion, Martha suggested in an off hand way, as though they were talking about recipes, that, “It’s common for there to be copycats. It’s even more common for them to desire to recreate the crime, so as to create more confusion.”

“Even by copying the details about escaping by way of rooftops?” Hannah retorted.

Martha stayed mute. Holding her breath as they entered the kitchen space. She paraded around the room, giving off the vibe that she was moving with predestined purpose. Grabbing a rag from here. Wiping down an area over there. Adjusting items on shelves that didn’t need adjusting.

Meanwhile, serving girls attended to stocking platters with various fruits and nuts, and also filling pitchers from a bucket brought in from the well. Some pitchers are filled with water and flowers. Some with water only.

"That's what the children saw," Hannah was still prattling on, despite all of the extra sets of eyes and ears. "A creature with something gross wrapped around its neck. That's what they said," Hannah insisted.

In a rush to leave, the serving girls, one by one, snatched up their platters and exited the kitchen space. Leaving Martha to keep up her silly charade pertaining to important housework. Hannah watched the woman of the house rush about the kitchen in a false frenzy. Martha was moving at such a quick pace that she accidentally knocked over a full clay pitcher of flowers and water, sending it to the mosaic floor, where it shattered in a piercing din. Clamor much too boisterous for this early hour of the morning.

Martha knelt to the mess and Hannah met her there. The old woman whispered more metallic breath her way, "I know it was your brother that did it." Martha stopped in the middle of picking up the jagged pieces of broken clay. Hannah continued, kneeling down and speaking right into Martha's face, "I know it was Lazarus that took that woman, that mother last night."

"You don't know anything," Martha choked out.

Hannah antagonized Martha further, by saying, "I've always known it was Lazarus behind everything. The goats. The missing people." She lowered her voice, as though they weren't alone, "Your sister's, um, lover."

Martha stared at the pallid old woman kneeling across from her. "You have no proof." Then, she tried to reason with Hannah by presenting the fact that Lazarus had just been there. Only a few nights prior. At dinner. Hannah had seen him there. Totally non-murderous and nothing gross wrapped around his neck.

"That's not a testament to his innocence," Hannah stated in a blunt retort. "Or yours."

With one hand full of shattered clay and another grasping fresh cut, drenched flowers, Martha stood. Even when Hannah stood up with her, Martha still looked down at the shrunken, older woman, and Martha was not a tall woman in the slightest.

"You sound very confident of your assumptions of my brother...and myself," Martha said.

Once again, Hannah grasped her shawl tighter at the point where her collarbones met her sternum. She turned her wrinkled chin up and in a stoic tone proclaimed, “I am. We **all** are very confident.”

Trying not to squeeze the jagged shards of clay in her hand, Martha spoke with a tender, enthusiastic tenor, “Great. Then produce your definitive proof.”

Hannah stalled. Looking about the kitchen space, she grumbled something unintelligible under her breath.

“I’m sorry,” Martha leaned in, “What was that you said?”

“I said I don't have any,” Hannah muttered. Then, she added in a mumble, “At the moment.”

Triumphant, eyes ablaze, Martha sucked in a short, sharp breath through her nostrils, and stated, “That’s what I thought.”

“But, Martha,” Hannah tried.

“Silence!” Martha shrewdly reprimanded the old woman, who had once been like family to her. She continued in a cadence that sounded as though she had a bad taste in her mouth, “Rumors. Gossip. Assumptions.”

“Mar-,” Hannah tried again.

Taking an imposing step forward, Martha spoke over Hannah’s attempt to quell her rising anger, “I said SILENCE!”

Hannah bit down on her wrinkled lips to keep herself from vocalizing any further interruptions. Her set of saddened chicory colored eyes cast themselves towards the water puddled at their feet. A single tear fell from the tip of her chin and rippled the surface of the spilled flower water.

“Rumors, gossip and assumptions,” Martha repeated Hannah’s infractions to her,"That's the caliber of loyalty I would expect from a total stranger.” This stung Hannah, because it was meant to. “How am I supposed to run this house with lies being spread about me, ultimately usurping my authority, behind my back?”

“I, uh, I don't, um,” Hannah started.

“Yes?” Martha coaxed her. Like she was trying to get a child to admit to an embarrassing wrongdoing.

Hannah started again, in earnest, trying to sound sincere, “I may, uh, have made some, uh, um, accusations that were, um, premature.”

“Premature?” Martha asked angrily. “You mean to say downright wrong?”

“Yes,” the frail old woman acquiesced. “Yes, um, I'm sorry." Hannah tried to straighten herself up proudly, but her bottom lip quivered during her next statement, "I have wronged you with my slander. Do with me what you wish."

Victory! Martha tried to suppress a grin and keep her focus intense. It was a challenge to keep the joy out of her voice, but she was confident in her tone, "First, you're going to clear my name and my brother's name with all of the staff."

Hannah nodded in subtle little ups and downs, then said, "Alright, um-"

"No um! Just do it! Or I will relieve you of your service to this household!" Martha threatened.

Big, medium brown eyes were awash in quivering little pools of tears. The old woman's heart was a clenching fist in her chest.

Martha pressed on, "Second, I plan on stepping out today. Mary is in her room sleeping. I have instructed **everyone** to not give her any wine to drink."

Through a bleary set of puffy, black eyes, Hannah stated, "She'll be a tempest."

'Probably," Martha agreed. "But, that is **your** problem today. Yes?"

Hannah bowed her head low. "Yes."

"Good," Martha said, gesturing with the fresh cut flowers in her right hand. "Now, finally, what am I to everyone in this house?"

Unsure as to the point of Martha's question, Hannah remained silent. Feeling like no answer was better than the wrong answer. Her creased mouth worked at some semblance of a response, but only brief hums and grunts were produced from the old woman.

Martha giggled in deception and pressed the old woman, "Come on, Hannah. It's not a trick question. What am I to everyone in this household?"

Venturing to give the correct answer, Hannah tried, "The, uh, Lady of the House?"

"Precisely," Martha said. "Now, one more question." Hannah waited with her head lowered, like a whipped pet. Martha allowed the air to thicken with the anticipation radiating off the poor old woman in waves.

Why am I enjoying this? Martha wondered to herself in a passing, uncontrollable thought.

Hannah glanced up to see what was keeping the question barred behind Martha's grinning teeth. Turns out, it was just for the sake of drawing out a certain pleasure afforded at the cost of the old woman's dignity.

Martha asked Hannah, "What do you think you are to me?"
"I'm your loyal servant," Hannah replied.
"Good, good," Martha said, as she let the clay shards and flowers fall from her hands to the doused floor again. "Clean up this mess, servant."
With that, Martha edged past Hannah with a quick goodbye in the form of, "I will return later. Remember, no wine for Mary."
Once Martha was gone from the kitchen space, Hannah braced herself against the nearest tabletop and sobbed streams of salty tears. Letting the teardrops fall and add to the mess that she would later clean.

viii

A comfortable, warm late Tuesday morning found Martha and Phillip, dismounted from their horses, walking side by side, down the well traveled, worn route leading to the family tomb. They each led their mounts by the bridle in a dawdling, unhurried pace. Taking some generous moments to wander around a tree trunk. Flirt with one another playfully. Maybe steal a sinful intimate touch, along with a kiss or two.

Even if she weren't spinning in this newborn relationship of theirs, Martha felt better by just being away from the house. A freedom she felt from not having to deal with Hannah and the coalition of servants under her spell. Plus, she was aware of a lightness in her breast, or maybe it was a sense of relief, from not being around her burdensome, alcoholic sister, Mary.

During their trek to the crypt, in between the chunks of time they were devoting to physical affection for one another, they also managed to shimmy in some entertaining conversation. Martha regaled Phillip with the tale about Mary smuggling wine in a water skin yesterday, resulting in Martha ordering the whole household to be compliant in a detox for her. Plus, it resulted in a mandatory staff attended whipping of the two servants, guilty of subjugation, for furnishing Mary with the perniciously disguised wine.

"Oh Mary," Phillip rumbled with a palpable sadness expressed through his baritone.

"I know!" Martha agreed eagerly. Taking a ponderous moment to gaze at this man she had known since childhood and, for the first time, see his soul as a compliment to her own. She felt a pull to him like no other. Maybe that was because Phillip, through most of this figurative tumultuous storm that her life had become, had been like a lighthouse to her. A strong beacon for her to anchor to. Unfortunately, it had taken all of the recent events for her to realize that she was, no doubt, coming to love him.

Continuing on, a flustered Martha shallowly delved into the mutinous difficulties she was experiencing with her house staff, in particular, with Hannah.

"Why?" Phillip asked. "She's just a harmless, frail old woman"

Martha answered him back with a playful bump of her hip against his outer thigh and a question, "Where is it written that you grow more innocent as you age? You don't know! That woman has had years to perfect the art of a devious nature."

Phillip laughed in a low, thrumming pulse from his barrel chest and kissed her upon the forehead. He tried to pull her off to the side of the path again for more fun, newly discovered canoodling. She pushed him off, as a part of the frisky courtship dance, that was a timeless diagram in the lesson of chase and conquer. A coy ritual which would perpetually unfurl long after they were dead and gone.Until time immemorial.

Sauntering down the trail and getting closer to their destination, with their pinkies curled around one another's, Phillip asked Martha about her visit to the tomb the previous day, "Well, other than Mary's covert boozing-," Martha giggled at his joke, "-how was the rest of your visit to the tomb yesterday?"

"Bizarre," she admitted, clearing her throat. The giggling mirth disappeared from her voice. "Lazarus was different than he was at the dinner."

"Different? How?" Phillip asked, feeling a notion of dread rising up in his chest.

"His actions were...unpredictable," Martha stated. "I don't know. I was expecting…" she trailed off with something too low to hear.

"What?" Phillip asked. "I didn't catch that last part."

"I said I was expecting some semblance of how he was the night before," Martha said. Then she clarified further, not that Phillip needed it, "You know. At dinner. Like how he was talking and carrying on a conversation."

Phillip broke their contact through their pinky fingers, to wave away an inquisitive bee that had floated down to see if he was something that it could in one way or another pollinate. "Maybe that had something to do with The Messiah's presence," Phillip offered, as the fuzzy bee drifted away from the lazy swatting of his big hand and back up to the blossoms. "He did seem to have a...calming effect on your brother."

"I don't know," Martha said again, with the inflection of her words leaning towards morose. "I was just hoping and praying so much for things to be getting better."

Phillip's big, calloused hand clasped her small, delicate one. Thoughts of what he saw and learned in Capernaum needled at the back of his conscience. Looking down at her looking up at him, with two lines of worry creasing her brow, he tried to say something reassuring and logical, "Nothing is predictable about what you're going through. Nothing can be expected. Because no one else has gone through it. Right?"

Martha nodded in a soft, affirming up and down. Turning over his words in silent concurrence, but not sounding fully convinced when she whispered a constricted agreement through brimming tears, "Right."

Phillip put his arm around her shoulder and added, "Maybe this is a test from God."

It was then that the wind changed course and blew the unmistakable stench of death right into their faces. Inducing a gag reflex from Phillip. Prompting Martha to rub his back in a soothing manner while he doubled over, retching. Once he had composed himself, they proceeded towards the warning scent. On very high alert now, they slowed their already sluggish pace down even more, to a trepid crawl.

The horses Tsalav (Aramaic for turtle) and Hilazon (Aramaic for snail) saw it before Martha and Phillip did. Both horses began to snort, screech, shake their heads and stamp their front hooves in objection to the human's efforts to drag them on any further.

Phillip walked both horses back up the trail a little ways and tethered them to the base of an old, large olive tree. It took a few moments to calm the beasts down, but before long, he had rejoined Martha and they continued in a careful, measured gait towards the repelling smell of decomposed flesh.

Their faces were covered by the sleeves of their robes. Martha held her breath and took quick snippets of the foul air as little as possible. Covering Martha in a protective gesture, Phillip held his brawny arm wrapped around her shoulders. She fit like a seed tucked in a pod within his big, bulky frame. No matter what, Phillip was assuring that whatever was going to happen, he wanted it to happen to him.

From a distance, they could both see the courtyard and the sealed tomb beyond. Unfiltered sunlight completely drenched the scene, giving it an almost oasis-like quality. It was a calming, peaceful, visual of two short rows of mature, sun dappled trees, framing a short stone pathway. This sight from afar, gave quite the elysium contrast to the reality that was happening much closer.

Before Martha, along with Phillip could lay eyes on them, a trio of shabby, bloody beaked vultures beneath an olive tree hissed, flapped and squawked at the advancing interlopers. This stopped both Phillip and Martha dead in their tracks. Their eyes darted all over what they were looking at with utter disbelief. After a speechless, disorienting moment, once their eyes had focused and their brains had processed what they were looking at, a fresh wave of new horror set in.

Leaving Martha frozen, holding her breath and planted to the spot where she stood while Phillip crept forward cautiously. Curiosity to know disgusting finer details gave him the motivating force to put one foot in front of the other. The vultures watched Phillip coming closer, their slick, featherless heads were fully caked in a gross, bloody viscera. Two of the three, in furious response, alighted asynchronously up to the nearest branch above the meal when Phillip reached a certain intolerable proximity. A stubborn third vulture remained by the feast. All three scavenging birds threatened and tried to intimidate Phillip to get away from their prize.

The prize being a mostly mutilated horse covered in greedy, glutinous flies. Still tied to a tree by the reins, causing its lipless mouth and skinned neck to skew up and at an unnatural angle, while the rest of what was left of its carcass was laid lifeless upon its side. Gruesome large, human looking bite marks were sprinkled across its starboard side and posterior. Whole slabs of meat had been removed, as well as most of the organs, leaving the body hollow. The front hooves had both been truncated up to where its breast had been. Sizable chunks of removed hide, and what little hide there was left, being blood splattered made it difficult to determine the color of the horse. If it weren't for a single spotless ear, a portion of the splattered mane and the tail, no one would've been able to tell that it had been a pale horse at one time.

Martha startled Phillip into a dramatic flinch, by walking up with soft, inaudible steps and saying, "What could've done that?"

"Good God!" Phillip said in reaction to being snuck up on. Once he realized it was Martha just joining up with him, his eyes returned to the carcass.

While turning over Martha's question in his mind, Phillip's eyes flicked from one of the human-like bite marks to the next. It looked as though the horse had been attacked by a single, bloodthirsty, savage human. Or a pack of wild, hungry-for-horsemeat humans.

"I don't kn-," Phillip started, but then abruptly cut himself off upon noticing something peculiar sticking out of the bloody mess of the horse's neck.

Puzzled, he cocked his head to the side, squinting and trying to identify what he was seeing amidst the spent carnage. From where he was standing, (a little over three cubits from the carcass), he couldn't quite make out what it was. It managed to blend in very well with all of the surrounding slimy bits and pieces. Glistening as well, but sporting a hard line rigidity, that helped it stand out among the supple, torn meat.

"What did you say?" Martha asked.

"Ssshhh!" Phillip tried to shush her politely, but it still came off short and rude.

He had to get closer. When he began to encroach further, the last remaining vulture at the feast saw him and snagged one last dangling bite, before doing a little hop glide, to where he joined his brethren on a low branch. There, all three, in no uncertain terms, staunchly opposed his presence and his dwindling proximity to their rotting smorgasbord.

Pushing through the dense cloud of flies to get to the object was horrendous for Phillip. The thousands of insects swarmed him. Landing on any exposed skin and tasting his sweat greedily. Trying to fly up through the bottom of his sleeves and base of his robe. Phillip thrashed and weaved his way up to the horse. He could feel hundreds of little winged bodies hit against his free hand when he swatted from side to side.

Upon reaching the horse, Phillip grasped the hard object and pulled, finding that it was lodged securely. He yanked with his free hand, while trying to keep most of his face covered with his sleeve. It didn't budge. With more force applied, he yanked again, causing the carcass to shift upon the ground a little and evoking a protesting squawk from a couple of the perched vultures. However, this did achieve a quick skid of movement from the embedded object, before it seized once more.

Phillip took a glance back to Martha, who was standing where he had stepped away from her. Her eyes looked back at him in intense anticipation above the sleeve that she held to her face.

"What is it?" Martha called to him. Muffled.

In a nonverbal response, Phillip shook his head from side to side and shrugged his broad shoulders, then returned to the task of trying to dislodge the item. With his one free hand, he tried to pull again at the piece, backing it out of the entry point just a smidge more.

He pulled again.

This time nothing.

Again.

Nothing.

In a final effort, he regrettably had to incorporate both hands into the pulling, leaving his full face exposed. Flies tried to flood into his ears, nose, mouth and eyes. He held his breath, shut his eyes tight and pulled. Nothing.

Again.

A little scrape of movement.

Again, nothing.

Again, a larger scrape.

Then, digging his feet into the ground, with all of his back and leg muscles engaged, Phillip yanked and strained against the item. The sight of blobby stars bloomed behind his eyelids. He could feel his veins bulging from his arms, neck and temples. When it came loose, at last, he was thrown backwards by the massive force of his own momentum. Coming to land on his butt and back. Sprawled out. Laborious breaths were sucking in and blowing out the foul air.

In an instant, he was almost up to his feet, lurching towards Martha. Away from the rancid carcass. Clutching the item in his hand.

They both meandered far away, upwind of the dead horse, along with its billowing putresence. Allowing the vultures and flies to return to their rotten meal, undisturbed.

Once they were clear of the scene, they stopped by a tree within spitting distance of the courtyard. Phillip turned the piece over in his hands. It was a knife. A large, wooden handled, curved blade. Both Phillip and Martha recognized it for what it was. A *Maakeleth*. Normally used for work in the Abottoir at the Temple. But, what was it doing all of the way out here? And why had it been stuck into a horse's neck in such a brutal fashion?

"A man did this," Phillip said in disbelief, looking between the knife and then back at the decimated horse they had just passed. Repeating, "A man did this," as though to help conflate the reality of the statement with truth. Using the repetition of the phrase as a sort of canticle. An exercise to help his own mind accept what was humanly possible, no matter how far flung and depraved.

"How could a man do that?" Martha asked.

"He would have to be possessed," Phillip answered gravely. Signaling where his thought process was leading him, by turning his head and looking right up through the courtyard to the enormous stone sealing the entrance to the tomb.

Under her breath, Martha gave a weak attempt at a defense for her implicated brother, "Lazarus isn't possessed." However, an inner voice was recalling relevant snippets of her talk with Hannah earlier today, *I know it was your brother that did it...I've always known it was Lazarus behind everything.*

For the sake of her own eroding hope, her mind raced and grasped for explanations and exonerations. Who did that horse belong to? Where were they now? The tomb is sealed. A single rider, maybe two, with all the might they could muster, would not even be able to move that tombstone one baby pinky fingerbreadth. Maybe there were more on foot traveling with the riders. At this point, all that they had was speculation. Anything was possible.

Through the thin veil of these flimsy, misdirecting questions and theories, legible collages of recent, terrifying events played out in stark contrast. The goats, reminding her of the horse carcass they had just seen. The cannibalism of the child that first night. Mary's unfortunate lover. Dozens of innocent people, over the course of weeks, taken in the middle of the night by a ghoul. Allegedly, her brother. Lazarus. If she were to be honest with herself, the evidence to Phillip's statement about possession was getting harder and harder to refute.

Meanwhile, while her mind had been racing, Phillip had walked over to the archway of the threshold to the courtyard. He had taken the knife he pulled from the horse and stuck it in his belt, letting it press against his hip. A pained look had contoured his usual handsome features into a grimace of hateful repulsion.

Martha came up beside Phillip and he said,"It looks different in the daytime."

"Different, how?" Martha asked.

"I don't know," Phillip answered without looking at her. His eyes tracing up and over the curve of the archway. "Somehow it seems more...sinister in the daylight."

"There is nothing to fear," Martha said in a weak display of resolve that was unconvincing even to herself.

Now Phillip pulled his attention away from studying the ominous courtyard and looked at her with an expression of blatant disbelief, as if she had said that some of that horse meat looked tasty back there. His head swiveled in little, almost imperceptible, movements from side to side. In a swift flare of motion, Phillip slipped the soiled knife from his belt. This action let the gruesome details of the congealed blood smeared upon the blade and the tiny bits of matted horse hide pressed against the top of the handle, shine in the sun.

Phillip challenged Martha, "You think there's nothing to fear? Look at this!" He held up the knife in both open palms. "Look at that!" He pointed back up the path. "Martha, I'm sorry, but there is something...evil out here."

"By 'something' I take it you're referring to Lazarus?" Martha said, sounding like she was heading towards anger. She recycled the line of argument she used with Hannah, "After seeing how Lazarus was at the dinner, you still feel this way?"

Phillip strained to reason with her, "Martha, I honestly think Jesus had something to do with that."

Martha fumed without any further coherent rebuttal. She paced and, in a petulant, childish way kicked the hard packed dirt on the pathway. There were multiple different ways she tried to start the same sentence, *Jesus...He doesn't...So, you think...Lazarus isn't...* Working her twitching mouth for the right words to dash his theory to pieces.

Phillip's heart ached and went out to her. She seemed to be stuck in the first stage of death normally reserved for the short, passing phase of denial. Her mind appeared to be a perfect subject willing to overlook simple facts in favor of reality.

"Martha," Phillip said in a tender voice. Offering his big hand out to her.

Martha's face had turned a shade of crimson that was a usual shade for roses. Her eyes bulged and she blurted out, "Watch!" Then, she stormed away through the detrimental archway threshold. Stomping hard to convey her broiling anger through her gait.

Following her through, Phillip immediately felt a mighty weight bogging down upon his body and spirit. An onerous, oppressive atmosphere that desired to push and pull whoever trespassed into a dismal physical and spiritual descending. A feeling like invisible hands were shoving his head mercilessly down into his collarbones. Every breath taken in created a sizzling, burning sensation in his esophagus and lungs. He suddenly wanted to puke all over the courtyard pathway. Each blink for the briefest of moments soothed his stinging, burning eyes. His skin crawled with an unseen, rashy irritation.

"Martha," he called to her back. "Martha, stop!"

Martha was almost to the tombstone. Moving as though she were traversing waist high snow. Pushing off with each difficult step, like she was dragging an ocean vessel's anchor behind her.

She threw herself at the tombstone upon reaching it. Slapping with both hands and in a wild syncopation at the warm limestone. Calling out to her brother on the other side. Her words were becoming thicker in her throat with every word, "Lazarus?! Lazarus come out and show us!" The increasing stinging in her palms didn't even register. "Show us that you're all better!!"

Phillip caught up to her and spun her around. Upon doing so, he saw that rivers of tears were streaming down her face. Snot revealed itself in the form of a translucent, green bubble, inflating and deflating, peeking out of her left nostril. Martha's speech had devolved into an incoherent, watery blathering.

Phillip gathered her up in a safeguarding embrace. Burying her deep in his formidable chest. Trying to pacify her with calm shushing and cooing.

Talking low and gentle, allowing his voice to rumble hypnotically through his breast, vibrating against her head.

Muffled from within his arms, Martha kept saying, "I just..I just wanted my brother back." A dollop of snot dribbled down to her lip and there was a great, rippling snort.

"I know. Ssshhh. I know," Phillip stroked the back of her head.

Rapid, muted slapping, that sounded as though it were generated from multiple sets of hands, could be heard coming from the interior of the crypt. Even on the exterior, the hitting on the thick, carved stone by the resident on the inside sounded painful. As if Lazarus were most definitely breaking its rigored fingers and phalanges.

When she heard Lazarus smacking the inner face of the tombstone, Martha cried harder from down in the burrow of Phillip's chest, "That's what happened yesterday." *SNIFF!!* "When we all came out here."

For a few long, unbroken moments, the disharmonious, staccato slapping continued. Too fast and hard for one human to achieve, let alone maintain for this length of time. Suddenly, just as quick as it started, it ceased.

Martha held her breath and Phillip stared with wide, frightened eyes. Unsure of what was going to come next. Once again, the grains of sand fell like weightless, lazy feathers in the metaphorical hourglass they were currently in. Leaves nearly froze solid in their rustling on the branches. Wind lingered like a languid, lover's touch as it passed over their irritated skin.

In a slow, calculated roll, the sun-dappled tombstone grinded against the outer wall of the crypt. The sound of the friction between two massive stones was definite. Shortly, the movement came to a stop after affording the resident only a small dark corner of the entry to peek out of.

Phillip narrowed his wide, frightened gaze down to a couple of shrewd slits. Inside of the crypt, there was a familiar, unobtrusive, reddish-orange flicker of a torch, coming from behind a partial outline of a darkened silhouette. Two shining points of reflection, resembling the sparkle of diamonds in a dark mine, accounted for a pair of feverish, pitch black eyes. A few glistening, backlit, elusive features hovered above and below the wild set of eyes, but Phillip couldn't make out what they were. Thick clouds of flies buzzed in and out of the small opening in cyclical droves.

The reek arrived next. Wafting out slowly and deliberate towards them. A stench that made the dead horse carcass up the path seem like a fragrant flower patch. A fetid concentration of decay that was an assault on their senses. Martha caught herself a most unpleasant whiff before Phillip did, but not by much. In response, he lurched involuntarily from his diaphragm and she immersed her face deeper into his chest.

"Good God!" Phillip exclaimed out loud through gritted teeth.

For a weird moment, with her eyes closed, Martha felt as if she were moving. She felt as though she were experiencing some strange out of body experience. It resembled an ethereal, gentle rocking that was reminiscent of being transported backwards on a long set of giraffe legs. However, she was facing forwards in the direction she felt she was headed. Almost mistaking this for a dream or a vision. Opening her eyes, she instantly came to realize that she **was** moving. Not by her own accord. She was being carried back to the courtyard entrance by Phillip. He had lifted her up from the ground, letting her feet dangle, and was now backpedaling them out of there as fast as he could, under the atmospheric circumstances that the courtyard enforced.

From inside the tomb, a single voice cried out, *"Martha! Martha, help!"* To Martha's hopeful ears, it sounded so close to how her brother once did. A long time ago. When he was a little boy. *"Help! Martha! Help me!!"* From inside the folds of Phillip's robe, she turned and looked back at the tomb with a longing to help. There was an understandable maternal piece of her that wanted so badly to believe that voice. A feeling that could be likened to a welling up, refreshing spring rose in her breast. A feeling that clouded over her eyes and demanded she go back to nurture whatever need her brother had.

"Don't listen Martha," Phillip commanded gruffly. "That's not your brother."

"MARTHA!" The childish imposter voice rose in its anguish. *"PLEASE HELP ME! MARTHA!!"*

Lazarus' oldest sister twisted herself around in Phillip's arms to answer the call from her baby brother. "Yes, Lazarus I hear you! I hear you!!" Martha called back. She wriggled an arm free from underneath Phillip's bicep, to reach back to the partially open tomb.

Phillip gripped her tighter and attempted to pick up the pace, despite the unrelenting duress this unholy place imposed. "No, Martha! No!!" He growled in exertion, as they passed the second set of trees.

"MARTHA! HELP ME!" The singular counterfeit voice, shifting from a child's to an adult's, called out. Sounding like her brother from only half a dozen full moons ago. Moaning with a heartbreaking cadence. *"MARTHA! I LOVE YOU!!"*

"LAZARUS!!" Martha screamed. She was twisted around and reaching back with both hands extended towards the crypt. "I LOVE YOU, BROTHER!!!"

Passing up the last set of trees before the courtyard threshold, Martha tried to squirm out of Phillip's grasp. Pushing down on the top of his collarbones with both hands and trying to squeeze up, out of his arms. Phillip manhandled Martha a bit and whisked her around like an inanimate bail of hay. Tossing her over his shoulder. "NO, MARTHA!! IT'S NOT LAZARUS!!!" He yelled at her through the misty spell that had been cast over her eyes and ears. Phillip was grunting and sweating while prying each foot from the ground with each impossible step. In the back of his mind, he could have sworn to the feeling of snatching roots or skeletal hands wrapping around his ankles and calves. Trying to hold him in place. Every muscle in his body burned from the effort of just putting one foot in front of the other.

Martha beat upon Phillip's upper back with the side of her small fists. Her foggy, enchanted eyes poured out tears for her helpless baby brother. "Let go! Lazarus needs me!!"

"MMMMAAAAARRRRTTTHHAAAA!! HHHEEEELLLPP MMMEEEE!!!" Lazarus roared across the courtyard from behind the stone. Sounding as though it were being put through the most mind bending torture.

When Phillip finally crossed the cursed courtyard threshold with Martha over his shoulder, the pale film over her eyes dissipated, like a wisp of smoke in a gale. Their skin pleasantly rested. Their eyes cooled and soothed. The oppressive force weighing down had relented. Her ears opened and she heard inhuman, demonic laughing coming from across the courtyard. *"HAHAHAHAHA!!!"*

Martha wiped tears from her face and seemed disoriented. She put the heel of her palm to her forehead, and said, as if waking from a dream, "Lazarus?"

Already on his feet, Phillip extended his hand down to her. She tenuously accepted his hand and rose up to her unsteady feet. Teetering at first.

Acting groggy and discombobulated. She allowed herself to be enveloped into and suspended up in his arms.

"See?" Phillip spoke low down to the top of her head. Steaming up her follicles. "That's not Lazarus. That's...something else. Something evil."

"Something else? Something evil." Martha spoke as though emerging from a deep sleep. With the demented laughter resonating out of the tomb behind them, Martha felt like she was still trapped in a fever dream. Without a word, she was escorted by Phillip back past the carcass to their tethered horses. She remained in her hazy, speechless daze the whole way home. Once there, she allowed Phillip to talk to her some more, in private, about their strange afternoon and how to proceed from here. Before saying goodbye, Phillip accentuated their time together with a final one-sided kiss on her numb,lifeless lips.

As though she were sleepwalking, Martha wandered without a word past familiar, eager faces and their soundless moving mouths. Past their concerned expressions. Past their prying questions. Until at long last, she was alone in her room. While still fully clothed and unwashed, she pulled the covers over her head. Shutting out the entire world.

"Arms held out in your **Jesus Christ** pose. Thorns and shroud, like it's the coming of The Lord. And I swear to you I would never feed you pain. But you're staring at me like I'm driving the nails."-Soundgarden, **Jesus Christ** Pose

Part V: Revelation

i

Nisan twelve. Two days before the Day of Preparation. Wednesday. Normally on a day such as this, the Temple would be packed to capacity with worshippers. There would be vast, lengthy lines combining all of the sinners, the diseased, and the destitute. It wouldn't be out of the ordinary for some leprosy ridden mutants to be creeping through the crowds, jingling obnoxious bells and waving horrific stumps up over their noseless faces, shouting a mushmouthed warning of, *Unclean! Unclean!* At this most special time of year, beasts of all sizes would typically be either braying or screeching during the sacrifices that were commonly happening morning, noon and night. As was considered regular, Priests would be covered in a thick coat of animal blood, garments torn asunder from a recent sacrificial performance. On any other ordinary Nisan thirteen, the Temple coffers would be overflowing in great, sparkling mounds of pilfered booty.

This year was by all accounts different. By comparison to previous years, this year the Temple looked almost deserted. Besides the required Pharisees, the Sadducees, Members of the Sanhedrin and patrolling pairs of Roman soldiers, there had only been a handful of worshippers that had come in for Temple services. All manner of stocked beast was in a current state of thriving in the Abottoir, unknowingly waiting for their turn, if any, with the *Maakeleth.* The coffers could've been mistaken for having been pilfered themselves, judging by how barren they were. For heaven's sake, Caiaphas had barely seen a half a dozen lepers within the Temple walls so far this week!

In response to the alarming diminished attendance, and, especially the coffers, Gamaliel had announced an emergency, mandatory meeting. All hands on deck. At once. In the Chamber of Hewn Stones, of course.

As was expected, Annas assumed the presiding duties of the Av Beit Din. Two gleaming white, shellacked, bovine femur bones were clutched in each richly adorned hand. Jutting down, almost touching the floor. Ready for the clacking. From his hunched position by Gamaliel, he was surveying the faces of his gathered peers. Comparing the level of palpable collective worry, based on demeanor and volume of what was being said.

Gamaliel, although in this Chamber, Nasi, sat in the tallest throne at the center of the dias. Looking not a day under two hundred years old. Stooped over, positioning his ancient chin over his archaic knees. Sporting a wispy, cobweb-like consistency of beard, that was the same impossible shade of white as a summer cloud. The wrinkled folds sagging down over each eyelid were so pronounced, that only a thin letterbox of vision was afforded to him. In the midst of mumbled conversation he thought he was having with Annas, without any warning, an inconsistent, wet cough would burst from the old man. An awful sound that rattled in his chest until it broke loose. Then, as was his habit, he would chew with gumption upon the slimy blob, as though testing its viscosity, before swallowing it back down.

The Chamber was filled with anxious Pharisees, nervous Sadducees and agitated Members of the Sanhedrin. Talk in the Chamber revolved around what was being said in the streets, amongst their absent constituents. Gossip, apparently, had been racing from mouth to ear of the man, Jesus of Nazareth, raising another man, Lazarus, from the grave. Promising people a better alternative pathway to God, where the miracles were tangible. Also free. This explained why this year, the holy beacon of the Temple was so terribly absent of all of the forlorn unsavories, with their pitiful hope and precious coin, seeking their false salvation.

CLACK! CLACK! CLACK!

The call of the bones snapped everyone's attention away from their current conversations to the center of the dias. Echoing voices died down to sporadic murmurs, leaving a repeating resonance bouncing from wall to wall.

"Please take your seats," Gamaliel grumbled, but still projected in the cavernous space.

Fine robes shuffled. Supple, leather sandals slapped. A few mild murmurs of *Pardon me,* were spoken in passing. Seats were taken. Rings and phylactery boxes were adjusted. Some throats were cleared and sniffs were sniffed.

From his seated position, Gamaliel said, "We will commence this meeting after approaching Almighty God for His blessing."

Nearly six dozen men stood or knelt after already having taken their seats. Jeweled hands were either clasped like meek servants do at the waist, heads bowed above, or extended out to each side, palms up, faces up in a posture of performative piousness.

A bald stenographer sat motionless, like a piece of furniture. Seated crossed-legged and compact in his usual spot on the floor, beside the feet of Gamaliel. Ready to capture every nuance of this meeting of all of the Holy Men in the Temple in permanent lampblack ink.

"Most High God, we humbly come before you to thank you for what has be-" A nasty, liquid cough bubbled up offensively in Gamaliel's throat, interrupting the prayer. Halting the pen. Once Gamaliel had chewed with satisfaction and swallowed what he had coughed up, he mumbled a quick, *Excuse me,* then continued in the prayer, "-thank you for what has been provided today and ask that you bless this meeting of the Greater Sanhedrin. Make our decisions wise and our judgements swift. Amen."

There was a concurrent rumbling of, "Amen." More brief shuffling as everyone took their seats. All except for one, Caiaphas noticed. James' seat was vacant. One missing out of seventy-one. This made him acutely aware that he hadn't seen the young Priest since he sent him off on his fool's errand of confirming the death of Lazarus.

Nasi began to drone, setting the statue like stenographer in motion, scribbling, "We are gathered here to discuss the recent, significant drop in our patronage."

Multiple men jumped to their feet and began to shout out of turn, claiming, *Jesus is to blame!* and *His miracles have charmed the masses!* or *He is no*

Son of God!! Their voices overlapped one another in the echoing. Bouncing from wall to floor to the ceiling, distorting the next set of spoken words. Over and over, until it all blended into an incoherent stream of yelling.

"QUIET!!" Av Beit Din roared out effectively.

CLACK! CLACK! CLACK!

Sharp, piercing notes from the femur bones being struck together penetrated through the babbling, frothing commotion, like a *Maakeleth* through surprised, unyielding flesh. Acting as one, the Priests shut their mouths concomitantly. Biting their own lips, they looked to Av Beit Din standing by the ancient Nasi. Unsyncopated, one by one, those inflamed by their collected passion for the Temple, or, a more accurate statement would be, inflamed by the missing masses and their coin, took their seats again.

Nasi, again, spoke low, once the echoing had died down to a residual hum. "We are not going to make any progress shouting over one another, brothers."

Still bedecked in all of the gold and the jewels that he had been flaunting all week, Caiaphas stood, but exhibited the proper decorum reserved for this Chamber. He patiently waited to be recognized with his long, spidery fingers intertwined. His smug expression was softly lit from underneath by the basic, slow shifting pattern of the jewels on the Breastplate. Ruby fading into sapphire. A tepid and lifeless Urim and Thummim laid dormant in the front pockets of the dirty, unwashed Ephod.

"Ah, Rabbi ben Caiaphas, you have the-," Nasi rumbled, but interrupted himself by hacking up a sopping snack, to which he habitually nibbled. Some of the holy men yacked in loud disgust when they caught sight of the thick, pale green expectorant stretch from between top and bottom row of Nasi's toothless mouth.

Caiaphas didn't wait for Nasi's coughing outburst to fully transpire. Claiming his time on the floor, his high voice rang out in the Chamber like a broken bell, "Yes! The rumors are true! This is all Jesus' fault!!"

This incited a furor that exploded from most of those gathered. They leapt from their seats, shook their fists and yelled as a fomenting mob would. Their voices were unmistakably in affirmation to Caiaphas' accusation, but were all obvoluted, like leaves, and obfuscating on top of one another.

Caiaphas sat, pleased with his inflammatory rhetoric and the results it was producing. In the commotion, he caught Av Beit Din's eye and signaled with his own eyes to the empty seat where James' butt was supposed to be.

A small, serious nod from his father-in-law, once up and down, telegraphed, *I know.*

Modest Nicodemus, with a tasteful amount of jewels and a solid cotton beard, now rose from his seat. With his small coalition of half a dozen assembled in tight support behind him, he challenged The High Priest of the Year, "What does this mean? Jesus is to blame? Blame for what?"

The younger, eager Sadducee, Stephen, jumped from his own seat to fervently debate Nicodemus, "He has coerced our worshippers! They are bewitched by his tricks!"

"What tricks?" Joseph of Arimathea spoke in defiance from beside Nicodemus. "A verifiable resurrection? Healing the sick and the lame? Giving a different brand of hope to the poor and downtrodden?"

Nicodemus added to this, "Coerced? Maybe our message and the results that this Temple is producing are weak in comparison."

Stephen seethed, "You both sound converted! Like you're a couple of his devoted disciples!!"

Nicodemus could see this easily spiraling out from a robust debate into an emotional and violent exercise. Plus, his opinions about Jesus were very unpopular and outnumbered in this present company. He raised his hands in passive rebuttal. Holding them up at chest height, palms showing. He replied by trying to reason, "All we're saying is, perhaps we've become lazy in our efforts to resonate with the people. They are obviously responding to the message Jesus of Nazareth speaks."

Before Stephen or anyone else could react to this, Caiaphas seized the opportunity to screech, "It makes no matter! He will be dealt with shortly! Then, our Temple will return to its former glory with 'the people'." A purposeful inflection was applied to how he pronounced 'the people'. Plainly, this was meant as a jab against Nicodemus and his sympathetic humanity towards their constituents.

Nicodemus squinted and questioned, "What do you mean, 'dealt with'? What are you planning?"

"Nothing," Caiaphas lied in a flippant waving off of his overly jeweled, elongated hand. "Radicals, like Jesus, step out of line and break the Law in due time. It's only a matter of waiting until he oversteps the bounds laid down by the Law."

"Here! Here!" Stephen cheered and clapped his hands together vigorously, making a sharp, metallic clicking from his rings smacking together.

Likewise, this sent most of the room into a resounding, lasting applause. Echoing the Chamber with a sound likened to being at the bottom of a cascading, powerful waterfall. Nicodemus had tried what he could to defend the innocent man, Jesus of Nazareth. Joseph of Arimathea, too. But, they were defeated just by their sheer lack of numbers compared to the rest of the dias. From across the Chamber, Caiaphas smugly smirked at them in victory.

CLACK! CLACK! CLACK! CLACK! CLACK!

The cheering and uproar in the Chamber died down, leaving a warbling fade of triumph. All gathered took their seats and once again, adopted an air of civility.

Nasi sided with the majority when he spoke, saying, "Thank you Rabbi ben Caiaphas for your words of reasoning. Of course this, Jesus, is only a popular, passing fad with the people for the moment. Whereas, the Temple is eternal."

Joseph of Arimathea stood and without being properly recognized, spoke freely, "But, what ab-,"

CLACK! CLACK! CLACK!

Av Beit Din roared, "Sit down! You have not been recognized!!"

Joseph instantly clapped back, "May I be recognized?"

"NO!!!" Av Beit Din yelled. And not just Av Beit Din, but also Caiaphas and a large swath of those on the dias all yelled back. Decorum be damned!

Joseph sat back down next to Nicodemus. Pouting, while his old friend assured him with comforting words and patted his forearm upon the armrest. Joseph's knuckles were white as he gripped the carved stone in anger.

Nasi continued now, "All will work itself out for the Temple's glory, which is God's glory. We will be patient and wait for this Jesus, this...this...radical to break the Law, as he most certainly will." The ancient, old man brought a pale, weak fist up to his toothless mouth and cleared his throat. Everyone in the Chamber nervously anticipated another saturated coughing fit, slash snack. Thankfully, none came. Nasi continued on, "Then he can be brought to swift justice. And our worshippers will return to our open arms."

The following applause that transpired from most of the dais was not raucous. More subdued and pretentious. Like they already knew that this was going to be the outcome. They knew they couldn't beat Jesus' message and miracles with a message of their own that spoke and transcended with the people. So, that only left them with one option. Jesus and his message, in their puny little minds, had to be eliminated.

After the collective applause had died down, some boring updates on unimportant administrative issues followed. Nasi finished off the meeting with another droning, recycled, word for word prayer.

Upon the official adjournment of the meeting, Nicodemus propelled from his seat towards Caiaphas. Stomping fast to cover the wide distance to the other side of the dias. There, Caiaphas was surrounded by a group of his adoring peers. The gems upon his Breastplate cycled through a calm, simple pattern. From carbuncle to diamond.

Diamond to emerald.

Nicodemus, with Joseph clipping at his heels, pushed through the barrier of bodies. Offering muttering pardons of, *Excuse me. Pardon me.* Nudging Pharisees, Sadducees and Members of the Sanhedrin aside. At last, coming face to face with Caiaphas in the center.

"What are you planning?" Nicodemus confronted him.

The gemstones picked up their pace and changed to a more complex, zigzagging pattern. Caiaphas' eyes burned like two torrid lava pits when he said in a cheerful tone, "I told you, Nicodemus. Nothing." The Urim cooled, but Caiaphas had become accustomed to ignoring them.

"I don't believe you," Nicodemus said behind clamped, bared teeth. Ironically this statement from Nicodemus caused the Thummim to warm and buzz in the right pocket of the Ephod.

Again, Caiaphas paid the signal given from the stone no mind and leaned in close to Nicodemus. He said, "I don't care what you believe, sympathizer. Now get out of my face!"

He pushed past Nicodemus and Joseph, through his fellow peers, out to where Annas was waiting, holding a stupidly tall walking stick. They made haste out of the Chamber, leaning in close to one another and talking in low, conspiratorial tones as they departed. By their body language, they both seemed perturbed, at least. Quick, sharp, jabbing gestures made it seem as though there were agitation coupled with their words.

Nicodemus watched them leave. The two real leaders of the Temple. Gamaliel was just a puppet figurehead to appease the masses, while Caiaphas and Annas moved the chess pieces behind the veil. There was an undeniable feeling of a shadow being cast over the future, in a sense of dreadful foreboding. Nicodemus couldn't quite put it into words what he felt was possible of coming to pass in the days ahead. However, he was positive that it would have a crushing impact of monumental proportions upon everything that he ever knew of the world.

ii

Night in The Garden of Gethsemane. Past the Brook of Kidron on Nisan thirteen. The day before the Day of Preparation. What would come to be known as Maundy Thursday.

Following the dinner with his twelve, Jesus had brought his closest apostles, Peter, John and James, with him out to the Garden. To keep watch while he prayed in private to his Heavenly Father.

Earlier in the evening, he had confronted Judas in front of all in attendance, by telling them, *One of you will betray me.* Most of the men started to plead with Jesus and argue amongst themselves as to who was the betrayer. During the commotion, Peter leaned over to Jesus and asked him who it was. Jesus told him that whomever he gave the piece of bread to, was the one guilty of the betrayal. He followed these words by promptly dipping a piece of bread in oil and presenting it to Judas. Judas took the piece of sop and they say Satan then entered into him. Afterwards Jesus said to him, *What you are about to do, do quickly.* Judas then stormed out of the Last Supper without another word. Confused, some of the apostles thought Jesus was telling Judas, since he was in charge of the purse, to go and get everything they would need for the feast. Jesus, however, felt dread in the pit of his stomach, that the plot of his betrayal was surely coming to its terrifying fruition.

At present, tucked beneath the boughs of surrounding olive trees, bathed in an ethereal beam of unfiltered, last quarter moonlight, Jesus knelt. Hunched over, he was trembling and sweating from every pore. His slippery hands wrung themselves together in extreme distress. A damp, dirty mop of hair sat limply above his wild eyes. Frantic, unbroken prayers shook his voice in trill, warbling cantillations.

"Dear, Heavenly Father, I know it is not my will, but yours that must be done," Jesus shook. Tears bled from his eyes. "But, please allow this cup to pass from me. However Father, if I must drink of it, provide me with the strength to carry out what must be done. I am scared Father. Amen."

Jesus wiped at his face and sniffed. Exhausted, he stood and walked back through the trees to where he had left Peter, John and James on watch. Since they didn't know what to expect, they were all armed. There was no telling how Judas was going to do the actual betraying.

When Jesus came to where he had left them to keep watch, he found all three fast asleep at the base of an ancient olive tree. Anger, but mostly sadness bloomed in his chest and he woke them all by saying, "Can't you stay awake to watch with me one hour?" They all sat up and rubbed the sleep from their eyes. Before they could give a lame excuse, Jesus instructed them to, "Watch and pray, so that you will not fall into temptation. Remember, that the spirit is willing, but the flesh is weak."

Leaving them in half awake, stumbling confusion, The Lord slipped back through the trees to where he had previously been praying. Kneeling again, he broke into another anguished prayer to his Heavenly Father, "Father! I beg you to let this cup pass from me!"

Above him a branch creaked, as if weight were being placed upon it. Jesus continued, "Though, I know it is your will, Father." Soft wind changed its course and carried with it an alarming essence of decay. "Not mine."

Michael, the name was somewhat uttered from overhead. It could've just as easily been mistaken for an innocent breeze soughing through the leaves of the grove.

Jesus opened his eyes. Over his sweaty, intertwined knuckles he cast his stinging eyes upward. Overhead, in the branches, something was moving. Glimpses of pale skin and dingy fabric passed by in quick, flashing blurs.

Michael, the name was then spoken, plain as day. Definitely, not an innocent breeze soughing.

Jesus instantly shifted over to the spirit realm. By calling upon The Holy Spirit he ignited a holy fire, scorching the air around him. His eyes became a glowing white sclera only. An aquatic shifting of his robes and hair swirled invisibly about him. In a booming, spiritual voice, he called out, “Belial?! How?!!”

From behind him came a single voice that sounded like his old friend, Lazarus, back when he was alive. It simply stated, *“They are sleeping.”*

For a moment, Jesus didn’t know what it was referring to. Then, it dawned on him and he withdrew from the spirit realm. Dousing his holy fire and bringing back a stillness to his hair and garments. Returning to a deep brown iris and a pupil in his eyes again. In one, swift motion, he sprung up from his kneeling position and raced back to where he had last left Peter, James, and John. A part of Jesus feared he would find all three torn to bloody, unrecognizable shreds.

Thankfully and also irritatingly, he found them alive and asleep. “Peter! James! John!” Jesus yelled, snapping their eyes open. Sitting up, they all looked around like they were lost and didn’t know what direction to go. Peter, still half asleep, tried numerous unsuccessful attempts to unsheath his sword. “Stay vigilant! I told you to pray to not fall into the temptation of the weak flesh! Pray with me!!” Jesus commanded.

The Messiah led them in prayer for strength, vigilance and, overall, alertness. He left them again, going back to the area he had been using for prayer to God. Searching the canopy up above and all around for signs of Lazarus. His mind already raced and he tried to make sense of what had just happened. Maybe it had been a hallucination. A strange, guilty byproduct of the intense mental and emotional agony he was under.

Once convinced that he was alone again, Jesus fell to his knees again and approached God in prayer. “Heavenly Father, hear me! You are the Most High and your wisdom is unsurpassed. This is your will, Father!!" A severe pang of powerful emotion struck Jesus, causing his shoulders to shake up and down from giving in to a painful weeping. He sniffed and wiped at his eyes, then continued, “Not mine. I am your servant and will see it through. But, if you should see fit for this cup to pa-,”

Mmmiiiicccchhhaaaeeellll. The interrupting, sluggish pronunciation of his Heavenly name slid and seeped all throughout the boughs, like an air born, toxic, sludgy ooze. It was delivered through haunting whispering echoes as it swirled all around and above Jesus.

In response, the Lord imbued himself with the power of The Holy Spirit and rekindled his spiritual blaze. His eyes shifted back to a complete, glowing white. Again, in a lazy way, Jesus’ hair and robes whipped all about his physical body, as his feet lifted without a sound from the Earth's surface. Blood beaded, like dark rubies, at his temples. A strange, physical phenomena called hematidrosis, where blood is exuded through the pores, denoting an experience of extreme stress.

"LAZARUS!!" Jesus bellowed, while rotating. Turning in a slow circle. He hovered a full handbreadth above the ground. "TELL ME THE NAME OF YOUR NEW DEMON!!"

Jesus' pure white, intense eyes scanned amongst the branches. A creak from behind the Lord caused him to spin in the direction from whence it came. He only caught the barest, fleeting glimpse of a gross, billowing robe and a pale calf, with an equally pale foot attached. Judging by its trajectory, it was circling around to Jesus' left hand side. Fast.

Revolving himself counterclockwise in midair, following the track that the leg and calf were on, Jesus lost sight of the evil phantom among the overhead boughs and leaves. But, he was still hearing the cracking of rigored joints, the resistant creaking of thick branches, and the shuffling leaves all around him. There was also a surrounding, singular voice devoted to the repeating of the name, *Michael.*

Obviously, this new demon parading around in Lazarus' body, wearing it like it was a fine, new robe, wanted to taunt Jesus. In a sense, it wanted to toy with The Lord. This one wasn't as dumb as the last one was.

Jesus stopped turning around in a tight circle. He closed his eyes and listened calmly to the commotion happening up above and all around. From behind his eyelids it sounded like a turbulent, swirling maelstrom of the most psychotic bedlam.

MichaelMichaelMichaelMichaelMichael!!

By drawing in and concentrating a gargantuan swath of the power from The Holy Spirit, Jesus shot out an omnidirectional scorching shockwave of holy fire. The blast spread out and rose from Jesus like a halo of angelic fire, lifting up from him in a solid, straight vertical cylinder all the way up to the Heavens.

This enormous shot tagged Lazarus, evoking a demonic squeal of pain. Ceasing the monotonous reciting of *Michael,* as well as all of the tumultuous activity overhead.

"TELL ME YOUR NAME, DEMON!!!" Jesus boomed towards the direction from which the squeal came.

Now from a lower vantage point and from off to Jesus' right hand side, there were signs of movement among the obscuring tree trunks. Then a single plucked vocal chord spoke, *"Your-Father-calls-for-your-return."*

Turning towards the hideous, sinister manipulation of a voice, Jesus challenged back with truth, "You know nothing of My Father."

Now closer from behind him, the dithering fiddling of vocal chords said, *Death-was-not-yours-to-meddle-with.Only-your-Father-can-combine-flesh-and-spirit. You-can-only-raise-flesh."*

Spinning to the source of the itinerant words, Jesus spotted Lazarus. Partially exposed from behind a tree trunk. Naked except for a filthy, blood stained robe resembling the one Andrew had left at the tomb in lieu of a death shroud. A plump, distended belly, that looked like a stretched, pregnant belly amidst a late third trimester with twins, poked out repulsively. Unidentifiable, moist looking neckwear hung loosely and cascaded down in front of its pallid, broken chest. Its mouth was smeared scarlet and spread wide in a rictus grin. One totally black, onyx eye stared wide and unblinking above the hardened black scab of skin that slashed across its cheek in a diagonal strip of puckered necrotic flesh. Its hair and fingernails had grown very long, the former being slicked back with a substance much like what was smeared all across its face.

"Tell me your name then demon, and let Death put Lazarus to rest!" Jesus offered. Without being able to see the evil spirit within the body of Lazarus, Jesus wasn't able to rebuke it from the body.

Fading backwards into the darkness beneath the thick foliage of the grove, the demon within Lazarus plucked a reply, *"No. Your-Father-calls."*

"Lazarus!" Jesus warned. "Lazarus, don't do this!!" He shot out another, smaller wave of holy fire towards the tree Lazarus had been partially concealed by. There was no demonic squeal of pain that resulted this time, though.

Instead, from off to his right Jesus heard a fading combination of the incessant chant of the name *MichaelMichaelMichael* resume, a menacing chuckle and the plucked vocal chord say, *"Your-betrayal-draws-near, Son-of-God."*

"Lazarus!" Jesus called. A strong breeze came through the Garden and cleared the air of Lazarus' putrid essence. "Lazarus!!"

There was no answer from the phantom. It was out there now, in the night. Jesus' resurrected creature. Flesh brought to chaotic, destructive life.

Jesus lowered back down to the ground. Irises and pupils became a part of his eyes again. His hair and robes hung limp and lifeless once again. In an involuntary response to the coolness he now felt on his exposed skin, Jesus wiped his forehead with a shaky hand. Smudging the droplets of blood that he had been sweating out. There wasn't any surprise to him when he looked at his own blood streaked across the back of his hand. He just touched his head again with his fingertips to confirm the blood and also, to check for a painless wound.

When no cut or scrape could be found, he fell to his knees again and prayed to God. Asking for something much different this time than for this cup to pass on from him. Upon finishing up and saying Amen, he stood. Then he spent a few moments fixing his robes, and wiping tears from his eyes with the sleeve of his robe. He would not be found disheveled and weeping for his oncoming betrayal.

Upon returning to his three closest apostles, he found them asleep once again. Jesus slumped his shoulders and hung his head down low in expected disappointment. From not too far away in the Garden, he now heard the sounds of many voices. A large crowd approached with torches, weapons and malicious intent.

"Are you still sleeping and resting?" Jesus firmly asked. Roughly rousing Peter, John and James from their slumber. They sat up, stretched, yawned and muttered some weak excuses for their sleepiness, while an orange glow from many torches became visible.

"Nevermind your excuses. Behold! The hour has come!" Jesus stated in a display of inhuman fearlessness. "The Son of Man is being betrayed into the hands of sinners. Rise, let us go!! My betrayer draws near!!!"

iii

Late night, or early morning. However it was viewed, it was Nisan fourteen. The Day of Preparation. What would come to be known as Good Friday. Hundreds of aloof Passover lambs were to be sacrificed at the Temple today, in a way, preserving tradition. Judas was at the Temple, too, after having been turned away from Caiaphas' palace earlier in the night.

Satan had withdrawn from Judas' heart after having him say, "Rabbi," and planting the Kiss of Betrayal in the Garden. But it was too late to reverse the course that had been set in motion. The armed Temple guards, Roman soldiers, Priests, elders and scribes, who had been led there by Judas, now seized Jesus. In a show of reactional, irrational, yet loyal bravado Peter drew his sword and sliced off Caiaphas' servant, Malchus' ear. Threatening screams, as well as all kinds of bladed and blunt weapons were brandished. Without being asked, Jesus put his hand upon Malchus and healed his wound back to new. However, even after Jesus miraculously healed the severed ear, they still arrested The Son of God and carted him off to Annas' house for questioning.

Judas fled from the scene he had created, into the camouflage of the night, away from the fury of his former apostle brothers. As if on cue, a low fog had now crept into the grove, like a snail covered in molasses. The moonlight from the last quarter moon dimmed as a rogue cloud drifted over its pale, craterous face.

Peter, John and James chased after Judas, until, by Judas' blind luck, they lost him amidst the sea of aged, gnarled tree trunks. In reluctance to give up on the search for their traitorous "brother", the three infuriated apostles then backtracked to the path and followed the incited mob to Annas' house. Judas watched them give up on their pursuit of him from beneath the cloak of an olive tree and the blanket of soupy mist. Without thinking, he decided to follow them following the mob to Annas' house.

Then, hours later, after skirting around the perimeter of Annas' house, and then getting turned away from Caiaphas' palace, Judas found himself early morning in the Temple. Aimlessly, he wandered around with a tainted bag full of silver blood money. Delirious and devastated, with no one but himself to blame. He was bordering on dramatic hysterics. Muttering to himself. Grief stricken. With a full awareness that he was witnessing his sanity slipping. Most would say he hadn't even started to get his just desserts. He deserved much, much more for the betrayal of The Son of God.

Stationary islands of illumination pulsed with heat from ensconced torches lining the wall and torch stands placed every two hundred square cubits. Tiny, mobile islands of light belonging to hand held lanterns or lamps, being carried around at shoulder height, by Priests and soldiers alike. The Priests walked like nefarious, busy graverobbers to and from the Abottoir, making preparations for the lamb's big day. Bored, tired soldiers and guards ambled around the perimeter like mindless zombies. Shuffling and trudging on unsteady feet. Leaning heavily upon their *Pilum,* long spears.

Judas held the satchel of silver coins before him in both hands, as though offering it to whoever would take it. The top was open wide, revealing the booty. Tears leaked down into his bushy beard. He was rambling and sobbing as he approached a pair of the floating lanterns being held by a couple of the nocturnal Priests. Some middling elders and scribes were peppered in around the Priests. Nothing more than framed faces floating in the darkness. Sharing in the outskirts of the Priest's lamplight, like opportunistic, tag-along moths.

Lumbering out of the dark up to the Priests, presenting the open bag of silver, Judas cried, "Help me!"

This obviously startled the small, quiet, tight group, causing them all to either jump or cry out. One of the older Priests exclaimed aloud, "Good Heavens!"

"Help me," Judas repeated. A little calmer.

The older Priest's eyes flicked down to the open satchel that was held between them. Bathed in the warm gift of soft lamplight, he returned his attention back to the manic eyed patron that had wandered in at this ungodly hour. "We are not performing any atonement sacrifices today on the Day of Preparation," the older Priest said in a way, as though he'd recited it a million times before.

"I have sinned by betraying innocent blood!!" Judas screamed, fresh tears now falling down his much aggrieved face.

"Blood money," one of the elders murmured while looking down his nose at the open bag of silver.

The second, slightly younger looking Priest dismissed Judas' remorse, by saying, "What is that to us? You are the betrayer. You see to it!"

As though acting through an operation of a hive mind, the small group of Priests, elders and scribes stepped away all at once. Heading straight in the direction of the Abottoir. Dismissing Judas to the dark. Mouth open. Stunned. Still holding out his blood money. Thirty pieces of silver. Truly, a pithy price to be bargained for one's own precious soul.

Anger and despair boiled up in Judas. He tossed the booty, satchel and all, with a loud, explosive clatter across the Temple floor. The sound being even more abrasive upon the eardrums at this tranquil hour. Then, he ran out of the Temple, headed south towards Gehenna. To what would later become known as Potter's Field.

Once there, in the modest moonlight, Judas spotted a high tree, with a long, outcropping branch that hung out over a decent cliff drop. In that moment, it all became so clear to him what he had to do. What needed to be done, in order to try and atone himself for the unforgivable wrong he had committed. Not to mention, Judas Iscariot was coming to the absolute, irrefutable realization that he, in no way, shape, or form could ever live with himself, after what he'd done.

Destiny pulled him closer to the tree. While moving in an impulsive, automatic way, Judas sobbed and removed his clothes down to his dingy undergarments. He then took his dirty, roughspun robes and threw them over the overhanging branch. In an efficient way, he went about tying the top portion of the fabric into a half hitch knot and cinching it up tight around the branch. Then, after fashioning the low hanging fabric into a soft shackle knot, Judas took a shaky breath and slipped it over his own head.

From there, it was just a soft, pushing off. Just a small perfunctory step from the edge and the knot around his neck tightened. He was dangling. Swinging back and forth in gentle sways. Neck bent at an awkward angle, but not broken. Peacefully strangling. Bright, blobby stars began forming and blooming at the periphery of his sight. After a meaningless internal prayer, Judas closed his eyes, like he was ready to let go and drift away.

If Judas' airway wasn't completely constricted, he might have caught the warning whiff of rancid meat. He might have gagged and been clued into a harmful presence closing in. Instead, Judas didn't become aware of

Lazarus' company until the horrific ghoul was creeping down the long, outcropping branch he had hung himself from.

Judas' eyes shot open and he looked up to see the epitome of all of his nightmares come to life. Maggots squirmed all over it. It was crawling down the branch towards where he hung. A set of sable eyes and a diagonal streak of charred, blackened flesh advanced quickly. It had a horrific, blood smeared mouth set into a pallid complexion. Lengthy, thinning hair had been pasted back with a thick layer of congealed blood and viscera. A partial set of dehydrated intestines were wrapped around the neck as a kind of twisted trophy. Long, rust rimmed fingernails dug into the bark of the objecting, creaking branch as it dragged along a revolting, capacious, distended belly.

Creak! Creak!

Dangling helpless, Judas' hands held onto the wrapped knot of bunched, twisted fabric around his constricted throat. Judas struggled and rotated in jerky, little half circles. Kicking and bucking his nude legs wildly. Piss ran in generous golden rivers down his inner thighs, being flicked in all directions from his toes.

Creak! Creak! Creak! Snap!!!

From the combined weight of both of their bodies, the long, hanging branch broke off of the tree completely and they plummeted together. This quick moment expanded to encompass many disturbing details. Including how the horrible, demonic creature rode the branch and Judas' body all the way down, with a massive grin malforming its maw into a pit of hideous joy. Judas would've screamed in terror if his esophagus wasn't constricted by his thwarted suicide attempt.

His body was the first to impact against the jagged rocks below, completely shattering his bones, but breaking the fall of his passenger ghoul and the branch. In a gory burst, Judas' insides had exploded from his body, leaving him looking like a cracked open pomegranate.

The absolute last horrendous thing Judas Iscariot's conscious, mortal mind saw and comprehended before he died, was the grotesque creature that he knew was Lazarus, playing gleefully with his guts. It was lovingly nuzzling up with Judas' organs and viscera. With both hands full, it was rubbing Judas' spleen, liver and stomach all over its face in a loving way, like a satisfied feline with an intoxicating batch of potent catnip.

Then Lazarus began to consume Judas while he was still alive.

iv

Phillip's feet seemed like they couldn't carry him fast enough. Even with the sun early in its ascent, the tragic news of Jesus' sudden arrest was already percolating in the air. As he ran to the house of Martha, in passing, Phillip could overhear snippets of conversations being held on the very subject.

- you hear? Jesus has been-

- to Pilate for trial-

- be crucified for sure-

It wasn't anything new that Phillip hadn't already heard. Jesus had been arrested in the middle of the night. Taken to Annas' house for questioning. Then to Caiaphas' palace, where The High Priest and The Sanhedrin awaited with more interrogative questioning, which continued for a few hours in the palace dungeon. At the present time, Jesus was being forced to wear a crown of thorns and receiving his one sided trial in front of an incited throng at Pontius Pilate's Praetorium.

After pushing through a growing flow of people heading to spectate the trial, Phillip arrived at his destination at about the second hour (8am). His muscles ached from weaving through unsavory pockets of people and sprinting in between their increasing numbers. Sweat dripped from his nose and beard in steady droplets. From this early perspiration, a burning and stinging sensation sizzled at the corners of his eyes.

Jacob stood before the main entrance, flanked by the same two guards that had backed him up the other night at the big dinner. The blade of his two-handed broadsword caught the morning sunlight and reflected it back in large, brilliant, scintillating flashes. Its sharp, chipped tip was pointed straight down into the dirt, while Jacob's thick, tanned, criss-crossed forearms rested upon the butt of the wrapped, leather hilt. Upon seeing Phillip trotting towards him, out of breath, Jacob greeted him like an old friend, "Hey Phillip. How are you, my brother? No sign of Martha yet this morning. Sorry."

"She...still...hasn't...come out?" Phillip asked between great, deep quaffs of air.

Jacob shook his head and lifted his shoulders in a lazy shrug, like he didn't have a care in the world on this morning of all mornings. "No, my friend. What's it been? Three days now?" Phillip had his hands braced upon his knees and his head hung down with his eyes squeezed shut. Jacob observed and mentioned, "Hey! Are you still carrying that *Maakeleth*? Better not let the Priests see you with that!"

Phillip ignored him. His breathing had returned to somewhat normal, when he demanded, "I must see her...at once! Mary as well." When neither Jacob nor the guards budged, Phillip added with considerable vehemence, "It is of the utmost importance, Jacob!"

With his dirty pinky nail, Jacob picked at something leftover from either last night's dinner or this morning's breakfast, behind his canine. After picking it out, inspecting it closely and then putting it back in his mouth to nibble, he said as nonchalant as could be, "See, my friend, that's the thing. I know you're close with the ladies of the house. Especially Martha. Am I right?" He gave Phillip a quick little, insider wink and Phillip recoiled. Offended. Jacob's tone then went to bordering on cocky, when he said, "But, they **are** the Ladies of the House and when they say they're not accepting any visitors, they're not accepting an-,"

"Jesus is on trial, you dummy!" Phillip cut off the much younger, not to mention shorter, by at least a handbreadth juvenile. "Pilate is going to crucify him!"

Jacob's demeanor changed in an instant, from total misplaced arrogance to being dumbstruck and catatonic. He just stood there like an astounded statue with his mouth hanging open. Stuck trying to formulate a sound and only managing to blink stupidly.

"Out of my way," Phillip growled and pushed his way past the shocked young man. Phillip acknowledged an inner, fleeting moment of feeling bad for insulting the young guard, but it vanished as quickly as it had appeared. He knew Jacob's heart was in the right place, but there wasn't a second to lose.

Once inside, Phillip noted a palpable uneasiness in the air. A dissonance in the harmony. The house appeared abandoned. Clean, though. Really clean. As though no one had been living in the living areas and the maids were just going through the motions of cleaning what was already spotless.

Stepping into the atrium, he saw Mary, sitting by a gurgling, peaceful fountain. She looked sick, but somehow better than she had in a while. There was a slight twinkle that had returned to her eyes. They had been dimmed by her self-inflicted debauchery for the longest time. In her hands, she was experiencing a moderate, noticeable tremor. This is what would later become known as a symptom of Delirium Tremens.

When Mary saw Phillip enter the shaded area, she beamed and rose from her seat by the bubbling water, calling his name out loud, "Phillip!"

"Mary!" Phillip rushed to her, foregoing any greeting formalities. "We must gather Martha and go!"

It was at this moment, that a wave of emotion from the gravity of what this morning had entailed hit him. They embraced in a quick wrapping of arms around one another and a nonexistent peck on the cheek, but that was it. Phillip withdrew from her. Wiping at his tearful eyes. She would never admit to herself that, in a weird sense of jealous honesty, she wanted more emotion in the embrace than what was given.

Seeing the moisture in his eyes, she became concerned and asked, "What's the matter, Phillip?"

Instead of a warm reunion, he rushed her off in the direction of Martha's bedroom, leading her like a brute, by using his meathook hand to grasp high up on her arm. He still walked ahead of her in brisk, long strides to make haste and, also to conceal his brimming tears. With a thickened voice he caught her up to speed on what was going on. She shrieked in actual physical pain upon hearing the horrible news of the fate of their Lord.

They both took big, fast steps up to the exterior of Martha's locked door. With a shaky hand, Mary already held out the skeleton key to unlock it, but Phillip, bullishly, banged on the door and called through, "Martha!? It's Phillip! Jesus has been arrested!!"

"Martha!?" Mary called. Her tremors caused the tip of the key to dance all around the black, dancing keyhole. "Damn," Mary muttered at the hindrance of her symptoms. "Martha!!?"

At random, a couple of maids drifted across the end of the hallway. Sloshing, sudsy buckets and fresh, dripping rags in their hands. Probably on their way for another monotonous scrub on the already immaculate clean kitchen. They twitched their attention towards what Mary and Phillip were up to, but did not linger to assist or even greet.

Mary had bent over, bringing her eyesight level with the keyhole. With both hands trembling, she was trying to steady the key and guide it into the keyhole. A look of concentrated determination furrowed her brow and drew her eyes narrow.

"Martha!?" Phillip slapped the door with his open palm, rattling it on its hinges. "It's Jesus! He's to be crucified!"

"No!" A muffled shriek came from inside the room. "It can't be!!"

The door was unlocked and pulled ajar wide by Martha from the inside. Phillip and Mary entered to see Martha stick her face directly into a basin of cloudy water. Blowing bubbles and sloshing the contents over the brim. She was wearing the same exact thing Phillip had last seen her in on Tuesday. Even with the windows thrown wide open, the smell of urine, defecation, body odor and bad breath was overwhelming. Strangely, a platter had been placed atop a pitcher tucked into the corner of the room, hinting at where Martha was doing some of her bathroom business.

Suddenly, Martha came up and wiped her face with the sleeves of her stinky robe, before disappearing behind a gorgeous room divider. The three screens displayed an intricately whiddled depiction of a small flock of Hoopoe birds lifting in unison from the ground. A large, flaming, rising sun, flanked by a tasteful placement of wispy clouds, rose omnipotent behind the birds. Lifting with them.

While changing behind the screen, Phillip rapidly spoke of everything he knew that had taken place overnight, and into this morning. Mary peppered in little emotional outbursts as the details of Jesus' demise were laid bare. Martha exhaled the anxious breath she had been holding, as she finished changing and stepped out.

A simple, striped indigo robe framed her grieving, pretty face. She donned her stacked up, towering, painful emotions like a funeral mask. Phillip swooped her up in a quick, but fierce embrace. When Martha saw Mary, more to the point, when she saw that Mary wasn't sloppy and inebriated, Martha hugged her baby sister as tight as she could. Whispering into Mary's ear a few tender, heartfelt sentiments of love and pride.

When they let go of each other, Martha swiped at her fresh tears and rallied, "There's no time to waste. Let's go to Our Lord."

V

Unusually thick, grey overcast had rolled in as the morning hours elapsed. Angry-looking, stained clouds hung low and felt as though they could come crashing down to the surface of the Earth at any moment. A muggy, drowning humidity saturated the very air and extracted sweat from every single pore, causing dry clothing to stick to balmy skin, like an annoying paste. Just enough to make the climate miserable without any promise in the forecast of rain.

Golgotha meant Place of the Skull. It was located outside the city of Jerusalem's walls. This is where the crucifixion took place. Many had gathered around for the grisly public viewing. Some were crying and wailing out loud in the midst of the tortuous atrocities taking place before their eyes. Others mocked or hurled insults at the victims nailed up to their crosses, along with their sympathizers in the crowd. Soldiers stood by to keep the peace and carry out the gruesome crucifixion, per the "acting" Governor of Judea, Pontius Pilate's orders.

Phillip, Martha and Mary arrived close to noon at the tumultuous, mournful scene. Three large beam crosses had been erected tall and wretched after the condemned had been fastened to them. At the foot of the center cross, they spotted Jesus' mother. She was surrounded by other women and John, Jesus' most loved disciple. From her knees she was reaching out to her dying son, up on the cross, and weeping in hoarse, uncontrollable brays. All of those who loved Jesus and were assembled around his mother, were weeping openly and laying their hands upon her, so as to provide comfort in some menial way. But, to be truthful, there was no comfort to be doled out or received on this day.

Two outer crosses held up in gruesome display two groaning men. Gestas, the unrepentant and Dismas, the repentant. Their voices strained and cracked in excruciating agony. The beaten, rolled over, drachma-sized nail heads, pinning their hands and feet gleamed like dull currency in the lack of direct sunlight. Juicy squirts of fresh blood trickled in plentiful bourns from their outstretched nailed hands and overlapped feet. Their exposed chests hitched in violent, little spasms from the slow suffocation they were going through, by being dragged forward from the weight of their upper body's pulling against their hands attached to the cross. As was usual in places of abundant death, flies congregated and feasted in ravenous, dense clusters. Crowding in around the open wounds. Crows perched and pecked at the not-yet-dead flesh with concise, bloodied beaks. Snatching little hors d'oeuvres of the living meat and skin in greedy, early rips. Cawing obnoxiously in between tasty, warm bites, as if to say to those they snacked on, *What is taking you so long? Why don't you just die already!?*

As a centerpiece among the three experiencing crucifixion, Jesus' cross was taller by a full cubit. Holding him higher, like a first place trophy over the two sinners he was associated with. Branches from the spiny jujube tree, which would later become known as The Christ's Thorn, had been twisted and made into a crown. In evil mockery, this morning, between the scourging and being led out here, to Golgotha, this "crown" had been forced down painfully over the top of Jesus' head by Roman soldiers. Some of these wounds continued to bleed, due to the spines having been driven so deep past his mortal subcutaneous skin. Black and blue flesh puffed out around his eye. The bridge of his nose was split. Bloodied skin hung in torn tapestry tatters all over his back from the whipping he had endured hours earlier. The shards of bone and chunks of discarded, sharpened metal that had been woven into the thongs of the whip, had ripped back large portions of his skin and meat, even exposing his ribcage in spots.

Above his head, on the cross, a wooden plaque had been affixed. Four letters were inscribed upon the Titulus Crucis. "INRI". In the Latin tongue, it read, *Iesus Nazarenus Rex Iudaeorum.* Translated it said, Jesus of Nazareth, King of the Jews.

When The Lord caught sight of his beloved friends arriving, he cried out to them, "Mary! Martha! I have been forsaken!!"

The sight of what had been done to The Messiah caused both sisters to weaken in their knees. Which led to them wobbling. Kneeling. Then, joining with Jesus' mother and the others, on the ground, in their profuse weeping.

"Oh Jesus!" Phillip bellowed with wild, unchained emotion. "How could this be?!"

Tears spilled in cascading torrents from Martha's eyes when she asked their Messiah, "Why Lord?! When you are powerful enough to release yourself from these bonds of your torture and demise?!"

Through a bout of labored, difficult breathing, Jesus answered, "Martha...this is...my...Father's will. I am... the Lamb to...be... ransomed."

"My Lord!" Martha blubbered through copious tears and snot. "What are we to do without you?!"

"Dear Martha," Jesus spoke in short, clipped syllables. "I am...always with you." He sucked in a sharp intake of air through his bared teeth, as rekindled, incredible pain bloomed like raging wildfire all over his physical body. "I...will...al...al...ways," Jesus faltered.

"Don't talk, Lord. Please!" Martha implored past her sister Mary's bawling to the side of her. "My Lord, please!" Phillip's big meathook hands wrapped like entangling octopus tentacles around her shoulders. On her back, Martha could feel the shaky rise and fall of Phillip's big barrel chest hitching. He was trying to breathe normally, while heaving amidst the tidal wave of emotion.

Withdrawing his gaze from the Heavens above, Jesus regained a sliver of vigor and replied, "No...I prayed to...My Father about you. I asked Him to...to give you...Divine Strength."

"Divine Strength?" Martha asked back.

"Yes," Jesus confirmed. "You must complete...what I...I...what I started."

"But, Messiah!" Martha cried. "What if I can't do it?"

"You must!" Jesus commanded with some of the last of his conviction. In a rapid draining though, his strength waned and his head lolled about between his collarbones. "You...simply...must," Jesus' subsequent speech trailed off as he appeared to fade from consciousness.

Those in witness to this, didn't find the exchange of words between Jesus and Martha suspicious at all. They all purely assumed that Jesus was talking to Martha in reference to his unfinished ministry.

Phillip, Martha and Mary, however, knew the exact subject of what their Lord spoke of. His resurrected, failed experiment, Lazarus. His creature. Lazarus had to be dealt with. It wasn't a total failure though, seeing as how Jesus did use the witness of the resurrection as a fatal blow to the belief that people had held for so long in The Temple. Now it was known and would resonate throughout the entire world that the Glory of God was real and available to all through His Son, Jesus Christ. Besides this silver lining,

Martha, Phillip and Mary were very well aware that tomorrow was the Sabbath, as well. So, whatever they eventually decided to do about Lazarus, it would have to happen tonight.

For the next few hours, they remained at the bleeding feet of their crucified Lord. Jesus would weave in and out of sporadic, lucid moments. Passing out for large periods of time in between brief, difficult conversations. At around the ninth hour (3PM), the sky darkened to a deep, slate grey and Jesus declared in a hoarse croak, "I thirst!"

Earlier Jesus had been offered wine mixed with gall (myrrh or wormwood), but after a minor taste, he refused the narcotic-laced drink. Not wanting to dull his senses. He desired to face his suffering with all of his faculties intact.

Now, at the request of Jesus, some of the soldiers took a sponge and soaked it in posca, or sour wine. A common soldier's drink. They placed the dripping sponge upon the end of a stalk of hyssop and lifted it to The Lord's dry, cracked lips. To which, Jesus accepted gratefully.

After satiating his thirst, Jesus lifted his face to the black Heavens and declared with the last of his mortal strength, "It is finished!!"

Upon these final words being spoken, Jesus' spirit lifted. His head then bowed and his mortal body went limp. There was a breathless second where everyone in attendance anticipated him to become animated and speak again. Expecting that this was another unconscious pocket of time for The Lord.

Instead, the Earth became animated by beginning to tremor and shake violently underneath everyone. Gargantuan rocks split and crumbled. Crypts cracked open, spilling forth their dead. At the Temple, it was reported that the veil that separated the Holy of Holies ripped itself in half, all the way down the middle. This symbolized God abolishing his previous covenant with The Temple.

Jesus of Nazareth. The King of the Jews. The Son of God, was dead.

Following this realization, came a series of brutal actions captured in a fuzzy blur of time. Amidst the screaming and wailing, crurifragium was committed by a faceless soldier taking an oversized, two-handed mallet and breaking the legs of the two criminals on their crosses. Hastening the death of Gestas and Dismas, by transferring all of their weight to their arms. Dislocating their shoulders. Making breathing impossible.

Coming to Jesus in the center and suspecting he was already dead, a Roman soldier named Longinus called for his Lance from his Praefecti. He approached the lifeless, hanging body of the Lord. Taking his spear in hand, Longinus, thrust upwards and pierced the side of Jesus. Sending up a new wave of horrified gasps and screams from all in attendance that loved Jesus. When Longinus removed the spear, water and blood poured out of the incision, like a gory fountain spout.

For a few blank moments, as though from out of her own body, Martha watched the scene play out before her. From her breathless catatonia, she saw a younger Pharisee, named Joseph of Arimathea, catch some of the blood and water pouring from Jesus' side in a plain, clay goblet. She saw the older Pharisee, Nicodemus, crying out in the open for the loss of his friend, Jesus. As though trapped behind a watery veil, words were spoken to her, but they only came through as garbled streams of enunciations. Numb, tear filled, fierce embraces were exchanged in slow motion, drawn out dream sequences.

Only when the strange overcast of the afternoon began to lighten and the soldiers were lowering the crosses down, did reality and Martha appear to align with one another again. Completely out of tears, just left with the anger and emptiness of loss, she now felt a surging determination to carry out the charge that Jesus had entrusted her with.

In her mind, a vague sense of a plan for how to deal with Lazarus was beginning to form. It was going to have to be solely up to her, Mary, and Phillip. No one else could be involved. Hope was not a strong factor in her plan for the three of them, going up against the corpse of her brother under the control of a psychotic, murderous demon. Regardless of the outcome of confronting her baby brother, Lazarus, it was going to be finished.

Tonight.

vi

When Martha had first met her baby brother, she was five years old. Mary was two. It had all happened on one unplanned day, he just arrived to Martha, balanced and extended out on her mother's proffering hands. Pink fair skin. Bald and swaddled. He was a little, perfect bundled up human.

"Support his head," Martha's mother advised with a soft, flowery giggle. "His little neck muscles aren't strong yet."

The baby boy was lowered down and set like a delicate egg into the crook of Martha's arm. There, sister and brother alike, studied one another for some time. While little Mary ran around, creating all sorts of chaos, Martha sat and held her new baby brother in quiet reverence. She was wholly unaware of a dumbstruck half smile creeping across her face. It was impossible for her young, immature mind to fully fathom and appreciate the amount of joy she was feeling.

With a pair of big, brown eyes, she looked up at her mother who was smiling down in maternal warmth at her, and asked, "What's his name?"

"His name is Lazarus," Martha's mother answered.

"Wazzrusss!" Mary happily yelled. Their mother snatched the toddler up from the floor. Little Mary squealed in delight as her mother then, playfully kissed and fake munched all over the little girl's neck, cheek and ear.

Martha and Lazarus stared at one another some more. Time dissolved into an abstract, subjective concept that only applied to anyone unsatisfied with the present. A strong, protective nature within Martha desired to be soft and treat the tiny baby in her arms like a delicate piece of pottery or an age old scroll. Another equally huge emotion in Martha wanted to squeeze this new, tiny perfect thing so hard and so fierce that his head would pop off!

Baby Lazarus' expression changed from concerned serious observation, to an incredibly adorable, beaming toothless smile. This sight melted Martha's heart into a quivering, sodden puddle. Creating a sweet ache in her chest, that she would later reminisce, was when he became a part of her life, forever.

Overjoyed, Martha smiled back down at little, baby Lazarus and kissed him on his soft cheek. Her nose took a greedy whiff of that one and only baby smell. She held that sweet scent in her lungs for as long as she could, before letting it go. Then, she laughed out loud and kissed him again. Sneaking in another pleasant sniff. Once more she repeated the process. This began her lifelong habit of holding her breath. All of the way into her adult life, she would use the memory of holding onto the scent of Lazarus' baby smell as a kind of security blanket.

"He likes you," Martha's mother said, while taking a seat next to her. With a soft touch she stroked the tiny, fragile crown of Lazarus' peach fuzzy little noggin. "You're his big sister. That means you have a big responsibility."

"What's re-resp-re-?" Martha asked, trying with difficulty to pronounce the big word.

"Re-spon-si-bi-li-ty," Martha's mother interjected and sounded out the word phonetically. "It means something you have to do. Like a duty."

"Doodee! Doodee!" Mary yelled, laughing and pointing at her bottom. Then, she bolted past where they sat as fast as her little legs could propel her. Dusting all three of them with the smell of her freshly soiled undergarments.

"Ugh! Hannah!" Martha's mother called.

In a prompt amount of time, Hannah entered the room. Their mother instructed the middle aged servant, Hannah, to take Mary away for her bath. Unamused, Hannah chased after Mary, as she giggled, ran and continued to fumigate the area. After a lengthy pursuit, Hannah had gotten ahold of little Mary and was carrying her out of the room. Looking over Hannah's shoulder, Mary stuck her hand up and waved, "Bye-bye, Wazzrusss!"

During this time baby Lazarus had begun to fuss. Martha's mother had taken him back and placed his tiny face against her humongous breast, waiting for him to latch onto the nipple. She was murmuring in a soothing, low voice to the baby, saying, "Come on. I've seen you do it before."

Once she felt that Lazarus had a good latch, Martha's mother returned to the subject, "So, responsibility."

"Responsibilily!" Martha repeated, a little tongue-tied at the end.

"That's right!" Her mother encouraged. "As a big sister, you have the responsibility to take care of your younger sister and also…"

Martha's mother left the blank at the end of the sentence on purpose. She was trying to coax the right answer from her oldest daughter, without giving away too much. While little Martha grappled for what her mom was asking, her mother flicked her eyes, as a hint, down to the baby boy breastfeeding.

"My baby brother!" Martha burst, making the connection at last.

"Yes!" Her mother said. She was gliding her hand over the top of the infant's head. Barely grazing the peach fuzz. Making tenuous contact with the baby's downy crown. Lazarus' eyes were closed, but his mouth would occasionally work at a few lethargic sucks from mommy's knocker. "Besides, isn't he just the sweetest thing?"

<u>vii</u>

"What are you thinking about?" Phillip asked. Startling Martha out of her fond, heartbreaking memory.

"Oh! Nothing. I was just remembering something," Martha answered. She trailed off, adding, "Something from when I was very young."

It was very early in the morning. Mere hours until the start of the Sabbath, marking the end of this Holy Week. There was a short, thick fog that laid like an opaque tarp across the pathway. Underneath the plentiful, shading boughs of ancient olive trees, the way ahead was bathed in a few permitted beams of filtered light provided from the last quarter moon and a sky full of stars. Jerusalem (Eurasian) Scops-owls hooted spookily from the deep, less traveled parts of the grove. Their calls echoed in an isolated, haunting way.

Fearful, the trio shambled. Keeping very close with one another. Their feet disappeared into the soup of fog, just above the ankle. Scared and ambivalent about what they were about to attempt, they pressed on through the cursed olive grove.

Armed.

Martha and Mary both carried winnowing forks (*Mizreh*) that they had lifted from their own livery. Phillip, on the other hand, in his right hand held a razor sharp, unsheathed *Machaira*. Also, tucked into his belt, on the left, rode the pilfered *Maakeleth* as a secondary, backup weapon. Hopefully, it wouldn't have to come to the point of using the blades and pitchforks, out of the necessity of self defense. Only to initially incapacitate.

According to their combined rudimentary plan, the sun would be their main weapon used. This lane of strategy was based on what Phillip had gleaned of Abigail and her similar situation in Capernaum. Not to mention, the burn that occurred on Lazarus' face from direct contact with sunlight shining in through the window of Mary's room. The long and short was, they just had to keep Lazarus from entering the crypt, his cradle, before sunrise.

"Ugh! What is that smell?" Mary declared in loud offense. Raising a sleeve to cover her nose and mouth.

A faint smell of death acted as a sinister precursor to the horse carcass that Phillip and Martha had anticipated on seeing again. Even in this minimal light, beneath the canopy, the sight of the stripped horse skeleton laying on its side, halfway submerged in the fog, was massively jarring. The leather bridle that the poor animal had been tethered to the tree with had snapped and broken away. Apparently, its skull and neck were intended to be frozen for the rest of eternity in the awkward position of being tweaked upward to the Heavens. Every last scrap of carrion had been totally gnawed from the bones. Most likely, the plethora of scavenging birds, insects and nocturnal beasts had been returning to pick off the corpse, until there was nothing edible left.

With an attitude of complete disinterest, Phillip and Martha skirted wide around the skeleton, making their way at a steady clip up the path to the tomb courtyard. Inside, they were just thankful that the scene of the horse's demise was drier and less populated this time around. Mary, however, edged up to what was left and poured over the finer, macabre details of the carcass with visible disgust and horror upon her face.

"Martha? Phillip? Did you see this?" Mary started asking. There was a notable tremble in her voice. Was it from the Delirium Tremens? Or from fright? The answer was: probably both.

"We saw it the last time we came out here," Martha said with as much volume as she dared over her shoulder. Up ahead, she could just make out the nebulous, familiar archway rising up out of the thick mist.

Phillip added on with a gross fact, by saying, "There was more of it to see then."

"Come on, Mary," Martha called from father up the path.

Mary spent another long moment gazing into the infinite, abyssal eye sockets of the horse skull. She let her eyes drift down to the double row of teeth exposed in a full grin. Then, to the breast, where the bones for the front set legs should've been.

In a state of warped horror, her mind desperately wondered, Why? Why had her baby brother passed away so early? Why was his corpse being used to wreak all of this havoc? Why all of the death?! Why did all of this happen?!!

Finally, Mary broke away from her trance and caught back up with Phillip, who was walking hand in hand with Martha. Overhead branches groaned and hummed. Soft wind blew noisily through the leaves, whistling and wheezing. Distant hooting from the obscurity of the woods, caused their three sets of eyes to dart this way and that.

They were all on ultra high alert. It was very well realized, but strictly unspoken amongst themselves, that Lazarus could be virtually anywhere. He could be creeping around somewhere in their vicinity. Watching them. Stalking them. Planning. Just waiting for the right moment to pounce!

As she pressed further on, Martha held onto her breath. The habit she had picked up ever since smelling the iconic baby smell coming off of the crown of her infant brother. She had reserved hopes of one day catching that smell and holding it deep in her lungs again. Hopes for that scent to come from the fuzzy, little heads of her own infant children. In all honesty, there had been many recent fantasies of having these dream children with the brave man that walked ahead of her, right now. Courageous and bold, Phillip led the way up to the crypt. All while knowing damn well exactly what kind of evil waited for them on the inside. If that didn't account for a true testament of love, then she didn't know what would.

They emerged from underneath the canopy. In the full light of the partial moon and stars, looking up the stone pathway, through the eerie dimness, they all beheld the tombstone rolled wide and to the side. This revealed the short, black, rectangular opening. It was always meant to be a quaint, secluded place of peaceful eternal repose. Now, it resembled something more akin to a viper burrow. Ominous and concealing something unmatched in its deadliness down below.

Bright, neon blooms began to form at the edge of her periphery and Martha exhaled the breath that she had been holding. The pitchfork became very heavy in her numb fingers, and it came close to rolling out of her grip. After a few rounds of big breaths, taken in through the nose and blown out through the mouth, her vision focused.

"Are we ready to finish this task?" Martha asked.

Both Phillip and Mary nodded in angry, quick affirmations. Fear pinned their eyelids to their eyebrows. Sweat formed on their faces and bodies, despite the coolness of the hour. Adrenaline coursed in their veins, like lava flowing down the face of a mountain.

Martha then looked to Phillip and asked, "Phillip, will you lead us in an uplifting prayer?"

Surprised by her request, although flattered as well, Phillip replied with a simple, "Of course, Martha."

He then took the double edged sword he carried and tucked it up, underneath his armpit. Bowing his head, he gripped one of each of their hands in both of his. With a passionate inflection to his tone, he approached the Most High, "Dear Heavenly Father, we humbly come before you today to say, 'Thank you'. Thank you for this new day that you have given us. Thank you for accepting us as sinners. Thank you for the strength that you will provide to us, to do what must be done. Most of all, thank you for your Son, Jesus, who gave his life in ransom today. Amen."

"Amen," Martha and Mary concurred in somber unison.

Afterward, Phillip gave Mary a light, brotherly kiss upon her forehead and promptly wiped off his lips. Then, it was Martha's turn. Phillip astonished both sisters and seized Martha by her shoulders. Then, he looked deep into her eyes and placed a fat, shameless smacker square on her lips, causing the pitchfork she carried to jut out at an odd angle from in between them. Not like Phillip or Martha noticed, though. For a lengthy five to ten seconds, they were completely oblivious to anything but each other and their shared transcendent, parted lip lock.

"Whoa!" Mary said, as though from some far away, distant dimension.

This spectacular kiss possessed the capacity to both weaken and empower Martha. Transforming her legs into a couple of overcooked noodles and her resolve into a mighty shield. She felt a resonating confidence now, that wasn't there before. She felt as if she were floating. She felt as though she would happily follow Phillip through fire, all the way to the deepest, darkest pit of Hell.

In all honesty, that kind of described where they all stood right now. Shoulder to shoulder before a darkened threshold that felt as though it were the fragile barrier between a world full of flourishing life and a mucky sewer with nothing but death running through its toxic channels.

"Are you ready?" Phillip asked with his signature deep rumble.

"I am," Martha answered and stepped into the cursed courtyard first. Following close on her heels, Phillip and Mary crossed beneath the archway as well.

Upon entry, all three immediately felt the strange sensation of being physically pushed and pulled down. A bogging, like their feet were caught in sucking mud. The notion that thousands of insects were crawling all over their skin was bordering on maddening. There was also an itchy burn that crackled and stung, giving a sense that fresh squeezed urine had been dabbed at the corners of their eyes.

Little piles of human bones were crudely stacked up along the interior, low stone wall and trunks of the mature trees. They rose up out of the clinging ground fog like clusters of hideous, deformed, inedible mushrooms. The Bethany buffet was most certainly open and, it was clear, Lazarus was going back for thirds and fourths.

With a near paralyzing trepidation, they came up to the entrance of the crypt. Loud, crunching footsteps announced their encroachment. All of them expected a surprise ambush, in the form of a stark naked zombie leaping out of the dark. Their weapons were held poised at the ready.

From inside the crypt antechamber, a thick, nauseating smell, like an overturned graveyard, seeped out to assault their noses in concentrated slow churning wafts. Besides the fragrance, the air within the chamber felt like it had substance to it. It was lukewarm and thick. Like a paste to be squished between the tongue and the roof of the mouth. Joyful flies and fleshy, pink maggots swarmed all about in a perpetual feast.

A splash of acidic vomit shot up to the back of Mary's throat. With some difficulty, she managed to keep it down. Swallowing the spew burned her esophagus harshly and brought quivering tears up into her eyes. She dropped her pitchfork and turned away from the cradle entry, with her nose lifted high, trying to procure the tiniest bit of fresh air.

At the back of his palate, Phillip could taste the rancid blood that was plastered all over the floor, walls and ceiling inside. This forced him to double over and dry heave violently. Brazen flies attacked his facial orifices by the hundreds, causing him to wave his hands, spit and snort, on top of his involuntary lurching.

Martha held her breath and peeked inside the ground level chamber of the tomb. She could feel the emanating putrescence trying to permeate into her lungs through her mouth and nostrils. The incredible stench bit at her eyeballs and tried to squirm into her ears. A thin slit of vision through her squinting eyelids provided her with the sight of an elongated rhombus of a soft, orange flicker within a field of black. It was the light of a single, meager flame that danced from down below. Shining up from the stairs leading down to the lower chamber.

"Lazarus?" Martha croaked out and they all tensed. Weapons raised and ready to strike.

They waited for any response other than the loud drone of the millions of flies. Alas, an answer from their intended target, Lazarus, never came. That didn't mean a version of possum wasn't being played. This very well could be a trap, and they were behaving like dumb, enticed crows following a treacherous trail of breadcrumbs.

"Lazarus?!" Martha called down into the lower tomb louder.

"Lazarus?!!" Mary yelled at a louder volume than her sister had just called.

Phillip stepped into the upper level of the crypt and walked over to the steps. A sick amount of flies buzzed all over and covered most of his body. Peering down into the dimly lit lower level, he barked down from behind his sleeve, "Lazarus! Come out!!"

Rapidly, he scooted back out of the antechamber and rejoined them, where they waited outside of the crypt a moment longer. His blade was held high in anticipation of making a slash, stab or thrust. Both women were shaky, but ready to jab and puncture with their winnowing forks.

A hint of a lightening to the sky in the East, brought the suggestion of dawn with it. Like a heartfelt promise yet to be fulfilled. The moon was still high in its descent, but the stars were beginning to disappear. Colors like rose, lavender and navy blue were becoming a part of the horizon in a way that only a loving God could conjure regularly.

Spitting and waving away at the aggressive clouds of flies, while referring to her brother, Mary said, "He's not here."

Eyeing the shifting change in colors eastward, Martha stated in an ominous tone, "But, he will be. Soon."

"This is great!" Phillip said, a small smile on his face. Both women looked at him as though he had a screw loose.

"What is?" Mary asked.

Phillip explained, "Well, if he's not here, then we can lie in wait and ambush him."

"You want to lie in wait? In there?" Mary asked incredulously.

Phillip looked again within the empty ground level chamber. When he turned back to Mary, he shrugged his shoulders and admitted, "Well, yes." He went on further to explain, "It will give us the element of surprise."

"I'm not going in there," Mary stated plainly. "It's repulsive!"

"So you want to stay out here where Lazarus can see you from a furlong away?" Phillip challenged. Their window of time for further consideration and contemplation was closing. Morning was on its way, as it seemed the Earth's steady rotation towards the sun had sped up. Various hues of purple, pink and peach had been added to the roster of colors blooming from the destined sunrise.

Phillip didn't wait for an answer. Instead, he ducked down a little, covered his face and stepped into the crypt. He chose to press his back up against the wall just inside the opening. Holding his sharpened sword across his body in a position ready to either incapacitate or decapitate.

With the seconds ticking away, Martha said to her sister, "Come on, Mary. Please! It won't be for long. Look! The sun is almost up."

Mary stood, gripping her pitchfork. Shaking her head from side to side. Indecisive and stubborn.

Martha came up close, right to her sister's face, and begged, "Please, Mary. This is hard enough without you being difficult." Spoken like a true older sister, getting in the last word. She then left her and stepped inside the fetid tomb, following Phillip.

Mary heard the unwavering buzz of the flies and cringed. The puke she had swallowed was back on deck, ready for its public debut and causing her mouth to over salivate. Likewise, from off to her left, deep within the grove, there was an odd sound. A discordant, distant screeching that overlapped and confused itself in the ear. Closely following this sound, she could see dozens of various birds lifting themselves on startled, flapping wings. Their little, feathered bodies rose in number above the top of the trees.

Petrified and filled with a strong foreboding sense of dread, Mary followed her sister into the dim, buzzing, putrid enclosure. She sprayed the vomit she had been holding back all across the floor, the second she came inside. Flies and maggots alike swarmed all over the fresh, hot, chunky puddle. Even a few of the nasty buggers managed to fly into her briefly open mouth, dredging up a new gush of puke that she then added to her previous spew.

"Sshhh!" Martha shushed from beside Phillip on the other side of the entry.

Phillip leaned over a little to peek from the top corner of the opening, looking out upon the courtyard. The thick carpet of fog was beginning to thin and dissipate, showing that there were far more bones spread out beneath the mist, than what had been piled up above it against the walls and trees.

Suddenly, from out of the grove, a spectacle of horror emerged. It lumbered along on a twisted, broken leg, bent at an impossible angle. A soiled, rust colored robe was draped over its bony shoulders and billowed all around its revolting, naked body. Between a pair of pale, scrawny thighs, a lifeless grey penis dangled from a balding thatch of crusty pubic hair. Its distended, splitting belly protruded out in disgusting proportions, making its crushed chest seem even more depleted. A thick wound coil of dried entrails circled its neck, like a psychotic cannibal's necklace. Slick, brownish red gelatinous gobs of blood and feces smeared its mouth and smoothed back its long hair. Solid, black unfocused eyes looked to nowhere and at nothing in particular. Slung over its shoulder, was the nude, headless body of what was recently a woman. Hitcher flies twizzled in lazy maneuvers about both of the dead human bodies.

"Oh my God," Phillip uttered via a shaky whisper, when he saw what was coming towards them in terrifying detail.

Mary was peering out of the corner of the entry on the opposite side of Phillip and Martha. Seeing the same version of her baby brother, transformed into this demonic ragdoll, trudging up the limestone path to its cradle. Behind Lazarus a spectacular morning sky blazed and threatened beautifully. Blinding light bordered on the bottom by the pitch black, shredded silhouette of the rough treeline. The obverse crown of the sun was on the cusp of announcing another triumphant daybreak.

Once Lazarus reached the second row of trees in the courtyard, Phillip and Mary pulled back from their vantage points and pinned their backs tight against the moist inner walls. Three pairs of ears strained to hear past the incessant buzzing of the billions, maybe trillions, of flies. Gradually, the terrible *shuffle-drag* of its footsteps could be heard getting closer.

shuffle-drag

Closer.

shuffle-drag

Closer.

shuffle-drag

Close.

Down low near the entrance, a pair of dead, gray feet, one twisted sideways and propped up on the inner ankle, appeared. They trudged up to the cradle entry and stopped. Waiting there. Kind of leaning and swaying from one side to the next.

Inside, their weapons were held high. Muscles were tensed up to the point of aching. Sweat streamed down into their eyes. Adrenaline screamed through their veins. Hordes of greedy flies swarmed all over them and regurgitated.

Lazarus shifted the headless body it carried on its shoulder and made to bend down to enter the antechamber. Once its disgusting head came into view, Phillip let out a loud, maniacal battle cry and swung his *Machaira* with all of his strength. The intent was either to incapacitate or decapitate. Instead, an iffy aim in the dimly lit chamber, sent the blade deep into the torso of Lazarus. Shattering the collarbone on Lazarus' left side and slicing right into the lung.

Without a scream, or a yell, or even a peep, Lazarus dropped what was to be his next meal, and seized Phillip by the scruff of the neck. With a monumental amount of power, it threw Phillip out of its sacred cradle, where he landed halfway back out in the courtyard.

Phillip crash landed on the stone pathway with a dull *Thud!* Knocking the wind out of him completely. Above him, he saw a cool to warm color palette becoming warmer by the second.

The body of Lazarus turned towards Phillip. Once it was facing him, it grabbed the sword by the tip of the blade that was sticking out its torso and removed it with a sickening squelch. Upon removal of the *Machaira* Lazarus, the ghoul, let it fall to the ground with a sharp, ringing clatter. Gross, sludgy blood and aged viscera coated part of the blade, like used tar.

Baring its rotten teeth while its eyes remained black and unfocused, Lazarus shot off from the Earth's surface. In a shameless spread eagle position it flew through the air. The confiscated robe trailed and stuck out behind it stiffly. Long, filthy claws extended and reached down to Phillip, like a bird of prey brandishing razor-like talons at the peak of the hunt.

The sisters ran out of the crypt and saw Lazarus' white buttocks flying through the air and coming to land on Phillip. A serious struggle ensued. Lazarus slashed at Phillip's chest and arms while trying to bite him. Phillip's left hand held Lazarus' chomping mouth as far away as possible. The big man's palm pushed with all of his might up against the chin. Meanwhile, his right hand tugged on the handle of the *Maakeleth.* The knife was stuck at a weird angle between his body and the ground. Phillip bucked his hips, while trying to free the secondary weapon. At last, it came free and Phillip sliced horizontally at the bulging stomach, releasing a cache of undigested, consumed human (maybe some horse, too) meat. The abhorrent slop drained out of Lazarus' stomach and dumped all over the front of Phillip.

Lazarus screamed. Not from pain, though. More out of frustration. At the edge of the courtyard, a solid border of sunlight advanced slowly and sluggish, carrying the break of day with it. At the present moment, daylight was passing the archway and creeping up to the first row of trees in the courtyard.

Mary and Martha lunged forward and buried their pitchforks into each side of Lazarus' back. Where the kidneys were located. The sharp tines disappeared all of the way up to the perpendicular root.

Lazarus stood and spun to the women with both handles of the winnowing forks sticking out from behind it, like two porcupine quills. Solid black eyes seemed to stare straight through them to its cradle.

In a haunting voice that could've been mistaken from when Lazarus was a little boy of four years old, the corpse spoke innocently, "Mary. Martha. Why?"

"NQ!!" Mary screamed. Despite the mind bending terror, her mind registered seeing that the plodding sunlight had spread near to the second set of trees in the courtyard.

From behind Lazarus, Phillip stood up tall. Rotten meat slipped from off the front of him and fell, making audible, nauseating *Plops!* as they hit the ground. A mean grimace had pulled down the corners of Phillip's mouth. Long sets of deep scratches on his chest and arms bled in profuse dribbles. Scores of slashes that were in groups of three or four throbbed in extreme pain. Drawing on that present pain and all of the emotional despair that had been caused by this thing ever since its resurrection, Phillip swung the curved knife with both hands. A deep grunt accompanied the swing that was intended to take off the head of Lazarus, like Herod had done to John the Baptist. Instead of Lazarus ending up fully decapitated, Phillip had only plunged the blade in sideways and drove it in as far as halfway, where it met with the spinal cord.

Its black, lifeless eyes were somehow capable of still expressing shock. In utter disbelief, Lazarus brought its hands up to the knife in its neck, where this body had been stabbed through before by brave, stupid James. It touched gingerly around the area and tried to assess the damage that had been done to it. Gentle prodding at the deep, single slice didn't take long to turn into its frantic pawing and snarling.

With the warmth of the sun and its glorious rays nearly upon them, the three triumphantly beheld Lazarus gargling and choking. Making a real spectacle of itself. Clawing in helpless desperation at the inflicted wound. Slicing its fingers to ribbons on the sharp, exposed blade of the *Maakeleth.*

Phillip smiled, raised his hands up to the sky and announced, "It is done!" Upon lowering his eyes, he caught Martha's stupefied gaze over Lazarus' shoulder. Phillip winked at her in victorious assurance. Filling her up with that trademark confidence that made her feel invincible.

That's when, in an unexpected turn of events, the body of Lazarus spun around, on the good leg, and took a violent swipe at Phillip's unprotected neck. Long nails connected and successfully gouged out the entire throat of Phillip in one attempt, leaving the mortal man with a look of surprised confusion upon his face. Phillip's hands shot up to his throat and felt his own hot blood gushing out of him. Then, he slumped to his knees and fell over to his side.

"NNNNNNNNNNOOOOOOOOOOOOOOOOO!!!!" Martha screamed. But, her voice cut off with machined precision at the end of her scream, as she became imbued with an infinitely strong spirit. The Holy Spirit. Her tearful brown irises and black pupils faded from her eyes, leaving pure white, glowing sclera. Both her garments and hair lifted. Swirling, as though in a dream, all about her body, giving off the effect of being tousled and shifted underwater. Streaks of lightning crackled powerfully out of her eyes and all about her body. In the same manner as taking a simple step up, she lifted gently from the surface of the Earth and levitated, like an angel.

Gobsmacked by what she was seeing, Mary looked at her sister floating a full handbreadth above the ground. A strange sense of déjà vu came over her, as though she had seen this, or something similar to it, in a memory of a dream. Or a nightmare. Her eyes flicked over to the possessed, decimated body of her brother, who was already cowering from fright. Past Lazarus, laid Phillip, bleeding out in a pool of his own blood. Without thinking, Mary bolted for the encroaching border of sunlight and Phillip's convulsing, draining body. Skidding into a slide, then taking his head and placing it in her lap. She stroked his sweaty hair back.

The nefarious demon manipulated the vocal cords in her brother's dead body to sound like the nostalgic voice of a young baby boy that Martha once knew and loved. These vocal cords said in a perfect mimic, "Martha, please! I'm your brother!!"

In Martha's head and all through her body she could hear and feel the clear, reverberating voice of Jesus, saying, "My Father has bestowed my Strength upon you!" Finish it, Martha!!"

Immense power flowed all through her from her toes, to her fingertips, to the top of her head. A feeling that was akin to an enormous expanding within her being. Filling her up to the point where she thought her skin would split apart and let all of the blinding light within her spill out. In her ears, there was a static like fizzle. The very air around her crackled and electrified with the power that was emanating from her.

"Martha! You wouldn't hurt your brother would you?!" Lazarus asked in that heartbreaking child's voice from her memories. Behind Lazarus, the sunlight had passed up the last set of mature trees and bathed the dying body of Phillip in its glory. Mary looked on in anguished disbelief.

Righteous anger filled up Martha completely and she flexed the power of The Holy Spirit to project a concentrated blast of angelic fire at the horrible demon within her brother's corpse. Upon connecting, the demon shrieked. It felt extreme, searing pain, at last, and took a step back towards the deadly approach of daybreak. In a weak defense, it held up its mutilated hands.

Phillip's primary weapon that he had brought with him, the *Machaira*, lifted on its own accord off of the ground, from where the demon had tossed it earlier. Guided upon invisible ghost hands, the sword joined and became enveloped in Martha's grip. The blade then lit aflame in a pale, transparent, radiating color wheel. Giving off the impression of quicksilver shimmering. Like the metal of the blade itself had become molten.

Martha bore down over the cowering body of Lazarus. Pinning it between the advancing morning sunlight and her newly endowed power. She gave it another blast of some scorching Divine fire and forced it to its knees. The power pouring out of her blew its stiffened hair and robe back and charred the skin to a crispy black on the forehead and cheekbones. With the gift of vision into the spirit realm, her eyes caught sight of the demon's face. It was a frenzied, translucent crimson spirit squirming inside of her brother's corpse. Upon seeing the familiar, kingly face of the known spirit that had been twisted by centuries of a degenerate desire for mindless chaos and a penchant for homicidal lunacy, there was a shared spark of recognition shared between Martha's consciousness and the spirit of The Lord.

"Finish it!" Jesus' voice boomed like the lofty voice of a deity in her head.

Martha gathered all of the power that had been granted to her and balled it up into one final, destroying blast. The force of this immense power pushed the body of Lazarus a full handbreadth into the ground, cracking the ancient limestone pathway and crushing every bone in its body into crumbling shards. Once it was struck by the full might of the Holy Spirit, the red, familiar demon inside Lazarus howled out painfully from where it was sunk in the ground. In a display of ultimate weakened futility, Lazarus tried to move under the massive power pushing against it. Minor twitching of the hands, feet and neck were the most that it could accomplish under the severe duress being imposed.

Martha opened her mouth to speak. Her tongue and lips moved in the enunciating of the following words, although it was Jesus' eternal, strong voice that came out in a final, conclusive rebuke, **"I COMMAND YOU DEMON, IN THE NAME OF MY FATHER, COME OUT! MOLOCH!!!"**

"AAAAAAAAAAAAAAAHHHHHHHHHHHHHHHHHHHHHH!!!" The ear splitting sound of the second demon being exorcized caused Mary's eardrums to throb to where she thought they would burst. Her index fingers flew up and jammed into her ear canals. There was a moment where she wondered if she would be left deaf after this, from the gross abuse of decibels.

All of the strange, evil, grimy characteristics that had hung over their family's sacred resting place instantly lifted. The disorienting sickness created. The oppressive pushing down upon their necks and pulling from under at their ankles. The maddening fuzzy, biting quality that agitated the air itself. The stinging and burning in their eyes and lungs. It was all gone. It felt as though something massive and otherworldly had been banished from this ground. Like a demonic portal had been slammed shut.

In the distance, startled flocks of birds shot up from the brightening treeline all around. Their little wings flapping furiously to facilitate an escape from the indescribable sound of terror.

Without waiting another second, in a swift, fluid motion, Martha took the *Machaira* in her right hand and swung it in a wide arch. The aim was for her brother's neck. To finish the decapitation that Phillip had started. Her eyes closed before the impact of the strike and there, in vivid detail, behind her eyelids, was the image of her infant brother's big, beaming, toothless grin directed up at her from the crook of her arms. A bittersweet memory now to be murdered by her hand.

The blade imbued with the Divine Fire of The Holy Spirit cut true.

After the lopping, the head of Lazarus rolled away from the body, towards where Mary held Phillip's own dying body, in the sunlight. As the harrowed, afflicted head of Lazarus tumbled into the daylight, the notion that it would burst into flames upon exposure, was stymied. The head was just a head again, and behind it, the body of Lazarus fell and went limp. Like a sack of grain.

Lifeless.

At last.

Praise God.

Martha's grip relaxed and she let the sword fall with a heavy *CLANG!* to the stone path. Human black pupils and brown irises had returned as a part of her eyes. Her feet touched down to the Earth's surface again. The quixotic shifting of her robes and hair had ceased, as the endowed Holy

Spirit lifted her body. Upon becoming just Martha again, she sprinted over to her sister and her dying love.

Phillip's eyes were unfocused as he was almost gone. Short, ragged gargling breaths were becoming segmented. Large pauses that stretched out in between signs of life were becoming more frequent from him.

Martha saw the state that he was in and wailed in the morning light aloud, knowing he was well beyond saving. She was a veritable pool of tears and snot as she kissed his face all over. Some of his blood became smeared across her chin and lips from her affections.

Phillip experienced a final lucid moment and his eyes focused on Martha's face. With a weak hand, he tried to reach up Martha's cheek with his bloody fingers. His mouth appeared to be trying to say something to her. His tongue kept pressing to his upper row of teeth, like whatever he was trying to say started with the letter "L".

Martha grabbed his hand, put it to her cheek as a gesture of pure love and devotion. Wanting to hold on to the feeling of his warm, calloused hand for as long as possible. She nodded *Yes* in affirmation. Then whispered to him, "I love you too, Phillip."

A hint of a smile curled Phillip's lips. With the barest nod up and down in silent agreement and reciprocation of their shared love for one another, he sighed out. Happy that he, at least, got to tell her once. Then, he closed his eyes and died.

Martha burst into uninhibited, ugly lamenting. Freely wailing over the beheaded corpse of her brother on one side of her and her true love, dead in her lap on the other. Not to mention, the still fresh, intense emotional pain from witnessing Jesus being crucified only fifteen hours ago. Her tears represented all of the pain and all of the heartache that she had been stuffing down for weeks, ever since her brother initially died.

Mary scooted over to where Martha still held Phillip's head in her lap and put her arms around her sister. Unabashed, she joined Martha in her immense grief and sadness. The glorious morning sunlight glinted off of the falling tears running down each of their cheeks. Turning their waterworks into streams of cascading diamonds.

Physically, the day was promising to be bright and warm. Mentally? Emotionally? To Mary and Martha, no matter how summer-like everything appeared, it would be nothing for them but a bleak, frosty forecast for the unforeseeable future.

viii

They buried Phillip the following day, on Sunday. Martha prepared the body with methodical, loving care. Washing it. Drying it off. Then, she wrapped it with spices, herbs and sacred cloth. Upon setting his corpse into the arcosolium, Martha could swear she had heard Jesus' voice say to her, in reference to Phillip, "This is my faithful servant, whom I have approved of and accepted into my bosom."

On the same day as Phillip's burial, in Akeldama, also known as the Field of Blood, Judas Iscariot's body was found. "Burst apart" is how it was described as being found. Eyewitnesses speculate that his body must've hung all day Friday and Saturday until the branch broke at some point. Letting his body crash and explode upon its impact with the jagged rocks below.

The sisters chose to burn the mangled, bisected body of their brother in a ritual of purification intended to cleanse the soul. After praying for the salvation of Lazarus, the sisters lit the pyre and watched the body burn until it was nothing but ashes. There was no approving message from the Heavens this time, as there was with Phillip's. So that just left Martha and Mary reliant on good, old dependable steadfast hope. Hope that their brother's soul had already been accepted into God's grace and favor, before his body was used for such atrocities. Hope was the best that they would ever have, until finding out for themselves.

Jesus, as is well known, was raised on Monday and stayed amongst his followers for three days, before returning back to his Heavenly Father. This offered another, more powerful witness for many to be convinced to trust in the Lord and leave the declining influence of the Temple, with their greedy, empty Priests behind.

Mary and Martha never married. Instead, they kept proselytizing in the name of their Lord, helping to spread the word and the birth of Christianity. For years they followed the disciples and apostles, becoming quite the anglers when it came to being "fishers of men".

Years later, in 46 A.D., Caiaphas bloodthirsty quest for power ended with his skinny body laid out on his death bed. Sweating buckets. Writhing his slippery legs against one another, like eels in an aquarium. Twisting and pulling his damp sheets up to his chin. His mind burned with a fatal fever. For weeks he remained in this condition. Babbling and jabbering in a geriatric, high-pitched wheeze. All the way up until the day of his death, with the fever burning to the core of his brain. He would rant for hours and hours on end, to tired ears and empty rooms about Jesus. The Apostles. Romans. Pontius Pilate. The Ephod, The Urim and the Thummim. Caleb. James. Annas. Abductions. Murders. Mary and Martha.

And, most of all...the horror that was the Resurrection of Lazarus.

The End

www.ingramcontent.com/pod-product-compliance
Lightning Source LLC
LaVergne TN
LVHW010600100826
845148LV00014B/2790